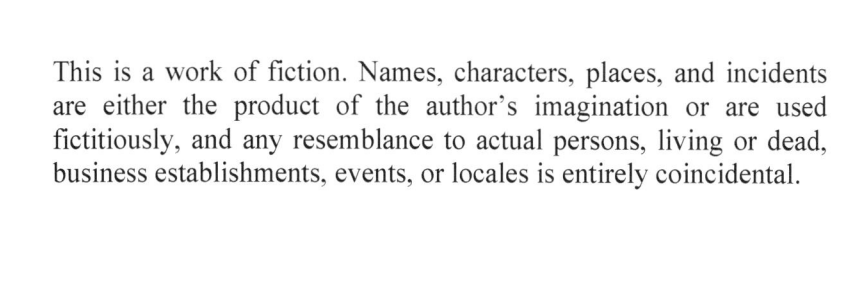

This is a work of fiction. Names, characters, places, and incidents are either the product of the author's imagination or are used fictitiously, and any resemblance to actual persons, living or dead, business establishments, events, or locales is entirely coincidental.

ANEURYSM

by

CHRISTOPHER SMYTHIES

TO ELISABETTA

ACKNOWLEDGEMENT

A special word of gratitude to my editor, Giulia Smythies,
and my cover designer, Stephanie Smythies,
for their invaluable help in creating this novel.
I would also like to thank my three younger children,
Francesca, Michael, and Chiara,
for their love and support.

1

A Rolls Royce Phantom quietly idled in downtown Seattle's darkest alley. In the back seat, the shadowy figure of a woman raised a cigarette to her thin, pale lips. Her cheeks sucked hollow and the burning tobacco beyond her fingers flared orange. Soft light permeated the gloom, briefly illuminating a pillbox chapeau with birdcage veil, a grim mouth, and an explosion of fiery red hair.

At her side a tiny black Chihuahua was strapped into a custom-built Bucket Booster pet car seat that dispensed Perrier water and Honey Nut Cheerios at the touch of a paw-friendly button. He was atrociously ugly with bulbous black eyes, an upturned nose, and a tuft of scraggly hair that sprouted awkwardly from the center of his forehead. Every once in a while he looked up at his mistress and whimpered for attention.

"Minimus . . ." the woman breathed with a thick, vaporous voice, savoring her dog's name as if it were an exotic delicacy. She crinkled her lips into a tight circle and blew a long stream of acrid smoke into his face. "Why won't Defendant Thompson settle? Do you really suppose the name Maxine Doggette means nothing to him?"

Minimus narrowed his eyes into slits and snorted.

The young man in the driver's seat was Billy Barlow, a recent graduate from some third-rate law school in the middle of nowhere. He was excessively tall and lanky; somebody who couldn't fit comfortably into any car and was hunched over the steering wheel like an arthritic buzzard. Chubby cheeks and a receding chin gave his face an unfortunate dopey look. Tonight, at least his eyes were wary and alert. They flitted between his wristwatch and Maxine in the rear-view mirror as he anxiously awaited her signal.

"If we don't go now, Ms. Doggette," he said, gripping the gearshift, "we'll fall behind schedule."

Maxine tapped her cigarette sharply with a bony forefinger and knocked loose a long, bending column of ash. Ever since she had hired Billy to work for her law firm a few weeks before, she had been having doubts about the wisdom of her choice. The overgrown goofball had an insatiable appetite for glory, always driveling on about becoming America's most celebrated medical malpractice attorney one day. Usually she burned through feckless novices like him with as much unbridled enthusiasm as she devoured medical practices, sacking them for the flimsiest of reasons. Billy, however, was more ambitious than most and this time she decided on a different approach: keep him on a tight leash, watch him closely, and thwart any attempt he made to advance his career.

As they say, better the devil you know than the devil you don't.

Maxine took one last drag from her cigarette and crushed it mercilessly into an ashtray. "All right," she said, expelling carcinogens from the deepest recesses of her lungs. "Let's go."

"Yes, ma'am!" said Billy, thrusting the gearshift into drive and guiding the Rolls towards the street. Once the sidewalk was clear of pedestrians he pulled out of the alley and eased into traffic.

On this evening Seattle was bracing for the latest low pressure system to spiral in from the Pacific Ocean. Fluorescent lights in thousands of office windows were going out as workers abandoned their desks and headed home early. Bundled up in overcoats, they emptied into the streets and scuttled away, gripping their umbrellas tightly against the driving rain. Cars poured out of parking garages and buses loaded up passengers. Dancing traffic lights splashed dazzling red, yellow, and green paint across canvases of wet asphalt. Rivers of white headlights and red taillights flowed through the mix before snaking towards distant suburbs.

As Billy drove, Maxine cast her thoughts back to the day when she had summoned her new employee to her office and informed him that her case against Giles Thompson, a local neurosurgeon, might collapse. She had ordered him to investigate whether the man had any personal weaknesses that she could exploit.

Billy resented the assignment, mumbling something about wanting to file his very first med-mal lawsuit instead. However, he knew better than to launch his career with argument with his boss and reluctantly agreed to tail Thompson. On the first night he observed him sitting in a hotel bar with a leather briefcase on the floor by his side. He engaged a middle-aged brunette woman in conversation, bought her a couple of drinks, then discretely escorted her to an elevator. Not more than fifteen minutes later, just as Billy was about to go home, the woman suddenly reappeared in the lobby with fearful eyes, tangled hair, and blood trickling down the side of her face. She bolted from the hotel and fled into the night.

Two nights later, Billy followed Thompson back to the same bar and watched him strike up a conversation with another woman, a blond this time. Once again he quickly gained her confidence and took her upstairs, briefcase in hand. Just like the brunette before her, she burst into the lobby a few minutes later with knotted, bloody hair and headed straight for the exit.

After the same thing happened a third time, Billy reported to Maxine that Thompson was a prolific womanizer and was having more affairs than anyone could have imagined. And there was more: while he had no trouble picking women up in hotel bars, somehow he was scaring them witless after only a few minutes alone with them in his room. Messing up their hair too. And why were their scalps bleeding? Perhaps the answer lay inside the mysterious briefcase he always carried around with him. Billy worried aloud that Thompson was too dangerous a target to pursue any further and suggested Maxine might be wise to accept the loss.

As she normally did whenever Billy expressed his opinion, Maxine ignored him completely. She had planned long and hard for this mission. Now was the time for some old-fashioned blackmail, not a spineless retreat. Even if her pimply-faced assistant had good reason to be concerned, she was sure she could defend herself against whatever mischief Thompson was perpetrating. Indeed, she relished the idea of pummeling that weasel and giving him a bouquet of bruises to take home as a souvenir.

After they had driven a few blocks, Maxine tapped Billy sharply on the shoulder. "You may give me my disguise now," she said.

Billy reached for a black leather bag and passed it back to her. "Everything's in there."

Maxine pressed a button in the center console. A beam of bright light cut through drifting wisps of blue smoke and shone upon her skull-like face, turning her skin sallow. Minimus looked at her in adoration, his head sprinkled with a fine layer of ash.

She opened the bag and saw the things she had prepared earlier back at the office: a plastic nametag, an admission ticket to the neurosurgery banquet tonight, an Excelsior cardkey for Room 709, and a long brown wig. She took out the nametag first and read it aloud. "Jessica Dunlap, R.N. Nurse member, Bradley Radcliffe Association of International Neurosurgeons (BRAIN). Sounds sufficiently authentic, wouldn't you agree?"

"Yes, ma'am."

Maxine pinned it to the black evening gown she was wearing and reached into the bag again. "And here's the ticket," she said, holding up a white card with a bar code printed across its front.

"How did you get one of those?" asked Billy, keeping his eyes on the road ahead.

"Odeus Horman procured it for me," said Maxine, turning it over in her hands.

"Dr. Horman?" Billy frowned. "He's the neurosurgeon you usually hire to give expert testimony. Isn't he your friend?"

"*Friend?*" snapped Maxine. "Odeus Horman may be a neurosurgeon who's willing to say anything under oath for the right price, but don't ever call him my friend!"

"I-I'm sorry, Ms. Doggette," stammered Billy, his face reddening. He broke into a dry, hacking cough as he always did whenever he was stressed. "He comes by the office quite often. I thought you and he . . . Well, you know what I mean. It wasn't my intention to—"

"Forget about it," said Maxine acidly. She took the cardkey out of the bag next, double-checked the room number, then dropped it into her purse along with the ticket. Lastly she removed the pillbox chapeau from her head and slipped on the wig. When she positioned herself directly under the dome light the shadows across her face stretched downwards.

"How do I look?" she asked, tucking an errant lock of hair out of sight.

Billy's face loomed larger in the rearview mirror. The curvature of the glass made his chubby cheeks chubbier and receding chin even smaller. "My God, Ms. Doggette!" he gasped. "Nobody will recognize you now!"

Not even Minimus. He shrank into his Bucket Booster and growled.

"You poor little thing," said Maxine, affectionately petting him. "Did I scare you? Have a treat. It'll make you feel better." She pressed the button in his car seat. A Cheerio flew down a plastic chute and landed into a receptacle near his mouth. He gobbled it up with relish and licked the crumbs from his lips.

Beaming with satisfaction, Maxine pinned her chapeau back on and fine-tuned her veil.

"And now my jewels."

She reached behind her neck, elbows sticking out, and unclasped her sparkling necklace. Into the purse it went. Several diamond rings, a brooch, and a pair of emerald earrings soon followed. Tonight she was supposed to be an overworked, underpaid nurse. If anybody noticed her rock collection they might grow suspicious.

"We should go over my plan again," she said, producing a tube of lipstick. She opened the top and twisted the bottom. "Just to be sure."

Billy cleared his throat. "The banquet is being held in the Grand Ballroom," he said. "Find Defendant Thompson but only make contact when he's alone. After you've softened him up a bit, take him to room 709. You won't forget the number, will you?"

Maxine didn't bother dignifying such an inane question with an answer. Instead, she held up a vanity mirror and turned a critical eye to her lips.

"The cardkey will let you in," Billy hurried on. "There's a large floral arrangement on a table in the corner. I hid a micro video camera among the stems. It's activated by a motion detector and will start recording when you enter the room. A small green light means it's working. Don't worry about running out of time. It stores up to four hours of video."

"This won't take four hours," muttered Maxine, her lips blossoming red. "Not even four minutes."

"When you're done with him," said Billy, "get out quickly. Take the camera with you if you can. If not, I'll swing by later and pick it up." He coughed his dry, hacking cough once again, a signal that something was bothering him.

"What is it, Billy?"

"Ms. Doggette, I have to confess I'm really nervous about this mission tonight."

Maxine's lips smacked together with a moist, sticky sound.

"What if your wig comes off in the middle of things?" he fretted. "If Defendant Thompson finds out who you are, he could accuse you of extortion. Hell, you could even be disbarred!"

"Bumps on a pickle," said Maxine, inspecting her handiwork in the mirror.

"And what if he refuses to settle?"

"He'll make his insurance company settle all right. I have no doubt about that. The alternative could be a nasty divorce—a much more personal and costly proposition for him."

"But there are risks!"

"There are *always* risks," said Maxine, closing her lipstick tube and dropping it back into her purse. "I'll never admit this in public, Billy—especially not in front of any doctor—but even the most carefully conceived plans can go wrong. Badly wrong."

Like the time long ago, remembered Maxine with a sudden ache in her heart, when she was anxious to become a doctor herself. Twelve medical schools reviewed her application and firmly rejected her. When the last one told her, unnecessarily harshly, that she was wasting her time and not to bother applying again, she was filled with vindictive demons yearning for revenge. She enrolled in nursing school where she learned just enough about medicine to be dangerous, then law school where she focused on medical malpractice. After spending a few years suing any old doctor, she decided to specialize in those at the pinnacle of the food chain—neurosurgeons. She pursued them with sadistic pleasure, less interested in winning cases for her clients as she was in making her enemies pay.

Now, after so much hard work building her practice, *she* was the one who possessed real power, not them. Her lawsuits—or at least the mere threat of them—had done more to influence the course of modern medicine than any silly operation ever had.

After a long, brooding silence, Maxine looked past the swishing wiper blades and spotted the Excelsior hotel a hundred yards away, filling more and more of the windshield as they approached. Countless rooms were stacked on top of each other, reaching into the clouds. She studied their checkered pattern of light and wondered how many other scandals were being hatched behind tightly closed curtains that night.

Several white buses were parked in front of the main entrance, disgorging passengers onto the wet sidewalk, mostly men dressed in black tie with a few elegant women hanging off their arms. They wasted no time seeking shelter from the stormy weather, filing past the uniformed doormen and disappearing into the hotel.

Were they *neurosurgeons*?

Maxine fumbled inside her purse for a pair of pearl opera glasses and held them up to her eyes. She scrutinized their faces as if she was the commander of a German U-boat at periscope depth, peering through the mire of the North Atlantic and assessing an enemy convoy before launching an attack.

They *were*! No mistake about it! The smugness in the eyes, the way they strutted about, expensive clothes, Italian shoes, gold watches—classic hallmarks, obvious even from this range.

As if she needed confirmation, she spotted nametags like hers pinned to their lapels and BRAIN signs taped to the front windows of the buses. She twiddled the focus knob between thumb and forefinger and imagined crosshairs moving from person to person.

Somewhere over there, she mused, was Thompson, foolishly unaware of the threat lurking nearby. The thought of having such a tactical advantage over him sent a tingling sensation down her spine.

"Pull over, Billy" said Maxine, tossing the opera glasses back into her purse. "Best not to get too close."

Billy parked the Rolls Royce across the street from the hotel. A black cat sitting on top of a nearby garbage can eyed them suspiciously.

Maxine turned to her dog. "Let's roll, Minimus," she said, undoing his straps.

Minimus was preoccupied by the cat outside.

She held her purse open and poked him in the ribs. "Get in, will you? We don't have all day."

He paid no attention to her.

Maxine was seized by a pang of jealousy. "Oh for goodness' sake!" she said, plucking him out of his Bucket Booster. "Since when were *you* ever interested in cats?" She slung him into her purse and snapped the clasp shut after him. She adjusted her wig one last time, then opened her door and stepped into the blustery street outside. "Wait right here, Billy. I won't be long."

"Ma'am!" he cried, rolling down his window and waving a small, collapsible umbrella. "You'll need this!"

He was too late. Maxine was already deployed, churning towards the neurosurgeons with the accuracy and destructive power of a torpedo.

2

Hugh Montrose, Chairman of the Department of Neurosurgery at Columbia Medical Center, felt like an alien arthropod from another galaxy.

A mask covered his nose and mouth, a hood his hair, ears, and neck, and a paper gown the rest of him. A headlight crowned his head, its two fiber-optic cables merging at the bridge of his nose. They were plugged into a light source behind him, glowed neon blue, and cast a dazzling light wherever he looked. The loupes in front of his eyes magnified the operative field by a factor of 2.5 and protected his porous parts from splashing blood.

Hugh was basking in the peace of the operating room, his personal sanctuary from the distractions of the world. On the schedule today: a craniotomy—surgery that involved opening the skull to gain access to the brain inside. He'd already drilled four burr holes and sawed three sides of a square between them. The fourth cut was supposed to go under the temporalis muscle and was difficult to make. He therefore wedged the sharp end of a chisel into the middle one of the three he'd already completed and, using the bone edge as a fulcrum, jerked the handle abruptly downwards. A trapdoor of bone, known as the bone flap, popped up with a loud, splintering *crack*—a mouthwatering sound that heralded the intracranial part of the operation.

Underneath, he exposed the dura mater—tough mother in Latin—a thick membrane that wrapped around the central nervous system as tightly as a glove. A #15 scalpel blade cut through it with antithetical ease and soon the bright beam of his headlight was dancing playfully over the moist, pulsating surface of the brain.

Hugh looked up. Above him were the forward-slanting windows of a soundproof observation booth. The twelve seats inside were occupied not by neurosurgical pilgrims from all over the world as was usually the case but by local journalists who were covering the annual BRAIN meeting this year. He had invited them to watch an aneurysm operation and report on the experience.

"Can everybody hear me?" Hugh asked, speaking into a microphone clipped to the neck of his scrubs.

The spectators nodded and gave him a thumbs-up.

"Thank you very much for coming," he began, returning his attention to the operative field. "Today I'm taking you with me on the most exciting adventure in neurosurgery—hunting down and killing a dangerous brain aneurysm. As you probably know, an aneurysm is a weak spot in the wall of an artery that slowly expands into something round that looks like a berry. That's why they're sometimes called berry aneurysms. A neck connects it to the normal circulation. The one we're going after today is medium-sized with a diameter of eight millimeters."

Hugh took a couple of brain retractors from the scrub tech and placed them under the frontal and temporal lobes. When he found his landmarks—the long, stringy olfactory nerve, the thicker optic, and a plaque-encrusted internal carotid artery—he fastened the retractors into position and stepped back from the field.

"Okay, let's bring in the operating microscope so the folks upstairs can see everything up close and personal."

The circulating nurse removed Hugh's loupes and headlight, set them aside, and pushed a three hundred thousand and fifty thousand dollar Leica M720 OH5 into position. Hugh removed the perforated pieces of sterile drape that protected the eyepieces, nestled up close, and peered through. The view he saw was transmitted to high-definition monitors mounted throughout the operating room and the booth above.

And what a spectacular view it was!

The intricate structures he had seen earlier blossomed into sharply focused, colorful, and incredibly detailed anatomy. Tiny red arteries and purple veins tangled playfully across the brainscape before dividing over and over again like the branches of a tree, carrying nutrients to an infinitely complicated world of cells, molecules, and atoms. Delicate membranes hung like misty veils and swayed gracefully in the crystal clear cerebral spinal fluid that welled from deep cisterns. Nerve fibers shimmered with iridescence as they coursed within the olfactory and optic nerves, conveying a trillion pixels of information from the outside world to regions unknown. It was a strange and wondrous jungle like none other in creation, bursting with beauty and having an essence as mysterious as life itself.

"Impressive, isn't it?" said Hugh, glancing at the spectators above him. They were riveted to their monitors, soaking in the view as if they had been blind all their lives and were now seeing for the first time. "As many times as I see this, I'll never get used to it."

Hugh worked in silence for a while and resumed his narrative only when it was safe to do so. "Once in a while we stumble across aneurysms by chance when we're doing CT's and MRI's for some unrelated reason like head trauma. Most of the time, however, they're discovered when they suddenly rupture. What provokes them? Usually a spike in blood pressure. That could mean running for a bus, exercising in a gym, having sexual intercourse, or any number of things. This gentleman happened to be watching the Seattle Mariners lose another baseball game on television."

Muffled laughter filtered down from the observation booth.

"Whatever the final straw," continued Hugh, "aneurysms usually leak a little blood first—something called a subarachnoid hemorrhage. Typical symptoms: severe headache, nausea, vomiting, photophobia, and a stiff neck. If nothing is done they can bleed again, only much worse the second time. Or they can disintegrate completely, blasting blood through the brain with the force of a fire hydrant, destroying centers that control movement, sensation, speech, vision, and memory. Twenty-five percent of all hemorrhages plunge into a coma and die. Another twenty-five percent die within three months. The rest survive. Of those, more than half are left with some sort of disability."

Hugh grew aware of somebody standing behind him and glanced over his shoulder. Richard Elliott, his junior neurosurgical resident, had just finished scrubbing and was holding out his arms. Brown soap bubbles dripped from his elbows as he waited for the scrub nurse to hand him a drying towel.

Richard had a pale, doughy face from spending too much time inside the hospital. When he wore a mask only his eyes were visible—two bleary, bloodshot globes embedded within heavy circles of exhaustion. As tired as he looked, however, Hugh felt that residents these days didn't have it so bad. By law, their total number of work hours was limited to eighty per week and no more than twenty-four could be spent consecutively in the hospital. In comparison, when Hugh was a resident he had worked as many as one hundred and fifty hours per week, leaving only eighteen to go home, reacquaint himself with his wife, Caroline, and get some sleep. Those were the days when he had plowed through the endless grind like an arctic icebreaker. The key to survival: being so much in love with operating on the brain that he was willing to risk self-destruction in the process of learning how. It was all worthwhile in the end. With so much experience under his belt, Hugh felt that there was little at the end of his training that he hadn't seen or didn't know how to do.

He wished he could be as confident about the current crop of residents graduating from training programs.

"Allow me to introduce Dr. Richard Elliott," Hugh said into his microphone for the benefit of his audience.

Richard waved at the windows above him. A few of the friendlier journalists tore their eyes from the monitors and waved back.

"What are you doing here?" Hugh asked him. "I thought you were planning to sneak out of the hospital and catch some of the BRAIN meeting."

"I was," replied Richard, accepting a towel from the scrub tech and drying himself, "until I heard you were operating on an aneurysm. Thought I'd give you a hand. When you're finished I'll close so you can leave early."

"Why should I want to leave early?" asked Hugh without taking his eyes from his dissection. "I like it here."

"Come on, Dr. Montrose! You're being awarded the Radcliffe Trophy at the banquet tonight! You can't miss the presentation!"

"I'm not planning to be late."

"Not if I can help it," said Richard, tossing aside his towel. He wriggled into a paper gown, snapped on a pair of rubber gloves, and took up his usual position next to Hugh.

"Ladies and gentlemen," said Hugh, pressing the zoom button with his thumb. The anatomy made a quantum leap towards him. "Please fasten your seatbelts and enjoy the ride. This is where things can sometimes get a little wild."

In his formative years he had always felt dryness in his mouth and a pounding heart at this stage of the operation. With thousands of such cases under his belt, however, the hormones of fright and flight had long lost their potency and he entered aneurysm country with silent confidence.

He probed with his micro-dissector and searched for the safest way forward. The internal carotid divided into two branches: the middle and anterior cerebral arteries. He followed the latter and crept along it as if he were a big game hunter on safari, approaching the den of a wounded lion.

"Aneurysms can be either coiled or clipped," he continued, almost whispering now. "Coiling them involves threading a catheter from an artery in the groin to the head and filling them with a tiny wire that clots them off. Clipping means having a conventional brain operation to isolate them from the parent artery with a small clip. Each technique has its pros and cons. Today, for a variety of reasons, I decided to go with—"

Suddenly the aneurysm lashed out with unrestrained fury.

Blood rushed from the depths in a turbulent, swirling flood and obscured everything in sight. Once it reached the opening in the skull, it overflowed the edges of the scalp and ran down the drapes in forked rivers of red.

Hugh instantly forgot the journalists and locked his mind onto the problem. His eyes came alive, hardly daring to blink in case he missed anything. His hands were perfectly steady and his breathing regular. Anybody closely observing him would never have guessed he was in the midst of a calamity.

"The aneurysm has ruptured," he calmly announced as if he was the commander of Apollo 13 informing Houston he had a problem. He reached for a larger sucker with his left hand and dunked its end into the cauldron of roiling blood before him. Richard followed his lead. Both drank long and deep as if parched by a terrible thirst. The clear plastic tubes that snaked over the drapes flashed red and spat their guts into a suction canister at the foot of the table.

"Start transfusing and stay ahead two units. Drop the systolic blood pressure to ninety. Give me a temporary."

The scrub tech fixed a gold clip to the end of an applier and placed it into Hugh's outstretched hand. It glinted in the bright lights as he passed it into the head.

"No good," said Hugh, withdrawing it again. "Bleeding too fast. I need a cottonoid."

Richard handed him a tiny cotton pad. Hugh gripped one end with a pair of bayoneted forceps, sunk it into the blood, and guided it towards the source of the bleeding. Using his other hand he held his sucker against the cottonoid, applied pressure, and worked to stem the flow.

"How much blood has he lost?" he asked.

"Five hundred cc's," replied the anesthesiologist, reading the numbers along one side of the suction canister.

About a pint in only two or three minutes. At this rate the patient didn't stand a chance.

Hugh picked up the pace and soon gained some measure of control. The hemorrhaging eased just enough for him to see the anterior cerebral artery once again. This time, when he passed his temporary clip into the head, he was able to clamp the vessel between its blades—equivalent to shutting off the water main in a house. The suction quickly caught up with the blood loss and anatomical landmarks all around re-emerged like rocks in an outgoing tide. The patient was no longer in imminent danger of bleeding to death. Instead, critical areas of his brain were now being deprived of oxygen.

The race was still on.

"The anterior cerebral is occluded," said Hugh. His hands moved quickly, making full use of the dozens of micro-instruments at his disposal. With Richard helping him, he cleared away debris and resumed his advance. More arteries came into view. Some were large enough to have names and supplied distant areas of the brain. Others, generically known as perforators, were tiny but no less important. Each was essential to identify and preserve. Soon he reached the aneurysm itself, crouching in a tangle of pulsating tendrils. With the temporary clip in position upstream it appeared weakened and vulnerable. Bright red backflow oozed from an ugly gash in its side.

"There it is!" he whispered in awe as if he thought it was a beautiful sight to behold. "Blood loss?"

"Two thousand cc's."

Time to strangle the bastard.

Hugh focused on its neck. Successfully compress it with a permanent clip and the patient would live. Tear it accidentally and the patient might die.

He studied the approach, calculating angles and distances. When he was certain of his intentions, he held out a hand.

"Permanent straight, please."

The scrub tech passed him a clip applier. This time the clip fixed to its end was silver. Gingerly he inched his weapon of choice closer to his target. Something didn't feel quite right and he veered off at the last moment.

"I'll have to use my left," he said, passing the applier to his non-dominant hand.

Now he was better able to slide the clip, ever so carefully, into position. Once he was sure he was deep enough without trapping any perforators he released a spring and the jaws closed.

The aneurysm withered and died.

Hugh immediately removed the temporary he had used to occlude the anterior cerebral artery. Blood surged towards the aneurysm but was blocked from filling it and flowed harmlessly by. As he prodded and probed its pale carcass with his dissector, he allowed himself a brief moment of triumph.

"The aneurysm is clipped," he announced, pushing away the microscope. "Raise the blood pressure back to normal. The likelihood of another rupture is almost zero. From now on, he can watch as many Mariner games as he wants."

Seizing his opportunity to do some operating of his own, Richard pressed closer to the operative field and removed the retractors from under the frontal and temporal lobes. "You'd better go now, Dr. Montrose," he said, gently nudging his boss out of the way. "Not much time before the banquet starts."

"You're not trying to get rid of me, are you?"

"Of course not, sir," said Richard, already searching for small bleeders.

As he stepped back and stretched, Hugh checked on the journalists in the booth above. Half of them had left, leaving their notebooks and pencils scattered around. Those who remained were either slumped over with their heads buried in their hands or were still gaping at the monitors, their faces pale and haggard. One had just finished vomiting into a brown paper bag and was wiping his mouth with the back of his hand.

"I wonder what kind of articles we'll be reading in the newspapers tomorrow," he said.

Richard looked up from his work, followed Hugh's gaze, and chuckled when he saw the journalists. "And that wasn't even a bad case," he said. "Imagine if they had seen one of those!"

Hugh ripped away his paper gown and set it aside. "Next time," he said, popping off his rubber gloves and catapulting them one by one—*thwack! thwack!*—into the trash on the other side of the room, "I'll try to remember to warn them."

3

As Maxine prowled around the Grand Ballroom, disguised in her wig and carrying Minimus in her purse, she searched the growing crowd around her.

Outside the hotel, the neurosurgeons had seemed as sophisticated and aloof as the gods of Mount Olympus. Here, gliding quietly amongst them, Maxine saw their flaws as clearly as the birdcage veil in front of her eyes. Data from her extensive research in the field showed that the amount they swaggered, boasted, and drank was directly proportional to their vulnerability to lawsuits. That meant almost everybody around her qualified as a worthwhile target. Being so close to so many potential defendants, she felt a buzz of electricity running under her skin as if she was an arsonist strolling through a tinder dry forest. She had to constantly remind herself that she wasn't here for a glorious, mind-blowing sue-fest but to target one specific man: Defendant Giles Thompson.

She compared the people around her with his photograph she had filed away in her memory. Medium height, one hundred and eighty pounds, dark hair. After a while she spotted a strong possibility in a far corner. She set off in his direction, studying him closely as she approached. He had a lean face, dimpled chin, thin moustache—just about right, she reckoned. Like all the other men in the ballroom, he was dressed in black tie. Unlike the others, however, he was quite alone.

Yes, it *was* him! The brown leather briefcase by his feet confirmed it beyond a shadow of a doubt. On the surface he was handsome and looked intelligent. Small wonder those women in the hotel bar were so ready to accompany him to his room! Maxine's sensitive antennas, however, picked up a trace of cruelty in his eyes which she found disturbing. If she had been one of those women she would have told him to go and—

"Hello," he said with a smile when she reached him.

"Hello," she answered back, her eyes luminous and filled with purpose. "Are you a neurosurgeon?"

"Yes. Are you?"

"Me?" she cried, pointing to herself. "Heavens no! Just a nurse." An incomplete résumé to be sure, but one that would suffice for now.

"You don't look like any kind of nurse I know."

"Why not?" asked Maxine, alarmed her disguise might not be good enough.

"I've never seen a nurse wear one of those things before," he said, pointing at her birdcage veil.

So it was only the veil. "Maybe I'm not just any kind of nurse," she replied, her confidence quickly restored. "My name is Jessica. What's yours?"

Thompson held out his hand. "Giles Thompson."

"I *love* your name, Giles," crooned Maxine, shaking his hand without letting go. "So distinctive! Is there a *Mrs*. Giles Thompson in the picture somewhere?"

"There could be," he answered, his smile fading. "Why do you want to know?"

Her grip on him intensified. "Because," she said, batting her eyelashes, "if you're married, I'd like to hear all about your affairs."

Thompson's pale lips parted in astonishment. "What makes you think I have affairs?" he asked.

"All men have affairs," said Maxine, now toying casually with his sleeve. "It's a perfectly natural thing, you know." Two fingers slowly up his arm, one step at a time. "How about you?" she asked, raising an eyebrow into the air and pegging him down with a stare. "I hope you're not going to prove me wrong." She slid her hand across his shoulder and fondled an earlobe. "Come on, Giles," she cooed. "You can tell *me* your secrets. You have nothing to be afraid of."

The cruelty in Thompson's eyes changed to unmistakable hunger. Beads of perspiration dampened his forehead. "Here?"

"No," said Maxine. "Upstairs where it's private . . . and more comfortable."

"Alright Jessica," said Thompson, grabbing his briefcase. "Let's go."

Maxine led him out of the ballroom and into the lobby of the hotel. An elevator whisked them to the seventh floor. Using her cardkey, she opened the door to room 709, went in, and located the flowers in the corner. A tiny green light among the stems confirmed that the video camera was recording.

Maxine set aside her purse and turned around to face Thompson. Eager to complete her mission as soon as possible, she wriggled out of her dress, unhooked her bra, and kicked away her shoes. When she lowered her panties she was naked except for chapeau and veil. The hair on her head was brown, and yet the curly triangle between her legs was flaming red. The incongruity didn't matter. Thompson was hopelessly entangled in her trap and was in no state of mind to notice.

"Now I'm ready for *anything*," she said, deploying her sultriest voice.

"Even for this?" said Thompson, fumbling open the latch to his case. He lifted out a large metal contraption with two arms and three sharp spikes, two on one of the arms and one on the other—a brutal device that looked as if it belonged in a medieval torture chamber.

Maxine's eyes bulged. "What the hell is *that*?" she blurted, staring at it in horror.

"It's a Mayfield clamp," he answered, caressing it lovingly with his fingertips. "Some people prefer to call it the Crown of Thorns. Better name for it, wouldn't you agree? Conveys more of a sense of pain and suffering."

"That's the ghastliest thing I've ever seen! What's it for?"

"I use it to fix patients' heads to the operating table," he explained, his eyes gleaming. "That way I can keep them perfectly still so I can work on their brains. Listen to the sound it makes when I—"

Thompson drove the two arms of the clamp together. A pawl ran down a bar of metal teeth, cranking out a loud ratcheting noise. His brown eyes turned to glass, rolled into his head, and fluttered closed. "Have you ever heard anything so *erotic* in your life?" he moaned between clenched teeth.

Maxine cringed. She could think of many ways to describe the Crown of Thorns but 'erotic' wasn't one of them. Maybe Billy had known all along about the contents of the briefcase. Her cheeks burned at the thought that she might have been deceived, either intentionally or as a result of gross incompetence. No matter, she decided. She would deal with that gutless twerp later. For now, she would handle this particular neurosurgeon with the same resourcefulness she always used when things didn't go quite as planned.

She went up to Thompson, removed his black bow tie, and manufactured an enticing smile. "Oh Giles," she whispered as her fingers sought out his shirt buttons and loosened them one by one. "I've dreamed of something like this for such a long time!"

"Me too!" said Thompson, groping her buttock with a sweaty hand.

"That feels wonderful, Giles," responded Maxine. She raised her hands to his neck and, in a single deft movement, slipped his shirt from his shoulders. He let go of her and drew his arm through the sleeve.

Very delicately so as not to impale herself, Maxine eased the Crown of Thorns from his other hand, lowered it to the floor, and kicked it under the bed as far as she could. *Her* head wasn't getting clamped tonight. Of that much she was certain.

Thompson opened his mouth to speak. Before he could say anything, Maxine pressed her lips to his and plunged her tongue into his mouth. Guttural sounds arose from the deepest parts of his throat. When she released him she laid a silencing finger against his lips.

"Don't talk!" she whispered. "Just relax and let me do everything." She climbed onto the bed and pulled him after her. She removed his trousers, lowered his underwear, and entwined herself around him like a snake.

Thompson hadn't given up on the Crown of Thorns. He reached over the edge of the mattress with his arm and stretched his fingers towards the floor.

"Look what I can do, Big Boy!" Maxine cried, desperate to hold his attention. She climbed onto all fours and growled like a tiger, displaying her fingernails and scratching the air. Perhaps a little tacky and contrived, but it was all she could think up right now.

Thompson was unimpressed. He propped himself up on an elbow and sighed impatiently. "Jessica, why don't you let me get the—"

Maxine pounced on him with a roar and straddled him with her legs. Soon the headboard was slapping loudly against the wall. Some poor schmuck might have been trying to sleep in the next room but she didn't care. All that mattered was to make this look good for the video camera. Gripping her chapeau with both hands so her wig would stay firmly on her head, she moaned and groaned as if drowning in pleasure. The thrill she felt was not sexual in nature but from knowing her case was almost in the bag.

"Let me clamp you *now*!" implored Thompson as he gasped for air.

No need to overdo things, Maxine decided. What jilted wife could bear to watch more than a few seconds of this? She abruptly dismounted Thompson and clambered off the bed.

"Oh yes, Jessica! Get the clamp! It's underneath somewhere!"

Maxine had no intention of getting the clamp. Instead, she hurried over to where her bra, panties, and dress lay scattered across the floor. Definitely time to get out of there.

"Okay, *I'll* get it then!" said Thompson, swinging his legs over the edge of the mattress. He dropped to his knees and searched under the bed, his bony bottom waving around in the air. "I know it's here! I saw it go under!"

Maxine quickly pulled on her clothes.

"There it is!" Thompson yelled triumphantly, reaching as far as he could. "Almost got it!"

Maxine picked up her purse, checked to see if Minimus was still inside, then slung the strap over her shoulder.

Thompson scrambled to his feet with the Crown of Thorns in his hand just as Maxine was slipping on her shoes. When he saw what she was doing, he frowned.

"Why are you dressed?" he asked.

"I'm leaving," said Maxine, straightening her chapeau.

"*Leaving*?" he shouted. "You *can't* leave! I haven't clamped you yet!"

Maxine threw Thompson a look of utter contempt. "Bye-bye, pervert," she said. "If you have to use that thing, clamp your own goddamned head!" With a sense of satisfaction that only comes with a brilliantly executed mission, she walked over to the door and opened it.

If Maxine had run, not walked, she might have made a clean getaway. As it was, she didn't even set foot outside the room.

Thompson moved so fast she didn't see him coming. With a yell he caught her from behind and knocked her down. Her purse struck the floor and Minimus popped out. Before Maxine could stop him, he bolted through the doorway and escaped into the hallway outside. The sound of yapping receded into the distance.

"Minimus!" shrieked Maxine. "Come back here!"

Thompson climbed on top of Maxine and pinned her down with a knee to the chest. "Aren't you forgetting something?" he asked, breaking into laughter which grew louder and more diabolical the closer the spikes came to her scalp.

"Let me go!" she shouted angrily, kicking her legs around and ripping her flimsy dress.

"Don't get so worked up, Jessica!" said Thompson, positioning the Crown of Thorns over her head. "It'll only make it harder on you."

"I want my dog back!"

"Relax and enjoy the pain!"

Maxine gripped Thompson by his shoulders and glared at him, her eyes filled with hatred. "Why don't you relax and enjoy *this* pain, you bastard!"

She buried her foot in his crotch with a sickening thud. He bellowed in agony, dropped the Crown of Thorns, and tumbled off her.

Maxine struggled to her feet. There was no time to retrieve the video camera. Instead, she escaped from the room, hollering frantically for Minimus.

4

On the evening of the BRAIN banquet, the Excelsior Hotel was abuzz.

Hundreds of gentlemen in black tie and ladies wearing colorful evening gowns poured into the lobby from different directions like the tributaries of a mighty river. They flowed across huge carpets and swirled around plush furniture, creating eddies that bubbled with lively conversation. After they finished rekindling old friendships and exchanging the latest gossip, they yielded to the force of gravity once again and gushed towards the Grand Ballroom.

On one bank of this river stood a woman with long, dark hair and a slender face. She was wearing a blue satin dress with a white shawl draped over her shoulders. Her soft, hazel eyes scanned the faces that passed by. Two teenage girls stood close to her, both of whom bore a striking resemblance to her and could only have been her daughters.

A bald man with a beaked nose stalked through the lobby, struggling against the current. Every few steps his head bobbed up and twisted in a different direction as if he were looking for somebody. His beady brown eyes fell on the woman for a moment, then he changed course and pushed towards her. A collection of colorful ribbons hung from his chest like the feathers of an exotic bird.

"Excuse me," he said, shaking a rolled-up program at her. "Are you Caroline Montrose?"

"Yes, I am," answered the woman, turning to face him.

"I'm Sam Stevens, president of BRAIN. It's my job to make sure that everything goes smoothly around here. It's something I take very seriously."

"Then I suppose you're wondering where my husband is," said Caroline.

"You guessed correctly!" spluttered Stevens. "We agreed to meet an hour ago!"

The older of the two girls at Caroline's side spoke up. "He's at home watching a baseball game," she said with a mischievous grin. "It should be over by midnight."

Stevens' eyebrows arched high.

"And after that he'll probably go straight to bed," chimed the other girl, following her sister's lead.

Caroline gave her daughters a look of disapproval, then reassured Stevens with a smile. "Hugh called me a few minutes ago to say he just finished a case and is on his way," she said.

Stevens was far from relieved. "Just finished a case?" he cried incredulously, pulling a handkerchief out of his breast pocket and mopping his brow. "What kind of case?"

"An aneurysm."

"*What?*" The handkerchief slipped from Stevens' grasp and fell to the floor. "He operated on an aneurysm right before the presentation ceremony?" he asked. "Why didn't he ask one of his partners to do it for him?"

"Hugh, give away an aneurysm? Not likely."

"He clips aneurysms every day of the week," Stevens declared huffily. "A banquet in his honor comes along once in a lifetime. Where's his sense of priorities?"

"Don't worry," said Caroline. "He'll be here soon."

Stevens picked up his handkerchief and started to go. Before he got very far, however, he turned around to deliver a parting shot. "My year in office has gone by without a single hitch," he said. "Only a couple of hours remain before the president-elect takes over. If anything goes wrong tonight I'll . . . I'll have a stroke! My legacy is something I take very seriously!"

Caroline returned her attention to the people moving through the lobby of the Excelsior. Their numbers were thinning and the flow had become a trickle. She watched Stevens bustling amongst the stragglers, waving his program around and herding them into the ballroom. Soon there was nobody left to bother and so he paced up and down just inside the front entrance, his eyes darting between the rainy street outside and his wristwatch.

Hugh arrived with minutes to spare. He carried an umbrella and was wearing a heavy black overcoat spattered with raindrops.

"*There* you are!" said Stevens, pouncing on him. "I was sure you weren't coming!"

"Sorry, Sam," said Hugh. "I was detained by an aneurysm. Damned thing decided to rupture just as I was getting close. Bled like stink."

"Tell me about it later. Right now we've got to—"

"You should have been there," continued Hugh, lifting his umbrella and pointing it at the BRAIN president. "I used a straight clip. Slipped both jaws into position and—"

"Hey!" cried Stevens, eyeing the tip of the umbrella as it inched towards his neck. "Do I look like an aneurysm?"

Hugh sized him up. His head was smooth, round, red with rage, and looked like it might burst at any moment.

"As a matter of fact . . ." he began, then thought better of it and lowered his weapon. The drama of the operating room flickered and died.

Caroline walked up to her husband, followed by her daughters.

"Hi there," said Hugh with a big smile, kissing her fondly on the cheek. "Sam, this is my wife, Caroline. And those are—"

"I've already met everybody," said Stevens, glancing at his watch once more. "Now let's go. There isn't much time."

Fussing around like a mother hen, he ushered Hugh and his family into the crowded Grand Ballroom. He led them past scores of round tables laden with dinnerware and flowers and showed them to their places at the front. Standing on a stage, brightly illuminated by spotlights that shone down from catwalks in the ceiling, was a heavy wooden refectory table covered with an elaborately embroidered cloth. Set on top, in an exalted position front and center, was a large shiny silver cup with two curved handles and a wooden base—the Radcliffe Trophy, once the treasured possession of Professor Sir Bradley Radcliffe himself, the British neurosurgeon who founded BRAIN some seventy years before. Awarded annually to a member who had somehow distinguished themselves, it was widely considered to be the holy grail of neurosurgery. Seated in a semicircle around the refectory table, just outside the pool of light and amongst the shadows, were BRAIN's senior officers, all august men who, like Stevens, were wearing colorful ribbons on their chests. A menagerie of feathered friends.

Stevens stood behind a podium at one end of the stage and extracted some notes from his inside pocket. He shook them open and slipped on a pair of reading glasses. When the house lights dimmed, he looked up and faced a significant percentage of the world's neurosurgeons stretching into the distance.

"Ladies and gentlemen," he began, clearing his throat. "I would like to start by—"

Suddenly a loud *fizz* followed by an even louder *pop* erupted from the audiovisual desk at the back of the ballroom. A mushroom cloud billowed into the air and a photograph in triplicate flashed onto the three giant screens above the stage—a naked two-year-old boy sitting in a bucket, looking impishly at the camera. There was no doubt who he was. The face was just the same, only a lot younger.

Recognizing himself, Hugh turned bright red.

Everybody exploded into laughter. Stevens gesticulated towards the technicians, mouthing at them to get the picture off the screens. Despite their frantic efforts, the same image reappeared over and over again.

Hugh pointed an accusing finger at Caroline. "You did this on purpose!" he sputtered playfully.

"They weren't supposed to show that one!" she cried, tears of mirth flowing from her eyes.

The technicians had obviously lost control over their computers. After an embarrassing length of time they were finally able to get rid of Hugh and replace him with an old photograph of Sir Bradley himself, looking far from amused. Stevens removed his glasses with a trembling hand, closed his eyes, and looked for a moment as if he was praying. When he was finished, he lifted his head and spoke into the microphone again.

"If this is the worst thing that happens tonight," he said as he put his glasses back on, "I think I might survive. Hugh, while we're waiting for things to get straightened out, please come up here and get your award."

The crowd broke into applause. Like a winner at the Oscars, Hugh left his seat amongst a flurry of backslapping and handshakes. He bounded up the steps into the lights, shook Stevens' hand, and accepted the Radcliffe Trophy from him. Gazing over the vast sea of darkness in front of him, he waited until the accolades died down. When the clapping ended he set the trophy on the podium, adjusted the microphone, and gestured to the screen above him.

"Now that everybody knows what I look like without my clothes on," he began, "I'm not sure there's much left I can tell you."

More laughter and applause. When it was quiet again, Hugh resumed speaking. "Being a neurosurgeon must be the most gratifying work a human being can do," he said, feeling the beginnings of a lump rising in his throat. "Over the years I've operated on a lot of patients with ruptured aneurysms and you'd think I'd be used to it by now."

Hugh paused and raised finger in the air. "Not true. Every aneurysm is like a brand new—"

A strident yapping noise suddenly filled the ballroom.

Hugh was startled by the interruption. He shielded his eyes from the lights above and searched for the source of the disturbance. Finding nothing out of the ordinary, he pulled the microphone closer to him.

"Every aneurysm is like a brand new experience," he continued, speaking more forcefully. "Something different about the hemorrhage, a variation in the anatomy, a different family sitting in the surgery waiting room—"

The yapping grew louder. A buzz of indignation rose into the air.

Hugh plowed on, raising his voice to a near shout. "As far as I'm concerned, if our work as neurosurgeons ever becomes routine, then we shouldn't be—"

The dog, wherever it was, became even more frenzied. Hugh looked again and spotted a group of people around a table at the back leaping to their feet and scrambling around. The same thing happened at a closer table, then another and another until a trajectory of commotion appeared to be racing directly towards him.

After a few moments he finally pinpointed the problem: the tiniest dog he had ever seen. Could it be a Chihuahua? He was running as fast as he could, his legs no more than a blur. When he crossed a wooden dance floor at the foot of the stage he lost his footing, landed on his belly, and went spinning into somebody's handbag.

A shriek ripped through the ballroom like the tree-bending shockwave from a nuclear detonation.

"*MINIMUS!*"

Numb with bewilderment, everybody turned to face the rear. A skinny woman in a tight dress was standing in an open doorway, no more than a black silhouette against the lights of the hallway behind. Her chest was moving up and down as if she had overexerted herself and was trying to catch her breath.

"*Come back here this instant!*" she shouted, jabbing a finger at a spot on the carpet right in front of her.

Minimus ignited his afterburners. He skidded around a small orchestra, shot up some steps, and ran onto the stage.

The woman was either so deranged in her mind or so preoccupied with catching her dog—or perhaps both—that she was completely oblivious to the stunned people watching from the darkness all around. She hobbled after Minimus as fast as her high heels would permit, colliding with chairs and tables she probably couldn't see. Instead of avoiding the orchestra as the dog had done, she plowed straight through it, scattering musicians and stepping on instruments. She clambered up the steps to the stage, shook off a tambourine that was lodged around an ankle, and stumbled into the lights.

Once he saw the woman clearly, Hugh could scarcely believe his eyes. A brown wig was squatting lopsided on her head, only partially covering her curly red hair underneath. Loosely attached was a crumpled pillbox chapeau. The accompanying birdcage veil was ripped down the middle and covered more of her ears than her eyes. Her dress was also torn in many places, exposing slithers of flushed, sweaty skin. The cups covering her small breasts shifted around her heaving chest. A purse swung from the crook in her arm.

When she spotted her dog, she hoisted her dress above her gnarly knees so she could move better, took a few wobbly steps forward, and slowly backed him into a corner.

"Heeere, doggy-doggy," she said in a sweet, enticing voice, beckoning with a craggy finger as she crept towards him. "Niiice, doggy-doggy." She produced something small and edible from her purse and held it out between thumb and forefinger. "Look what I have for you, Minimus! Your favorite treat! A Honey Nut Cheerio!"

Minimus wasn't interested. With a new outburst of yapping he bolted from the corner, ran between the woman's teetering legs, and made a break for it. When she lunged for him her feet were caught in a loop of electrical cord. She fell hard and broke off one of her high heels.

"*Fuck this!*"

She yanked off both shoes and sent them whizzing into the trombone section of the orchestra.

Somehow Minimus became airborne and landed on the refectory table. He scrambled across it, his sharp toenails ripping threads from the embroidered cloth as he went.

Without the slightest consideration why it was there or to whom it belonged, the woman snatched the Radcliffe Trophy off the podium. As everybody watched in open-mouthed shock, she chased her dog with it, brandishing it in the air like a battle-axe. When she was within range, she turned the venerated cup upside down and slammed it hard onto the refectory table in an ambitious attempt to trap him underneath. He was too quick for her and scampered out of reach. She went after him in hot pursuit, bringing it crashing down again and again, each time missing him by a mile. Eventually she saw the futility of what she was doing and hurled the battered remains of the cup into a distant corner.

Pink-faced and winded, she looked around for something bigger to use. That's when she first noticed the semi-circle of BRAIN officers seated nearby.

"Who are *you*?" she said, reaching up with both hands and pulling the preposterous wig tighter onto her head. When nobody answered she shaded her eyes against the lights above and caught sight of the rows upon rows of crowded tables below her. "And who are *they*?"

A man jumped to his feet and pointed a shaking finger at the woman. "I know who *she* is!" he shouted. "I'd recognize that face anywhere! It's *The Dog!*"

Two thousand gasps sucked the air out of the ballroom.

Like everybody around him, Hugh knew exactly who The Dog was: Maxine Doggette, a wealthy heiress who once wanted to be a doctor but was rejected by multiple medical schools. As if to get her revenge, she turned to nursing and law instead and became a nurse attorney who specialized in medical malpractice. Her predatory behavior around neurosurgeons was legendary. She had targeted one of his partners at Columbia a couple of years ago. Afterwards the poor man sat slumped for hours in the surgery lounge like a shell-shocked soldier, telling anybody who would listen that The Dog was the strangest, nastiest creature—human or otherwise—he had ever encountered. His stories of her bizarre behavior were so outrageous they were hard to believe. Had she really flashed him under the table in order to destroy his concentration during a deposition? Was it true that she paid a spectator in the public benches to fake a seizure and distract jurors during his lawyer's opening statement? Was she responsible for surreptitiously slipping a remote control fart machine into his pocket and activating it while he was being cross-examined on the stand? By the end of a six-week trial, the poor man had taken to the bottle and was having serious problems with his marriage. Hugh had often wondered what kind of lawyer could drive somebody around the bend. Now here she was, not even ten yards away. He would soon find out for himself.

More people rose from their seats and shook their fists at her. "Get her out of here!" cried one. "Stone her!" howled another. There were catcalls and insults, boos and jeers. The rising tide of anger gathered strength and engulfed the stage.

In the midst of her enemies, identified and exposed, The Dog defiantly squared her shoulders, stuck out her chin, and stood her ground.

As BRAIN president, Sam Stevens was in the best position to defuse the situation. Unfortunately he was locked in a state of catatonic apoplexy over what was happening and was completely incapable of doing anything to help. He picked the Radcliffe Trophy off the floor and slowly turned it over in his hands. The damage was heartbreaking; dents everywhere, both handles twisted into pretzels, half of the wooden base split off. He pulled a handkerchief from his pocket and for a moment Hugh thought he was going to burst into tears. He dusted off the cup instead as if that would fix everything, and then shuffled mindlessly off the stage, his precious legacy sealed forever.

With Stevens' departure Hugh suddenly felt the onus of leadership land squarely on himself. When he thought about it, the way forward seemed clear enough.

First, Minimus.

He went over to the refectory table and gathered him into his hands.

Ew, what a hideous dog! he thought, getting a close look at his lumpy, lopsided face, misshapen body, and chicken bone legs; a genetic mutation that Mother Nature had neglected to miscarry. Not all was bad though. He couldn't help but notice a certain paradoxical cuteness about him, especially when he looked up with those large, supplicant eyes of his. The poor animal was shivering with fright and his heart pitter-pattered like the inner workings of a pocket watch.

Hugh carefully approached Maxine. Her grey eyes locked onto him as if guided by an early warning radar system programmed into her brain. They were so intense and accusing he had the creepy feeling he was guilty of something before he'd had the chance to utter a word.

"Yours, I presume," he said, cautiously holding out the dog at arm's length as if offering a tasty snack to a wolf.

Maxine snatched Minimus away and pitched him headfirst into her purse. "And who are you?" she asked.

"Hugh Montrose."

Maxine eyeballed him. "You're afraid of me," she eventually concluded.

Hugh was puzzled. "Why should I be afraid of you?" he asked.

Maxine stretched herself to her maximum height like a rooster preparing to crow. "Because I'm Maxine Doggette," she said, her voice engorged with self-importance, "the Queen of Med-Mal."

"Makes no difference to me," said Hugh, struggling to keep his cool. "As far as I'm concerned—"

"I *know* you're afraid of me," she responded, fighting for superiority. "All doctors are. There's no reason why you should be any different. I suppose you'll now want to be on my Do Not Sue list for returning my dog."

"Do Not Sue list?" asked Hugh, looking at her steadily in the eye. "What's that?"

"It's a privileged group of doctors I've promised never to sue."

"Put *me* on your Do Not Sue list," mocked a bold voice from the back row of tables, "and I'll take *you* off my Do Not Cut list!"

Laughter erupted throughout the ballroom.

Maxine whipped around to face a thousand neurosurgeons and their spouses, her eyes shining with malevolence. "Go ahead!" she shouted, shaking a balled fist in the air. "Make fun of me! See if I care! One day the joke will be on you, my friends! I won't rest until I've sued each and every one of you! *Then* you'll be sorry! You'd better learn to respect me because I'm *never* going away!"

A chorus of *oooh*'s arose from the rabble-rousers in the crowd, a demonstration of bravado meant to prove they weren't scared. The laughter that followed, however, was scattered and shallow, suggesting more than a few, at least, believed her threats were plausible.

The situation was quickly deteriorating. Hugh knew he had to do something without further delay. He spotted a big, strong security guard standing near the stage and frantically waved him forward.

"Get rid of that dreadful woman!" he quietly told him when he was closer.

Maxine suddenly whirled around and glared at Hugh, her face flushed as if he had just slapped her. "I heard that!" she shouted. "You called me dreadful!"

The security guard approached Maxine. She pushed him aside and confronted Hugh.

"You can forget about my Do Not Sue list!" she shouted, spraying him with saliva. "First chance I get, I'll slam you with such a nasty lawsuit you'll wish you'd never been born!"

The guard advanced on Maxine again. "Step this way, ma'am!" he growled angrily.

Maxine wasn't finished with Hugh yet. She swept off her wig, displaying the dazzling red hair underneath like a peacock fanning its feathers. "From now on I'll be right behind you wherever you go," she warned him, sticking her face into his. "I'll be watching your every move and waiting for you to make a mistake! Just one itsy-bitsy mistake! That's all I'll need! Then you'll think twice before you call me dreadful again!"

Hugh stared at The Dog in shock and disbelief. He had been exposed to her for only a few minutes and already his heart was racing. How could anybody spend weeks shut up with her in a courtroom? No wonder his partner at Columbia had gone nuts!

"Tonight you've gate-crashed our banquet, smashed our precious trophy, and threatened everybody here with lawsuits," he told her, clenching both hands into fists. "Why don't you leave before you make an even bigger fool of yourself than you already have?"

Maxine turned a dark shade of puce and wound herself up as if getting ready to let loose a punch. The guard grabbed her just in time, pinioned both her arms behind her back, and frog-marched her kicking and screaming off the stage. When he reached one of the ballroom's side doors, he propelled her out and told her to get lost.

5

Maxine found Billy where she left him, parked across the street from the Excelsior Hotel. Earlier she had looked elegant in her evening gown and felt completely in control; a professional woman who knew what she wanted and how to get it. Now when she stormed towards him she was wigless, bare-footed, and dressed in little more than rags. When he caught sight of her he froze with bewilderment. Only when she piled into the back seat of the Rolls Royce and ordered him to take her home did he finally lurch into action.

As Billy drove, Maxine angrily told him what happened. Yes, she had located Defendant Thompson and yes, as expected, she had no difficulty luring him to the room upstairs. When she got down to business, however, he had opened his briefcase and produced some ghastly clamping device he used in surgery. He had actually wanted to attach it to her head! Many men had weird sexual deviancies, but his was the worst!

"You knew about that clamp, *didn't* you!" shouted Maxine.

"No!" cried Billy, recoiling in horror. "I had no idea!"

"You're lying! You thought you'd keep it a secret and play a sick joke on me!"

"That's not true! I swear it!"

Maxine whipped Minimus out of her purse and clung to him like a security blanket, muttering something about dogs being the only things in this world she could trust. "I suppose there's no sense arguing with you, Billy," she said, searching Minimus' fathomless eyes for their usual calming effect. "I'll never be able to prove anything. At least I never felt personally threatened. Just kicked him where it hurts the most and made my escape. Anyhow—all that seems so unimportant now, considering what happened next."

"What happened next?" asked Billy, eager to move off the subject of ghastly clamping devices.

Maxine told him how Minimus had tumbled from her purse and ran out of the room. She chased him through the hotel and eventually caught up with him in the Grand Ballroom where BRAIN was conducting some kind of ghoulish ritual. There she met a neurosurgeon who introduced himself as Hugh Montrose. The two had a confrontation and Montrose insulted her in a particularly personal and offensive way.

"He made a mockery of me in front of two thousand people!" fumed Maxine, curling a set of spidery fingers around Minimus.

"No!"

"And as if that wasn't enough," added Maxine, "he also had the insolence to throw me out! Me! Maxine Doggette! Manhandled by a security guard! Can you believe it? I've never been treated so atrociously in my life!"

Which was not true at all, she realized as soon as the words left her mouth. By far the worst treatment she had ever received started at the tender age of eight after she lost her mother and father in a tragic plane crash and was subsequently transferred to the care of a cold and heartless great-aunt, her only remaining relative. Agatha Doggette wasn't rich like Maxine's parents and lived her declining years in a constant state of seething jealousy. When her grandniece showed up on her doorstep one day with a small suitcase in one hand, a red-headed rag doll named Rosie in the other, and a hundred million dollars safely tucked away in a trust fund, the repugnant woman went out of her way to be as mean as possible.

Maxine's life changed dramatically. Her parents had loved to read her fairy tales and let her fertile imagination run wild. Afterwards she dressed in colorful, frilly clothes, put on make-up, costume jewelry, and perfume, and played the part of a beautiful princess who lived in a castle. In stark contrast, Aunt Agatha was about as warm and loving as an icicle and never spent much time with her at all. She threw away all of Maxine's playthings and forced her to do endless chores instead. No sleepovers, birthday parties, television, movies, or anything else that was fun. When Maxine broke the rules, as she was prone to do quite often, her great-aunt punished her by locking her in a dark, musty basement for hours on end. In the beginning Maxine handled it bravely by pretending an evil witch cast a spell over her and had thrown her into the castle dungeons. Eventually, though, harsh realities asserted themselves and she mourned for her dead parents every day.

That man Montrose made a big mistake when he called me dreadful, simmered Maxine, gripping Minimus tighter around his middle. Any other word and she might have shrugged it off. People were always saying unpleasant things about her, either behind her back or directly to her face, and by now she was used to it. But the word he chose had been the exact same one Aunt Agatha used that terrible day on the ferry only a few short months after Maxine moved in with her. The two of them were heading to a funeral on the Kitsap Peninsula and were halfway between Seattle and Bremerton when Maxine accidentally dropped her great-aunt's camera overboard. In response, Aunt Agatha was as hateful and malicious as any human being could ever be.

"You're a dreadful little girl!" she screamed, grabbing Rosie away from Maxine. "See how *you* like it!" And then she actually did the unthinkable: fling Rosie into the Puget Sound after the camera. "Absolutely *dreadful*!"

Maxine watched in shock as Rosie, bobbing up and down in the ferry's wake, was swiftly carried away. She ran to the stern and almost jumped from the railing when a deckhand restrained her at the last moment.

"Let me go!" she had screamed, struggling to free herself. "I want my Rosie back!"

The ferry neither stopped nor turned around. Rosie became a dot amongst the distant waves, then finally disappeared from view altogether.

Maxine was never the same again.

Aunt Agatha's cruelty and constant criticizing ground on for years. Maxine grew up believing she was seriously flawed and that the fault was all hers. Filled with feelings of shame and guilt, she shunned friendships and spent most of her time alone. In college, after her aunt had died and gone to hell, she tried to rescue what little was left of her self-esteem by applying to medical school. Her plan might have worked if those admissions committees had looked on her kindly instead of slamming the door in her face, proving themselves just as callous as her aunt had ever been.

Damn those doctors! Let them join Aunt Agatha in hell and burn for all eternity!

"Ms. Doggette!" cried Billy. "Stop squeezing so hard! Minimus can't breathe!"

Maxine looked down. Minimus' body was ballooning purple on either side of her hand.

"Oh my goodness!" she cried, quickly releasing him. He tumbled into her lap, looking dazed and gasping for air.

After her failure to get into medical school Maxine reached a new low. Sometimes she developed relationships but they never lasted very long. She deliberately destroyed them to avoid getting hurt while simultaneously giving herself some semblance of control over her life. While in nursing school she became all those things that normal people detested: demanding, fickle, hormonal, unpredictable, and maneuvering—qualities that made it easy for her to subsequently gain admission to law school. After she graduated her legal career took off reasonably well and yet she became more socially isolated than ever before. With neither friends nor family around, she was always looking for new ways to cope. One day she found an adorable teacup Chihuahua at the Humane Society. She rescued him from certain death, took him home, and quickly discovered that harmless little dogs made much better companions than humans ever did.

"If I let Montrose get away with it," said Maxine, prodding Minimus back to life with a finger, "all those neurosurgeons will think I'm all bark and no bite! I'll never be able to force another settlement again! Don't you see? I have no choice but to make an example of him!"

"Yes, ma'am!"

"Listen to me, Billy. I've got a new assignment for you. It's top priority so put everything else on the back burner. Find out everything you can about Montrose: how many times he's been sued for malpractice, what kind of insurance he has, how big his personal assets are. I want information on his marriage, his children, and his affairs. Conduct the same kind of investigation that you did on Defendant Thompson. Look for his weaknesses. Dig up one I can use against him."

"*Another* of your investigations?"

Maxine looked at Billy sharply. "Do you have a problem with that?"

Billy's surly eyes said yes. He obviously wanted to sue doctors, not spy on them. When he grunted his reply, however, he managed to make it sound like a no.

"Good," said Maxine. "And one more thing: go by the hotel room later and retrieve the video camera. I didn't have time to get it myself."

"Yes, ma'am."

"And no peeking!"

"No, ma'am."

Maxine lit a cigarette to signal she was finished talking and wanted a rest. As Billy drove on in sulky silence, she occasionally glanced down to check on Minimus. He was breathing easier now and had returned to his usual black color. If she ever managed to make good on her threats to throttle Montrose with a major lawsuit one day, she would make certain the insolent bastard was not so fortunate.

6

The tennis ball, when it came, flew far over Julie Winter's head and splashed into the shallow waters of the Puget Sound behind her.

She planted her hands on her hips and looked down Alki beach with an open-mouthed sense of wonder. Patrick, her thirteen-year-old son, had just thrown the ball. He must have been standing at least fifty yards away and was grinning with obvious pride. She hadn't realized he was so strong and made a mental note to tell her husband Gary about it when they returned home. Maybe he should contact the school's baseball coach. The team could use a good right arm.

"I'll get it!" shouted Patrick in a ridiculously deep voice. It had only recently broken and Julie was still couldn't get used to the change.

He stepped forward, his bare feet scuffing through the soft grey sand.

"No, I will!" shouted his fifteen-year-old sister, Jennifer, as she kicked away her sandals and broke into a run. The sea breeze caught her long, dark hair and it streamed horizontally behind her.

"Oh no you don't!" cried Patrick with a sudden burst of speed.

Jennifer looked over her shoulder and shrieked when she saw him coming. "It's mine!" she shouted. "Go away!"

Brother and sister raced towards the tennis ball, but in the end it was Rolo, the family's chocolate Labrador, who reached it first.

He swept in from nowhere, ran into the foamy surf, and snatched the ball from the water with his mouth. He returned to Julie, shook himself off, and dropped it in front of her.

"I win!" laughed Julie, triumphantly holding the wet ball in the air.

Patrick took it from her, wound himself up like a real pitcher, and threw it as hard as he could. It soared into the clear blue sky and almost struck a passing seagull.

"Come on, Jennifer!" he shouted, giving his laughing, stumbling, breathless sister a push in the right direction. "Last one there's a rotten egg!"

Julie watched Patrick and Jennifer take off again and followed at a leisurely pace. Rolo strolled along beside her, his tongue lolling from his mouth. It was a good idea to come to this place today, she decided. Recently her children had been stressed from all the usual teenager pressures—school work, keeping up with their peers, overwhelming extracurricular schedules—and were constantly at each others' throats; bickering, complaining, making everybody around them miserable. Today, the family reached a new low. Parents loudly accused children of being spoiled rotten, selfish, lazy, and rude. Children accused parents of having no understanding whatsoever of their problems. Seemed like a good time for everybody to call a truce and go to Alki for some fresh air.

So far, thank God, it was working. As soon as Jennifer and Patrick were chasing the tennis ball around the beach they reverted back to their normal, happy selves. Julie felt enormous relief and hoped the truce would last as long as possible.

Many other families were also outdoors on this fine Saturday afternoon—possibly for the same reasons. As usual, the view from Seattle's prettiest beach was spectacular. A freighter piled high with orange containers slowly moved against a backdrop of a low-lying shore rimmed with trees. In the distance, the snow-tipped peaks of the vast, empty Olympic Peninsula rose dramatically into the sky.

Julie resolved to bring her third grade class here on a field trip one day. No self-respecting school teacher should pass up the opportunity to show their students such a beautiful place as this.

Patrick's booming voice interrupted her thoughts. "Mom!" he called.

Julie saw him huddling with Jennifer beside a pile of large rocks. "What's the matter?" she asked.

"Come here, Mom! We need your help!"

Julie walked up the beach to join her children.

"The ball went in there," said Jennifer, pointing into a dark crevice.

"Did you try reaching in?" asked Julie, peering between the rocks.

"Yes. It's too far."

"Here, let me try." Julie balanced herself on two boulders and slipped her arm between them. She explored the cold, wet sand with her hand. Patrick and Jennifer watched her with uncertainty.

"Almost got it!" she said, feeling the course texture of the ball with her fingertips. She stretched her body as far as she could. Her muscles strained from the exertion. "Just another millimeter and—"

An intense pain instantly exploded somewhere in her lower back. She fell backwards onto the sand, gasping for breath and unable to move.

"Mom! What happened?" said Jennifer, scrambling over.

The pain was the most intense Julie had ever experienced. "My back!" she cried.

Patrick scuffled up next to his sister. "We should call Dad, Jennifer," he said with a worried look.

"No, don't!" interceded Julie. "He's at work and hates to be interrupted."

The truth, she knew, was more complicated than that. Her husband, Gary, was a physics teacher at the local high school and was giving a special weekend tutorial to some of his students who were about to take their SAT's. Unfortunately the principal was a tyrant and was always threatening disciplinary action if his staff took any liberties. Leaving the classroom to go to the beach, even under these circumstances, would definitely qualify.

"I don't care," said Jennifer, searching her pockets for her cell phone. "This is an emergency." She dialed her father's cell number. He answered after the first ring.

"Jennifer?"

"Hi, Dad," she replied with tension in her voice. "Mom hurt her back at the beach and we—"

"Hurt her back?" interrupted Gary, sounding alarmed. "How?"

"Reaching for a tennis ball."

"Put her on the line."

Jennifer held the phone up to her mother's ear. "He wants to talk to you, Mom."

Gary's voice sounded far away. "Julie? Honey? Are you alright?"

"Yes," gasped Julie. "I'm fine, Gary. But I don't think I can drive home like this." A bolt of lightning crackled down her legs and she drew in a short, sharp breath.

"I'm coming to get you right now."

"No! You'll get into trouble!"

"You're more important than any stupid tutorial. I'll be there as soon as I can."

Twenty minutes later an old beat-up Ford Explorer raced into the beach parking lot and screeched to a halt. The driver's door flew open and Gary jumped out. He leapt over a tangle of driftwood and hurried to where Julie and the kids were waiting.

Julie looked up, wincing in pain. She saw her husband's face above her. He had wavy brown hair down to his shoulders, a long, untidy beard, and small, delicate nose. His normally friendly and easy-going blue eyes were serious and down to business.

"Do you think you can walk?" asked Gary, dropping to his knees beside her.

"Maybe," said Julie.

"Here, let's get you to the car," said Gary, putting one arm around her waist and gently helping her to her feet.

"*Owww*, Gary! Watch out! That *hurts*!"

"Easy now!" he said, steadying her. "Let's go real slow. One step at a time."

With Gary on one side and Patrick on the other, Julie slowly hobbled across the beach towards the parking lot. Rolo loped after them, holding the tennis ball in his mouth and looking sad.

"What about Mom's car?" asked Jennifer as they approached the parking lot.

"We'll just have to fetch it later," said Gary. "Right now, we need to get her home."

The trip took much longer than it usually did. Julie lay slumped in the back seat, crying out every time he went over a bump. Her children sat on either side of her and stared solemnly out of the windows.

When they eventually arrived home, Julie crawled into bed and Gary reluctantly returned to work.

Julie remained incapacitated for the rest of the weekend.

Jennifer and Patrick had never seen their mother in so much pain. They crept around the house like mice, afraid of disturbing her. Gary searched the internet for help, found a medical website, and investigated the subject of low back problems. He soon learned that the initial treatment for this sort of problem was bed rest, heat, ice, and massage.

When he followed the website's advice, however, Julie's pain only worsened. On Sunday evening he entered the darkened bedroom, stepped over Rolo, and eased himself onto the edge of the bed.

"You won't be able to go to work tomorrow like this," he said simply.

Julie looked up at him from amongst her pillows. "I know," she agreed, grimacing with frustration. "I'll call in later and tell them to arrange for a substitute teacher."

"If this isn't better by the morning, I'll skip work too and take you to see a doctor."

Julie shook her head. "No," she said. "Go to work and stay out of trouble with your principal. Besides, I don't want to see any doctors. I'm almost as afraid of them as I am of the pain. God knows where things might lead. It'll be expensive too and we don't exactly have the money. No, I'll just stay at home and wait until the things get better on their own."

"But just *look* at you, Julie," replied Gary, adjusting the pillows under her head. "You can't even move. It's important to get this checked out. Don't forget, summer is right around the corner. We have to get you back on your feet by then."

Julie acknowledged he had a point. The family's annual vacation was promising to be something special. Every summer they drove their camper, affectionately named Harvey the RV, around the country to visit national parks. This year they were planning to go to Yellowstone for the first time. They had organized the trip in great detail and it was hard to imagine canceling because of some trouble with back pain.

"But who would I see?" asked Julie. "We've never needed a doctor for something like this before."

"There's a family practice clinic at the shopping center down the street," said Gary. "We can make an appointment with somebody there."

"Are you sure? It's so hard to know who we can trust. Maybe if we waited a little longer, things might—"

"No, Julie! You *have* to see a doctor! You need to get well as soon as possible. You won't if we don't take care of this properly."

Julie brightened a bit. "I suppose you're right," she said with a faint smile.

"Of course I am," said Gary. "Now get some rest. I'll check on you later to see if you need anything. Okay?"

"Okay."

When Gary was gone, Julie closed her eyes and let out a long, deep sigh. So, she was actually going to see a family physician about her back pain. There was no denying she was nervous about the prospect. But what was the worst thing that could happen?

No definitive answer came to mind—just a tiny, persistent

voice warning her to stay home.

The next morning Gary took Julie to see Dr. Taylor, the family physician at the local shopping center. He led her by the arm into the waiting room and helped her into a well-worn chair. Once she was settled, he threaded his way past half a dozen elderly people and made his way to the reception desk.

"Good morning," he said, smiling nervously at a young blond woman who was painting her fingernails. "I'm Gary Winter. My wife has an appointment with—"

"Fill out these registration forms," she said, pushing some papers in his direction.

While Gary busied himself with the paperwork, Julie looked around the waiting room with growing unease. The patients weren't simply elderly. They were *ancient*. Some of them gripped plastic bags full of prescription bottles with their withered, bony hands. She had nothing in common with these people. Was this the right place for her? She was thinking about heading for the exit when she looked down a long, hallway behind the reception desk and was astonished by what she thought she saw. Was that really a—

"Julie!"

A nurse in blue scrubs and white sneakers was standing by an open doorway.

Gary helped his wife to her feet and escorted her across the waiting room. When they reached the nurse, he held out the forms he'd been filling out. "I'm sorry," he said, "but I haven't quite finished—"

"No matter," said the nurse. "It's only paperwork. Give it to the receptionist."

Gary did as he was told, then put his arm around his wife and guided her down the hallway.

"It *is* a skull!" said Julie, pointing at the thing that she had seen from the waiting room.

It certainly was, Gary noted. Not a real one though. And not homo sapiens either. They were looking at a model of a Neanderthal skull with big, empty eye sockets, a flat face, and a small sac-like cranium. Underneath was a sign that identified it as having originally come from the head of a trial lawyer.

Neither Gary nor Julie felt like laughing.

The nurse waited for them outside an examination cubicle. "Step in here, please!" she said, waving them along.

Once all three were inside the tiny room, the nurse wrapped a cuff around Julie's arm, pumped it up, and took her blood pressure. By now Julie was so nervous she felt a powerful *thud-thud-thud* in the crook of her arm as the mercury dropped. When the nurse was finished she left the room and shut the door behind her. Julie waited in tense silence, holding Gary's hand and closely monitoring the sounds of the clinic outside.

After an interminable fifteen minutes the door suddenly opened and a man with slick black hair, a thick moustache, and white lab coat stepped in. A stethoscope was draped around his neck. He was pushing along a computer on wheels that was almost as tall as him and resembled an android.

"I'm Dr. Taylor," said the man, sitting on a stool and bringing his computer closer. He pulled a lever underneath somewhere and lowered the monitor screen to eye level. "Now what seems to be the problem?"

"My back is hurting," explained Julie, gingerly laying a hand over the painful areas. "It's so bad, sometimes I can hardly—"

"When did it start?" interrupted Taylor, busy checking little boxes with a mouse.

"Saturday. I was at the beach with my children, Patrick and—"

"What have you done about it so far?"

"We looked up information on the internet and—"

"Excellent," said Taylor, clicking ENTER. "I'm now going to perform some tests on you, Julie. Just sit tight for a minute." He proceeded to poke and prod her with various instruments while muttering strange, incomprehensible things. When he was finished, he returned his attention to the computer and started typing. Gary peaked over his shoulder and tried to follow what he was doing. When Taylor noticed, he clicked REDUCE and Julie's information zipped safely into an obscure corner of the screen.

"Obviously you need an MRI scan," he announced.

"Do you think it's that serious?" asked Julie, incredulously.

"Yes, I do," said Taylor, standing up. He pulled the lever again and the computer rose with him. "You can get one done this afternoon. My receptionist will organize it for you. Come back tomorrow and I'll give you the results. Now I'd better go. Lots of data entry to do before the next patient. If I don't get started now, I'll never finish in time."

And with that, he and his computer left the cubicle.

Bewildered, the Winters sat around for a couple of minutes, then followed him out.

"Gary," whispered Julie as they passed the skull in the hallway again. "Do you think that this is the right doctor for me?"

"I hope so, Julie," said Gary. "At the very least, he can tell us where to go from here."

They returned to the waiting room. Gary approached the receptionist and braced himself for the bill.

The next day, Gary took Julie back to Dr. Taylor's office, MRI disc in hand. They were both filled with anxiety about the information it contained and said little as they were escorted back to the same examination cubicle as before.

When the doctor appeared he was once again accompanied by his computer on wheels. Today his face was speckled with dark cookie crumbs. He took the MRI from Gary, inserted into the disc drive, and read the report when it came up.

"Bad news, I'm afraid," he said, ominously shaking his head.

Julie reached for her husband and held his hand for support. "Bad news?" she asked with a small, frightened voice.

He pointed to his monitor. "You've got six bulging discs in your back."

"Bulging discs?"

"Discs are the padding between the vertebrae," Taylor explained. "They enable you to bend your spine. As you've aged six of yours have become worn and degenerated."

"Worn and degenerated?"

"Here, let me show you." He reached into a pocket, took out six Double Stuf Oreo cookies, and held them one on top of the other.

Gary and Julie looked on with confusion.

"Imagine the dark brown biscuit parts are the bones in your spine," he said, pointing to them. "The white creamy centers are your discs. Now look what happens when I recreate a harmful situation. If I apply pressure like this . . ." He squeezed the stack of Oreos together. ". . . something has to give." Soft cream oozed out in all directions. "That's what your back looks like."

Gary and Julie stared at him in shock.

"Nothing a surgeon can't fix," said Taylor, popping the top two Oreos into his mouth and crunching them with his teeth. "Go and see Dr. Frank Clegg. He's an orthopedic surgeon at the Emerald Spine Institute."

"But surely I don't need surgery!" cried Julie with alarm.

"That's not for me to say," said Taylor, brushing loose crumbs from his lab coat. "He'll tell you what to do." He tapped on his keyboard. "There! The referral's already made." Without another word, he dropped the surviving Oreos back into his pocket and left, pulling his computer along behind him.

7

Billy festered in his windowless office at the Doggette law firm, high up a skyscraper in downtown Seattle. He cradled his jaw in the palm of one hand and stared apathetically at a computer screen.

God he was tired, he thought as he blinked his weary eyes and yawned. He spent the last few days researching Hugh Montrose's life and hadn't slept nearly enough. None of his professors in school ever mentioned that lawyers had to work so hard. If only he could go back to his apartment right now and climb into bed!

His eyes wandered over to a framed photograph of Maxine. He snapped the picture a couple of years ago when she had visited his law school to deliver a lecture that would forever change his life. The topic: ethical dilemmas in the practice of medical malpractice law. She set out to prove that it was okay for lawyers to violate all ethical boundaries in order to enrich themselves. Her theories were so outrageous that even the American Trial Lawyers Association had accused her of immorality. Billy, on the other hand, was so inspired he decided to become a superstar in the world of medical malpractice. He couldn't wait to sue a bunch of doctors and make buckets of money! When he interviewed for the position at Maxine's law firm, he told her that he wanted to file his first lawsuit without delay. She agreed to his terms but reneged as soon as he signed his contract and ordered him to rake up muck on Giles Thompson instead. What was the point? An ordinary private investigator could do the same thing. Did she want him to wither away and die like the potted plant next to his desk? When he finally summoned the nerve to complain, she said all medical malpractice attorneys had to learn the business from the bottom up and knowing how to discover the opposition's weaknesses was the best place to start.

And now this! Another chickenshit investigation. This time some neurosurgeon named Hugh Montrose. When would she give him what he wanted?

Somewhere underneath the piles of notes on his desk, a telephone rang. Billy found it and picked up the receiver. "Hello?" he answered.

"Billy," said a husky voice on the other end of the line. It was Maxine.

"Yes, ma'am?"

"Report to me immediately."

"Yes, ma'am."

Billy gathered up the loose papers on his desk and hurried from his office. When he reached Maxine's door his weariness was already forgotten. He paused a moment to give his beating heart a chance to settle down, took a deep breath, and knocked.

"Enter!"

Billy pushed open the door and stepped inside. Every time he visited Maxine's private office the sense of wonder it stirred within him never diminished. The place was huge, with more square footage than the rest of her space put together. Tall windows afforded a spectacular view over the Puget Sound, the Olympic and Cascade mountain ranges, and Mount Rainier. Wooden shelves filled with leather-bound law books and autographed photos of famous politicians lined the walls. Prominently displayed under overhead spotlights was a framed document that certified Maxine as a Super Lawyer for the state of Washington. Hanging next to it was an issue of the magazine *Suing for Dollars* with her haughtiest, I'm-a-hotshot-nurse-attorney-who-takes-no-prisoners face displayed on its front cover.

When a woman was worth an estimated two hundred million dollars, her money, so it seemed, could buy anything.

Even if she was as eccentric as Maxine Doggette.

One day, Billy resolved, *he* would have an office like this, only even bigger and more impressive. The walls would be decorated with dozens of Super Lawyer certificates and his face would be smiling from the cover of *Time*, not *Suing for Dollars*.

Maxine was at her desk, dressed in a smart designer pantsuit. She wore a different outfit every day of the year, always brightly colored and full of frills. Her wardrobe back home must have stretched for miles and been worth a fortune. She was holding the video camera from the Excelsior Hotel in her hands and snapped shut the viewing screen the instant Billy appeared. Judging from the look of revulsion across her face, he had the feeling that she had just been watching herself cavorting in the sack with Defendant Thompson.

"Everything turned out okay?" asked Billy, nodding towards the camera.

"Better than expected," said Maxine, putting it inside her top desk drawer and firmly shutting it. "He'll cooperate now. I'm sure of it."

Minimus was in his favorite spot: atop Maxine's desk, reclined on a burgundy-colored velvet cushion monogrammed with a fancy gold M. She picked him up, flipped him upside down like a waffle iron, and laid him in her lap. Taking one of his paws in her hands, she inspected his toenails closely.

"Sit down," she told Billy without looking up.

Billy lowered himself into a hard, wooden chair in front of her desk. Feeling like a schoolboy who had been summoned to the principal's office, he fiddled and squirmed as he waited.

Maxine produced a pair of doggy nail clippers and positioned its sharp jaws around Minimus' biggest, nastiest toenail. "Tell me what you've found on . . ." She squeezed the handles hard together. ". . . *Montrose!*" With a loud click, the nail separated from the rest of her dog and disappeared downrange.

Billy leafed through the papers in his hands and cleared his throat. "He's fifty years old," he said, "and the chairman of neurosurgery at Columbia Medical Center. Best known for his work on brain aneurysms. He operates on at least two hundred of them every year and publishes tons of research papers on the subject. In fact, according to the newspapers, he was awarded a special prize at the banquet the other night for his lifetime accomplishments. The journalists who wrote the articles were quite effusive about his surgical skills. Seems like he invited them to observe an operation."

Maxine's face darkened as she searched for the next largest toenail. "Journalists are such an impressionable bunch of ignoramuses," she muttered grumpily. "Now tell me something that might interest me."

Billy hurried on to a fresh page of notes. "How about this?" he said. "He's never been sued for medical malpractice before."

"Ah-hah!" cried Maxine. "So he's a . . ." Once again she squeezed the clipper handles. Another loud click. ". . . *virgin*!"

Billy ducked as a second toenail sailed over his head. "Yes, ma'am," he said. "That's unusual, isn't it?"

"Extremely!" said Maxine. "Most neurosurgeons get peppered with lawsuits throughout their careers. Sometimes the cases are usually so frivolous they're quickly dropped. Others are settled to make them go away. Only rarely do they lead to a trial. But a virgin? At *his* age? What luck! I *love* virgins! Full of righteous indignation at being named. Always prattling on about how important their *un*important reputations are. They're the ones who get the queasiest and lose their stomachs when things get rough." She moved on to a third toenail. "What did you find out about his insurance policy?"

"His malpractice carrier is Grand National. A premium of one hundred and twenty thousand dollars a year buys him a million dollars of coverage per claim."

Maxine looked up. "Only a million?" she said, her mouth widening into a vile grin. "This is sounding better all the time!"

"What's so good about that?" asked Billy.

"A million's not nearly enough for what I have planned for him," replied Maxine, returning her attention to Minimus. "When the jury makes its *multi*-million dollar award against him he'll be left high and dry. I'll just help myself to his personal assets and garnish his wages for the next hundred years. He *does* have personal assets, doesn't he? Significant ones, I hope."

"He owns a million dollar house in Bellevue," replied Billy. "Paid off his mortgage ten years ago. No second home. Three modest cars. If he's wealthy, he doesn't flaunt it."

"I guarantee you he's got plenty of money stashed away somewhere," said Maxine. "All neurosurgeons do. Won't do him any good though. Somehow I'll eventually . . . *find it*!" She squeezed the clippers for the third time. The resulting projectile ricocheted off the top of her desk and zinged into a corner.

"Now tell me what kind of doctor he is," said Maxine, putting away the clippers and flourishing a nail file in her hand.

"He's a neurosurgeon," said Billy flatly. "I thought you already knew that."

"What I *meant* was," said Maxine rolling her eyes at his innate stupidity, "what's he like?"

"Oh I see," said Billy, hurriedly flipping to another page of notes. "He's generally well respected by his colleagues around the hospital. A pleasant, friendly kind of guy. Unpretentious. An ego of modest proportions. Definitely not your typical neurosurgeon. Always on time for his cases and responds within minutes to the emergency room. A responsible professional. His patients rate him pretty highly too, giving him top grades in all categories. Their surveys also say he knows his business and takes their problems seriously. Always willing to listen and go the extra mile to provide good care."

Maxine scowled at the positive tone of Billy's answer. "What about his personal life?" she asked, returning her attention to the first toenail again and rasping away with her file.

"He has been married to a woman named Caroline for the past twenty-five years," he answered, deciphering the scribbles before him. "Two teenaged daughters, both in high school."

"Any affairs? Dalliances with the nurses at the hospital? Mistresses? I mean, is he anything like Defendant Thompson? I have to know his vulnerabilities!"

Billy hesitated before he replied. "That sort of thing is kind of difficult to ascertain from the internet," he finally said with an apologetic look.

"I'm sure it is," agreed Maxine, finding the next toenail and bearing down even harder with her file. "But you must have formulated an opinion of your own."

"Well, I have." Billy coughed nervously. "I'm sorry, Ms. Doggette, but you won't like it."

"Go on."

"He's a family man who doesn't have affairs. Not a whiff of cheating within a hundred miles of him."

For the next couple of minutes Maxine touched up remaining rough spots, sulking as she digested Billy's information. Eventually she blew a cloud of fresh nail dust off her dog, put away the file, and regarded Billy with calculating eyes.

"Maybe things aren't as bad as all that," she said. "So he follows a straight and narrow path, probably because he hates criticism and conflict. Imagine what'll happen when I slam a virgin like him with his first mega-lawsuit! How will he cope with a steady barrage of *nothing but* criticism and conflict month after month for a couple of years? Not very well, I'd wager."

"But how will you catch him being negligent?" asked Billy.

"Negligence per se is not required," answered Maxine. "Just a confluence of events that could be interpreted as negligence by a handful of half-witted morons sitting in a jury box."

"Okay, so how do you find a . . . a confluence of events?"

"It'll be difficult," said Maxine grimly, "but not impossible."

"Ma'am?"

"Listen, Billy," said Maxine. "A medical malpractice powerhouse like me thrives on a steady supply of reliable information on medical mistakes. You don't think I wait for disgruntled patients to dribble into my waiting room one at a time, do you? If that was the way I did things, I'd be no better off than the millions of lawyers down *there*." She jerked her thumb towards the teeming metropolis far below. "No—unless I'm the lead dog, the view will always be the same. That's why I've taken an avant-garde approach and developed special techniques for obtaining the information I need."

Maxine opened the desk drawer where she had put the video camera and took out a black leather notebook. She handed it to Billy and told him to look inside. He saw scores of names written in her flowery handwriting, a few of which were followed by either an MD or an RN. Next to each name was a telephone number.

"Who are these people?" asked Billy, licking his thumb and flipping through the pages.

"They work in the health care industry," she explained. "Not just doctors and nurses either. In there you'll find hospital administrators, billing accountants, information technologists, industrial injury case managers, therapists, social workers, chart reviewers, and so on. All have two things in common: unprecedented access to medical records and a serious shortage of money. They pass me the information I need to keep my law practice healthy and in exchange I give them the dollars they need to pay their bills. It's an equitable arrangement. Everybody comes away satisfied. Except defendants, of course, and I can't say anybody spends much time worrying about *them*."

"A network of informants!" cried Billy.

"That's right!" said Maxine, retrieving her notebook and throwing it back into the drawer. "My favorites are the people who work at health insurance companies. They're the ones who were corrupt enough to tell me about Defendant Thompson. Even provided me with his social security number and mother's maiden name for no extra charge. How's that for service? With regard to Montrose, we're in luck. One of my informants is an anesthesiologist who works with him at Columbia Medical Center. I think it's time to give Dr. Henry Harrison a call."

"You'll have him spy on Dr. Montrose in the operating room and report any medical mistakes?"

"Say, you catch on fast!" cried Maxine. "It won't be long before he'll witness something. Nobody's perfect. Not even Montrose."

Billy clapped his hands together. "That's brilliant!" he declared.

Maxine positively glowed. "I know," she said smugly.

Billy saw an opportunity to bring up an important issue. He coughed nervously and cleared a throat that suddenly felt as dry as desert sand. "Ms. Doggette . . ."

"Yes?"

"When will you let me file a lawsuit against a doctor? I've seen how it's done and it looks pretty easy to me."

Maxine gave Billy an icy look. "It's much more difficult than you think," she admonished him. "I had to work hard for years before I learned how. You need a lot more experience before I can allow you to—"

"But where will I get the experience?" interrupted Billy.

"The courtroom."

"And when will I—"

"Billy!" cried Maxine. "Listen to me! First, you start off examining a treating physician—somebody other than the defendant who was unlucky enough to get mixed up in the case. After that I'll give you a medical expert—an outside physician who's paid to say how things should have been done differently. When I'm satisfied you know how to handle both of those, you move to the next step: examining the defendant himself. That can be tricky sometimes. Requires a steady nerve and a quick mind. Next, you get an opening statement or a closing argument. Only then are you qualified to sue your very own doctor. You have to work your way up the ladder like everybody else, young man. Not begin right at the top. My rules on this subject are very clear."

"So when will you let me examine a treating physician in court?" asked Billy, unable to hide the disappointment in his voice.

"When the time is right," answered Maxine impatiently, "and not a moment before. Now stop pestering me about it. Go back to your office and pay attention to more important things. Keep searching for information on Montrose! Visit his hospital and ask questions about him. Be discrete! If he goes out at night, follow him and see where he goes. Don't let him out of your sight. Do you hear me?"

Billy knew it was pointless to press an issue as inconsequential to Maxine as his career. Sometimes she was as tough as Minimus' toenails and never yielded to badgering.

"Yes, ma'am. I hear you loud and clear."

8

Gary and Julie looked in awe at the gleaming glass and steel tower of the Emerald Spine Institute. They saw an imposing façade with two curved wings spread to either side like welcoming arms, inviting mere mortals to put aside their fears and walk through the front door.

Come unto me all ye who are suffering back pain and I will give you relief, the building seemed to be saying.

Inside, the lobby was several stories high, decorated with elegant furniture, exotic trees, and tinkling fountains. Feeling as if they were visiting a five-star hotel and not a hospital, they walked past fish tanks big enough for beluga whales, rode up an escalator, and found themselves in a waiting room where glass cabinets displayed surgical instruments. After they had filled out their paperwork and had written a check for the co-pay, they sat down in plush seats and waited anxiously for their appointment.

The night before, they had searched the internet and learned that the Emerald Spine Institute was an internationally recognized center of excellence. According to the website, the institute's experienced board-certified physicians were each a leader in their field and provided unsurpassed patient care. The emphasis was on conservative management and minimally invasive techniques that allowed patients with debilitating back pain to return to an active life in the least amount of time.

Below such reassuring words were dozens of pictures of distinguished doctors in their neatly pressed white lab coats, each paired with a biographical paragraph that gushed on about their worldly accomplishments. Dr. Frank Clegg's face, however, was strangely missing. In its place, a brief note stated that no current photograph was available. His biography proclaimed that *Western*

Washington magazine had honored him several years in a row by including him in its annual list of Best MD's.

"Are you here to see Dr. Clegg?"

Gary and Julie looked up from their magazines and saw a nearby woman smiling at them. She was in her forties and was wearing a necklace of wooden beads.

"Yes," said Julie, wincing from a fresh spasm in her back.

"You look very uncomfortable," she said sympathetically. "Well, at least you're in the right place. Dr. Clegg, God bless his soul, is a wonderful doctor. The best in the business. I had back pain too, but he fixed me completely. I've never felt so good in my life."

"How did he do it?" asked Gary.

"I had an operation," said the woman, eager to share her experience. "A lumbar fusion. Best decision I ever made."

Julie shot her husband a look full of doubt. "An operation is *not* what I had in mind," she said to the woman, although she could have been addressing Gary.

"Oh, they're not that bad!" laughed the woman. "Just a day or two of pain until everything heals. Nothing a little morphine can't handle."

"Julie, you have to keep an open mind," said Gary. "Your top priority right now should be to get better. If having an operation is what it's going to take, you have to accept that."

"That's right!" agreed the woman. "It took me a bit to get used to the idea, but I came round soon enough and here I am! Good as new!"

A nurse with long blond hair and green scrubs called out Julie's name. Gary and Julie followed her into a small, windowless examination room where another computer on wheels was parked in a corner. Pinned to the walls were posters of human beings without their skins on, showing where the various bones, muscles, and nerves were located.

After a few minutes, the door opened and the doctor walked in.

As soon as Gary and Julie saw Dr. Frank Clegg in the flesh they understood why somebody thought it best to omit his photograph from the institute's website. His head was shaped like the Neanderthal skull they had seen in Dr. Taylor's clinic—sloping forehead, prominent brow, hollow eyes, flat nose, high cheekbones, and protruding teeth as big as clothes-pegs. His hair was short and stubbly and cauliflower ears stuck out from the sides. His body was powerfully built with big, bulging muscles. He had long arms, simian hands, and fingers the size of bananas. The white coat he was wearing was as big as the sails on a yacht, embroidered with his name and festooned with badges.

"You obviously need a complete work-up," he announced in a deep throaty voice after listening to a brief history. "I'll order a thoracic MRI, lumbar CT myelogram, and EMG's of the lower extremities."

"All that?" asked Gary, trying to remember what the internet had said about tests. "Didn't she already have an MRI scan?"

"Lumbar, not thoracic. The more information, the better."

"But that'll take weeks!" protested Julie.

"Here, we do them in a single day. How does today work for you?"

"Today?" exclaimed Julie. "But I—"

"When you're finished, come back here and I'll tell you what to do."

Julie wasn't sure how to respond. The kids had to be collected from school and driven to various after-school activities. There was always so much to do. On the other hand, she could definitely see the advantage to getting some quick answers.

"Alright," she sighed. "Leave me here, Gary. Go and take care of the kids. Pick me up later when you have time."

Before Julie could change her mind she was whisked off to the radiology department, a maze of corridors and rooms stuffed with complicated machines that must have cost a fortune. Her first stop was MRI where she lay on a narrow table and was slid into the yawning mouth of a scanner. She remained as still as possible for half an hour while the machine clanged and clattered like the percussion section of an orchestra.

Next, she had a myelogram and discovered what it was like to have a three inch long needle sunk into the small of her back. Clear, colorless spinal fluid dripped out and was collected into a test tube. A label with Julie's name was stuck to the outside of the glass and the specimen was sent to the lab. Metrizamide dye was injected into the spinal canal via the same needle and she was bombarded with X-rays from many different directions. A technologist with long red fingernails and her hair in a bun told her when she could and couldn't breathe.

After the department of radiology came the department of electromyography where a man with thick glasses laid her on a couch, poked sharp little electrodes into her legs, and zapped her with enough electricity to make her muscles twitch. He recorded spikes and squiggles into a computer and added his report to Julie's electronic chart.

Finally, towards the end of the afternoon, Julie returned to the orthopedics clinic, black and blue from being poked all day and anxious to hear Clegg's analysis of her condition.

Clegg didn't keep her waiting. When he entered the examination cubicle he went over to the computer in the corner and started typing on its keyboard. The reports from Julie's studies came up on the screen. He read them slowly, his eyes dark and serious. When he was finished he shook his head slowly from side to side, just as Dr. Taylor had done.

A swarm of butterflies fluttered through Julie's abdomen and she wished Gary was there to hold her hand.

Clegg pinned her down with his eyes. "I'm afraid surgery is your only option," he told her bluntly.

The words punched Julie in the gut. The color drained from her face and she gripped the arms of her chair. "So it's serious then?" she asked weakly, her knuckles turning white.

"Yes. I'll show you." Clegg tapped on the keyboard again and a series of X-rays and MRI's appeared. "These are your studies. You have six bad discs in your back. The worst is the bottom one at the L5-S1 level, right . . ." He pointed to the screen. ". . . here."

Julie had no idea what she was looking at.

"That's where your pain is coming from," explained Clegg. "If you don't do anything about it soon, it could cause serious problems and cripple you for life. A lumbar fusion will save you a lot of trouble."

Julie swallowed hard.

"Don't be alarmed," said Clegg. "We'll implant titanium screws and rods into your back, then add some bone harvested from your hip. Over time, the two bones on either side of the disc space will fuse together."

When Julie heard the gory details she grew faint. "What about the other discs?" she asked.

"They don't look as bad," answered Clegg, sticking his finger into an ear and twisting. "We can save those for another time. Don't worry. We do so many fusions these days the procedure has become quite routine. The pain is sure to go away."

"It will?"

"Definitely," said Clegg, flicking something away. "I guarantee it."

There was an awkward pause before Julie spoke again. "Do you think I should get a second opinion?" she asked, hoping she wasn't giving offense.

Clegg's eyes flashed angrily. "You don't trust me?"

Julie reddened with embarrassment. "Oh I trust you, Dr. Clegg," she said quickly. "You come highly recommended."

"Good," said Clegg, softening a little. "Then a second opinion shouldn't be necessary, should it? Besides, if you see ten different surgeons, they'll all agree with me. You'll have the operation here, at Emerald. We have the most advanced operating rooms in the world. Overhead microscopes, intraoperative MRI scanners, navigation computer systems. You name it, we've got it. No expense spared."

As Julie began to turn the possibility of surgery over in her mind, she heard a soft knock on the door.

"Yes?" barked Clegg.

A nurse's head protruded into the room. "Dr. Clegg, the husband is here."

Clegg's face flashed with annoyance as if he knew he would have to repeat everything. Whatever irritation Julie may have glimpsed, however, was quickly cloaked with a big, toothy, smile. "Show him in," he said.

Gary hurried into the room looking windswept and haggard. "What's the news, doctor?" he asked Clegg anxiously.

"I was just telling your wife she needs an operation," said Clegg, offering Gary a chair.

"Really?" asked Gary, sitting down and grasping Julie's hand. "Are you sure?"

"Absolutely. Let me explain why."

Clegg went over the details once again. When he finished answering questions, he brought up a calendar on the monitor and clicked through its pages. "The sooner we schedule her, the better. I'm thinking June 28th."

"But that's only next week!" spluttered Julie.

"I'm completely booked up July and August," said Clegg solemnly as if being busy was a terrible thing. "It's either now or September. By then, it might be too late."

Gary squeezed Julie's hand. "Remember what we talked about this morning in the waiting room?" he said. "If the doctor says you need surgery, then that's what you must do. He's the expert and should know."

Julie pictured the woman with the wooden beads who had started that particular conversation. She had been so enthusiastic about her own operation. Perhaps Gary was right and she was reacting too negatively to the situation.

Julie closed her eyes and took a deep breath. "Alright, I'll do it," she said.

Gary smiled with relief.

"Excellent!" declared Clegg, making a mark on an electronic calendar with his mouse. "You won't regret it, Julie. I can promise you won't regret it at all."

9

Hugh Montrose's resident at Columbia Medical Center, Richard Elliott, backed away from the operative field and gaped in mute horror at the unfolding disaster before him.

The patient beneath the drapes, Mr. Walter Brown, was full of cancer. The problem started in his lungs a year ago and had spread to his bones, liver, and God only knew where else. Not long afterwards a gobstopper-sized metastasis was found growing in his brain. Dr. Montrose saw him in his clinic and scheduled him for a craniotomy.

The tumor had different plans.

The day before he was supposed to have surgery, Mr. Brown was gripped by a terrifying seizure and his condition plummeted. He was rushed to the emergency room and Richard was summoned. He had already been working sixteen hours straight and, as usual, was exhausted. He wanted to ask one of his fellow residents to fill in for him and head for the call room for a life-sustaining nap instead, but everybody had reached the limit on their hours and had already gone home. When he evaluated Mr. Brown he figured an emergency operation to remove the tumor was the proper thing to do.

"Go ahead and get started," Hugh had told him over the telephone after listening to him present the case. "Expose the brain and locate the tumor. Don't take it out until I get there."

"You'll let me open the head on my own?" Richard had asked, feeling a surge of excitement. Suddenly he wasn't so tired anymore.

"Are you comfortable with it?" asked Hugh.

Richard had assisted with plenty of craniotomies before and had even done a few under supervision. This, however, was the first time he had been given permission to fly solo. He knew he was capable and was anxious to prove himself.

"Yes!" he said enthusiastically. "I'll handle it! Thanks a lot!"

Running on adrenaline fumes alone, Richard had drilled four burr holes in Mr. Brown's skull with a craniotome, a tool whose business end resembled the multi-toothed drill bit used on oil rigs. He connected them using a saw, intermittently altering the angle of the hand piece as he had been taught. When he had removed the bone flap, he gripped it firmly between his fingers, taking special care not to drop the damn thing on the floor—something for which he would certainly lose style points.

So far, so good.

Next, he had opened the underlying dura with a fine pair of scissors. When he saw the exposed brain underneath, he felt the stirrings of a real neurosurgeon. His self-confidence soared high into the sky, only to return to earth soon afterwards with a resounding crash.

He couldn't find the tumor.

Richard had pushed a metal probe over and over again into the brain and watched its centimeter markings being swallowed one by one. No matter how many times he tried or how deep he went, his fingertips couldn't sense the telltale resistance he was looking for.

With each failed attempt, the nausea in the pit of his abdomen grew worse. He had eventually cast aside the stupid probe and used the bipolar and sucker instead, a much cruder way of finding a tumor but one that covered more ground in less time. He had excavated through the brain to no avail and now it resembled pureed bananas and raspberry sauce.

What a disaster!

Richard's self-confidence was shattered. He had been harshly reminded, yet again, that neurosurgical operations were far more difficult than they looked. When his attending, Dr. Montrose, breezed through challenging cases it was not because he had learned his skills by osmosis—reading textbooks and listening to lectures—

but because he had fought hard in the front line trenches day and night for years and learned from the thousands of patients he had treated.

Experience was everything in neurosurgery. Each time Richard dared to believe he was making modest progress, a catastrophe had to happen.

"I've killed him!" Richard muttered under his mask. "I swear to God I've killed him!"

The anesthesiologist, Dr. Henry Harrison, was a short round man who wore wire-rimmed glasses with thick lenses. Normally he stayed out of sight and silently passed gas for hours on end. When trouble broke out, however, his magnified eyes had appeared above the ether screen like a pair of rising moons and were now closely monitoring the situation.

"He'll never wake up after what I've done to him," continued Richard. "I should have put a gun to his head and pulled the trigger. The result would have been the same."

A sucker slid off the drapes. He tried to catch it but wasn't quick enough. It stopped just short of the ground and dangled at the end of its plastic tubing.

"Shit!" he swore. "Now look what I've done!"

Val, the circulating nurse, hurried over to a set of glass wall cabinets. "I'll get you another," she said helpfully.

"I just don't understand," said Richard, fighting back tears of frustration. "It's a whopper in the middle of the frontal lobe. Right . . . there!" He prodded the brain with his finger, making it wobble like Jell-o. "I've looked everywhere and it's not where it's supposed to be!"

Val handed new tubing to the scrub tech, Lori, and helped her get the system up and running. When the sound of rushing air returned, Richard snatched the new sucker off the tray table and resumed poking around. The brain shuddered and shook. A chunk the size of Rhode Island suddenly disappeared up the tubing with a loud *slurp*, sounding just like dregs of an ice cream sundae going up a straw.

"Whoa!" cried Richard. "Turn it down!"

"Okay, okay," said Val, twisting knobs on a nearby wall and making things hiss. "Keep your hair on!"

Harrison's magnified eyes hovering over the ether screen grew even larger.

"Sometimes I wonder why I ever went into neurosurgery," Richard whined as he resumed his fruitless search. "Sure I knew it would be hard, but not *this* hard. I thought I was tough enough, but now I'm not so sure. How was I to know I'd be spending so much time in the hospital working my butt off? My wife never gets to see me any more. The kids don't even know who I am. If I was smart I would resign my position and go into something else."

"Why don't you then?" asked Val.

"Dr. Montrose keeps encouraging me to stick with it," said Richard. "He tells me that he understands how I feel; one day it'll all seem worthwhile. It doesn't seem right to quit when he's always so supportive. Call his office, Val. Ask him to come. I can't handle this case any longer."

"You're not the only one," said Val, reaching for a phone.

* * *

While Richard Elliott was ransacking Mr. Brown's brain for an elusive tumor, Hugh Montrose was sitting in his office with his feet on his desk, taking a break from his clinic down the hall. He gazed at the Radcliffe Trophy in a display cabinet opposite him. The silver cup had been lovingly restored since Maxine Doggette had famously pulverized it at the last BRAIN meeting. Now it looked as good as new and served as a secret hiding place for M&M's.

Today Hugh was seeing a variety of cases—everything from incidental aneurysms and brain tumors to herniated lumbar discs and carpal tunnel syndrome. Many neurosurgeons disliked clinics to the extent that they wished they were almost anywhere else. Hugh felt differently. As he saw it, most patients were good, honest folks who found themselves in difficult, hard-to-understand situations and were simply looking for help. If he didn't enjoy being around people who were less fortunate than himself, why had he bothered to go into medicine in the first place? He welcomed even the most challenging patients—those with no money, no education, and plenty of grievances. He would patiently sit with them and their families and explain complicated issues in simple terms. He answered all their questions and made sure they didn't leave until they had a good understanding of what was going on.

The phone rang. It was Sandra, his office manager.

"Val is on line one, sir."

He picked up the receiver. "Yes, Val. What do you need?"

"You, sir."

"Has Dr. Elliott found the tumor yet?"

"No, he's hopelessly lost."

A voice rose above the background sounds of the operating room. "You don't have to put it *that* way!"

"He needs your help, Dr. Montrose," Val persisted.

"On my way."

Five minutes later Hugh swept into Richard's operating room with the confidence of a concert pianist making his way to center stage. Val and Lori heaved sighs of relief. Harrison's big, round eyes slowly set behind the ether screen.

"My God, what have you done to his brain?" asked Hugh, inspecting his resident's handiwork. "It looks like the pizza I had for lunch."

"I've been searching for the tumor," Richard explained in a small voice, "but it's not there. And I've looked *everywhere*."

"That much I can tell." Hugh brushed past Val, approached the MRI scans hanging on the X-ray view box, and checked them.

"Take a look at those films," he said, stepping away after only a few seconds. "See anything wrong?"

"No . . ."

"*I* can," said Hugh with a knowing gleam in his eye. "They've been hung backwards."

There was a deep, resonant silence as Richard's soul shriveled up and plunged into hell. Only the whooshing of the anesthesia machine was heard, its bellows blowing gases into a pair of cancer-ridden lungs.

"Oh my God!" he eventually moaned. "I opened the wrong side of the head!"

"Yep," said Hugh, removing the films from the view box one by one, reversing them, then snapping them back into place. "Looks like you have trouble telling the difference between left and right. My daughters had the same problem when they were about five years old."

"How could I *do* such a thing!" cried Richard, dropping his sucker onto the floor again.

"Fix that mess and zip him back up. You'll have better luck finding the tumor if you look on the opposite side."

"Aren't you going to scrub in?"

"*You* dug yourself into this hole," Hugh told Richard. "Now *you* can dig yourself out again. I won't always be around to rescue you when you're in trouble. This is the time to learn how to handle complications, not when you're in practice by yourself."

"Oh Lord, what have I done?" groaned Richard.

"You've just taught yourself an important lesson," said Hugh, heading back towards the door. "There are two sides to a human brain. Don't get them confused."

"Where are you going?"

"Back to my clinic."

"What about the family? What are you going to tell *them*?"

"The truth, of course."

"But they might sue!"

Hugh stopped in his tracks, paused for a second, then slowly wheeled around to face Richard. "What would you have me tell them?" he asked. "'Good news: we located the tumor and removed it. Even better news: we thoroughly searched the other side and found nothing there.' Is that what you have in mind?"

"Something like that, sure," said Richard, cracking a sheepish grin.

"I don't think so," said Hugh, straight-faced and serious. "*Never* try to cover up your mistakes when you talk to families. They have a right to know everything that happens during their loved one's surgery."

"Yes, sir," replied Richard, his smile gone.

By early evening, Mr. Brown and his tumor had been successfully separated. One was in the ICU waking up and asking for a cold beer while the other was pickling in a jar of formalin, waiting to be sectioned, stained, and examined under a microscope.

The happy result was proof of the extraordinary resilience of the human brain under full frontal assault by a tired and disoriented neurosurgery resident. The only hint that not quite *everything* had quite gone to plan was a pair of mirror-image incisions on both sides of Mr. Brown's shaven head.

10

Julie drifted through the darkness with her naked body flexed into a kneeling position and her arms outstretched as if prostrate before an altar. Her vital signs—blood pressure, heart rate, respiration—were controlled from afar via a complicated system of wires and tubes. Relieved of such life-sustaining responsibilities, her mind roamed blissfully free.

She felt incredible peace and prayed it would never end.

"Julie!"

She was rolled onto her back, straightened out, and blanketed by delicious warmth. The darkness gave birth to a point of brilliant white light only inches from her face. It grew larger and brighter, then swayed from side to side like a pendulum. Julie's eyes swam lazily after it, unable to comprehend what they were seeing.

Leave me alone. I feel so good.

"Your surgery is over!"

The sound of powerful suction filled her ears. A plastic tube snaked down her throat, searching for secretions. She gagged and convulsed, begging it to stop. Next she heard a steady hissing and felt cool moisture wafting against her lips. Fingers gripped her under the jaw and extended her neck. A wall accelerated smoothly past as if she was in a subway car leaving a station.

"You're waking up, Julie," a soothing voice spoke into her ear. "You're on the way to the recovery room."

The wall slowed and stopped. Blurry figures bustled around, poking and prodding her. A deep, throbbing pain radiated from her low back into both legs.

The voice spoke again. "You're doing just fine," it said.

Julie's mind fought back. *No, I'm not doing just fine! My back's in pain! Horrible pain! Leave me alone! Let me go back to sleep!*

When Julie finally emerged from the fog of anesthesia, she found herself in a quiet, clean hospital room. A man was sitting in a chair beside her bed, holding a magazine and staring vacantly at the pages before him as of his mind was either too preoccupied or too tired to read. At first her vision drifted in and out of focus and she was unable to discern the details of his face. Eventually they coalesced together and she recognized the long brown hair arranged into a pony tail, an untidy beard, and blue eyes.

"Gary?"

At the sound of his name her husband threw away the magazine, scooted to the edge of the chair, and gathered her hand from the bed sheets. "Finally you're awake!"

"What time is it?"

"Five o'clock. You've been in surgery for eight hours."

"Eight hours?" cried Julie, struggling onto her elbows. "Why did it take so long? Something go wrong?"

Gary coaxed her back down. "No, nothing went wrong," he reassured her. "Dr. Clegg called to say it was a success."

Julie eased into her pillows. "Thank God!" she said with a sigh of relief.

"Tell me how you're feeling," said Gary, gingerly tucking in the sheets around her.

Julie's eyes momentarily lost their focus as she ran an internal check. "Hurts like hell," she said, returning her attention to her husband, "but it's a different kind of pain than I had before."

Gary pointed to a black button at the end of a cord. "The nurses told me that if you press this you'll make a machine inject morphine into your vein."

"I'll have some now!" Julie reached over and pushed it with her thumb. A patient-controlled analgesia pump attached to a nearby IV pole made a friendly whirring sound.

"The worst is over now, Julie," said Gary with a smile. "All you have to do now is rest and heal up. Then you can get back to your life and put your pain behind you."

Julie repositioned her head on her pillow and winced.

"What's the matter?" asked Gary, hoping he hadn't spoken too soon.

"It's my neck."

"I don't understand," muttered Gary. "Why your neck?"

A Filipino nurse provided a plausible answer when she came to take Julie's vital signs. "It's from the way you were positioned during surgery," she said as she pumped up the blood pressure cuff. "Nothing to worry about. Happens all the time. Okay?"

In the evening Gary brought the children to the hospital for a visit. Jennifer brought her mother's old-fashioned alarm clock and set it down on her bed table. Patrick lent her his favorite Teddy bear, Edward. Gary showed Julie a huge GET WELL poster covered in pictures drawn by her students at school. He taped it onto the wall where she could see it from her bed.

As they talked and watched television, Julie's episodes of neck pain gradually intensified like the flickers of lightning from an approaching storm. After an hour Gary noticed her growing discomfort and decided to take the children home again so their mother could get some rest.

"I'm sorry I'm not feeling well," murmured Julie, her eyelids growing heavy from the morphine.

Gary kissed her on the cheek. "The nurses are close at hand in case you need anything."

"Here's Edward," said Patrick, carefully placing the bear next to his mother.

"Thank you for being such a good family," said Julie with barely a whisper.

"Sometimes not as good as we should be," Jennifer confessed. "The ordinary, everyday stresses get too much to handle. That's when Patrick and I take it out on each other."

"It's okay," said Julie. "You're still young and have a lot to learn."

"We love you, Mom," said Patrick.

"I love you too."

As soon as her family was gone, Julie's eyes fell shut and her mind drifted. The last sound she heard before falling asleep was the steady, hypnotic ticking of her clock.

Tick . . . tock . . . tick . . . tock . . .

Julie woke up with a start. The numbing effects of morphine had worn off and the pain in her neck was much worse now. She reached for the call button but somehow lost control of her arm and knocked her clock off the bed table. It fell to the floor and erupted into life.

"Shit!"

The loud clanging of the alarm bell lasted for a long time before it gradually wound down, gasped a terminal ding or two, and died.

Julie reached for the light switch in her bed's side rail but her fingers refused to move.

"What the . . ."

She tested her legs. They wouldn't move either. And what was that ponderous numbness that made her sheets feel . . . No, wait—she couldn't feel them at all! Something was wrong!

Panic exploded inside her.

Julie's heart was racing now. She called out but the door to her room was closed and nobody came. Her eyes read the digital clock on the TV. A few minutes before midnight. The nurse should be coming soon to take her vital signs. She had no choice but to wait.

At one o'clock, after anxiously watching the clock for more than an hour, the door finally flew open and a formidable nurse appeared, so monolithic in her overall dimensions that the light from the hallway outside was momentarily eclipsed as she entered. Like all the other nurses in the hospital, she was pushing along a computer on wheels, identical to the ones in Dr. Taylor and Clegg's offices. She plodded over to the bed. A face carved from steel and concrete emerged from the gloom. Fumes of cheap perfume seemed to coil around Julie's chest and squeeze it tight.

"Who are you?" she gasped, searching for a nametag.

The nurse flashed a mouthful of gold. "Me Bogdana, nightshift nurse," she said with a thick, Russian accent. "Time for vital signs."

"There's something wrong with me. My neck is killing me and I—"

The nurse thrust a thermometer into her mouth. "No talk!" she commanded.

After a few seconds the thermometer beeped. Bogdana retrieved it and read the digital numbers along its side, her Brezhnev eyebrows knotted together. She stuffed it back into her pocket and slowly, laboriously entered the numbers into her computer.

"And I can't move my—"

"I take pulse now," interrupted Bogdana as she took hold of Julie's wrist. She held it in a bear-like grip and locked her eyes onto a tiny wristwatch.

Julie was not so easily put off. "My arms and legs!" she persisted. "They're not moving! And my whole body feels numb too. I tell you: there's something—"

"Shhh!"

Julie reluctantly fell silent and didn't speak again until Bogdana had dropped her wrist and was once again typing on her keyboard. "What's happened to me," she asked.

"Not now. Bogdana busy with computer."

"I want some answers!"

"Wait!"

"No! I *won't* wait!"

Bogdana stopped what she was doing and gave Julie a long, cold look. "More morphine make you feel better," she eventually said. Without waiting for permission she reached for the pump's black button.

"But I don't want any more morphine!"

Bogdana pressed the button anyway.

"What have you done?" cried Julie, watching in horror as a bubble of air inside the IV tubing advanced a few menacing inches towards her arm. "You did that just to shut me up!"

"Have extra."

"No!"

Bogdana pressed the button again. The bubble zipped under Julie's skin and into her body. "Now go to sleep," she said, "and let Bogdana take care of computer."

Julie was about to start yelling when her mind was suddenly assaulted by the first wave of morphine. She succumbed to its power and was soundly asleep within seconds.

Julie's room was still dark when she awoke to a loud *crunch* and saw a monstrous shadow beside her bed. Bogdana was trying to move around quietly and was having as much success as a Soviet tank in a Venetian glass showroom.

"Nurse?"

The big nurse froze. "You awake?"

"Now I am."

Bogdana bent over, picked up a piece of flattened wreckage, and deposited it on the bed table.

"My alarm clock!" cried Julie. "You stepped on it!"

"Floor not good place to keep things."

"You could have been more careful!" Julie tried to reach for her clock's remains and was harshly reminded that something was seriously wrong with her arms. "All right!" she surrendered. "Forget about it! Just check me out, will you? I can't move."

Bogdana looked annoyed as if checking a patient was the last thing she imagined she would ever have to do as a nurse. "Show me," she said.

Julie wiggled her shoulders and made her arms flop around uselessly.

"Move hands."

"I'm trying!" said Julie. "They won't do anything."

"Legs?"

"They won't do anything either!"

Bogdana pinched Julie's arm until the skin turned white. "You feel?"

"No."

She did the same to her inner thigh. "Now?"

"No."

She dragged a dirty fingernail up her belly. "Tell me when you feel."

At first, Julie said nothing. When Bogdana reached the level of her upper breastbone, however, she suddenly cried out in pain. "What's the matter with me?" she whimpered.

Bogdana shrugged and muttered something in Russian.

"I want to speak to my husband!"

"I call Doctor," she said, stepping away. "Okay?"

"No, it's *not* okay! Get my husband on the—"

"Wait here."

Julie protested but found herself addressing Bogdana's massive backside as it seesawed away. A few moments later she was once again alone. In the dim light she noticed Edward at her side. The stuffed animal represented everything warm and loving in her life and she instinctively reached for him. Her arm, however, still wouldn't work right and her fingers refused to move. She swept him from the bed and watched helplessly as he tumbled into a dark corner.

An hour later, just as dawn's grey light was brightening the sky outside the window, Clegg arrived. He approached Julie's bed cautiously as though he was afraid of what he might find there. Grunting instructions, he tested the strength of each major muscle group in her arms and legs. He checked the extent of her numbness with a safety pin and tapped on her knees with a reflex hammer. When he was finished, he pursed his lips and shook his head.

"What's going on?" Julie asked, her voice trembling. "I want to know!"

Clegg opened his mouth to answer but couldn't find the words. He backed out of the room and sank into a chair at the charting table outside.

Julie craned her neck and saw him staring in her direction. The stunned look in his eyes spoke plainly enough.

Something was very, *very* wrong.

11

The phone on Hugh's desk rang. He put down his Dictaphone and picked up the receiver.

"Yes?"

"I have Dr. Clegg on the line for you, sir," said Sandra, his office manager.

"Oh God," Hugh moaned softly to himself. "Not him!"

Hugh pictured the big, ugly orthopedic surgeon in his mind. A real knuckle-dragger, that one. His nickname amongst the members of the medical staff was Bonehead. It was generally assumed that his brain, if indeed he possessed one at all, was very small and that his head was almost entirely made out of bone. Hugh had often caught himself studying his amazing skull with professional interest, secretly hoping to get his hands on it one day so he could display it in his office.

Bonehead's natural habitat was the Emerald Spine Institute, yet another of those so-called centers of excellence that masqueraded as places of higher learning and stocked their clinics with specialists like live lobsters in a restaurant. Nowadays they were sprouting up all over the country, each one counting on their grandiloquent title to attract patients with money. Hugh had a more appropriate name for the place. A little less lofty and a lot closer to the truth.

The Fusion Factory.

Every day, boxcar-loads of patients passed through its front door. Anybody qualified for surgery—the oldest, fattest, unhealthiest, most psychologically damaged, most previously operated on, most industrially injured, most litigated . . . It didn't matter what kind of baggage they lugged around with them. They were only required to have something that resembled a spine between their heads and their tails and complaints that could be vaguely related to it.

First they were examined, MRI scanned, CT scanned, X-rayed, poked with needles, and zapped with electricity. Then they were shunted off to surgery where they were slit open, hammered, chiseled, screwed, plated, fused, and sewn up again. Post-operatively they were shunted back to radiology for more MRI's, CT's, and X-rays. If anything imperfect was found—a screw slightly off target, a plate a few millimeters too short or too long—it was back to the OR again for another round of surgery.

After a few days, when every nutritious dollar had been extracted from their insurance companies, the patients were taken to the discharge area in wheelchairs and crapped out the back door.

Frank Clegg—Frankie, alias Bonehead—was at the epicenter of the whole lousy scam. Frankie and the Fusion Factory. He implanted enough titanium per annum to build a railroad from one coast to the other. If he couldn't find space for any more, he'd take it out again.

Put it in one year, take it out the next.

Put it in.

Take it out.

In—out.

In—out.

How did a brute like him manage to attract so many patients?

For one thing, his name was listed in *Western Washington* magazine's annual Best MD's issue. When the public read that rag they were led to believe that the man was indeed an orthopedic surgeon worthy of their ailing spines. After all, he had been nominated by his peers for the honor. If *they* didn't know, who would? Hugh, however, knew that the truth was far more complicated than that. Nominations depended less on the altruistic behavior of physicians than it did on their compliance with multiple emails from hospital administrators urging them to vote. The more they did so, the more likely their colleagues would be chosen, and the more money the hospitals would make when patients came flocking for care. Bonehead was particularly adept at bullying others into voting, especially for *him*. Hence his name found its way onto the list year after year. Hugh had always ignored such heavy-handed lobbying efforts, confiding in Caroline that the only time he would ever vote for Bonehead was if the magazine ever published a Worst MD's issue.

Another reason Bonehead was busy: for some unfathomable reason, few of his patients obtained second opinions. Maybe they were overwhelmed by his prestige and the wealth of the place where he worked. Once they were promised a pain-free existence they stopped listening and didn't bother to ask questions. They were only interested in signing the consent form and getting it over with.

And then, of course, a rumor had made the rounds that Bonehead paid people to sit in his waiting room, impersonate his post-op patients, and sing his praises. The idea, presumably, was to sway the more skittish customers towards having surgery and was so outrageous, so unethical, so *Cleggish*, Hugh actually believed it.

And now Bonehead was on the telephone. It couldn't be anything good.

"Why's he calling?" asked Hugh.

"He wants to transfer a patient to you," she replied.

"Let one wriggle off the hook? I don't believe it!"

"Shall I tell him you're on vacation in the middle of the Sahara?"

"No, I'd better speak to him." One click later, Hugh heard hot and heavy breathing on the other end of the line.

"Got a great case for you, my friend," announced Bonehead in his deep, raspy voice.

Hugh winced. The 'my friend' part smacked of desperation. "Hello, Frank," he said. "What kind of case?"

"Yesterday I did a lumbar fusion for a forty-something year old woman with low back pain," explained Bonehead. "Quite routine. No complications, until the middle of last night when she suddenly became . . ." He gave a little cough of embarrassment. ". . . quadriplegic."

"*Quadri*plegic? Or do you mean *para*plegic?"

"Definitely *quadri*plegic," said Bonehead, emphasizing the quadri part of the word as if a fully paralyzed patient was far more desirable to receive in transfer than one who was only half paralyzed. "Both arms and both legs—toast."

Hugh knew that any problem at the site of a lumbar fusion surgery, such as a post-operative clot, might result in paralysis, but only of the legs. If the arms were also involved, it could only mean that something had gone wrong in the neck.

"What happened?" he asked.

"We scanned her and found an incidental tumor in the cervical spinal cord," answered Bonehead, confirming Hugh's theory. "Look at the films and see for yourself."

Hugh's fingers danced across his computer's keyboard and entered a password into Emerald's online radiology system.

"The radiologist says it's an ependymoma," continued Bonehead, "whatever the hell *that* is. He says it's been slowly growing for a long time. You can't blame me for missing it. Anybody else would have done the same."

Hugh sighed. "It sounds like your patient was unlucky," he said charitably.

"*She* was unlucky?" shouted Clegg. "What about *me*? I do an elective back operation on some woman and the next thing I know she's a damned quad! How often does that happen? Now she'll hire some shit-for-brains lawyer who'll accuse me of negligence!"

Hugh wondered whether it was a good time to find an excuse to hang up. This conversation was not sitting well with him, particularly towards the end of a long day.

"What's the patient's name?" he asked, stretching his tolerance as far as it would go.

"I was afraid you might ask that. Let me see . . ." Hugh heard the rustling of papers. "Here we are. Winter. Julie Winter."

Hugh entered the patient's name into the computer and her radiology file popped up on the monitor. He saw a long list of plain X-rays, pre-op spine MRI's, a pre-op lumbar myelogram, a post-op lumbar myelogram and the most recent of all, done only an hour ago, a cervical MRI—enough studies to rake in a fortune for the Fusion Factory.

Hugh clicked on the latest cervical MRI.

Wow!

The spinal cord inside the woman's neck was grotesquely abnormal. Ordinary nervous tissue had been replaced by a mass that completely filled the spinal canal, obliterating normal anatomy. Instead of a normal smooth grey color, the cord was mottled with magnetic signals of varying density ranging from the purest white to the darkest black. A large cyst defined its upper limit and beyond that, a milky streak typical for swelling faded far into the brainstem.

This was a dangerous situation—that much was obvious. One that would require an operation. A *risky* operation.

Alarm bells clanged inside Hugh's head. An elective back operation that resulted in quadriplegia could easily lead to a lawsuit. If he accepted this patient, he might be unwittingly sucked into it. But was there really any danger to him personally? Surely not. The damage had already been done. No reasonable lawyer would sue him for something that had happened the night before.

"Listen," said Bonehead, lowering his voice and getting down to the meat and potatoes of his sales pitch. "A tumor inside the spinal cord is obviously something beyond the expertise of an orthopedic surgeon like me. Do you mind if I transfer her to Columbia? I know how much you relish this sort of thing. What do you say?"

Hugh studied the MRI pictures. On that particular point Bonehead was right. This *was* a technically challenging case—one he would love to do.

"Alright, Frank," he said, hoping he wasn't making a terrible mistake. "I'll accept her."

"Thank you!" said Clegg, sounding relieved. "I knew I could depend on you. You're a real friend!"

After he hung up, returned his attention to the computer screen. As long as Julie Winter's radiology file was open he thought he would peak at her original lumbar MRI. He was curious to know what had inspired Bonehead to operate on her back in the first place.

Within seconds of his command, her pictures were up and Hugh was leaning forward in his chair, studying them closely. What he saw was hardly surprising.

For a woman in her forties, the spine was completely normal.

12

Hugh received Julie Winter from the Fusion Factory only two hours after he agreed to accept her, warp speed compared to the time it usually took to transfer a quadriplegic patient from one hospital to another. She arrived just as he was finishing rounds outside the intensive care unit with his customary entourage. He led the way at the front of the pack, looking smart in a long, white lab coat, neatly starched and pressed. The chief resident walked to his right and two steps behind, wearing a shorter lab coat to denote his more junior rank. He held a list of Hugh's patients in his hand and served as his personal guide, telling him where they were, how they were doing, and what was planned for their care. Richard Elliott was next in the pecking order. He wore a short, scruffy lab coat and was responsible for carrying out orders from his superiors and making things happen. Behind Richard were a couple of medical students and a physician assistant—underlings who didn't speak unless spoken to. Right at the back was a nurse wearing a flowery blue uniform. She was pushing along a computer on wheels, also known by the acronym COW, that served as a mobile point of access to every patient's electronic medical record (EMR).

Hugh had not adapted well to the EMR revolution that had swept hospitals recently. Perhaps the concept may have made sense to politicians, geeks, salesmen, and the occasional save-the-rainforest activist but, as far as Hugh was concerned, it did absolutely nothing to improve patient care. Quite the opposite, in fact. Now doctors were forced to waste much of their valuable time struggling to understand computer systems that were counterintuitive and clashed with the way they had been trained to think. Nurses spent even more of their time trying to get information into and out of their COWs instead of giving patients hands-on care.

Hospitals threw away tens, sometimes hundreds of millions of dollars setting up and supporting the whole worthless enterprise—money that could otherwise be spent on saving lives. The older physicians who couldn't cope were retiring in significant numbers. The younger ones had no choice but to adapt. Hugh was one of them and regarded EMR as a major source of stress in his professional life.

Richard's pager went off. He called a number and was told the transfer had arrived from the Emerald Spine Institute. "Shall I go and work her up?" he asked the chief resident.

"No," interjected Hugh, suddenly stopping in his tracks. Everybody behind him slammed on the brakes, narrowly avoiding a massive pile-up. "I would like to see her first, on my own." Judging from what Bonehead had already told him, he knew this was not the best time to invade the patient's room with a bunch of coffee-toting, gum-chewing people in white coats. He would send his troops away and handle this delicate matter in the most humane and professional way he knew how.

A departmental chairman who wanted to make first contact with a new admission was about as rare as being struck by a meteorite from outer space while taking a nap in the call room. The chief resident and Richard exchanged looks of disbelief, then led the others away.

Hugh retreated into a quiet corner with the patient's medical chart. Fortunately the Emerald Spine Institute was in the middle of transitioning to EMR and all the important stuff—history and physical, progress notes, orders, op notes, consults, and some lab—were, for now, still preserved on paper. He opened the folder and began to read.

So, this was a forty-three-year-old white female named Julie Winter. Married, mother of two.

Just like Caroline.

This won't be easy, thought Hugh, feeling his heart beat faster.

The first document was a copy of Bonehead's initial letter to her primary care physician, Dr. Taylor, written a week ago.

Only a week?

True to Fusion Factory tradition, Bonehead had wasted little time scheduling her case. No sense making people wait for their operation when there was a chance they might be stolen by the competition across town.

What was the initial problem? Hugh scanned the page in front of him. The woman had been having low back pain for about two weeks.

Only two weeks?

Lower down on the page, the neurological exam was checked off as normal.

Normal?

That was obviously baloney. A cervical tumor as large as this one would have had plenty of telltale signs—spasticity, hyperreflexia, clonus, upgoing toes to name just a few. More than likely, Bonehead hadn't bothered to examine his patient.

Most people with a short history of an aching back and no objective neurological findings are offered conservative treatment such as physical therapy, massage, and steroid injections. Bonehead hadn't suggested any of those things. Instead, he had sent her for a battery of expensive tests—plain spine X-rays, MRI's of the lumbar spine and thoracic spines, EMG's and nerve conduction tests of the lower extremities, and a lumbar myelogram followed by a CT scan. The last test included a spinal tap which had an inherent risk of causing headaches, nausea—

Wait a minute.

Wait a goddamned minute!

After a spinal tap, the fluid would have been sent to the lab for routine chemical analysis. He flipped through the paperwork. A pink sheet of paper was loose and fell into his lap—the CSF results. He lifted it up and studied at the numbers. One of them caught his attention.

Protein........104.

Oh—my—God! Bonehead—you bumbling fool!

The implications of this discovery ricocheted around the inner table of his skull. A normal CSF protein level was forty. One hundred and four was really high and only meant one thing: a tumor was located somewhere in the central nervous system. If he had bothered to check the CSF result he would have discovered the tumor and referred the problem to a neurosurgeon for removal *before* it caused quadriplegia. The woman lying in the nearby ICU room, now paralyzed from her neck down, might have been spared the tragedy that befell her.

Hugh circled the number with a pen and wrote two exclamation marks next to it.

A brief look at the anesthesia record revealed that the operation had lasted eight hours—more than twice as long as it should have. Not surprising since Bonehead had half of the normal number of neuronal connections between his brain and his hands. Aside from being excruciatingly slow in the operating room he had never completely comprehended the delicate nature of nerves or the fragile dura that enveloped them and often tore into one or the other, or both. A spinal fluid leak might have dropped the pressure inside the spinal canal to dangerously low levels, jamming the tumor downwards like hammering a large peg into a small hole. Such an event would have led to an interruption of the blood supply to the spinal cord, infarction, and paralysis.

Hugh continued searching and learned more details about what happened. Sometime during the night a nurse at Emerald discovered the patient wasn't moving her arms and legs. To his credit, Bonehead responded promptly and saw her at 5:45 a.m. After examining her he scribbled a note into the chart indicating she was quadriplegic.

Okay, so far, thought Hugh. *But what did he do then?*

Evidently Bonehead had no clue that the neurological exam was pointing directly to his patient's neck as the source of the problem like a big blinking neon arrow for he had ordered another lumbar myelogram.

Hugh shook his head. No, no, *no!* Wrong test. Wrong part of the body. A medical student would have known better.

Not surprisingly, the myelogram was negative. Bonehead was clearly out of his depth. So what did he do next?

He consulted a neurologist.

Nice try, but another stupid mistake all the same. A catastrophic paralysis like this was well within the purview of a neurosurgeon, not a neurologist.

More time was wasted while a neurologist was found. When he finally arrived, he poked and prodded the patient using the diagnostic aids in the little black bag he always carried around with him. At least *he* had arrived at the correct conclusion, scribbling in the progress notes that she probably had a hitherto unknown tumor in her cervical spinal cord. He had recommended an MRI to prove it, followed closely by a neurosurgical consultation.

Already 9:00 a.m. and nothing meaningful had been accomplished.

Bonehead's flailing didn't end there. Clearly, an emergency situation existed, yet three hours passed before the patient was transported to the MRI scanner and another three before Hugh received the telephone call in his office.

Where had *Western Washington* magazine's distinguished Best MD been all that time? Clearing a path through the usual hospital inefficiencies and entanglements so his patient would be sure to get prompt attention? Not likely. Hugh bet Bonehead had spent the entire day hiding in his office like an invertebrate jellyfish, trying hard to expunge this mess from his mind.

Whatever miniscule chance this woman had of regaining any function in her arms and legs at 5:45 a.m. was most certainly eliminated by now, more than fifteen hours later.

Hugh put his pen back into his pocket, snapped the records shut, and wished he could dispatch one of his troops into the room to do the dirty work for him. Surely knowing how to break bad news to patients was an important part of residency training. Although sorely tempted to pass the buck, he knew it wouldn't be right. The circumstances were too appalling. This one, whether he liked it or not, was for him. He walked down the hall to Julie's room, steeled himself against whatever he might find inside, and knocked on the door.

Julie Winter was lying in her bed, a Teddy bear by her side. To his dismay, her straight black hair, high cheekbones, and large chestnut eyes reminded him of Caroline. How would he feel if such a cataclysm ever happened to his own wife? He quickly ejected the thought from his mind before it had a chance to take root.

A man with red, swollen eyes and a beard tangled into knots was pacing up and down beside Julie's bedside. When he saw Hugh enter, he rushed over and introduced himself.

"I'm Gary Winter," he said. "Julie's husband. You're the neurosurgeon, aren't you?"

"Yes, I'm Dr. Montrose."

"Thanks for coming! *Please* tell me there's something you can do for her."

Hugh put a consoling hand on the man's shoulder. "First, I need more information," he said. "Why don't we—"

"It's all my fault!" Gary suddenly cried. "I was the one who talked her into having back surgery! I should have kept my mouth shut! Why the hell didn't I?"

Hugh coaxed Gary into a chair. "Let's talk about it," he said, lowering himself onto the edge of the bed. "How are you feeling?" he asked Julie.

Julie looked up at him with big, scared eyes. "At least I'm not in pain any longer," she answered in the short, breathless phrases typical for quad-speak.

"Can you tell me what happened?"

"I stopped moving my arms and my legs," she said, shrugging her shoulders to demonstrate how little she could do.

"When did this happen?"

"In the middle of the night."

"And since then, have you stayed the same or are you getting worse?"

"The same."

"Are you quite sure?"

"Yes."

Gary sprang out of his chair. "What do you think, Dr. Montrose?" he asked, looking down at him with desperation in his eyes. "For God's sake, tell me there's something you can do for her!"

Hugh stood up. "Let me examine you," he said to Julie.

He proceeded with care, testing the motor and sensory functions in her limbs and tapping her tendons, looking for reflexes. He lowered Julie's blanket as far as her waist, and raised her gown so that he could have a good view of her lower chest and abdomen. Each time she drew in a breath her belly bulged out like a pregnancy, a common finding in quads. The intercostal muscles in her chest wall had been knocked out and her ventilation was being powered entirely by her diaphragm.

Hugh's findings confirmed that his patient's lowest level of normal functioning was C5. Her shoulders had good strength, but everything below that level was gone. He covered her up with the blanket and worked the problem.

Gary edged closer to Hugh. "What do you think, Doctor?" he asked.

"What has Dr. Clegg already told you?"

"He telephoned and said something about finding something wrong in Julie's neck," answered Gary. "He told me he was transferring her to your care. I had plenty of questions but he said you would answer them."

"And so I shall," said Hugh, returning to his place at the edge of the bed. "Yes, there *is* something wrong in Julie's neck. Dr. Clegg discovered a tumor inside the upper part of her spinal cord. It's probably been there a long time, slowly growing—"

"A long time?" asked Gary, sinking slowly back into his chair.

"Yes."

"How long?"

"Months, maybe years."

Gary was thunderstruck. "Then why the *hell* didn't we know about it before?" he cried.

Good question, thought Hugh, feeling vaguely responsible even though he'd had nothing to do with Julie's care until now. Omitting awkward details about sky-high spinal fluid proteins,

Bonehead's botched work-up, and how much of a klutz the man was in the operating room, he said, "The tumor is most likely what's called an epenydmoma. Because of its slow growth, it can get quite large before causing problems."

"Why did she become paralyzed last night?" asked Gary, wringing his hands.

"I don't know exactly," replied Hugh evasively. "Safe only to say it was something waiting to happen."

"Can you take it out?"

"Technically it's possible," said Hugh. "In my opinion, however, it's unwise to do so at this time. Julie's MRI shows a lot of swelling in the spinal cord. There's a substantial risk that immediate surgery could make her worse."

"Worse?" cried Gary. "Worse than *this*?"

"She could lose the ability to breathe," explained Hugh. "That would mean becoming dependent on mechanical ventilation. Or she could also lose the strength in her shoulders. No, my advice would be to give her an infusion of high dose steroids overnight to help reduce the swelling. In a couple of days, when the dust has settled and it's safer, we can remove the tumor."

"And after that, what are her chances of . . ." Gary's voice faded as if the implications of his next question had just dawned on him.

Hugh asked it for him. "What are her chances of her regaining any function in her arms and legs?"

Gary nodded.

Hugh drew in a deep breath. Bad news was always hard to deliver, no matter how many times he'd done it in the past. "The spinal cord tissue around this tumor has already been seriously damaged, I'm afraid," he said grimly.

"What does *that* mean?" asked Gary impatiently.

"It means the chance Julie has of regaining any function is very low."

"*How* low?"

"Almost zero." Hugh wanted to leave out the 'almost' and just say 'zero' but he couldn't deprive these nice people of the faintest glimmer of hope.

Gary closed his eyes and sunk his head into his hands. "Oh my God," he softly groaned. "I can't believe it! I talk her into having back surgery and *this* happens!"

Now Julie spoke up again. Her voice, as weak as it was, commanded attention. "Are you saying I'll be paralyzed for the rest of my life?" she asked.

Yes, that's precisely what I'm saying, thought Hugh. But there was never a good time to be quite so blunt.

"That may be true," he said instead. "But you *must* stay positive about the future."

As if he had just told her she would be better off dead, Julie suddenly unleashed a heart-rending howl of anguish followed by a string of uncontrollable sobs. Gary leapt out of his chair again, threw his arms around her, and tried in vain to console her. She continued to wail until the weakness of her breathing forced her into long spells of moaning interrupted by short, sharp gasps for air.

"I think we know what you mean, Doctor," said Gary as he clung to her. "Please . . . *Please* do whatever you can."

"I will," Hugh said, standing up. Definitely time to leave. "I promise I will."

Outside, Hugh leaned against the nurse's station and exhaled long and hard. He had always believed he could always, if necessary, construct an impregnable wall between himself and his patients.

Now he was no longer so sure.

When he felt stronger again, he found a COW grazing nearby, raised it to the right height, and started to type.

13

Maxine, dressed in a navy blue designer pantsuit, was seated at her desk in her office. A variety of make-up kits were open in front of her. She was fixing her face in a small mirror, a task that proved to be more challenging as the years went by. Minimus was reclined on his favorite cushion, quietly snacking on medium rare filet mignon cubes she had prepared for him.

"You sweet darling," said Maxine, blowing him a kiss.

He looked up from his food and beamed back at her.

Maxine returned her attention to the face in the mirror. Just as she was penciling a pair of arches for eyebrows and curling her eyelashes she noticed something new.

The eyelid on the right covered more of her eye than the one on the left.

She blinked and looked again. No doubt about it. The distance between the bottom of her eyelid and her pupil was definitely shorter on the right. And wasn't the pupil itself larger too? She switched her attention from one black circle to the other and back again.

Yes, it was.

Maxine attributed her discovery to the high levels of frustration she was being obliged to endure these days. The source of the problem: she was getting absolutely nowhere in her search for muck to use against Montrose. Billy had tailed him all over creation and yet had unearthed nothing. No loose girls in hotel bars, no drinking, no drugs, and no gambling. Nothing scandalous at all. *Yech*! How could anybody live such a dismally dull life?

Neither had she heard anything from Dr. Henry Harrison, her anesthesia spy at Columbia Medical Center. Presumably all of

Montrose's patients were doing well. Not a single botched case amongst them. How would she ever teach that man a lesson?

The telephone rang. Maxine put down her eyelash curler and picked up the receiver. Her receptionist was on the other end of the line.

"Dr. Harrison is here to see you, ma'am," she announced. "He says it's very important."

Speak of the devil! Harrison at last!

Maxine gleefully rubbed her hands together. "He's witnessed something I can use against Montrose!" she said to Minimus. "Why else would he come to see me?" She told her receptionist to send him right in, then opened a desk drawer and swept her make-up kits into it.

Harrison was a middle-aged man with a round, lumpy stomach. In striking contrast, his chest was hollow and his legs little more than pretzel sticks. He wore thick wire-rimmed glasses that magnified his eyes to twice their normal size, making him appear unmistakably owlish. He was wearing a deep purple jacket, a matching waistcoat with watch chain, and a yellow open-neck shirt.

"Dr. Harrison!" said Maxine, springing from her perch behind the desk and swooping towards her informant like a bird of prey. "What a pleasure to see you again!"

"You remember when you called me a few weeks ago and asked me to keep an eye on Dr. Montrose?" he asked.

"Of course I do," she said, alighting next to him. "Let me guess. He made a mistake!"

"A short while ago," said Harrison, lowering his voice an octave to reflect the high value of the information he was about to divulge, "I personally observed a junior neurosurgery resident at Columbia Medical Center do a craniotomy on a patient with a metastatic tumor. Believe it or not, the kid operated on the wrong side of the head. When he discovered the mistake he made a second opening on the correct side. The attending responsible for the case was Hugh Montrose. There! What do you think of that?"

Maxine's smile evaporated. "A wrong side surgery?"
"Yes!"

"Was the patient damaged?"

Harrison cast down his eyes.

"*Was the patient damaged?*"

"Regrettably . . . no."

Maxine suddenly turned conniption crimson. "*No damage?*" she shouted, flapping her arms into the air. "How *the hell* do you expect me to sue him when there wasn't any damage? I told you to dig up something serious, not a minor excursion into the wrong side of the brain!"

"It was still a mistake!" insisted Harrison. "And the best you'll ever find considering who you're going after. Tell the patient to invent symptoms if you have to! Chronic headaches, dizziness, memory loss! Things that can't be disproved!"

"I'm not going to waste my valuable time on a frivolous lawsuit like that!" screamed Maxine, picking up a decorative vase from her desk and raising it above her head. "For what? Ten or twenty thousand dollars? Maybe fifty at the most! Because that's all a stupid wrong-side surgery—*with no damage*—is going to get!" She flung the vase onto the floor, shattering it to pieces. "I want millions, not thousands! He must be made to suffer just like me! Now get out! And don't come back until Montrose has killed a patient! Or better yet, *paralyzed* one—somebody young and educated with decades of lost wages in their future! Do you understand me?"

Harrison fled from Maxine's office on his little stick-like legs.

Maxine went over to the wall where her diplomas were hanging and bashed her head hard against it. Her Super Lawyer certificate fell off its hook and crashed to the floor, breaking its glass. She collapsed into the chair behind her desk, an ugly bruise spreading across her forehead and steam blasting from her ears.

Why on earth was that miserable worm Montrose proving to be so difficult to sue? Defendant Thompson had been a pushover! At least *that* case had turned out well. Within hours of receiving a copy of Maxine's sex video he agreed to settle the case for a million dollars. Montrose, she knew, was far too straight-laced to fall for the same dirty trick. Putting on a wig and seducing somebody like him at a BRAIN banquet was unthinkable.

An idea suddenly occurred to her. A brilliant idea!

The Bellegrove Rehabilitation Center! Why hadn't she thought of it before?

Maxine returned to her desk, retrieved one of her make-up kits, and applied enough powder to her forehead to hide the bruise. "Stay here and finish your nice steak," she told Minimus when she was finished. "I'll be back soon." She gathered a sports bag from a closet, headed for Billy's office down the hall, and poked her head through his open doorway. "Come with me," she ordered. "We're going on a field trip."

Billy had been spending the day scouring the internet for any new information on Montrose and looked at her with tired, shifty eyes. "Yes, ma'am," he muttered unenthusiastically.

An hour later they were inside the spinal cord injury unit of the Bellegrove Rehab Center wearing white lab coats decorated with official-looking badges. Maxine had found a lonely COW that had wandered off by itself and was milking information from it. Billy stood nervously next to her, on the lookout in case anybody approached.

"Rehab centers are absolute goldmines for medical malpractice attorneys," said Maxine, busily typing on the keyboard. "Literally *stuffed* with paralyzed patients facing a lifetime of gargantuan medical bills. Sooner or later I'll find one who was treated by Montrose. Then we'll dig for anything we can use against him."

"But you shouldn't be searching through confidential records," said Billy. "What if you get caught?"

"I won't get caught," Maxine reassured him as she entered a password into the COW. "All I have to do is wear a white coat and a few phony ID's. Nobody will dare to challenge me."

"How can you be so sure?"

"Experience, Billy," said Maxine confidently. "I've come to this place so many times over the years the nurses have grown used to me. Sometimes they even offer me a cup of coffee. God knows who they think I am. There are so many faceless bureaucrats checking medical records for one stupid reason or another these days, I suppose I could be anybody."

Maxine clicked open another chart, her sixth so far. The patient was a man who'd become paraplegic after plowing his motorcycle into a tree on his way home from a bar. She was in the middle of copying his information into a yellow legal pad when she noticed the words duplicate into side-by-side images. Perplexed, she looked at her right hand and saw ten fingers instead of five.

Something was definitely wrong. Earlier her drooping eyelid, and now this.

"Are you okay, ma'am?" whispered Billy, peering at her.

Maxine saw two identical Billies standing in front of her. "I don't feel well," she told the one on the left.

"Do you want a break?" asked the Billies.

"No, I'm going home," said Maxine, stepping away from the COW. "Maybe I'll come back tomorrow when I'm better. Stay here and keep looking on your own for a while. Let me know if you find anything interesting."

"But I've no idea how to use these stupid things!"

"Neither do most of the doctors and nurses who work here."

"Yes, but—"

"I'm off. Goodbye."

Maxine walked away, clutching her legal pad with its precious harvest of potential plaintiffs.

Billy looked at the information on the computer screen with a helpless, sinking feeling in his gut. Everything was terribly complicated and made no sense. He was about to let the COW go free and follow Maxine when he noticed what looked like an old-fashioned paper chart laying on a desk outside a room just a short distance away. He went over, opened it up, and quickly realized that it came from the Emerald Spine Institute. Billy didn't care about its origin just so long as he could read it.

According to the chart, the patient inside the room was a woman named Julie Winter. Age: forty-three. Address: some street in west Seattle. He quickly scribbled down her information.

So what had happened to her?

He found the discharge summary and discovered she'd undergone a routine back operation at Emerald and became quadriplegic shortly afterwards.

This sounded promising. An elective surgery resulting in paralysis of her arms and legs? Hmmm . . . Very promising indeed!

He noted the name of the Emerald doctor, Frank Clegg MD. The day after the operation he had transferred his patient to Columbia Medical Center. And the name of the accepting physician?

Hugh Montrose MD!

Billy's heart leapt with excitement. This was exactly what Maxine was looking for!

A sheet of pink paper fluttered from the chart. He picked it up and saw that it was a lab slip reporting a chemical analysis on CSF, whatever *that* was. There were words like cell count & diff, glucose, and protein whose significance he didn't understand. One thing, however, caught his attention.

Protein……..104 was circled with heavy black ink. Two large exclamation marks stood to the side. Although the number didn't mean anything to him, apparently it had to *somebody*. As he considered the implications, he heard a woman's voice behind him.

"May I help you?"

Billy suddenly felt a surge of panic. He stuffed the lab report into his pocket and wheeled around to face a young nurse in a white uniform. She was herding along a COW of her own.

"I'm from the Joint Commission, doing a random spot check on chart documentation," he blurted, reciting the emergency response Maxine had made him memorize in the unlikely event he was challenged. "I've found at least four serious deficiencies in the last ten minutes."

"I already know who you are and what you're doing," said the nurse pleasantly. "The charge nurse told me. I only wanted to know if you need anything."

"If I need anything?"

"That's right."

Billy's heart slowed. "No, nothing right now," he said.
"Are you sure?"
Billy sized up the COW next to her and had a rare idea.
"Well, there *is* something," he said, "if it's not too much trouble. Could you make that computer of yours print a—"
"Her name is Daisy."
"Excuse me?"
"My COW prefers to be called Daisy."
"Oh, I see," said Billy, clearing his throat. "Well, could you make Daisy print a copy of the discharge summary from 204's hospitalization at Columbia Medical Center? I need to include it in my report."
"I can't make Daisy do anything," said the nurse with a sigh. "If I ask her really nicely though, she might—just *might*—cooperate." She typed something long and complicated into Daisy's keyboard, then left. After a few minutes she returned with some papers and handed them over. "Wasn't too difficult this time. You were lucky."

Billy thanked her and promised to omit her name from any disciplinary recommendations. As he walked away he quickly read the summary. Why had the patient become paralyzed? The answer soon became clear enough. There had been an incidental tumor in her cervical spinal cord. Somehow her back surgery had complicated the situation in a particularly disastrous way. Two days after her admission to Columbia, Montrose had performed an operation to remove it. The pathologist said it was an ep . . . epen . . . ependymo . . . ependymoma. The surgery had been successful but, as expected, no neurological function had returned. After a few days recuperating in the main hospital she was transferred to Bellegrove where she'd been ever since.

By the time Billy left through the front doors, his head was spinning with excitement. Trawling for clients in rehab centers was so easy! On the face of it, Julie Winter's case was crawling with opportunities. He couldn't wait to show Maxine what he had found! What better way was there to prove his abilities?

Now she would be forced to take him seriously and let him examine a treating physician in court!

14

Castle Doggette stood on a low hill overlooking a reservoir. Not one for modest understatement, Maxine had seen what she liked while at a lawyer's conference in England and had replicated the entire structure on her secluded estate outside Seattle.

Being filthy rich had some of its advantages.

Grey stone walls were crowned with a maze of steep slate roofs, parapets, and turrets that soared towards the sky. A pole stood on the pinnacle of the building and flew her flag—a coral red crown against a black background—whenever she was in residence. The interior featured high ceilings, wooden rafters, and heavily draped windows that allowed in only grey twilight. The Great Hall was the largest room with double doors at one end and a monolithic fireplace at the other. It was empty save for two solitary armchairs and an antique bookcase. A portrait of Maxine reclining naked on a leopard print couch hung over the mantelpiece.

The real Maxine Doggette, fully clothed in the same navy blue designer pantsuit she'd been wearing all day, was sitting in one of the armchairs. A dinner tray was set before her on a small collapsible table. On it was a plate of roast quail stuffed with white truffles. As she ate, she watched a TV-VCR combo perched on the top of an elaborately carved marble plant stand that was once owned by Lorenzo de Medici in the days of the Florentine Renaissance. Every once in a while she lifted a wine glass to her lips and sipped some chilled Chardonnay.

"How's your meal, Minimus?" she asked between mouthfuls. "Tasty enough for you?"

Minimus was in the other armchair enjoying the same dishes, only served in much smaller portions. He whimpered happily at the sound of his name and resumed eating.

Together they were watching an old videocassette recording of Maxine's early depositions. 1990 was a vintage year. One sweaty defendant after another appeared on the screen, nervously eyeing the camera as if they were facing the barrel of a machine gun. Maxine was somewhere off-camera, firing questions designed to blow gaping holes in their testimony. One after the other, the defendants succumbed to the onslaught and their mutilated bodies were dragged away by their lawyers. Her deposition videos were as precious to her as life itself, enabling her to relive the most triumphant moments of her career.

When Maxine finished her quail she switched off the television, lit a cigarette, and blew a stream of smoke high into the air. She looked at Minimus who was busily licking his balls for desert and saw him separate into a pair of identical side-by-side images—the same thing she had experienced while checking charts at the rehab center earlier that day. She blinked, rubbed her eyes, and looked again.

What was happening to her? Did she have a disease? She thought back to nursing school but couldn't remember what sorts of things caused double vision. She rose from the armchair and was about to go over to the bookcase to consult her nursing diagnosis handbook when a distant doorbell rang.

Fiddlesticks! Who could be bothering her at this late hour? She stubbed out her cigarette, picked up Minimus, and set off for the front door, her high heels clicking busily across the stone floor.

Billy was waiting outside—or rather, two Billies standing side by side, identical in every way.

"This isn't a good time!" she said before either of them had the chance to say anything. She gave the door a shove with her hand.

"I found something at the rehab center!" they said, jamming two right feet into the doorway before it slammed shut.

"What?"

The Billies spontaneously fused into one. "A patient treated by Montrose!"

"Montrose!" cried Maxine, breaking into a big smile. "Why didn't you say so in the first place? Do come in!" She held the door wide open for him.

Billy stepped inside the entrance hall. His mouth fell open when he saw its high ceiling, sweeping oak staircase, and iron chandelier large enough to hang in St. Peter's. "My God!" he said. "This place is huge!"

"I know," said Maxine, closing the door behind him.

"Do you live here alone?"

"No. I share the place with Minimus. Now tell me what you've found."

Billy drew closer to Maxine and peered at her eyes, looking from one to the other and back again.

"What are you doing?" she asked.

Billy edged nearer and cocked his head. "Are you okay, Ms. Doggette?" he asked, frowning.

"Of course I'm okay!" snapped Maxine. "Why do you want to know?"

"Your right eyelid is drooping."

So people were beginning to notice. Crap!

"I've been working too hard lately," she told him brusquely. "Now let's talk about more important matters. You've got something good, I hope. Not some worthless wrong-side surgery."

"I have something really good!" said Billy, smiling proudly. "Perhaps you should sit down before I break the news, Ms. Doggette."

Salivating with anticipation, Maxine led Billy into the Great Hall. Once inside the big room his eyes immediately locked onto her nude portrait. He was so distracted he walked straight into Lorenzo de Medici's marble plant stand. It toppled over, crushed Maxine's tray table, and shattered on the ground with an ear-splitting crash. The television tumbled away.

"You idiot!" shouted Maxine, running after it. "My video deposition tape's in there! It survived twenty years without a scratch! You spend less than thirty seconds in here and—"

"I'm sorry, Ms. Doggette!" gasped Billy, erupting into his usual dry, hacking cough. "I didn't see that marble thing! I'm sure your tape's okay though! Let me get it for you!"

"No!" shouted Maxine. "Stay where you are!" Clutching Minimus protectively, she stepped through the debris field, checked the television, and was relieved to see that the videocassette inside was undamaged.

"Thank God for that!" She took it out, went over to her armchair, and sat down. "Now tell me about Montrose's patient before you demolish my whole house!"

Billy nodded and cleared his throat. "Yes, ma'am," he said, carefully lowering himself into the other chair. "After you left me this afternoon, I found some old-fashioned paper medical records outside a patient's room."

"Go on," said Maxine, twiddling the tuft of hair on Minimus' forehead into knots.

"They belonged to a forty-three year old woman by the name of Julie Winter," he continued. "A few months ago she had low back pain and went to see a Dr. Frank Clegg at the Emerald Spine Institute. He's one of *Western Washington* magazine's Best MD's. Do you know him?"

"Yes . . ." answered Maxine, her eyes narrowing as she searched her memory. "A while ago I sued him twice—no, three times in a single year."

"Three times!" gasped Billy. "But he's an orthopedic surgeon. I thought you only sued neurosurgeons."

"Some days I'll sue anything that moves," said Maxine. "His lawyer told him not to take it personally but he wouldn't listen. By the time it was all over he was a changed man. Crushed beyond recognition!"

"Anyhow, Clegg performed an elective operation on the woman's back," continued Billy. "She was convalescing uneventfully until the night after surgery when she suddenly became quadriplegic."

"*Quadriplegic?*"

"Complete C5."

"Ah-hah!" Maxine felt a surge of excitement. She *adored* quads! They were the most pitiful victims imaginable—sawn off from the neck down and as helpless as beached whales. They required years of expensive care and invariably won the maximum compensation for their injury. She never found it hard to bring a jury to tears over their plight, especially if she propped them up in their elaborate wheelchairs and displayed them like the scarecrows they were. If all the possible medical malpractice cases in America were a deck of playing cards, a retained foreign body was the Two of Clubs, an amputation of the wrong limb—or a limb-off—was the Jack of Diamonds, and an accidental death was the Queen of Hearts.

A fresh quad, however, was the Ace of Spades.

The videocassette incident now forgotten, Maxine leaned towards Billy. "What happened next? I want to know every salacious detail!"

"Clegg transferred the patient to Montrose's service at Columbia Medical Center," said Billy, extracting some papers from the inside pocket of his jacket. He unfolded them and handed them over to Maxine with a big, satisfied smile. "Here's the discharge summary from that admission."

"How . . . how on earth did you get hold of this?" asked Maxine, leafing through the pages and confirming what they were.

"Oh, it wasn't difficult," replied Billy, trying hard not to sound too impressed with himself. "According to Montrose, Julie Winter became paralyzed from a tumor—something called an ep . . . epen . . . ependymo . . . ependymoma—inside her spinal cord. He saw her right away, but waited *two whole days* before taking her to surgery and removing it."

"How many days did you say?"

"Two!"

"Oo-ee!" whooped Maxine, tossing the papers into the air. "*That's* called a delay in treatment, something I can sue him for! Perfect!"

"He documents his reasons for delaying pretty thoroughly," continued Billy. "He says he waited so the swelling in the spinal cord would go down before he removed the tumor. Considered it safer that way. Less risk of making things worse. Does that make any sense to you, Ms. Doggette?"

"I don't care what he thought," said Maxine. "It's what the jury thinks that's important, and I can make them think anything. Especially if there was a delay for two days." Her eyes grew distant and pensive. "*Defendant* Montrose," she whispered softly to herself, weighing the individual syllables of the name as if each was a fleck of gold in a finely calibrated balance. The way they sounded together had an alluring ring. "*Winter vs. Montrose* will be my greatest triumph!" she suddenly declared, rising from her seat with Minimus in her hands. "When I bring him down, neurosurgeons everywhere will pay attention. Good job, Billy!"

"You really think so, Ms. Doggette?"

"Without a doubt!"

"Does that mean you'll let me examine my first treating physician now?"

Maxine's face fell a mile. "Why do you keep asking for the same darn thing? You're beginning to sound like a broken record."

"I deserve a reward!"

Maxine paced up and down in front of the fireplace. Ever since she hired Billy she had successfully kept the ambitious runt on a short leash. Now she was forced to admit that he had a valid point. He had made an important discovery. Maybe he did deserve something. But a treating physician all to himself? So soon in his career? Maybe it would be okay, she reluctantly decided. If he messed up, it probably wouldn't make any difference to the trial's outcome.

"Alright, Billy," she relented. "Clegg's a treating physician. I'll put you in charge of his testimony during the trial. There! Are you satisfied now?"

Billy leapt out of his seat. Bursting with effusive gratitude bordering on blind insanity, he threw his long arms around Maxine, almost knocking Minimus out of her hands. "Thank you, Ms. Doggette!" he spluttered, hugging her. "A treating physician all for myself! I can't wait to examine him!"

As far as Maxine was concerned, having physical contact with Billy was about as disgusting as stepping bare-footed into a fresh, steaming pile of Minimus poop. "Urrrgh!" she shouted, unpeeling his arms and scraping him off. "Don't touch me, you blockhead! Go home! We'll start work early in the morning."

Billy spent a nauseating amount of time telling Maxine how wonderful she was before she finally flushed him out the front door. When he was gone, she gave Minimus a celebratory hug.

"This is it!" she said to him. "At last, my precious doglet, this is really it!"

Minimus wagged his tail and yapped.

15

When the doorbell rang, Gary Winter was on his knees with his index finger buried deep inside his wife's rectum. A chunk of stool the size and consistency of a brick was stuck there and even though her anus was as flaccid as a coffee-dunked donut he was having difficulty reaching in far enough to scoop it out. As he kept trying, gas passed through the loose sphincter, not with the robust raspberry of healthy flatus but with the tired *pfffffffffff* of air escaping an inflatable mattress. The odor in the bathroom was stultifying. As accustomed to killer smells as Gary was by now, he was still starting to gag.

"Damn!" he swore, withdrawing his finger with a loud, succulent *schhhh-luck*. "The lawyer's here early!" He shifted his weight onto his heels and straightened his stiff back. Lubricating jelly dripped off his rubber glove and splattered onto the floor.

Julie was sitting on her specially adapted potty chair, naked except for a bra. Her pale and bloated body was hunched over, afflicted by ugly raw sores at every pressure point. Her atrophied legs stuck out in front and her hands lay uselessly across a belly that ballooned with each breath she drew.

Following her paralysis Julie fell into a long, deep depression. The specialists at the Bellegrove Rehab Center tried to cheer her up by claiming she was lucky to have some residual function in her upper arms. They taught her many things, among them how to eat with special implements strapped to her hands, how to get around in a wheelchair, and how to make telephone calls. She scorned their words of encouragement and dared them to trade places. What good were arms without hands? What was the purpose of life without the use of a body? When she tried to scream with frustration, her lungs were too weak and she was only able to moan.

When Julie returned home and was once again amongst familiar surroundings she gradually fell into a routine. The alarm clock rang every morning at five. Once Gary had showered and dressed himself he hoisted his wife out of bed with a lift that resembled a small crane and strapped her into the potty chair. He lay under her as if he was changing the oil on a car and evacuated her rectum with his finger. After that, he rolled her into the shower and washed her body with soap and her hair with shampoo. Julie felt horribly embarrassed and humiliated by the whole ordeal and could never get used to it.

Dressing took half an hour or more, a laborious process since she was no more cooperative than an infant. Gary began by putting her into support hose that prevented her female organs from turning inside out and dropping out of her pelvis. He would then strap a plastic bag to her leg to collect the urine that flowed down her in-dwelling catheter. Next he pulled on her clothes, trousers being the most difficult of all. Finally he brushed her teeth and combed her hair.

When Gary left for work, he usually left Julie sitting on her wheelchair by the living room windows where the sunshine fell across her and she could have a good view over the neighborhood. As she whiled away the time she would often think about the students at the elementary school where she used to work. At first she received frequent telephone updates from her replacement teacher and cards from the children. As the school year progressed, however, she heard less and less from them. Schedules were getting busier and Ms. Winter simply wasn't in the forefront of everybody's minds any longer.

While the children at school were slipping from her life, her own children, Patrick and Jennifer, seemed closer than ever. Somehow their family's tragedy had highlighted the relative insignificance of their former problems and had reoriented their values. They weren't constantly bickering any longer; nobody had to take them out to Alki Beach to help clear their heads. Instead, they spent as much time as possible with their mother, helping with her activities of daily living and often reading her stories. Whenever her children were kind to her, Julie wanted to reach out and hug them. Sometimes it was more than she could bear when she remembered she couldn't.

Gary felt horribly guilty about Julie's condition and had never forgiven himself for pushing her into having back surgery. If he hadn't insisted on it, he constantly reminded himself, she would probably still be walking. Consequently he bore the responsibility for taking care of her with iron resolve, never once complaining—not even in the middle of the most abysmal bowel protocols. On the surface he stayed cheerful and always gave her encouragement. Somewhere deep inside him, however, a sickening despair had taken root.

Julie slowly lifted her sagging head. "Did you say the lawyer is here?" she asked. "You mean that woman who called you the other day? What was her name?"

"Maxine Doggette," said Gary, carefully removing the soiled glove from his right hand and dropping it into a red trash container marked BIOHAZARD. "She claimed to be the best medical malpractice lawyer in town, with more experience suing doctors than anybody else."

"I wish we didn't have to sue anybody," said Julie, her voice mustering strength. "It's blood money."

"I know, I know," said Gary, standing at a sink and washing his hands with soap and water. "But we have to think of what's best for us. You're not working as a teacher any longer and what I make isn't enough to pay for everything."

"There must be a better way," said Julie with a forlorn sigh.

"Not as long as the situation is so serious," said Gary, ripping a paper towel from a roll and drying his hands. "Our finances are a complete mess. We're already falling behind on our house payments and we receive a threatening letter from the bank at least once a week. Things are only going to get worse. I'm missing a lot of work. One of these days the principal will tell me not to bother showing up any more. What the hell am I going to do then? A bad situation will get even worse."

The doorbell rang again.

"I better get that," said Gary, throwing the paper towel into a nearby trash can. "We need to hear Ms. Doggette's opinion about things. I'm sure she'll know what to do."

"You're not done with my bowels," said Julie anxiously.

"There's no time," said Gary as he headed down the hallway towards the front door. "I'll have to finish later."

"I could have an accident!"

"We'll have to take that chance."

*   *   *

Maxine and Billy stood on the Winters' front porch waiting for somebody to answer the door. Shock and awe was a tactic Maxine often used to recruit clients. Today she had put on a stunning canary-yellow outfit with a tight skirt and enough gold and jewels to make her resemble a Fabergé egg.

While she waited she looked around the property with undisguised disapproval. The house was seriously neglected. Paint was peeling from the wood siding, a window was broken, and weeds sprouted from the gutters. The surrounding garden might have looked pretty once with its sloping lawn edged by flowerbeds. No longer. Brambles had broken loose and their thick, prickly stems were running wild. Some of them had found an old abandoned RV and were growing up its dilapidated sides. Tender green shoots curled and twisted along its rusty windows as if trying to find a way inside.

By now, Maxine was experiencing chronic, unremitting double vision. She had looked up its potential causes in her nursing diagnostic handbook but had found nothing. When she searched on the internet, however, she was overwhelmed with a long list of diseases: cancer, multiple sclerosis, botulism—*botulism!*—Guillain-Barré syndrome (whatever *that* was), brain tumor, abscess, and so on. Next she looked up a drooping eyelid's potential causes and found another list equally long: diabetes, brain tumor (again), myasthenia gravis . . . Even exposure to the venom of a black mamba snake!

A troubling thought had crossed her mind: could Billy be trying to poison her? If so, what was his motive? Probably to destroy her practice in his quest to become supreme in the land of Med-Mal. She had made a note to keep a close eye on him at all times and to monitor her food carefully.

A chocolate Labrador poked his head around one corner of the house and growled at the visitors. Maxine bent down and made a face at him. The dog yelped with fright and took off with his tail between his legs.

The front door opened. A man with tired eyes and an untidy beard appeared. "Yes?"

"Mr. Winter? I'm Maxine Doggette, the lawyer you've been expecting." She shook his hand. "We spoke on the phone."

"Hello," he said, smiling. "Thanks for coming. I hope my dog, Rolo, didn't bother you too much."

"Not at all," said Maxine. "Easily taken care of. I brought along my assistant, Billy Barlow."

"Please follow me." Gary ushered Maxine and Billy into the living room and politely excused himself, saying something about helping his wife get ready.

While Gary was gone Maxine looked around the house, a shoebox compared to her own place and cluttered with cheap furniture. An obscene number of family photographs were on display and drab paintings hung on the walls. A long, narrow table was positioned against a wall with a row of wilting house plants arranged along its length. She swept her index finger across its surface, held it up for inspection, and frowned.

"Now, I want you to watch me carefully," she told Billy, rubbing the dust away with her thumb. "When I spoke to the Winters on the phone I sensed that they're the sort of people who are reluctant to sue doctors. You are about to learn how I handle potential clients who, for any number of asinine reasons, feel that way. The answer is a gentle, well thought-out approach."

"A gentle, well thought-out approach? Yes, ma'am. I'll remember that."

After an interminable wait, Julie finally guided her mechanized wheelchair into the room, followed by her husband. She was young, attractive, a wife, a mother, a teacher, and thoroughly paralyzed. The perfect plaintiff! Maxine's face liquefied into an expansive smile.

Once everybody was introduced and seated, Maxine came straight to the point. "As you already know," she said, clasping her hands together in her lap, "I'm an attorney who specializes in medical malpractice. I've had a great deal of experience in cases like yours and have saved countless struggling families from ruin. I heard about your tragic circumstances and immediately understood how much of a financial strain you must be under."

Julie and Gary nodded their agreement.

"Everybody knows quadriplegia is a terribly expensive condition," continued Maxine, "especially with all the special equipment and supplies that are necessary for daily living. Victims are forced to file lawsuits just to survive. I was wondering why you haven't filed one already. You *haven't*, have you?" Maxine pinned Gary down with a probing eye.

"No, we haven't," he replied. "Our doctors never did anything wrong."

Maxine rolled her eyes. "Liability lawsuits have nothing to do with right and wrong," she said, reciting one of the most fundamental principles of tort law. "And don't get the absurd notion that they somehow safeguard the quality of medical care either. They're all about money and only money. Those who have it, those who don't, and how much is transferred from one to the other. And it seems pretty obvious to me," she added pointedly as she looked around the room with disdain, "that you fall into the 'those who don't' category."

"You're right," said Gary. "We do."

"Good!" said Maxine with a look of delight that was quickly replaced with something more appropriately lugubrious. "I'm glad we established that important fact. In a serious situation like yours, the check is usually made out for an amount between five and ten million dollars. The money comes from some huge insurance company with billions in the bank. They wouldn't even notice the difference."

"We don't care so much about insurance companies," said Julie, glancing at her husband as she spoke. "Doctors are different though. They were kind to us. We don't want to hurt them."

"Hurt your doctors?" said Maxine, eyebrows raised high as if such a notion was patently absurd. "Oh, *pah-leeez*! They're taught in medical school to expect lawsuits and not to take them personally. In fact, if they're not sued, they worry that they're not being productive enough. I've seen some get quite depressed over it."

"But how can we sue them if there wasn't any negligence?" asked Julie.

"I agree Dr. *Clegg* didn't do anything wrong," said Maxine, her voice dripping with oodles of innuendo. "How could he have possibly known you had a tumor in your spinal cord?"

"He couldn't have," agreed Julie.

"Exactly!" said Maxine. "Montrose, however, is an entirely different matter."

Julie's eyes grew large and apprehensive. "What do you mean by that?" she asked.

"Look, Julie," said Maxine, leaning forward in her seat to make her sales pitch, "I've told you that I'm a medical malpractice attorney. But that's not all I am. I'm also a fully qualified registered nurse. In that regard, I stand head and shoulders above ordinary attorneys. When I reviewed your case a glaring question immediately came to my mind. Why did Montrose wait two days before he took out the tumor? It wouldn't be hard to persuade a jury that his delay in treatment deprived you of the only chance you had for regaining any function—"

Julie suddenly looked horrified. "Are you telling me a mistake was made?"

"No, not at all," said Maxine quickly, sensing the need to tread softly. "I don't believe for a second that you could have avoided your paralysis. It's what the jury believes that's important and over the years I've learned that they can be persuaded to believe *anything*."

Julie calmed a bit. "Sometimes I feel I can live with the way I am," she said, "but only if I believe the doctors did everything they could for me. If there's a lawsuit, people will ask questions. If somebody uncovers a mistake, I fear I won't be able to cope any longer. Maybe it's best to let sleeping dogs lie."

A powerful odor of stool suddenly filled the room.

Julie closed her eyes. "O God," she groaned. "Not *now*!"

Maxine's olfactory system reeled under the assault and she fought to stay composed. Billy, however, had no such self-discipline. Turning a light shade of green, he excused himself, walked smartly to the front door, and bolted outside.

Gary turned to Maxine. "I'm really sorry, Ms. Doggette," he said with an embarrassed smile. "I guess we won't be making any decisions today. Perhaps you'd better leave now so I can take care of Julie."

Maxine was horrified. If she left now, she might never have another chance to sign them up. Or even worse, some other lawyer might steal the case from her. The signature lawsuit of her career, *Winter vs. Montrose*, could end before it ever began!

"I can wait here until you're finished!" she cried, racking her brains to think of a way to buy more time with the Winters.

"This could take me a while," said Gary. "Why don't you come back another day?"

Retching sounds reached them from the garden.

An idea struck Maxine. "I can help you clean her up!" she offered without thinking through the implications.

"You?"

"As an RN I've had years of experience caring for the disabled," she quickly explained. To be sure it was a bald-faced lie. As soon as she graduated from nursing school she enrolled in law school, never showing the slightest interest in taking care of patients. The situation, however, called for desperate measures and these suckers would never know the truth anyhow. "If you'll let me help, I could make things easier for you. How about it?"

For a few moments Gary seemed transfixed, unable to believe her generous offer. Eventually he broke into a grateful smile. "All right then," he said, beckoning her over. "If you insist. Follow me."

Maxine jumped from her seat, grasped the handles of Julie's wheelchair, and pushed.

An hour later, Maxine hurried down the Winters' driveway as fast as her high heels and tight skirt permitted. She waved her skinny arms around in the air like a tightrope walker desperately trying to keep her balance. Her hair was a big tangle of knots and bounced around like a cheerleader's pom-pom as she swiftly approached her Rolls Royce. When she arrived, she threw herself breathlessly against the front passenger door and wrenched it open. She dove inside, slammed the door shut behind her, and locked it. Billy was in the driver's seat, staring at her with amazement. Minimus was sunbathing on the dashboard, an expression of soporific bliss stretched across his face.

"Drive, Billy!" she ordered, reaching for her seatbelt with a trembling hand and clicking it closed.

"Ma'am?"

"*Drive!*"

"Yes, ma'am!" Billy twisted the key in the ignition, started the engine, and trod on the accelerator. The engine roared, tires squealed, and the massive car fish-tailed into the street. Minimus was launched from the dashboard like a missile and flew head over heels into the back seat.

"I can't believe the things I'll do to get a client!" Maxine fumed, her chest heaving up and down as the road ahead hurtled past. "I swear I've never done anything so *disgusting* in my life! *Never!*"

"What did you do?" asked Billy.

"The woman was impacted," said Maxine. "I had to dig a bucket-load of shit out of her butt. Hard as rock it was too! The stink was awful! All the beautiful clothes I'm wearing will have to be burned! Urrrgh!" She suddenly turned on Billy, her teeth bared like a jackal. "And what the hell happened to you?"

Billy took his eyes off the road. "I . . . I—"

"Look out!"

A car was heading straight for them. Billy wrenched the steering wheel to the left. Minimus tumbled across the back seat to the right.

"Your behavior back there was unforgiveable! Throwing up like that! You could have ruined everything!"

"I'm sorry, Ms. Doggette!" cried Billy, wrenching the wheel the other way to stay on the road. Minimus tumbled to the left. "My stomach couldn't take it!"

Maxine grabbed her dog before he broke his neck and threw him into his Bucket Booster pet car seat. The sound of screeching tires whizzed past her right ear as Billy careened through a stop sign.

"My stomach couldn't take it either," she said, fastening buckles as quickly as she could, "but you didn't see *me* puking up my guts."

When Minimus was secure, Maxine exhaled a lungful of air and blew aside loose hair that had fallen over her face. For a moment, she said nothing. Then her mouth gradually spread into a cunning grin. "My self-sacrifice was well worth it though," she said, her eyes now shining. "Congratulate me, Billy! I've signed up the Winters!"

Billy whooped loudly and slapped the steering wheel with his hand. "How did you manage that?" he asked.

"While I was dynamiting my way through the impaction I had time to use my considerable powers of persuasion," explained Maxine. "Eventually they came around to my way of thinking and agreed to go ahead with a lawsuit against Montrose."

"That's brilliant!" bleated Billy. "Your gentle, well thought-out approach worked! Let's go and celebrate!"

Maxine searched Billy's face for any cheeky sarcasm but saw none. Evidently such a reaction required at least four brain cells to fire in the correct sequence—something clearly beyond his capabilities. Relieved he wasn't making fun of her, she turned serious and focused. "It's far too early for any celebrations," she cautioned. "There's a lot of hard work ahead. First, I'll file the paperwork at the courthouse. Then I'll make a copy of the medical records. It'll take a few acres of Amazon rainforest to do the job, but that can't be helped. Next I'll have to go through them page by page, analyzing each and every morsel of information. Odeus Horman will help me understand what it all means. I'll make him my neurosurgical expert."

"You think he'll agree to do the job?" asked Billy.

"Odeus?" said Maxine with a knowing smile. "Of course he will. That fat pig does whatever I tell him. Now slow down before you get us all killed."

16

Hugh Montrose stood on his front lawn with his feet firmly planted together, holding a cricket bat vertically in front of his legs. Feigned concentration was etched into his face.

Hugh's daughters, Anna and Marie, circled around him, taking turns to throw a tennis ball at his shins. By the rules of French cricket he was not allowed to move his feet as he defended his legs with the bat. His body became twisted and vulnerable as he faced his attackers.

Anna knelt on the grass and faked a couple of throws, trying to trick her father into swinging. Spotting an opportunity, she let go of the ball. Hugh hit it hard, sending it flying into the rhododendrons at the far end of the garden. Twix, the family's golden retriever, was standing in the outfield and chased after it. He snorted and sniffed around, eventually emerging with his trophy in his mouth.

"Twix!" shouted Anna. "Bring the ball back here! *Twix!*"

Twix promptly headed in the opposite direction.

"What do we do now?" moaned Marie, throwing up her arms in exasperation.

"Look around the garden for another ball," suggested Hugh, practicing a few swings with his bat.

Marie pouted with her hands on her hips and dragged her feet. When she saw Anna start searching amongst some rose bushes she followed her.

Hugh tossed the bat aside and ambled over to Caroline. She was sitting on a tartan blanket at the edge of the lawn, enjoying the last fragments of the sun that filtered through the surrounding trees. He lay down on the grass beside her and stretched out.

"How are you feeling, Hugh?" asked Caroline.

"Much better," he replied. "You were right. I needed a day off."

Columbia Medical Center had been a mass casualty zone lately, with the neurosurgery department, as usual, right in the thick of it. The local knife and gun clubs were at each other's throats again and had generously provided the operating room with a steady supply of penetrating head injuries. For three consecutive days and nights Hugh had been wielding his scalpels and suckers as if his own life depended on it, not just the lives of his patients. He removed shattered bone, blood clots, and bullets out of club members' brains as fast as he could, then patched up what was left and hoped for the best—all while his resident, Richard Elliott, commuted to and fro between the hospital and home, dutifully complying with the no-more-than-twenty-four-consecutive-hours rule. Some of the patients died. A few others became wards of the state; over-boiled Brussels sprouts gaping vacantly at the ceilings of their nursing homes. Most returned to the streets invigorated by the experience and eager to fight another day.

Twix suddenly bounded from the end of the garden, barking furiously.

Hugh looked down the driveway and saw an old Chevy Chevelle approaching. The roof was so rusty the car could have doubled as a bath tub in a rainstorm. The engine gurgled like an old motorboat and blue smoke billowed from the tailpipe. The car stopped in front of Hugh and momentarily disappeared in a cloud of noxious fumes.

When the air cleared, the driver, a scruffy young man, cracked open his window. A dozen metal rings of different shapes and sizes were hooked through various parts of his anatomy. Something round and plastic was inserted into an ear lobe, stretching open a hole large enough for a bus to drive through. Skulls, daggers, and coffins littered the exposed areas of his skin.

Hugh stood up and approached the car, waving his hand around to clear the air. "Can I help you?" he asked.

"You sure can," said the man with a sadistic grin. "Are you Dr. Hugh Montrose?"

"Yes."

"And is that your wife?" he asked, nodding towards Caroline who had just dispatched Twix into the back garden and was closing a small wooden gate behind him.

"Why don't you just tell me what you want?"

"I'm Jake the process server. And do I have something special for you! Let me see if I can find it." He turned his ignition key off. The engine sputtered and backfired before it died. He twisted around and rummaged through a pile of papers scattered across the back seat.

"What's a process—?"

"Here it is!" Jake sang out, extracting some papers and waving them about in the air. "There are always so many of them, they're hard to keep organized." He rolled down his window further. The smell of cigarette smoke and sweat assaulted Hugh's nose. "Today I have a summons and complaint to give you. Congratulations, man! You're being served!"

Hugh felt the ground disappear from underneath him. "Served?"

"Looks like you must have screwed up, Doc, because there's a Gary and Julie Winter who've filed a medical malpractice lawsuit and named you as a defendant. It says so right here in the complaint: *professional negligence, failure to obtain informed consent, personal injuries and damages*. Makes quite interesting reading. Thought about going to law school myself once—"

"Give me those!" snapped Hugh, reaching out.

Jake pushed the papers through the car window. Hugh took them and scanned the first few lines:

<u>*SUMMONS*</u>

*IN THE SUPERIOR COURT OF WASHINGTON
FOR THE COUNTY OF KING*

JULIE WINTER AND GARY WINTER, wife and husband, plaintiffs v. HUGH MONTROSE, individually and on behalf of the marital community composed of HUGH MONTROSE and CAROLINE MONTROSE, defendants. TO THE DEFENDANT (S): A lawsuit has been started against you in the above-entitled Court by JULIE WINTER AND GARY WINTER, plaintiffs.

Julie and Gary Winter? Hugh cast his mind back and pictured the face of a woman with long, dark hair like Caroline's. As the pixels of his memory coalesced, other features came into focus. She was paralyzed. Her hands and legs were useless. Her MRI scan had shown—

She was the one with the huge spinal cord tumor!

"Caroline!" Hugh called out.

"Yes?" she responded, ambling over.

"Take the children inside the house please."

Caroline looked at Jake with uncertainty. "Is there a problem?"

"Please let's not discuss it right now. Just do as I ask."

Uncertainty turned to apprehension. She quickly rounded up Anna and Marie and hustled them away.

When Hugh was alone with Jake, he glared at him angrily. "You've got some nerve coming to my home on a Sunday and humiliating me in front of my family!" he said, his voice shaking with emotion.

"Don't get pissed off with me, Doc," sniffed Jake. "I'm only doing my job."

"You could have taken these to my office!"

"It's closed today."

"Why didn't you come tomorrow?"

"I only work weekends." He glanced at his watch. "Shit, it's getting late. Better get going. Lots of other lawsuits to deliver. Enjoy your evening!"

Jake cranked his ignition. The car didn't start. He tried again. Still nothing. Just as Hugh was beginning to panic about the possibility of the creep getting stuck in his driveway, the engine blurted into life and another cloud of exhaust fumes polluted the neighborhood. The car backed out of the driveway and rattled off, leaving behind an ugly patch of oil on the ground.

When Jake was gone, Hugh examined the document.

> *Julie Winter came under care and treatment of defendant Hugh Montrose. As a direct result of defendants' negligence...*

Negligence?

> *... plaintiff Julie Winter was permanently and severely injured and disabled, and has sustained both general and special damages, in amounts to be proven at trial.*

Trial?

> *As a direct and proximate result of defendants' failure to obtain informed consent, plaintiff Julie Winter was permanently and severely injured and disabled.*

Hugh was horror-struck at the accusations against him. A cloud of butterflies swirled in his stomach. The wailing of a police siren rose and fell in the distance. Gripping the pages more tightly he quickly read on.

> *In order to defend against this lawsuit, you must respond to the complaint by stating your defense in writing within twenty (20) days or a default judgment may be entered against you without notice. If you wish to seek the advice of an attorney in this matter, you should do so promptly.*

> *Maxine Doggette (signed)*

Maxine Doggette?
The Dog!

Hugh remembered the BRAIN banquet when he was awarded the Radcliffe Trophy. That evening the Grand Ballroom had been filled with a couple of thousand people from all over the world. He had sat with his family at the table nearest the stage. His introduction began badly, with a photograph of him sitting stark naked in a bucket, his nads on full display.

What a bizarre entrance that woman had made!

First Minimus had come running in. Ugliest damned creature he'd ever seen. Then Maxine, bewigged, dressed in rags, and screeching her head off. The trophy didn't stand a chance. Why hadn't he done the smart thing and ignore her dog? She might never have learned his name. He might never have called her dreadful.

First chance I get, I'll slam you with such a nasty lawsuit you'll wish you'd never been born!

Those were her exact words, spoken with such force and clarity Hugh could still remember his shock and disbelief when he'd heard them. Now she had finally found a way to carry out her threat. He was staring at the papers in his hand when Caroline appeared at his side.

"What's going on, Hugh?" she asked.

"I'm being sued," said Hugh, feeling the weight of his words settle on his shoulders like a lead apron in surgery.

"Oh no . . ."

"And you too, officially."

"Me?"

"Washington is a communal property state and you're my wife."

"Who's suing us?"

"Julie Winter, a school teacher I saw some months ago. Perhaps a year. She became quadriplegic after an orthopedic surgeon operated on her and I was the one who . . ." Hugh faltered as the details came rushing back to him.

"What is it, Hugh?"

"Hold on." He hurriedly flipped through the pages, looking for Frank Clegg's name. It wasn't anywhere to be found. "But this doesn't make any sense!" he spluttered in disbelief. "Why isn't

Maxine Doggette suing *him*? He's the one who screwed up! Not me!"

"Maxine Doggette?" said Caroline, her eyes narrowing as she searched her memory. "Isn't that the woman who chased her tiny dog onto the stage at the BRAIN banquet?"

"Damned right it is!" choked Hugh. "She thinks suing neurosurgeons is a blood sport. She's totally loony tunes."

"She's crazy and you're innocent," said Caroline thoughtfully. "Sounds to me like a winning combination in your favor."

"I guess you're right," sighed Hugh. "It's just that . . . I've never been sued before and I've no idea what to expect. One thing's for sure: it really gets me riled up to read these nasty accusations against me." He brandished the papers in his hand.

"Oh, come on, Hugh," said Caroline, speaking plainly. "You knew something like this was bound to happen one day. Neurosurgeons get sued all the time. It's the price you have to pay for what you do. Don't take it personally."

"Easier said than done."

"Your insurance company will take care of everything for you." She put her arm around Hugh's shoulders and guided him towards the house. "They'll hire some hotshot lawyer to defend you; a knight in shining armor who'll gallop to your rescue and slay the fire-breathing dragon. I doubt it'll take more than a couple of phone calls to do the job."

"I'm sure you're probably right," muttered Hugh angrily under his breath.

"And now it's time to fix dinner," continued Caroline. "I've got some potatoes for you to peel. And don't forget to take the garbage out too. And when you've finished that, both kids need help with her homework. I hope you didn't think you were getting out of your chores just because of some stupid lawsuit."

"No, of course not," said Hugh as he followed his wife through the front door. "I didn't think that for a second."

17

When Hugh stepped into the lobby of Wilson, Kassel & Biggs in the Safeco Plaza Building forty-one floors above the Seattle streets, he was stunned by its sheer size and opulence. The reception area alone dwarfed his entire clinic.

Rich mahogany paneling covered the walls and recessed spotlights artfully illuminated rows of gold-framed oil paintings. A marble statue of a naked Greek goddess stood in an alcove of its own, her featureless white eyes watching a grand oak staircase that led to the floor below.

"May I help you?"

A blonde woman was sitting behind a distant desk. Hugh hiked across an acre of Persian Esfahan and handed her a business card. "Good morning. My name's Dr. Montrose. I have an appointment with Mr. Denmark . . ." Then he added, quite unnecessarily, ". . . for the next four hours."

The woman didn't offer the sympathy he was looking for. "I'll let him know you're here," she said, pressing a button on her intercom.

Hugh's cell phone rang. He snatched it off his belt and answered.

Richard Elliott was at the other end of the line. "I'm in the ER seeing a fifty-four year old white male who fell in the shower this morning and struck his head," he said. "When he arrived he was awake and alert. The CT scan showed a small amount of air under a small basilar skull fracture but nothing else. Now his headache is getting worse and he's slowly becoming more confused. What am I supposed to do?"

"Scan him again," said Hugh without hesitation.

"But he just got out of the scanner!" exclaimed Richard. "Aside from some bubbles of air under the brain, everything looks okay. Why run him through again?"

"Maybe he has a tension pneumocephalus." It was a rare condition Richard, with his no-more-than-eighty-hours-per-week experience, had likely never seen, so he added, "The skull fracture acts like a one-way valve. Air gets into the head but can't escape again. The pressure rises and the brain gets compressed."

"Alright," said Richard. "I'll order another CT." The line went dead.

"You're a very busy man," said the receptionist, hanging up her own phone.

"I know," said Hugh, scrolling through messages on his pager. "I certainly don't have time to hang around some lawyer's office all morning."

"Mr. Denmark said he won't be long."

Hugh clipped his pager back onto his belt, retreated to a nearby couch, and sat down. He looked out of the windows and spotted the light beige buildings of Columbia Medical Center a few blocks away. He imagined Richard in the ER drilling a hole into somebody's skull and wished he was by his side.

After a few minutes Hugh saw a handsome, solidly built man with broad shoulders, brilliant blue eyes, and dark hair walking resolutely towards him. He was immaculately dressed in an expensive suit and carried an air of competence about him. If this was the knight in shining armor Caroline had mentioned, Hugh was encouraged.

"Hi, I'm John Denmark," he said, taking Hugh's hand and shaking it enthusiastically. "Very pleased to meet you. Come into my office. We can talk there."

Hugh followed Denmark into a corner office with a stunning view of downtown Seattle and thought of his own place, little more than a broom closet with a brick wall outside the window. He didn't care. As far as he was concerned, the views through the microscope in the operating room beat anything he was ever likely to see out of a window.

"Thank you very much for coming this morning," said Denmark, slipping off his jacket and draping it over the back of his chair. "I'm sorry it's such a long appointment but there's plenty to talk about. Make yourself comfortable. Coffee?"

"No, thank you."

"I'll have some myself then." Denmark took a fish-shaped mug off a shelf. "Be back in a minute."

Hugh turned his attention to the city below. Cars packed with lawyers were jostling to get ahead in the morning rush hour. More lawyers crowded the sidewalks, walking between scattered parking lots and various office buildings. He looked through the windows of a nearby skyscraper and saw lawyers arriving at their desks, lawyers hanging up their coats, and lawyers turning on their computers. Everywhere he looked there were lawyers—faceless, nameless, and utterly depressing in their numbers. From this height, they looked like millions of army ants—no, *lawyer* ants, bustling about their meaningless lives.

Sickened by the view outside, Hugh looked around the office. Instead of lawyer ants he saw fish. A collection of stuffed salmon was mounted prominently on a wall, their glassy eyes coldly staring back at him. All around were framed photographs of Denmark in various fishing poses. In one, he was bracing himself at the stern of a big boat, reeling in something strong enough to bend his rod backwards. In another, he was standing in a beautiful mountain river, fly fishing for trout. Some had explanatory labels underneath: displaying his catch on a sun-drenched dock on the coast of Florida, receiving first prize for hooking the largest bass in an Alabama lake, ice-fishing on a frozen lake in Minnesota. Fishing books outnumbered law books on the shelves behind his desk and several *Field and Stream* magazines were scattered about.

So, his lawyer liked to fish.

Hugh had no interest whatsoever in fishing.

Where were the photographs of his lawyer's family? A wife perhaps? Some children? Hugh looked around and found nothing. Perhaps the fish in this office were his family.

Hugh wondered how he should pass the time while he waited—watching the lawyer-ants outside or making friends with the salmon on the wall.

No contest.

He went over to the wall and found the friendliest-looking one. According to a brass plaque underneath, he was a sixty pound king named Diego. Hugh was about to ask how his day was going when Denmark returned with a cup of coffee in his hand.

"Let's get started right away," he said, settling behind his desk. "Your medical malpractice insurance company, Grand National, asked me to—"

Hugh's cell phone rang again. "Excuse me," he said, answering the call and taking a seat.

Richard reported that Hugh was right. The follow-up CT showed that the collection of air inside his patient's head had indeed expanded. Since the volume inside the skull was fixed, the brain was obliged to shrink in order to make room and now resembled a walnut.

"Stick a tube into the head and let the air out," Hugh told him.

"You must be joking!"

"Nothing to it. Do it the same way you would put in a ventriculostomy to drain spinal fluid. You've done millions of those. Aim for the largest collection of air. When you're in the right place, listen carefully. You'll hear air escaping. It'll sound like the brain's farting."

When Hugh hung up, he saw Denmark looking at him strangely. Then his lawyer shrugged and sipped his coffee. "As I was explaining to you," he continued, "Grand National asked me to represent you in this lawsuit. I told them I was far too busy and couldn't possibly take the case." He produced an apple from a pocket and bit into it.

"Good. Does that mean I can leave now?"

"I was just about to hang up," continued Denmark, chewing away, "when they mentioned the name of the plaintiffs' attorney, Maxine Doggette." He made a face as if the apple was riddled with rotting worms. "She calls herself the Queen of Med-Mal. I prefer The Dog. Do you know who she is?"

"Everybody does."

"I've never known a stranger woman in my life," said Denmark, swallowing hard. "Lawyers like her give the rest of us a bad name. She thinks she's wreaking havoc amongst neurosurgeons but in the end she's really doing herself the most damage. Personally, I think she's bent on self-destruction."

"Just like an aneurysm," muttered Hugh.

"What did you say?"

"An aneurysm," repeated Hugh more clearly. "They self-destruct too."

"You're an expert on aneurysms, aren't you?"

Hugh nodded.

"Well, I consider myself an expert on The Dog," said Denmark, his eyes growing cool and distant. "I've been trying to muzzle her for years. Unfortunately, every time we fought in court she won the case."

"Oh great," said Hugh, slumping into his chair. "*That's* encouraging."

Denmark threw the rest of his apple into a waste paper basket as if he'd suddenly lost his appetite. "You would never believe the things she's done," he said, his blue eyes smoldering. "After I lost the last time I was desperate for one final chance to beat her. When Grand National contacted me the other day I couldn't believe my good fortune and immediately cleared the decks for you."

Hugh moved to the edge of his seat. "Maybe a chance to beat her is what *you* want," he said, "but I never want to see her again. You *must* get rid of this lawsuit for me, quickly and quietly. I should think a couple of well-placed phone calls ought to take care of it."

Denmark chuckled.

"What's so funny?"

"If only things were so simple," said Denmark, drinking more coffee."

"They're not?"

"There's a lot you don't understand."

"You think I'm naïve? I've seen plenty in my time, you know."

"Perhaps in an operating room, but not a courtroom. You have no idea what kind of trouble you're in."

Hugh felt rising warmth in his face. "What do you mean by that?"

"This isn't some piddling wrong-side case, you know," said Denmark, stabbing a finger directly at Hugh. "You've been accused of negligence by a quad."

"So?"

"Quads nearly always win their cases. This one also happens to be young, attractive, a wife, a mother, and a teacher. That makes your situation five times as serious."

"Are you telling me you can't make this lawsuit disappear?"

"Absolutely," said Denmark. "This is big. Really big. Over the next year or two you'll be spending a lot of time—"

"*Year or two?*" spluttered Hugh in disbelief. "I can't spend two years of my life dealing with that woman! I'll go stark raving crazy. And what about my practice? Who'll take care of my patients?"

Denmark was as yielding as a concrete bunker. "I won't keep you busy every minute of the day," he said, "except during the trial, of course. When you *are* with me, however, I'll expect your undivided attention."

Hugh's cell rang again. "This is the perfect example of what I'm talking about!" he said, pressing the button to answer it. "There's a patient in the emergency room right now and I'm here, wasting my time talking to you!"

It was Richard again. "I inserted a tube into the patient's head like you told me to and listened closely," he said. "Sorry, but no farting noises."

"Is he getting worse?" asked Hugh.

"Gradually, yes."

"On my way over. Give me a few minutes." Hugh hung up and climbed to his feet. "I'm sorry," he said to Denmark, "but we'll continue this discussion some other time. Maybe next week, if I'm free."

"Go if you must," said Denmark, raising his arms in surrender. "Maybe it won't make much difference just this once. But mark my words: if you allow your neurosurgery practice to take priority over this lawsuit, you'll pay a heavy price."

"Money!" said Hugh, heading towards the door. "It's always about money, isn't it? That's all you lawyers are interested in. Well, I'm not like you. I don't give a damn about money." He was already in the hallway outside when he heard Denmark's voice behind him as clear as a lead bullet dropping into a metal pan.

"Not even fourteen million dollars?"

Hugh froze in his tracks. "*How* much did you say?"

"Fourteen million," repeated Denmark, casually inspecting his fingernails. "I only ask because that's how much the Winters want."

Hugh slowly turned to face Denmark. "Fourteen *million*?"

"That's right. I have the plaintiffs' statement of damages right here." Denmark picked up a document from his desk and started reading. "One point two million for past economic damages—things like medical bills, in-home care services, equipment, and so on. Four million for future economic damages. They also would like to have one hundred and twenty thousand for a wheelchair-accessible RV. Apparently the Winters are camping enthusiasts and want to hit the road again. Non-economic damages add up to nine million. Seven point five million for Julie's grief, sadness, pain and suffering, anguish, emotional distress, depression, disability, disfigurement, and loss of enjoyment of life. One point five million for Gary's own grief, sadness, pain and suffering, loss of enjoyment of life, loss of spousal consortium due to his wife's quadriplegic condition, blah, blah, blah . . ."

"Spousal consortium?"

"The right of a husband to enjoy the conjugal affections of his wife."

"You mean sex?"

"Exactly."

"Even sex has a price tag?"

"Everything does, right down to the last paper clip. It's all here in black and white. If you don't believe me, take a look for yourself." Denmark tossed the document onto his desk.

Powerful forces sucked Hugh back into the office. "I don't have fourteen million dollars," he said, crumpling back into his chair. He left the papers in front of him untouched. "My malpractice policy has a maximum of only one million per occurrence."

"Well, that might just present a minor problem then," said Denmark, shaking his head from to side to side in a way Hugh found deeply troubling. "If the jury agrees with the plaintiffs, looks like you'll come up a little short, won't you? You'll have to pay the rest out of your personal assets. Your home will be put on the market and sold. Your possessions will be auctioned off and your wages will be garnished for the next bazillion years. While you and your family are panhandling in the streets, you can think of the Winters touring the country in their brand new wheelchair-accessible RV. Put *that* in your pipe and smoke it."

"Surely you're exaggerating!" said Hugh, searching for any signs of amusement in his attorney's eyes.

There weren't any.

"But why are they suing *me*?" Hugh's voice sounded dangerously close to a whine. "I did everything right!"

"Maxine must have gotten her hands on a neurosurgical expert who'll testify that you did everything wrong. Probably Odeus Horman, her usual testifier."

"Odeus?"

"Short for Odysseus. He'll claim you were negligent and did the opposite of what you should have done. Had you operated on her right away, Julie would never have been paralyzed."

"That's a damned lie!" Hugh exploded. A small collection of fishing rods stored discretely behind the door toppled over and fell onto the floor. "The tumor had destroyed her spinal cord more than fifteen hours earlier! I can't bring dead tissue back to life! Nobody can!"

Denmark calmly stood up and went over to his rods. "Horman will do his best to raise as many doubts in the minds of the jurors as possible," he explained, carefully picking them up one by one. "Maybe the tumor *hadn't* really destroyed her cord. Maybe Julie *wasn't* completely quadriplegic. Maybe you performed a substandard neurological examination. He'll make it sound as if you couldn't be bothered to give her a chance. You went home to have a nice, relaxing evening with your family while your patient's reversible paralysis became *ir*reversible. Then you delayed for two days and only operated on her when it suited you, long after it was too late."

"That's ludicrous!" shouted Hugh, suddenly feeling an overwhelming desire to strangle Odeus Horman, whoever he was.

"You may very well think so," said Denmark, putting his rods back behind the door as lovingly as a father tucking his children into bed. "So might every reasonable neurosurgeon in the country. Only the jury's opinion matters though, and there's no predicting what a bunch of chumps fresh off the street will think."

"I just don't understand," said Hugh, loosening his tie and undoing his collar button. "Clegg was the one who screwed up. He never checked the CSF lab result. Or if he did, he didn't understand its significance."

Denmark looked puzzled. "What CSF lab result?" he asked.

"From the lumbar myelogram Julie Winter had before surgery. The protein was really high, a telltale sign she had a tumor."

"I went through the medical records line by line, millimeter by millimeter. I didn't see anything about high levels of protein in the CSF."

"*I* did," said Hugh. "The day she was transferred to Columbia. I clearly remember a pink piece of paper. I even marked it with my pen. We'll have to track it down. Maybe the lab will have a record of it. It's the best evidence there is that Clegg's guilty, not me."

Denmark returned to his desk, picked up a pencil, and wrote a memo to himself. "If I haven't seen that lab slip," he mumbled, "perhaps The Dog hasn't either. That might explain why she neglected to name Clegg as a co-defendant."

Hugh looked at Denmark ruefully. "Mr. Denmark—"

"Call me John."

"I'm sorry about my snotty attitude, John," said Hugh, wearily rubbing his forehead to soothe a rising headache. "I'm not accustomed to this sort of thing. I hate to admit it, but it's tearing me apart inside. I wish I could stay, but there's a patient—"

"I understand," said Denmark with a forgiving smile. "Go and make his brain fart, or whatever it is you need to do. We'll meet again next week when you're feeling stronger."

"Seems like I don't have a choice."

"No. As a matter of fact, you don't."

Hugh rose from his chair and left the office again, this time feeling thoroughly defeated. Common sense and the truth were nowhere to be found in the lawyerly latrine into which he had been dropped. In this dark and stinking hole, the only thing in abundance was—what else?—bullshit.

* * *

When Hugh was gone, Denmark leaned back in his seat, locked his fingers behind his head, and reflected upon his newest client. First-time medical malpractice defendants always handled things so badly, he decided. It was sad to watch them lose their bright-eyed enthusiasm for their profession and transition into a twilight zone of cynicism and disillusionment. He worried whether he had been too rough on Hugh. To be sure, the demand for fourteen million had been shocking enough for him. In reality, though, the numbers meant nothing. Maxine could ask for a hundred million dollars, for the moon, for the *stars* and it wouldn't make a difference. The jury, and only the jury, decided how much money her clients would get.

No, something else was of much greater concern to him right now.

The Washington Supreme Court had decided to give the concept of trial-by-ambush a test run and randomly chose *Winter vs. Montrose* as the pilot case. That meant no process of discovery, no depositions, no snooping around to find out what the other side was up to. And on this specific occasion, no witness lists either. Trial-by-ambush was already law in Oregon and went a long way to reducing costs. The disadvantage: almost anything could happen, and lawyers hated uncertainty. With Maxine Doggette representing the plaintiffs, Denmark knew he wasn't simply facing uncertainty. He was up against the complete unknown.

Denmark returned his gaze to the view outside. The sun was rising higher above the jagged Cascades in the east, shortening the shadows that stretched across the city. Mount Rainier was a beacon of grace rising proudly into the crystal clear sky. His mind registered none of this beauty. He saw only one image rising above the landscape like a ghostly apparition—The Dog in all her supreme ugliness laughing at him, mocking him, goading him into yet another ignominious defeat.

18

Odeus Horman was so fat, Maxine was quite sure he weighed at least a ton. She was relieved when he finally finished his fortnightly ritual of thrusting and grunting and wobbled off her like an elephant seal sliding into the sea. Without him grinding her into her mattress any longer she could think more clearly and there was plenty on her mind.

She covered herself up with bedclothes and looked up at the vaulted heights of her bedroom as if the answers to her throbbing questions could be found there. She saw no answers, only a black bra, panties, garter belt, and stockings draped over the lazily rotating blades of a ceiling fan.

So *that's* where those things ended up!

For a while Maxine's principle neurosurgical expert lay incapacitated beside her, panting, wheezing, and reeking of sweat. Maxine felt compelled to say something before he fell asleep and started snoring which was his custom once spent. She had important things to discuss with him and not a whole lot of time.

"You were terrific," she said, reaching for a packet of cigarettes on her bed table and tapping one out.

Horman cranked open his plaque-encrusted eyes and looked at Maxine.

"What's wrong with you?" he asked, frowning.

"What do you mean?" asked Maxine, lighting up.

"Sometimes your right eyelid droops so low I can't even see the eye underneath."

Maxine exhaled and sent a cloud of smoke rolling towards the underwear above her. This was neither the time nor place to discuss her health problems. "Maybe I'm exhausted," she said. "Time to shorten these appointments."

"Exhausted in one eye and not the other?"

"Okay, so I've got cancer and I'm dying," she said, nonchalantly waving around her cigarette. "What's it to you?"

"It's ugly and distracting," he said. "That's what. For pity's sake, next time wear an eye patch. Or at least a pair of dark glasses."

"Enough about me," said Maxine, sitting up and looking at Horman with her one good eye. "How long have we been doing business, Odeus?"

"Years."

"How many cases?"

"Dozens."

Maxine inched closer and lowered her voice. "How much *sex*?" she breathed suggestively.

"The agreed amount. No more. No less."

"So tell me something," she said, prodding him in the chest. "Why *the hell* won't you sign the declaration against Defendant Montrose?"

Horman gazed into the distance as if he was carefully formulating a diplomatic answer to her question. After a few moments his eyes brightened and a smile spread across his face. He drew in a deep breath and bore down hard. Flatus of astonishing ripeness and duration erupted under the covers. "Beg your pardon," he said, exhaling and grinning his satisfaction. "Oysters for dinner."

Maxine quickly stubbed out her cigarette before it ignited an explosion. "I asked you a question," she said impatiently. "Are you going to answer or not?"

"As I've already told you," replied Horman, "I've reviewed the case and, in my opinion, he did exactly the right thing."

"What difference does *that* make?" sputtered Maxine. "You've assassinated plenty of neurosurgeons before who did exactly the right thing. As long as I let you dip your fountain pen into my inkwell once in a while, you'll sign any declaration I put in front of you."

"This time it's different, my dear," said Horman. "I can't say anything outrageous under oath anymore, at least not for a while, or there'll be trouble."

Maxine shook with frustration. "In God's name, what kind of trouble?"

Horman shifted position and released a stink of rotten eggs from under the covers. "Do you recall *Larson vs. Blackwell?*" he asked, rubbing a swampy armpit as if it might stimulate her memory.

"Of course I do," said Maxine, reaching for an aerosol can of air freshener on her bed table. She shook it hard, aimed directly at Horman, and fired.

"The defendant, Dr. Blackwell, committed suicide," he said, momentarily engulfed in a billowing cloud of lemon fragrance. "Shot himself in the chest in the middle of an operation."

"So?" said Maxine, putting away the can. "The man was emotionally disturbed."

"Not surprising, considering what you put him through."

"You share the blame, you know. After all, you *were* my neurosurgical expert."

"I really went out on a limb for you that time," said Horman, jabbing his finger at Maxine. "Told all kinds of lies under oath. After his suicide, Blackwell's partners became quite belligerent towards me and filed a formal complaint with BRAIN's Professional Conduct Committee. There was an investigation and a hearing. Yesterday it concluded that my testimony was indeed unprofessional and recommended that the board suspend my membership for a year."

"No!" shouted Maxine, sitting bolt upright. Her breasts sagged from her chest like two fried eggs.

"I'm afraid so, Maxine," said Horman. "The board will almost certainly approve the committee's recommendation. That means any more bogus testimony from me and I could be permanently canned."

"What a disaster!"

"How do you think *I* feel?" said Horman, sweeping the bedclothes aside. He climbed to his feet and reached for his clothes. "My credibility has been severely damaged. I may never be able to market my services again." He slipped on his shirt and worked with the buttons. "No, I'm afraid I have no choice but to play it straight, at least for a while. I can't testify against Hugh Montrose. Far too risky. Don't worry though. There are plenty of other guns for hire out there who'd be willing to do your dirty work for you."

"No time," said Maxine. "Montrose's defense lawyer has filed a motion for summary judgment. The hearing is scheduled for next week. If I can't produce a sworn declaration from a neurosurgeon by then, the judge will throw out the whole case."

"What's so bad about that?" he asked, wandering over to a window. He slipped on his tie and threw a knot into it. Outside, Mount Rainier towered in the distance, its glaciers turning pink in the setting sun. A bald eagle was circling above the reservoir. Suddenly it plummeted towards the water, snared a salmon, and flapped away. "Sink your talons into somebody else."

"I don't want somebody else!" snapped Maxine. "I want Montrose!"

Horman turned to look at Maxine. "Is it something personal?" he asked, raising an inquisitive eyebrow.

Maxine's face tinged red. "No, of course not," she said, averting her eyes.

"Quite sure?" asked Horman, eking out the truth. "Let me guess. You've been having an affair with him, haven't you? The two of you have gotten quite close, so now you want to hurt him before he hurts you."

"That's complete nonsense."

"Is it? That's what usually happens. Afterwards you end up hating yourself forever. I should know. I've had to deal with you when you're depressed and it hasn't been easy."

"Not this time," said Maxine. "He's just another arrogant doctor who thinks he can humiliate me and get away with it."

First Horman regarded her with skepticism, then returned an indifferent gaze to the view outside. After a few moments he held up an index finger as if checking the direction of the wind.

"*I* know . . ."

"You know what?"

"I know somebody who might help you on short notice."

"You *do*?" said Maxine with a glimmer of hope in her eyes. "That's great! Who?"

"Somebody I worked with a long time ago."

"A neurosurgeon?"

"Of course he's a neurosurgeon," replied Horman, stepping away from the window. He picked up a pair of tent-sized briefs from the floor, held them open in front of him, and peered in. First he frowned, then shrugged and stepped through the leg holes. "He trained me when I was a resident. Accomplished many other important things in his career too. Wrote a textbook and published tons of research papers. Even invented a few surgical instruments."

"What's his name?" asked Maxine, suddenly all businesslike.

"Professor Charles Mortimer," said Horman, pulling on his trousers.

Maxine opened a drawer in her bed table and retrieved a small address book. She licked her thumb and leafed through the pages. When she reached the M's she lifted up her right eyelid with a finger and searched the list of names.

"He's not in my directory of medical experts," she said after a minute or two.

"You won't find his name in your stupid directory," said Horman, zipping his fly and fastening his belt. "He's never testified before. Did I mention he's officially retired? He still conducts research at the Miami Veterans Administration hospital, although he hasn't published a paper in years." Horman looked about the bedroom. "Do you remember where I put my whip?"

"I don't want a retired neurosurgeon," said Maxine stubbornly, returning her book to the drawer and letting her eyelid drop back down. "The jury won't like it."

"Maxine, if you don't find an expert real soon you won't *have* a jury. You won't even have a case. You can't afford to be choosy, you know." He held out his hand. "My whip?"

Maxine reached under her pillow, pulled out a black leather cat-o'-nine-tails, and threw it onto the bed as if it were a venomous snake.

Horman picked it up, flicked it around a time or two, then dropped it into a bag he had brought with him. He pulled on his socks and shoes and slicked his greasy hair back with the palms of his hands. "Would you like me to arrange for you to meet him?"

Maxine pouted, then acquiesced with a reluctant nod.

Horman leant over, treated her to a potpourri of lemons and sweat, and planted a sloppy kiss on her cheek. "I'll give him a call in the morning," he said. "Now I'd better go."

"Aren't you forgetting something?"

Horman looked around the bedroom. "Am I?"

Maxine pointed straight up, indicating the collection of underwear hanging from the ceiling fan.

"Oh, my things," said Horman, breaking into a sheepish grin. "I suppose you'd have no use for them, my dear. A few sizes too big, eh?"

Maxine was not amused. "Fetch them down," she said. "Then get out of my sight."

When Horman was gone, Maxine reached under her pillow and produced a framed photograph of Minimus wearing his favorite collar—the one with a pink heart-shaped pendant.

"Sorry, my darling," she said, setting him onto her bed table in plain view. "I'm afraid he insisted."

19

Hugh's appointment with John Denmark was a watershed event in his career. Before that day of infamy, Hugh liked patients and their diseases were the enemy. In the tense months afterwards, diseases mattered little and the patients themselves became the enemy.

Once Hugh understood the seriousness of the lawsuit against him, practicing defensive medicine became an obsession. Every time he made a decision he threw his experience and judgment straight out of the window and picked the safest course of action purely from a liability point of view. As it so happened, the choice he made was usually the most expensive one too. No longer did he care about spending obscene amounts of money. Why should he? It wasn't his. He admitted people to the hospital when it wasn't necessary. When it *was* necessary he put them into the intensive care unit when a regular floor bed would have been sufficient. He ordered twice as many CT and MRI scans, lab tests, and consults than ever before, jacking up overall costs into the stratosphere. He documented everything into the medical record in great detail, letting the lawyers of the future know how thoroughly a history was taken, how well a neurological exam was performed, how closely the standard of care was followed. Whenever he finished an entry, he imagined how the page might look if blown up into a large poster and placed on an easel in front of a jury.

To his surprise, he discovered that most of his colleagues around the hospital—and, indeed, across the whole country—had already been practicing defensive medicine for a long time now. Nationwide the costs were running into the hundreds of billions of dollars, adding to debts piling up everywhere. Hugh remembered how, a few months before, he had sat in Denmark's office and described Maxine as an aneurysm, badly stressed and heading for self-destruction. A far more frightening analogy was one between an aneurysm and the United States of America; thousands of miles across, bloated beyond belief, and under enormous pressures from within. What would happen when the entire system ruptured? No clip would be large enough to contain the damage. The country's lifeblood would gush into the oceans, turning them red and heralding an economic depression the likes of which the world had never seen before.

Hugh stood in his office, holding the day's clinic schedule in his hand. He had spent the previous six hours slowly working his way down the list of names. All the patients had presented with one kind of threat or another and any mistake on his part could easily have led to litigation. In the morning he had been alert and managed to make all the right defensive moves. After he had finished with each one he crossed them off his schedule with a single stroke of his pen. As the day wore on, however, his paranoia had grown and the lines he made became heavier and more erratic. At the bottom of the list, the paper was nearly scratched to pieces.

Now only one patient remained, a woman named Joyce Parker. Hoping she would be an easy one for a change, he walked to the examination room down the hallway, knocked on the door, and entered.

Joyce was in her mid sixties and had frizzy grey hair that stuck out to the sides, giving her head a triangular appearance. Boobs built in Bangkok ballooned from her chest, stretching the skimpy pink leotards she was wearing to their limit. *Triangle with two circles.* A living, breathing Picasso.

Joyce told Hugh she had been rear-ended three years before and was now suing the other driver for giving her the *haw*rible pain she had been suffering from ever since. Everything hurt—back, arms, legs, groin, tailbone, feet, hands. She was also afflicted with patches of numbness in a variety of improbable places, intermittent incontinence of urine and stool, headaches, dizziness, and depression. Dozens of healthcare professionals had given her a wide range of explanations for her problems. Either none of them knew what was really wrong with her or they didn't want to say.

Joyce handed Hugh a thick stack of medical records and tattered X-ray jackets filled with scans. The most recent cervical, thoracic, and lumbar MRI's were only three months old. He looked through them and decided they were normal.

"I advise you to avoid surgery," said Hugh, after carefully examining her. "It'll only make you worse. Treat yourself conservatively and hopefully things will improve with time."

Joyce looked at him angrily through narrowed eyes. "I'm here to get answers and won't leave without them!" she insisted.

Hugh groaned. Yet another hostile patient! He snapped on his full body armor again and went into a high state of alert. He offered to order up-to-date spine MRI's—ten thousand dollars' worth—just in case there were any changes since the last ones were done.

"You think it's all in my head, *don't* you?" she said, beginning to cry.

He wanted to tell her yes, she was obviously unhinged. The woman needed a shrink, not a neurosurgeon. Telling the truth wouldn't do any good though. She obviously wanted to have an operation. If he said anything that reduced her chance of getting one her hostility would only worsen.

Hugh retreated and regrouped. "I would like to refer you for a second opinion," he said, removing the X-rays from the viewing box and slipping them back into their jacket. "Dr. Frank Clegg is an orthopedic surgeon who works at the Emerald Spine Institute."

And one who never met a patient he didn't want to cut.

"*That* awful man?" said Joyce, her eyes flashing defiance. "He's the one who referred me to you!"

Hugh stared at her in disbelief. *Bonehead* had sent her to him? The Fusion Factory had actually rejected a patient? When had *that* ever happened before? Hugh desperately scrambled for another solution to the problem. The answer quickly became abundantly clear.

The nuclear option.

"You're wasting my time," he said harshly. "Why don't you leave and save us both a lot of trouble?"

Joyce swelled toad-like with indignation. "What kind of doctor are you anyway?" she sobbed, snatching back her X-rays and medical records and gripping them tightly to her chest like a mother protecting her beloved children. "You're supposed to make my pain go away! Instead you've made it worse! All right, I'm leaving! And I'm *never* coming back!"

She fled the examination room.

Hoping he hadn't provoked her into filing a lawsuit against him, Hugh retreated to his office, shut the door behind him, and collapsed into his chair. Moments later he heard a sharp knock.

"Yes?"

Sandra, the office manager, entered and planted her hands on her hips. "What did you tell that poor woman?" she asked, glaring at him.

"I told her to get lost," said Hugh, kicking off his shoes.

"She was crying when she left!"

"You're confusing me with somebody who cares," he said, putting his feet on his desk. "Send her a certified letter discharging her from my practice."

"Dr. Montrose!" spluttered Sandra. "You used to be nice to your patients! What happened to you? Is it the lawsuit?"

The phone rang. Hugh picked up the receiver. "Hello?" he answered, shooing Sandra away.

The voice at the other end of the line was Dave Holz, a physician who worked in the ER at Columbia Medical Center. "You're the neurosurgeon on call, aren't you?" he asked.

"I suppose."

"Can I run a patient by you and see what you think?"

Hugh examined the liability risk as if he was standing at the edge of a frozen pond, trying to decide whether it was safe to walk across. He was being asked to give a curbside consult, meaning he didn't have to see the patient or document anything in the medical record; just give some free advice over the telephone. Such consults were common and sometimes saved patients a great deal of trouble and expense. He didn't see any harm in helping out and set the threat level at green.

"What's the case about?" he asked.

"I have a forty-two year old man who just walked in here with a long history of back pain," said Holz. "His neurological exam is completely normal. I didn't want to take any chances so I ran him through the MRI scanner. Thank God I did! Looks like he's got a big spine cancer surrounding his cord at T12. What should I do?"

Hugh's eyelids grew heavy. It had been a long morning. "You said he's neurological intact? No deficits whatsoever?"

"None. I'm sure of it."

"Then admit him to the internal medicine service," he yawned. "Get the interventional radiologists to obtain a biopsy to establish the diagnosis and ask the oncologists to coordinate his care. If the tumor's sensitive to radiation, maybe that's all he'll need. If not, then he should have an operation to take it out and stabilize his spine. In the meantime, watch his neurological status carefully. If it gets worse, let me know immediately. That's the way I would normally handle it."

Holz thanked him and hung up.

Hugh closed his eyes and let his mind drift. Moments later he found himself in a shadowy courtroom, cowering before a stern judge wearing black robes and a long white wig. A mob of men brandishing pitchforks and flaming torches occupied the jury box, agitating amongst themselves. Maxine was standing beside the plaintiff table, conducting a campaign of psychological warfare against him; drilling into him with her cold, grey eyes and gassing him with her perfume. A gold hummingbird brooch was pinned to her chest.

"So, you gave a curbside consult, did you?" she said, taking slow steps towards him.

"I was only trying to be helpful!" he cried, rattling the chains around his wrists.

"You didn't go to see the patient!" continued Maxine. "You didn't examine him! You didn't look at his X-rays! You didn't have adequate information! So when he eventually became paralyzed two weeks later after being seen and treated by ten other physicians it was ALL . . . YOUR . . . FAULT! Isn't that the truth?"

Hugh no longer knew what the truth was. By now it was badly mauled and hardly recognizable; a rotting corpse hanging from a noose, gently twisting one way and then another, depending on the direction of the wind.

"I wasn't asked to see the patient!" he shouted. "There was no doctor-patient relationship!"

"Yes there *was* a doctor-patient relationship!" the judge roared back. "You were the neurosurgeon on call for the ER! That's good enough for me! And I make the rules around here!" He turned to the jurors. "Gentlemen! How do you find the defendant?"

"Negligent, Your Honor!" they bayed, raising their pitchforks and torches into the air. "Negligent . . . negligent . . . negligent!"

"Speak louder! I can't hear you!"

The jury worked itself into a frenzy. *"Negligent . . . negligent . . . negligent!"*

"So be it! Defendant Montrose, the jury has found you guilty of gross negligence. You are hereby sentenced to have your blood sucked from your carotids until you are dead. May God have mercy on your soul!"

Hugh folded up and buried his face in his hands. All he had ever wanted to do was to take care of patients. Now one had destroyed him. The judge continued to speak but Hugh was too busy watching his life pass before his eyes to pay attention to what he was saying. Eventually a gavel banged and cheering filled the room around him. He recognized Denmark's voice whispering urgently into his ear.

"We'll appeal . . . We'll appeal . . . We'll appeal . . ."

Alas, it was too late for any appeals. Maxine's hummingbird brooch came to life and a long tongue streaked towards him. He felt a dash of stickiness against his chest and an irresistible tug as it winched him in. Maxine smiled with evil delight and opened her mouth. Blood was dripping from both incisors.

Hugh screamed.

"Dr. Montrose! Wake up, Dr. Montrose!"

Hugh's eyes flew open. His heart was racing and his face was covered in sweat. Sandra was shaking him and calling his name.

"Dr. Montrose!"

"I'm going mad!" Hugh shouted back. "*Mad!*"

"You were having a nightmare, Dr. Montrose! Just a nightmare! You're safe in your office!"

Hugh blinked his way back to reality. He looked around and saw his diplomas, his books, his computer; familiar things that helped to settle him down.

Not another nightmare! He was having too many of them these days. Invariably he would wake up in the middle of the night, yelling his head off and alarming Caroline. This was the first one he'd had in his office.

Hugh's eyes suddenly filled with alarm. "Oh my God!"

"What's the matter?"

"How long have I been asleep?" he asked, whipping his feet off the desk and sitting bolt upright.

"Only five minutes."

Hugh snatched his telephone, punched in the number for Columbia's ER, and demanded to speak to Dr. Holz immediately.

"Dave!" he cried when he heard him at the other end. "Remember that patient you just called me about? The one with the spinal tumor?"

"Sure."

"Is he still there?"

"Yes. We haven't admitted him yet."

"Thank God! Transfer him somewhere else! Use any excuse you want. I don't want to have anything to do with him. It's too risky!"

"Are you okay, Hugh?"

"Get rid of him!"

"Sure thing, Hugh. Right away."

Hugh hung up and heaved a huge sigh of relief. Just when he thought he knew everything about protecting himself from medical malpractice lawsuits, The Dog had appeared to him in a nightmare and had shown him a new way he could be sued.

Never *EVER* give curbside consults!

Hugh raised their threat level from green to red. Of course, such a decision was bound to cause patients untold inconvenience and expense, but he didn't care.

The only thing that mattered these days was perfecting the art of defensive medicine.

20

A few days after her bedroom appointment with Odeus Horman, Maxine took Billy and Minimus with her on an overnight flight to Miami. She bought a couple of first class tickets for herself and Minimus and appeared neat and well rested when she emerged from the plane the following morning. Billy, on the other hand, stumbled out tired and rumpled after spending the night at the back, wedged between two men the size of sumo wrestlers.

Maxine decided to follow Horman's advice and had strapped a black eye patch over her right eye. As she walked through the terminal she looked like a marauding pirate. Not altogether a bad thing, in her opinion, considering the nature of her law practice.

From the airport they took a limousine to the Miami VA hospital. When they arrived at their destination they passed through the main entrance and entered a bustling lobby. Marble columns and big, black wall directories gave the place the same government atmosphere as the King County Courthouse.

Both Maxine and Billy had brought along elephant bags— black cases on wheels that lawyers typically use for transporting documents. Billy's was nine months' pregnant with a copy of Julie Winter's medical records and weighed a ton. Maxine's served as a luxurious traveling carriage for Minimus, complete with a wire mesh window and padded walls. Exterior pockets carried his medications and grooming supplies.

After a few minutes waiting beneath a row of photographs of government officials ranging from the president of the United States to the local VA administrator they were met by a young man wearing a short white lab coat. "I'm Sven Johansen," he said, shaking their hands, "one of the neurosurgery residents. We spoke on the phone the other day."

"So where is he?" asked Maxine, scrutinizing the faces around her.

"Professor Mortimer? Certainly not here, in public. His laboratory is in the sub-sub-basement."

"The sub-sub-basement?" said Maxine with a sudden look of concern.

"That's correct," answered Sven, pointing a finger towards the floor. "Deep down there."

"Surely a man of the professor's stature doesn't conduct his research *below* ground level!"

"It's the best place for him. Everybody in the neurosurgery department decided *that* a long time ago. Is there a problem?"

"No, no . . ." said Maxine a little too quickly to be believable. "In general, I don't like basements." To be sure, it was an understatement. Ever since her childhood when her Aunt Agatha had often locked her up in one she avoided them whenever possible.

"Don't worry," said Sven. "I'll show you the way. You'll be fine." He led Maxine and Billy to a waiting elevator, punched a button, and stood back as the doors closed. The BB sign, the one below the B sign, eventually lit up.

"This is as far as the elevator goes," said Sven, stepping out. "We'll have to take the stairs the rest of the way. Follow me."

They were now in the bowels of the VA. A cluster of pipes ran alongside fluorescent lights in the ceiling and heavy machinery hummed behind cinder block walls. Large plastic bins on wheels were scattered around, some filled with laundry, others with bags of used medical supplies. They threaded their way down a long corridor and dipped into a stairwell at the end. Billy picked up his elephant bag and lugged it down the stairs, straining from the weight of the medical records inside. Sven offered to carry Maxine's but she pushed his hand away.

When they reached the bottom of the stairwell, they stood in front of a heavy fire door with a big red BBB stenciled onto it.

"This is the sub-sub-basement," said Sven, pushing the door open. He stepped back and allowed Maxine and Billy to pass through. "The professor's lab is at the end of the hallway," he said, pointing into the gloom. "You can't miss it."

"You're not coming?" asked Maxine.

Sven started back up the stairs. "Not today," he said cagily over his shoulder. The sound of his shoes grew fainter. A door slammed in the distance.

"That's weird," said Maxine. "I guess we'll just have to proceed without him."

The light was much dimmer at this level and a smell of rodents pervaded the atmosphere. Maxine produced a frilly handkerchief, held it over her nose, and crept down the hallway.

Billy tiptoed close behind. "Ms. Doggette," he said, "do you really think Professor Mortimer is the right man for the—"

"*Shhh!*" hushed Maxine, suddenly stopping dead in her tracks. "I hear something! Listen!"

Creak . . . creak . . . creak . . .

The sound of a rotating ceiling fan that had never been oiled.

A shiver went up Maxine's spine.

"What *is* it?" whispered Billy.

"I don't know," she said, peering into the darkness.

Minimus whined.

As Maxine probed closer, the noise intensified.

Creak . . . Creak . . . Creak . . .

It was coming from the other side of a low iron door at the end of the hallway.

Maxine drew in a deep breath, put her handkerchief away, and edged up to it. She knocked gently, then stepped back and waited. Her heart was thumping hard inside her chest.

After a few moments there was a loud click and the door slowly groaned open.

An ancient man wearing a dirty lab coat materialized like a phantom from the shadows. Indeed, he was so old, parts of him looked like they were already dead. Certainly his mummified eyes were devoid of any signs of life. His face was the color of ash, covered in sores and blemishes and sagging loosely over the fragile bones underneath. Long, white hair covered his head and fell around his ears in dirty tangles.

Maxine gaped at him. Was this prehistoric fossil her neurosurgical expert, the lynchpin of her case against Defendant Montrose? He must have been at least a hundred years old! If she allowed him to take the stand—assuming he was able to climb the step to get there—the jury would laugh her out of the courtroom.

"*You're* Professor Mortimer?" she asked incredulously.

He nodded faintly.

Maxine's heart sank. In her mind's eye she saw high explosives detonating under *Winter vs. Montrose* and the whole case collapsing amongst huge clouds of dust. Odeus had done this to her on purpose! Another one of those horrible jokes people liked to play on her!

"My name is Maxine Doggette," she said, putting on a brave face. "Surely you've heard of me."

Mortimer showed no signs he had.

"I'm a medical malpractice nurse attorney from Seattle. Dr. Odeus Horman, one of your former residents, referred me to you."

"Odeus Horman?" said Mortimer in a frail, high-pitched whine that spun through the air like a dying firework.

"Yes," said Maxine, feeling faint. His voice would sound pathetic in a courtroom. "He told me you might be interested in testifying as a—"

Mortimer suddenly turned and shuffled away.

Maxine and Billy looked at each other, uncertain what to do next. When Billy started backing away, Maxine reached up, seized him by the scruff of the neck, and yanked him through the doorway.

Once they were inside the lab, they saw a large wooden butcher block table illuminated by a single overhead light bulb. Darkness pervaded on all sides, making the overall size of the room impossible to fathom. A powerful stench exploded in their faces; a zeppelinful of nauseating gas. Here was the source of that rodent smell!

CREAK . . . CREAK . . . CREAK . . .

In the gloom they could barely make out dozens of cages set on black slate workbenches. As their eyes adjusted, they saw that they were filled with white mice running inside exercise wheels.

Maxine gasped. There were thousands of mice in this place, their red eyes shining like stars in an alien universe.

A camp bed was set up near the table, a rumpled sleeping bag thrown on top. Around it were scattered candles, spent matches, and piles of dirty clothes. Several framed diplomas lay on the ground face up, their glasses cracked as if somebody had stepped on them.

"My God!" she whispered, looking around in horror. "What *is* this place?"

Mortimer tottered over to a stool next to the butcher block table and sat down. He reached out with a claw-like hand, opened the door to a nearby cage, and grabbed a mouse. Keeping a firm grip on the little bundle of fur, kicking legs, and twitching whiskers, he picked up a pair of scissors, positioned the blades around its neck, and decapitated it. The head fell to the table, its whiskers now still. The rest of the mouse continued to kick and wriggle. Tiny squirts of blood pumped out of its body and sprayed through the air. Mortimer dropped the corpse into a garbage can by his feet and added the head to a pile of others inside a glass beaker.

"What are you doing?" cried Maxine, her nausea intensifying.

"Collecting mouse brains," droned Mortimer without taking his eyes off his work.

"But why?"

Mortimer wiped his bloody fingers across the front of his lab coat, leaving behind five red smears. "Research," he answered.

"But that's utterly disgusting!" said Billy.

Mortimer reached for the cage door again and extracted another mouse by its tail.

Maxine swallowed the bile rising in her throat. "Odeus spoke very highly of you," she said. "He told me you were a great neurosurgeon—"

"I *am* a great neurosurgeon!" shouted Mortimer, raising his hand into the air and slamming his mouse onto the table.

"Of course!" said Maxine. "How silly of me! He said you *are* a great neurosurgeon and that you would make an even greater neurosurgical expert if given the opportunity to testify. Would you like to hear about the lawsuit? My client is a woman who has been terribly wronged and is quadriplegic now because . . ."

Maxine tried to describe the case but Mortimer's scissor blades were hard at work again and he clearly wasn't listening. As she searched for the right words to capture his attention, she felt something warm and wet brushing against the back of her leg.

Startled, she jumped away. A mangy dog with large, doleful eyes was looking up at her. The top of his head was shaved down to the skin and a six-inch metal bolt protruded from his skull. Suture lines zigzagged away from it in all directions.

A four-legged Frankenstein.

Maxine rushed over to her elephant bag and covered its wire mesh window with outspread hands. "Don't look, Minimus!" she urgently warned him.

Minimus' whines escalated into howls.

Maxine realized it was pointless to explain anything to Mortimer about the case. *Winter vs. Montrose* was finished. Without a living, breathing neurosurgeon to testify for the plaintiffs, Denmark would tear her to shreds. She floundered about, desperately looking for a way to save the day.

And then an idea struck her! A truly outrageous idea!

"Professor Mortimer!" she cried, her eyes shining with inspiration. "I'm here to invite you to Seattle to give a lecture!"

Mortimer looked up from the carnage. "A lecture?"

"A lecture on your research!" Maxine pressed on. "It'll be the biggest thing to hit the neurosurgical world in years!"

"*Ms. Doggette!*" hissed Billy through gritted teeth. "What are you *doing*?"

Mortimer put down his scissors and blinked. "It will?"

Maxine ventured closer to Mortimer. "Not only am I a topnotch medical malpractice attorney," she told him, "but I also happen to represent the World Federation of Mouse Brain Research. Its most important members are gathering together for a special symposium in your honor. They want you to give the keynote lecture and explain your work. Afterwards there will be press conferences, television interviews, and book signings. Tell them you'll do it, Professor! Please accept this invitation!"

Billy frowned at Maxine. "A symposium?" he said. "You didn't tell *me* about any—"

Billy's voice faded as he noticed a transformation taking place deep inside Mortimer. A hint of light was now shining behind his eyes.

"A symposium in my honor?" he said, his lower lip beginning to twitch.

"Yes!" shouted Maxine, shaking him by the shoulders and feeling his skeleton rattling around inside his skin. "Just think where this will lead! You'll be famous! Your work will change the world! Can you imagine that?"

Mortimer's mouth opened up like an expanding sink-hole and twisted into something that resembled a smile.

Maxine hurriedly opened Billy's elephant bag and extracted some papers. "As you might expect," she said, whipping out a pen, "the symposium's Quality Assurance Committee has certain policies and procedures that have to be closely followed. First you must sign this declaration, confirming you understand the terms and conditions of the lecture."

Without reading a word, Mortimer took the pen and scrawled his signature somewhere near the bottom.

Maxine snatched the precious declaration from him and spirited it away. "You'll also have to travel to Seattle," she explained with a triumphant look in her eyes. "When the time comes, I'll send for you. Meanwhile, I'll leave my client's medical records here. You can peruse them when you're not busy with your research."

"A lecture!" cackled Mortimer, dipping both hands into the beaker before him and burrowing his fingers through the mouse heads. He scooped some out, raised them into the air on outstretched palms, and let them drop as if they were gold doubloons. "I'm going to give a lecture!"

Maxine turned to Billy. "Come on," she quietly said to him. "We've got what we came for. Let's get out of here before I throw up."

Billy unloaded the medical records from his elephant bag, then followed Maxine outside. When they were safely in the hallway, he tugged at Maxine's sleeve. "Ms. Doggette!"

"What is it?"

"I didn't know there was going to be a symposium."

"There isn't, you fool! But as long as *he* believes it, there's still a chance I can win the case."

"Oh, I see."

After a moment or two or deep thought, Billy spoke up again. "But what are you going to do when that fruitcake takes the stand and rambles on about mouse brains?"

"Stop worrying so much," she said, pooh-poohing away his concerns with her fingers. "You're forgetting who you work for. I'll come up with a plan. I always do. By the time I've finished with that repulsive creature, the jury will think he's God's gift to neurosurgery."

Maxine had deliberately made it sound as if things would be easy. Privately, however, she knew that Professor Charles Mortimer presented her with a major challenge—one requiring every ounce of imagination, audacity, and bare-faced effrontery at her disposal. Dealing with difficult situations was her strong suit. The more demanding they were, the better she performed. When all was said and done, she was confident that Professor Mortimer's metamorphosis from a crazy old man into a lethal expert witness would become the single most astonishing accomplishment the Kingdom of Med-Mal had ever known.

21

For most of its patrons, the *No Tomorrows Lounge* was the end of the road.

A ramshackle building with a corrugated iron roof and neon beer signs in the windows, it stood on a patch of barren wasteland somewhere between a trailer park and a truck stop.

Hugh sat alone in a red vinyl booth, hunched over a table. His tired eyes stared vacantly ahead. He was finishing his first beer and the alcohol was finally having its desired effect—erasing the pain he felt from losing touch with a profession he once loved. In the six months since he had been served the lawsuit, he had learned to hate ninety-nine percent of his patients. As his bitterness and cynicism worsened he began acting strangely, snapping at the residents instead of teaching them and making stupid mistakes in the operating room.

As he picked at a bowl of stale peanuts, Hugh shuddered to think what the future had in store for him.

A blonde dressed in skimpy clothes was circulating around the few drifters in the joint as they smoked and played pool, searching for the kind of love that earned hard cash. She sidled over to Hugh with a can of beer in her hand.

"Hi baby," she said, looking down at him with an alluring smile. "How's it going?"

Hugh said nothing.

"Well?" she asked as she waited for an answer. "Cat got your tongue?"

"Leave me alone," he grunted.

"I'm Candy," she said, scooting into the booth next to him. "Have I seen you here before?"

Hugh drained the last of his beer and pushed away the empty glass. "No," he said wearily.

"You shouldn't sit by yourself," said Candy, leaning closer and treating him to a generous view of her cleavage. "Every man needs a woman. How about having a little fun with me?"

"I don't want any fun," said Hugh, looking away.

"Sure you do," said Candy, caressing his arm. "What's your name?"

"Hugh."

"So, Hugh," said Candy, dropping her hand to his thigh. "What do you say? Want to forget your troubles?"

Hugh turned to look at Candy. Her hopeful face was etched with the lines of a person who had known hardship for many years. He had once empathized with downtrodden victims like her in his clinic, broken the barriers, and made them feel comfortable. Now he felt like he had become one of them himself.

"No," he said, pushing away her hand. "I'm not that kind of guy."

Candy's face colored and her eyes hardened. The moment quickly passed, however, and she quickly got back to business.

"Have another beer," she suggested. "It'll loosen you up. God knows you need it."

Hugh shook his head. "Better not," he said with a sigh. "I'm on call tonight."

Candy looked at him with surprise. "You've got a job?"

"You might call it that."

"What do you do?" she asked, taking a long draft from her beer.

"I'm a brain surgeon."

Beer exploded from Candy's mouth as if she was a can herself, shaken vigorously and popped open at high altitude.

"Oh my God!" she hooted. "A brain surgeon? The hell you are!"

"You don't believe me?"

"Of course not! Brain surgeons are smart, sophisticated people. You think I don't know that?"

The pager on Hugh's belt beeped urgently. "There goes that damn thing again," he said, reaching down for it. "They never stop calling me. Never!" He read the numbers on the display, pulled a cell-phone out of his pocket, and punched the keys. "Hello? This is Dr. Montrose. Did somebody page me?"

Dave Holz, the ER physician, was on the other end of the line. His voice was tinny and distant.

"I have a ninety-two year old Alzheimer's patient from a nursing home in Juneau, Alaska," he told him. "This morning she had a large intracranial hemorrhage and suddenly became comatose."

"So what's she doing here?" asked Hugh. "Don't they have somebody in Juneau who can take care of her?"

"No, they don't. At least not a neurosurgeon. So they loaded her into one of those flying intensive care units and sent her south. Her name's Pearl Peterson."

Hugh was impressed by the spectacularly expensive display of defensive medicine. The postage alone on this particular package must have cost the federal government tens of thousands of dollars. Those doctors in Juneau deserved a prize for wasting so much money.

"Alright, I'll come and have a look at her," he told Holz, then hung up. He saw Candy looking at him expectantly. "Sorry," he said to her. "Got to go. There's an old woman with a brain bleed in the ER." He dug deep into a pocket and scattered a handful of dollars across the table.

"You're no frickin' brain surgeon" said Candy, sneering at him.

"Sure I am. Check me out on the Columbia Medical Center website."

"Prove it to me now!"

Hugh searched the girl's disbelieving eyes. When he realized she was being serious he broke into a shrewd smile. "Alright," he said. "Why not? Come with me to the hospital. I'll show you what brain surgery is all about . . ." Then he added, as a melancholy afterthought, ". . . these days."

Hugh grabbed Candy's hand, led her from the booth, and headed for the exit. Once outside, he went to his car and opened the front passenger door for her.

"You know, there are easier ways to make me come to your apartment," she said as she climbed in.

"I don't have an apartment," said Hugh, shutting the door after her.

"Your hotel room then," she said when he settled into the driver's seat next to her.

"I don't have one of those either."

"Then where are we going?"

"Like I said: to the hospital. I'll prove to you who I am. That's what you want, isn't it?" Hugh inserted his key into the ignition, cranked the engine, and started driving.

At first Candy listed the various sexual services she provided and their corresponding prices as if Hugh was just another john, albeit one with more than the average imagination. When Columbia Medical Center appeared through the windshield in front of her, however, her voice trailed away as if she realized for the first time that there might be some truth to what he had been telling her.

Hugh parked his car in a PHYSICIAN "EMERGENCY" PARKING ONLY space outside the ER and walked through the swishing doors. Candy followed, looking nervously around her.

Inside, they were met by Holz, a man with a crew cut, horn-rimmed glasses, and a bow tie. "Thanks for coming," he said to Hugh. "Your head bleed is in Room 6." He frowned at Candy with her heavy make-up, skimpy clothes, and tattoos. "And who are you?" he asked.

Candy shrank away from him. "I'm Can—"

"Kennedy!" interrupted Hugh. "*Doctor* Kennedy. She's a medical student from the university. Just starting her third year. Never been in an ER before."

Candy's face filled with alarm. "I'm not a doctor!" she cried.

"We address all medical students as Doctor around here," explained Hugh. "No need to terrorize the patients if we don't have to."

"Welcome to Columbia Medical Center," said Holz, giving Candy a dubious smile.

Pearl Peterson looked every day of her ninety-two years; a shriveled carcass trying unsuccessfully to die a dignified death in twenty-first century America. Her eyes were closed and her skin was white as alabaster. A plastic tube emerged from her mouth and was attached to a machine that blew air into her lungs. A cluster of IV bags and clear plastic tubes hung from poles at the head of her bed, delivering fluids and medicines into her body.

Candy looked at her with reverence and respect.

Hugh barely noticed her. "So, Dr. Kennedy," he said, approaching the gurney and waving in the patient's general direction. "Tell me what you think is going on here."

"I-I don't know," she murmured, squinting at a monitor screen that displayed rows of squiggly lines.

"Don't they teach you anything in medical school?" he said with exasperation. "She's had a bleed in her brain. Isn't it obvious? Now examine her and tell me what you find."

Candy reached out to the woman with a hand. Her fingers hesitated over her wrinkly face, then brushed gently across her cheek.

"That's no way to examine a patient," said Hugh, stepping forward. "*This* is how it's done."

He pulled down a sheet and pinched a nipple. She scrunched her face into a frightful grimace and fought against the ventilator. The steady *beep . . . beep . . . beep* on the monitor became a *bip-bip-bip-bip-bip-bip-bip* and at least three different alarms exploded into life. Her arms and legs flailed around randomly while her eyes remained closed.

Candy instinctively crossed her arms over her own chest and shrank away in horror.

"She's making non-purposeful movements to noxious stimulation," explained Hugh. "Intubated, and no eye opening. I would give her a six on the Glasgow Coma Scale. That means her hamburger is pretty well cooked. So, Dr. Kennedy, what are we going to do next?"

"Did . . . Did she feel that?"

"Looks like she did. What's next?"

"I . . . I—"

"We check out the CT scan." Hugh waved towards some X-rays hanging on a viewing box. "See that big glob of white stuff in her frontal lobe? That's a blood clot. It's making the pressure inside her head go sky high. How do you propose we deal with it?"

Candy shrugged helplessly.

Hugh sighed impatiently as if a kindergarten student would have known the answer. "Duh!" he said, sounding like one of his teenaged daughters. "We'll open her up and take it out."

Candy blinked with disbelief. "You're going to operate on her?"

"Yep."

"But she's ninety-two years old! Why don't you let her die in peace?"

"Ninety-two, sixty-two, thirty-two . . . Age doesn't mean anything anymore." Hugh reached for a flashlight. He lifted an eyelid and shone it into an eye, checking pupillary reaction. "Nowadays, all patients are treated the same. Nobody dies in peace. It's far too risky." He checked the other pupil. "Might provoke all kinds of lawsuits."

Candy pulled Hugh closer. "How about her?" she asked. "How would *she* feel about that?"

"Pearl can't feel anything," said Hugh, switching off the flashlight and putting it aside. "I guarantee it."

"And how do *you* feel?"

Hugh looked at Candy with emptiness in his eyes. "I can't feel anything either. At least, not anymore."

When they reached surgery, Hugh snatched scrubs off a shelf, tossed them to Candy, and pointed towards a locker room. "Go in there and put these on," he told her.

"Hugh," said Candy with pleading eyes. "This has gone far enough. Take me back to the *No Tomorrows*. Please!"

"Do as I say!"

She scampered away.

Five minutes later, when they were both dressed in scrubs, Hugh helped her to put on booties, cap, and mask. When she was ready he led her down a sterile hallway, past stacks of surgical supplies, and into OR 8 where Val, Lori, and an anesthesiologist were preparing the case.

"Can I have your attention, everybody?" boomed Hugh. "Dr. Kennedy is a third year medical student from the university. She came to see what brain surgery is all about. She's never been in an operating room before, so keep her well away from anything sterile."

Candy headed for a corner of the OR and stood with her back flat against a cold, tiled wall. "Is this where I'm supposed to go?" she asked nervously.

"Don't be so squeamish. Stand right behind me."

"You're not serious!"

"You won't have to do anything," he said, checking the CT's hanging on a view box. "Just watch."

"Oh God!" whimpered Candy, stepping cautiously forward. "I can't believe this is happening!"

A couple of orderlies wheeled Pearl into the room on a gurney and transferred her onto the OR table. After the anesthesiologist had put her to sleep, Hugh took the Mayfield clamp off a table, opened it wide, and positioned the spikes around her head. He took a deep breath and drove them into her scalp until his biceps were bulging. Once he finished attaching her to the table, he whisked off her bluish-white hair with a pair of clippers. Within seconds she resembled a plucked buzzard.

The anesthesiologist inserted an arterial line for monitoring her blood pressure, a central venous line for her fluid volume, and an esophageal stethoscope to listen to her heart. Hugh washed his hands at the scrub sink outside, then returned to the room to gown and glove. Soon he was slicing through Pearl's scalp with a knife. A fine jet of blood sprayed a swarm of tiny red spots across the front of his gown.

Candy teetered.

"Stand closer, Dr. Kennedy," said Hugh. "Have a whiff of *this*!" When Candy's nose was within range, Hugh fired up the monopolar cautery. Pools of blood and liquid fat boiled and bubbled. Clouds of acrid blue smoke swirled from the wound.

Candy held her breath and screwed her eyes shut.

Next, the craniotome. He jammed it against the exposed skull, mashed a pedal with his foot, and bored four burr holes in quick succession. Bone disintegrated into a cream-colored paste. Venous blood welled up from below and turned it dark red. He smeared wax everywhere for hemostasis. Next he grabbed a cutting saw and guided the howling blade between the holes he'd just made. Bone dust kicked up behind it and floated through the air. Its rich smell was intoxicating and spurred him on. When he was finished, he lifted out the flap, tossed it aside, and cut open the dura with a scalpel.

"Behold, the human brain!" he announced with all the exaggeration of a Gothic melodrama.

Candy cracked open an eye just in time to see mushy brain fungating out of the opening like over-fermented dough bursting from a bread maker.

"Brain surgeons aren't quite what you imagined, eh, Dr. Kennedy?" said Hugh, hoovering up the soupy mess with two large-bore suckers, one in each hand. "Sorry to pop your bubble, but there's nothing smart or sophisticated about *this* business, I'm afraid. At least, not any longer. The lawyers are running hospitals now, just like they run the whole country. They're the ones who set the standards we're forced to live by. And this is how they expect us to do our jobs. The clot's got to be in here somewhere!" Hugh poked both suckers into the frontal lobe, stirred vigorously as if he was a chef mixing a pudding, and sent brain matter foaming down coils of transparent plastic tubing. "Where is the damned thing? What's wrong here?"

Hugh slammed his suckers onto Lori's instrument tray and went over to the X-ray viewing box. His face reflected milky blue light as he looked at the pictures.

After a few moments, his eyes rolled up into his head as the awful truth sunk in.

The writing on the films was backwards! He was on the wrong side of the head! The same idiotic, inexcusable mistake Richard Elliott had once made!

Hugh took a deep breath, gathered his strength, and swore as violently as he knew how; a primeval explosion of triple X-rated filth that blasted out of Room 8 and echoed down the spotless halls of the OR.

Candy staggered away from the operative field, sank to the floor behind the anesthesia machine, and threw up into her mask.

Val rushed to her side.

"I'm not a medical student!" Candy told her, choking and coughing. She wrenched off her mask and wiped vomit from her face. "I'm just some girl he picked up at a bar tonight. He forced me to come here because he wanted to prove he's a brain surgeon. I didn't ask for any of this. It was *his* idea. I swear!"

Hugh returned to the patient and snatched back his suckers. "I'll be damned if I'm sawing another hole on the other side of the head!" he shouted. "This time I'm going clear across the middle. Nobody will ever suspect a thing!"

As everybody watched with disbelief, Hugh thrust his suckers back into the craniotomy opening like a gunslinger with both barrels blazing. Large swaths of brain were vaporized in an instant. When he reached the falx, a thick membrane that separates one cerebral hemisphere from the other, he slashed a hole through it with a scalpel. On the other side he found what he was looking for: a blood clot that had the same general size, shape, and color as a beet root. He delivered it whole and dumped it with a loud *splat* in front of Lori.

Candy screamed and fled the room.

"Ladies and gentlemen," said Hugh, his chest heaving from exertion. "I have an important announcement to make: the operation has been a *complete* success! Go and tell *that* to the family!"

22

Hugh came perilously close to losing his privileges at Columbia Medical Center over the Pearl Peterson incident. Several hospital committees—Quality Assurance, Credentials, Executive, Ethics, and Surgery—met separately in emergency session to review the events of that night. In the end, Hugh's neck was saved by a miracle: Pearl actually woke up afterwards and, for the first time in months, returned to her normal gregarious self; alert, oriented, and lacking any trace of dementia. The pathologist reported the presence of a melanoma metastasis in the specimen that was sent to the lab. So it seemed the tumor was the source of her confusion all along. When it bled, as melanomas in the brain were prone to do, she spiraled into a coma. When both clot and tumor were removed, the indestructible old bird spiraled out again. Hugh successfully argued that he had suspected the true diagnosis all along and that he was only guilty of bringing an unauthorized person into the operating room. The matter soon blew over. Pearl flew commercial back to her overjoyed family in Juneau and the various committees moved on to more important things.

Denmark was not surprised when Hugh went to his office one day and told him what happened. He had seen similar bizarre behavior before and had no doubt about the diagnosis.

"Juris psychosis," he declared. "JP for short. I can recognize it a mile away."

"What's that?" asked Hugh, turning down an offer of coffee.

"A psychiatric condition most commonly diagnosed in physicians being sued for malpractice," answered Denmark, pouring a cup for himself. "Caused by over-exposure to the legal profession. Similar to post-traumatic stress disorder in combat veterans."

"What can you do for it?"

"There's only a single approved treatment: Preparation T, generically known as trial preparation.

"I've never heard of anything so preposterous in my life," scoffed Hugh.

He wasn't laughing for long. From that day on, at least twice a week, Denmark made him figuratively drop his pants, bend over, and receive a large enough dose of the toxic stuff to make him feel bloated for days.

Three months later Denmark ordered him to attend a mandatory mediation conference, known by a few as an ADR (Alternative Dispute Resolution) and by most as a BWOT (Big Waste of Time). He explained that it would be held on the eighth floor of the King County Courthouse in downtown Seattle. The defense team would hunker down in one jury room while the plaintiffs and their lawyers would do the same in another. A mediator would bounce between the two like a ping-pong ball and translate their threats and insults into civilized negotiation. The idea was to reach some kind of settlement in an attempt to avoid the time and expense of a trial. As Denmark aptly put it, a pay-off so they would piss off.

Medical malpractice lawsuits were often settled in such a manner. *Winter vs. Montrose*, however, was one that likely wouldn't be. Maxine Doggette was still loudly demanding the full fourteen million—not a single penny less—and was in a very uncompromising mood. Hugh's insurance company, Grand National, was equally pig-headed and would go no higher than a paltry ten thousand. How would the two sides ever find middle ground?

When the appointed hour arrived, Hugh went to the courthouse and craned his neck at the large, grey building with a strong sense of foreboding. Its stone walls were as solid as those of the Bastille and heavy iron bars covered the windows at street level. This was a place where lawyer ants lived, worked, and sometimes bred in restrooms when they thought nobody was looking. What Hugh needed right now was a giant can of bug killer. He wanted to seal all the windows, stick its nozzle through the front door, and exterminate every last one.

He walked through the Fourth Avenue entrance and joined a long line of lawyer ants who were sending their briefcases and handbags through an X-ray machine. Once he was clear of the metal detector, he walked down a marble hallway and stood in an oval-shaped foyer with twelve elevator doors. More lawyer ants and their clients huddled together in pairs, speaking with hushed voices and glancing furtively around.

A young black prisoner wearing an orange jumpsuit ambled towards Hugh. He was flanked by two big, strong Department of Adult and Juvenile Detention guards. His wrists and ankles were chained together and his eyes were listless and downcast. Hugh backed against a wall and watched the condemned man go by with unease. Even though he was facing a civil case and would not be tried as a criminal, he could feel the same chains locked tightly around his own limbs and the coolness of their steel against his skin. The prisoner's hopelessness was no different from his own and he felt an uncommon bond with him despite the world of cultural differences between them. In another life he might have had the courage to tell him that he understood what he was going through. In this one, however, the best he could do was to avert his eyes and move on.

Hugh rode an elevator up to the eighth floor. As he made his way down another marble hallway, he spotted a dark-haired woman seated in a mechanized wheelchair. A bearded man was walking beside her, reading name plaques on doors. The two people looked curiously familiar. When they were a few yards closer, he realized who they were.

Gary and Julie Winter!

Hugh froze. His heart was suddenly thumping in his chest. He had seen *them*, but had they seen *him*? Before he could find a place to hide, he had his answer.

Julie's voice was frail and thin. "Dr. Montrose?" she called. "Is that you?"

Hugh stiffened, then slowly turned around. He suspected there was a rule against talking to plaintiffs. Without any lawyers around to tell him what to do, however, he did what came most naturally to him.

"Yes, it is," he answered, expecting to see her face fill with hatred.

Julie nudged the joystick on her wheelchair forward with her withered right hand and slowly approached. Gary followed, his hands stuck awkwardly into his pockets.

Hugh had last seen his former patient about three months after he successfully removed the tumor from her spinal cord. Back then, she had only just begun her journey into the world of quadriplegia and had not yet lost much weight. Now, as she sat in her wheelchair in front of him, her wasted limbs and haggard face reminded him of a concentration camp inmate. He had felt burning anger when he remembered how easily Bonehead could have prevented her paralysis.

In contrast to her body, Julie's eyes were full of life. Rather than showing any hatred, they smiled up at him.

"Remember me?" she asked when she was closer.

"I remember," said Hugh, wishing he was somewhere else. *Anywhere* else.

"I almost didn't recognize you," said Julie. Even after so long, her breathing was still labored and she had to work hard to construct every sentence. "You've lost weight."

"You have too."

"It's nice to see you again."

Hugh did a double-take. "Nice to see me?" he asked, wondering whether he had heard correctly.

"Of course," said Julie as if it should have been obvious. "I will always be thankful for what you did for me. Not many people have the skill to remove a big tumor from a spinal cord. I was lucky to have you and Dr. Clegg as my doctors."

Hugh felt a surge of resentment. He thought of the elevated CSF protein. In his search for evidence, Denmark had contacted the

Emerald lab to see if it had a computerized record of the result. Unfortunately, it didn't.

Hugh folded his arms across his chest. "If you're so thankful, Mrs. Winter—"

"Julie, please."

"If you're so thankful, Julie," he said, making little effort to hide the contempt he felt for her, "why are you suing me?"

The light in Julie's eyes faded and she looked away, leaving Gary to answer the question.

"I'm glad you asked," he said, blushing. "After everything you've done for us, you deserve an honest answer. It's really quite simple. We need the money."

"So it's all about money," said Hugh, hardly surprised.

"I'm afraid so," said Gary with a heavy sigh. "When Julie became paralyzed, we had a respectable savings and retirement accounts. Now our money's getting really low. We've missed a couple of mortgage payments and the bank wasted no time sending us nasty letters. Last week my principal warned me I might lose my teaching job because of excessive absences. You see, often I have to rush home to take care of Julie."

"I'm very sorry to hear it," said Hugh, not feeling particularly sorry at all.

"For us, the future looks very dicey," said Gary. "We were forced to consult with a lawyer."

"So you picked Maxine Doggette?"

"Sometimes I get the feeling she picked us," said Gary without further explanation.

Hugh felt an urge to damn the consequences and blurt out the truth regarding *Winter vs. Montrose*—how Bonehead was to blame, not him. He wanted to tell Gary and Julie to let him off the hook and sue their bungling orthopedic surgeon instead. They were far more likely to get the money they needed. Instead, he bit his lip, bent his knees, and lowered himself to her level so he could look directly into her eyes.

"I don't blame you for trying to survive," he said, trying hard to contain his frustration. "But I cannot admit I did something wrong when I didn't. My lawyer will defend me to the bitter end."

"We understand that," said Julie. "We wouldn't expect you to do things any differently."

"Thanks. I appreciate—"

Suddenly a loud voice rumbled down the hallway. "For God's sake, Hugh, what are you *doing*?"

Hugh looked over his shoulder and saw a red-faced John Denmark striding down the hallway towards him, vigorously shaking some papers in his hand.

"You can't talk to *them*!" he bellowed. "It's absolutely forbidden!"

Hugh smiled apologetically at Julie. "Speaking of my lawyer," he told her, "here he is now." He straightened up again. "We were only having a harmless little chat, John."

"If The Dog caught you having a harmless little chat with the plaintiffs," he warned, positioning himself between Hugh and the Winters like an impenetrable wall, "there would be hell to pay!"

"Julie and Gary," said Hugh, "I would like to introduce you to John Denmark. Normally he's a little friendlier. John, meet the plaintiffs."

"Are you mad?" he said, nervously scanning the horizon for any sign of The Dog. "*I* can't talk to them either."

"Look, John," said Hugh impatiently, "the Winters need money. Lots of it. I understand their point of view but have a reputation to defend. I told them—"

"This is no way to conduct an ADR!" interrupted Denmark, now glaring at Hugh. "You must have *at least* two lawyers *and* a mediator between you and the other side!"

"Why don't we save time and discuss things directly?" suggested Hugh. "We're adults, aren't we? Surely we can find a way to—"

A devilish screech ripped through the courthouse. "*Jesus H. Christ*! What's going on here?"

Everybody swung around and for the first time since the BRAIN banquet Hugh laid eyes on Maxine Doggette. She was heading towards them in all her usual powder-puff glory. The feathery black and white outfit she was wearing and the eye patch over her right eye made her look like a swashbuckling ostrich.

"Damn!" Denmark quietly swore between clenched teeth. "Just what we need right now!"

"What *the hell* do you think you two are doing?" said Maxine, addressing Denmark and Hugh as she approached. A tall young man—her side-kick, Billy Barlow—teetered along behind her, a stack of legal files in his arms.

"Now, Maxine," Denmark began, "let's try to be mature and—"

"Never, *ever* talk directly to my clients!" she shouted back, drenching him with saliva. "Tell me what you were saying so I can assess the damage!"

Denmark was just opening his mouth to answer when Maxine abruptly turned to Gary and Julie.

"And you mustn't speak to *them* either," she said, prodding Gary on the chest with her finger. "You could give away secrets and screw up everything. If you've got something to say, go through me."

Hugh stepped forward to explain. "We were just—"

"Mr. Denmark!" barked Maxine, whipping around. "Kindly inform your client that if he wishes to say anything to me he has to go through you! It's forbidden for us to talk directly to each other!"

Denmark spoke to Hugh out of the corner of his mouth. "If you want to say anything to Ms. Doggette," he said quietly, "go through me."

"This is really childish," said Hugh.

Denmark gave Maxine a whimsical smile. "My client wants you to know that he thinks this is really childish," he told her.

"Ms. Doggette," interrupted Billy, standing in a corner like a lonely lamppost. "These files are *really* heavy. Can I put them down?"

Maxine ignored him and confronted Julie instead. "What were you talking about when I arrived?" she asked. "I demand to know!"

Julie answered in a tiny voice. "Dr. Montrose was just saying—"

"Don't refer to him as Doctor Montrose!" interrupted Maxine, jerking her head contemptuously in Hugh's direction. "He's *Defendant* Montrose to you."

Julie's tiny voice grew even tinier. "Defendant Montrose was just saying—"

"I know perfectly well what he was saying. He was attempting to coerce you into dropping this case." Maxine suddenly turned and glared at Hugh. "Confess, Defendant Montrose!"

Denmark politely coughed. "Uh . . . Maxine," he said. "You must speak to him through me. Remember?"

Maxine whirled around and faced Denmark. "Tell your client to confess!"

He looked over his shoulder at Hugh. "*Were* you trying to coerce her?" he asked.

"Of course I wasn't!" cried Hugh. "Julie, *you* tell her. She might believe me if you—"

Maxine suddenly broke in. "And if your client wants to talk to my client," she said, addressing Denmark, "he has to talk to you first, then you to me, then me to her. Isn't that clear enough?"

Denmark sighed wearily. "If you say so, Maxine."

"Now tell the Winters we're leaving. There's important work to be done."

"Tell them yourself. They're *your* clients."

Hopelessly confused, Maxine looked back and forth between Hugh and the Winters. When she realized her mistake she balled her fists and shook her arms. "Urrrgh! I'm wasting any more of my valuable time here." She waved Gary and Julie forward. "Come on—let's go upstairs and find our room!"

An elevator door opened and she marched into it. Gary and Julie smiled apologetically at Hugh and Denmark, then followed her in. Billy staggered on board with his legal files just as the doors were closing.

As predicted, the settlement conference yielded no settlement. Denmark quietly read the latest issue of *Field and Stream* in one room while Maxine kept a watchful eye on the Winters in another. An amiable off-duty judge bounced between opposing camps, carrying messages and trying to reason with them.

As plaintiff counsel, Maxine made an initial offer of thirteen million nine hundred and seventy-five thousand dollars—only a tiny bit less than her original demand. Denmark found it insulting and counter-offered a paltry twenty-five thousand dollars just to show how he felt. Maxine claimed such an absurdly small amount wouldn't even cover her copying costs. She grudgingly lowered her demand another twenty-five thousand dollars and let it be known that she was being more than generous. Denmark accused her of negotiating in bad faith and rejected the offer as being totally unreasonable. He dangled fifty thousand dollars in front of her like a hunk of fish bait and declared that it was his final offer. She threw back her head and laughed. After that, nobody budged. At the end of the conference, the parties went home dissatisfied and empty-handed.

A trial was now all but inevitable.

23

Billy Barlow sat in his office, holding a pink lab report in his hand. He had recently discovered it at the bottom of a lab coat pocket and remembered when it had fluttered loose from Julie Winter's Emerald Spine Institute records while he was snooping through the Bellegrove Rehabilitation Center. When Billy first saw it that day, he hadn't understood why somebody circled the Protein……..104 with heavy black ink and put two exclamation marks next to it. Now he had the unsettling feeling that he was missing something important. He spent hours looking up information online but couldn't grasp the medical jargon.

Billy considered approaching Maxine but was afraid she would be angry at him for not investigating sooner. Acutely aware of how critical this case was for the success of his career Billy decided to ask Dr. Frank Clegg instead, the treating physician he would question in the upcoming trial. He ought to know. After all, he had originally ordered the test. Billy had not yet met him and was biting his fingernails over the idea of talking to one of Maxine's former victims. Surely he would not have forgotten those three lawsuits against him. How would he react? After several minutes of indecision, Billy reached out a clammy hand, picked up the receiver, and dialed the Emerald Spine Institute.

When a secretary answered the phone, Billy timidly identified himself and asked to speak to Clegg. Moments later, he heard heavy breathing at the other end of the line.

"Dr. Clegg?" said Billy with as much confidence as he could muster.

A deep, sonorous voice answered. "Yes?"

"My name is Billy Barlow," he said, plowing into uncharted territory. "I'm calling you about *Winter vs. Montrose*. I'm planning to subpoena you to testify as one of the treating physicians in the case."

The breathing suddenly stopped. "*Winter vs. Montrose?*"

"That's correct," said Billy, feeling his confidence slip. "Uh . . . There are some questions I would like to ask you."

The voice at the other end of the line sounded more ominous now. "You work for . . . *that woman?*"

"You mean Ms. Doggette?"

"Yes."

Billy's heart sank. So Clegg hadn't forgotten! "Yes," Billy reluctantly confessed. "I suppose I do. When would be a good time to meet?"

Silence.

A full thirty seconds later the heavy breathing finally started up again. "Meet me at *Joe's Diner* on Capitol Hill in two hours."

Joe's Diner was a grimy dump that smelled strongly of saturated fats. Chrome-legged tables were arranged in rows across a linoleum floor, each with its own plastic ketchup bottle, salt shaker, and paper napkins. A group of construction workers in dirty work clothes and hard hats sat around eating lunch and drinking beer. Their conversation was loud and vulgar, but nobody cared.

When Billy arrived, he searched the dining area but didn't see anybody who fit his idea of an orthopedic surgeon. He was just about to breathe a sigh of relief and beat a retreat when he noticed a shadowy side-room. Nervously he approached it and peered in. At a table against the far wall he saw a huge man eating a cheeseburger and a mountain of French fries. He was wearing a tweed jacket and a yellow tie.

"Dr. Clegg?"

A pair of small, deeply-set eyes rolled up.

"I'm Billy Barlow," said Billy, going over to him. "We spoke on the phone."

Clegg looked at him briefly, then returned his attention to his food. "Sit down and order lunch," he said in the same deep voice Billy had heard earlier.

Billy eased himself into the seat opposite Clegg, watching him warily for any sudden moves. He needn't have been so concerned. The man was more interested in his cheeseburger than getting his revenge for those three lawsuits. The muscles in his temples alternatively bulged and relaxed, working like garbage truck pistons to crush his meat into rubble. As he chewed, juices bubbled from between his teeth and trickled down his chin.

"Thank you very much for meeting with me," said Billy, reaching for a menu. "I know you must be a very busy man."

Clegg mopped his chin with a paper napkin and grunted.

A top-heavy waitress came up to the table. "Hi there," she said, sliding a glass of ice water in front of Billy. "Our special today is the all-you-can-eat garlic fried chicken with onion rings and a buttered baked potato. The chili dog and dumplings is pretty good too. What'll it be?"

"I'll have what he's having," said Billy, pointing at Clegg's plate.

"One super-cheeseburger with extra fries coming right up," she said, retrieving the menu and leaving.

"Dr. Clegg, Ms. Doggette has assigned me the important task of handling your testimony in the upcoming trial against Dr. Montrose," said Billy, fingering his glass of water.

Clegg sank his teeth into his cheeseburger again and ripped loose a chunk of meat.

"I thought we ought to get to know each other so things will go smoothly when we're in trial," continued Billy, not sure whether Clegg was listening. "I would like to start by asking you a question." He reached into his pocket and dug around its deepest parts. When he eventually found what he was looking for, he yanked his hand out, spraying small pieces of litter into the air. "Tell me what you think of this." He placed the pink lab report onto the table and pushed it tentatively towards Clegg with his forefinger.

"What is it?" asked Clegg.

"It's evidence from the Emerald Spine Institute," answered Billy. "I found it amongst Julie Winter's medical records."

Clegg put down his food and wiped his greasy fingers clean with a paper napkin. He took the report from the table and looked over it as he chewed.

"These are CSF results from a myelogram," he said. "The patient's name is . . ." He held it sideways. ". . . Julie Winter. The ordering physician was . . . me. The numbers show—"

Clegg's massive jawbone suddenly froze.

"The protein was one hundred and four," said Billy. "Since you ordered the test, I figured you might know why somebody would circle that number and put exclamation marks next to it."

Clegg pinned Billy down with his eyes. "Does Maxine Doggette know anything about this?" he asked.

"No, not at all," said Billy. "You might say I'm conducting an independent investigation. So, what do the numbers mean? Can you tell me?"

"Hmmmph!" Clegg blinked a few times as if trying to formulate an answer. "I probably can."

"Obviously it must mean something important," said Billy.

"Let's see now," mumbled Clegg, fingering the pink paper. "Something important? I suppose it must. Maybe it means . . ." Suddenly his eyes brightened and his leathery face broke into a smile. "I know!" he said, surreptitiously slipping the report into his pocket. "It's really quite obvious!"

"What's obvious?" asked Billy, holding out his hand, palm up, and flexing the tips of his fingers.

Looking vexed, Clegg reached into his pocket and handed it back. "A normal value for protein in the CSF is about forty," he explained. "A hundred and four is very high."

Billy put the piece of paper safely away. "So?"

Clegg tentatively offered an explanation. "So, you see, there's a very complex process going on here. Basically, degenerated discs produce toxic break-down products irritate the nerves in the area and result in pain and inflammation."

"Pain and inflammation?" Billy slowly repeated as he tried to wrap his mind around unfamiliar concepts.

"Exactly!" cried Clegg, his smile broadening as his confidence grew. "The body fights back by manufacturing CSF proteins that counteract the effect of the toxins. The more pain, the more protein. In fact, a good physician can actually quantify how much back pain a patient has by measuring the CSF protein. All he has to do is to stick a needle into the spine, draw off some spinal fluid, and send it to the lab for analysis."

Billy rubbed his chin the way he had seen Maxine do it whenever she was deep in thought. He had always liked how it looked and spent hours honing the correct technique in front of his bathroom mirror. "The more pain, the higher the protein?" he asked.

"There's a direct correlation," said Clegg, "although I've rarely seen it go as high as one hundred and four. That's why I circled it and added two exclamation marks."

"*You* made those notations?"

"Of course I did," said Clegg as if Billy should have known all along. "The high number means she must have been in extreme pain. I decided she needed an operation right away before the toxins inflicted permanent damage. Do you understand what I'm telling you?"

Billy didn't have a clue and stared back with a blank expression.

"I see you do!" said Clegg. "You're really quite a smart attorney."

Billy blinked. "I am?"

"Not everybody with a law degree can understand difficult concepts like these."

"They can't?"

Clegg reached out with a big, powerful hand and clamped it onto Billy's shoulder. "Somebody as clever as you should come with me to the operating room sometime," he said, giving him a friendly squeeze with his fingers. "I would love to show you around."

"You would?"

"Absolutely!"

Billy felt strangely important and chided himself for being so nervous earlier. This meeting was turning out to be a resounding success! Despite Maxine's lawsuits against him years ago, Clegg was so ready to cooperate and be a friend!

Clegg released Billy's shoulder and returned his attention to his food. He picked up a plastic ketchup bottle, turned it upside down, and squeezed hard. The bottle farted, splattering a thick layer of ketchup over his French fries. He grabbed a batch of them with his fingers, crammed them into his mouth, and washed them down with a swig of beer.

Billy was still caught up in the moment. "I have a great idea!" he cried, snapping his fingers. "Why don't we go back to my office after lunch and do some trial preparation?"

"Trial preparation?" said Clegg, jerking his head up with alarm.

"Maxine says it's never too early," chirped Billy. "She recommends a regular schedule. Maybe two or three hours a week between now and the trial."

The waitress appeared with Billy's lunch order—a monster burger dripping with molten cheese. Big, soggy fries were haphazardly scattered around it. She set the plate in front of him and took off without a word.

Billy stared in awe at the mountain of food he had been given to eat. A hair amongst the stacks of fries caught his attention. He reached in with his thumb and forefinger, gingerly removed it, and identified it as a short and curly. Suspecting there might be others, he picked carefully through the rest of his food with a fork.

"I see we're going to get along just fine, Frank," he said as he searched. "I hope you don't mind if I call you Frank, Frank. I mean, I feel so positive about your testimony. I won't ask anything hostile or challenging, I can assure you. Just simple questions about the role you played in Julie Winter's care, the history you obtained, the results of your examination, the work-up you ordered, and maybe some details about the operation. I certainly won't want to know your professional opinion about anything. After all, you're not testifying as a medical expert. Just as a treating physician."

When he was certain there were no more hairs to be found, Billy gripped his cheeseburger with both hands and lifted it to his mouth. He looked up and was astonished to see that the seat opposite him was empty. Clegg's plate of food sat unfinished and abandoned on the table.

"Frank?" he said, lowering his burger again. "Where are you, Frank?" He looked around the dining area, then over towards the front door and the restrooms. There was no sign of him anywhere. "That's strange! Where did he go?"

For the next thirty minutes Billy ate his meal alone, hoping Clegg would shortly return. When he didn't, he paid both tabs and left, confused and disappointed.

24

A few days before the trial, Gary's principal finally fired him for missing too much work. It didn't matter that he was at home taking care of Julie. Even tragic circumstances such as his weren't an adequate excuse.

"I understand you're taking care of a paralyzed wife," the gray haired man told him from behind his desk, his voice cold and distant, "but I'm responsible for hundreds of students at this school and right now they're not learning any physics. I'm sorry. I wish things were different."

Gary drove home in a state of shock, paying little attention to traffic and almost colliding with another car. He had always worried about losing his job, but never thought it would actually happen. How was he going to break the news to Julie? What would Jennifer and Patrick say? Adding insult to injury, his old Ford Explorer broke down by the side of the road and he had to walk the last couple of miles home. A storm was rolling in from the Pacific Ocean, bringing with it gusty winds and sheets of cold rain. When he eventually reached his front door, he was dripping wet. He retrieved his keys from his pocket and let himself in.

Inside, the house was dark and empty.

"Julie?" he called as he squelched across the hall. "Jennifer? Patrick? Anybody home?"

No answer.

Strange. Julie was always home when he returned from work. And where were the kids? They should be home too, busy with chores and their homework. A quick search of the house confirmed that nobody was inside. He was just wondering what to do next when he looked out of a window and glimpsed a faint light at the bottom of the garden.

Gary stepped outside the front door and peered into the darkness. Yes, there it was again! Definitely a light. He strained his eyes and realized it was coming from Harvey the RV.

What was going on?

Once the source of endless family fun, the rusting hulk was now all but forgotten—a monument to a bygone era. Gary wanted to get rid of it but the tow truck operator wanted too much money. So it sat abandoned and forgotten, standing on flat tires and overrun with brambles.

Gary walked across the lawn towards Harvey. When he drew closer, he saw Julie's wheelchair parked outside. What was *that* doing here? He opened the door and looked inside.

He was shocked to find his family sitting around the dining table with a road map of the United States laid out in front of them. Julie was propped up in a corner, secured by a seatbelt. Jennifer was next to her, buttressing her mother's body so she wouldn't topple over. Patrick was across the table, holding a pencil in his hand. All three faces were illuminated by the soft light of a propane lantern. They were startled at first, then welcomed Gary with smiles.

"What on earth are you doing?" he demanded.

"Planning our camping trip to Yellowstone," said Patrick.

Gary winced. The Yellowstone trip was the one they never took, postponed because of Julie's original back pain and canceled altogether when she subsequently became quadriplegic. He had already told his children that there wouldn't be any more camping trips and to find something else to do with their summers—something practical like getting a job to help support the family. Obviously his message hadn't gotten through.

"You're wasting your time," he said angrily. "We'll never have the money for Yellowstone so put away the map and go back to the house."

Patrick's smile died.

"But, Dad," said Jennifer, taking a cue from her brother's crestfallen look. "Can't we at least dream about going? What harm is there in that? Maybe one day something will change. Anything can happen, you know."

"No!" shouted Gary, snatching the map off the table and flinging it away. "Nothing will ever change! Dreaming won't get you anything except a whole bunch of heartache and disappointment! You should stay away from this camper so you don't get screwy, unrealistic ideas!"

There was a long, awkward silence. Nobody had ever heard him speak with such bitterness before and they weren't sure how to respond. Eventually Julie spoke up. "It was my idea," she confessed. "I thought it would be fun to be together again inside Harvey just like the old days. And it was, until you showed up. I think it would have been better if you had joined us instead of yelling like that. Is something upsetting you?"

"No, of course not!" said Gary, burying his hands into his pockets. Then his shoulders slumped and he surrendered with a sigh. "Well, actually, there is."

"What?"

"Today I . . . I lost my job."

Julie closed her eyes as she absorbed the bad news. Jennifer and Patrick became still and quiet. A gust of wind moaned around the camper, sprinkling rain against the windows.

"As you might guess," continued Gary, crumpling into an armchair, "the principal said I've been missing too much work. The kids' physics scores are going downhill. As long as we can't afford a private nurse the situation is not likely to get any better. So he decided to let me go. Just like that. I'm sorry." He buried his head into his hands.

Jennifer went over to her father. She put her arms around him and gave him a warm, loving hug. "Don't be sorry, Dad," she said, looking into his moistening eyes. "We know you did your best. Sometimes things can get overwhelming for some families. Like now. For us. If we're strong we'll get through it."

"Do you even understand what we're facing?" Gary asked her bluntly.

"I think I do," she answered.

"No, you don't. Let me put you into the picture. First, there's—"

"Is this really necessary?" interrupted Julie. "Remember, they're only kids."

"They're old enough!" cried Gary. "First, there's our home. We've had a mortgage for years and have always made our payments on time. Until now. We missed a few recently and now the bank wants to start foreclosure proceedings against us."

"Foreclosure?" asked Patrick, frowning.

"They want to make us leave and sell our house to somebody else."

"But where would we go?"

"Where do people usually go when they've lost their house and have no money? The streets? A homeless shelter? Maybe we could put Harvey in a trailer park somewhere and live there. How should I know? This sort of thing has never happened to me before. Then there are your college savings."

"Mine?" asked Patrick.

"Both yours and your sister's," answered Gary. "Basically the money's gone. We've had to raid the account in order to pay bills. Unless you can find a scholarship somewhere, there won't be a college education in your future."

"Gary," said Julie, a tear trickling down her cheek. "That's enough. The kids understand more than you know."

"I could go on—"

"I don't care about our house!" interrupted Jennifer. "Let the bank have it! What's so bad about living in a trailer park? And I don't care about college either. Only my family means anything to me. That's you, Mom and Dad, and you, Patrick. I know we don't have much money, but we *are* surviving. Sometimes I wonder if we aren't doing better than we've ever done before."

"What are you saying?" cried Gary. "*Better* than before?"

"Look how hardship has pulled our family together!" said Jennifer. "Before, Patrick and I were always fighting and complaining about everything. Now we're much closer, trying to help each other out for a change. Don't you think so, Patrick?"

Patrick nodded his agreement.

"Jennifer's right," Julie said to Gary. "And nobody knows better than me. Over the last couple of years my children have done more growing up than most people do in a lifetime. How can I complain?"

At first Gary sat silently as he wrestled with the things he'd just heard. Then the pain behind his eyes suddenly melted away as he saw Julie, Jennifer, and Patrick in a different light. Of course they didn't care about his sudden joblessness! They only cared about the family. Nothing else mattered. Not poverty. Not homelessness. Not even quadriplegia. Feeling new threads of optimism flowing through him, he stood up from his armchair, picked the road map off the floor, and went to the table with it.

"Move over," he said to Patrick, spreading out the map in front of him. "So you're planning the trip to Yellowstone, are you? Show me what route you have in mind."

25

Hugh's brain sizzled and popped like bacon in a frying pan.

He was continuing to lose weight and now his clothes hung loosely from his body. When he sat down for meals with his family he picked at his napkin while barely touching his food. No amount of persuasion got him to eat. Even phone calls about freshly ruptured aneurysms in the emergency room weren't enough to rouse him. When he talked with the physicians at the other end of the line his voice was flat and disengaged and they often enquired whether something was wrong.

As each day passed, his weary eyes grew wearier and the bags under them baggier. Not even sleep was an escape. Every night he went to bed with a rock in the pit of his stomach only to wake up a few short hours later shouting and screaming in a pool of his own sweat.

Caroline had fled the marital bed long ago and sought refuge in the guest room.

On the eve of the trial, just as the sun was rising, she knocked on the door of the master bedroom. Hugh had been staring at the ceiling for five hours now and grunted permission for her to enter.

She cautiously opened the door and poked her head through. "Hi, Honey," she said gingerly. "You remember there's church this morning?"

"Oh God!" Hugh groaned and buried his head under a pillow.

"Frankly, I think it'll do you a lot of good."

"Mmgmph-mgmdm-mmbmph!"

"Sorry, I can't understand what you're saying under there."

Hugh lifted a corner of the pillow and peeked out. "You go," he told her. "I'll stay home and pray for my deliverance here."

Caroline took a few cautious steps into the bedroom. "Anna and Marie think you should go too."

"Anna and Marie? Why do *they* care?"

"Your lawsuit is all over the internet," Caroline explained. "Apparently their friends at school have been taunting them, saying that their father is a no-good quack who paralyzed a patient. You know how kids that age can be so cruel sometimes. The girls fight back, but the truth is they're not sure what to believe anymore. They just want their lives to get back to normal as soon as possible."

"I'd better talk to them," said Hugh, putting the pillow aside. He struggled out of bed and headed towards the door. "It's time they heard the real story from me."

"Later perhaps," said Caroline, standing in his way. "Right now it's time for church. Get cleaned up and put on some decent clothes. I'll wait for you downstairs."

One hour later Caroline drove Hugh to St. Anthony's Episcopal Church, a low-key place with a conservative membership. When they reached their destination, she pulled into the parking lot and navigated her way through groups of church-goers dressed in their Sunday best. Hugh glowered at them through the window and hated them for looking happy.

"For God's sake, Hugh," said Caroline. "You're embarrassing me."

Hugh stretched his surly face into a misshapen smile. When Caroline found an empty spot, she switched off the engine, climbed out of the car, and led Hugh into church. Rows of wooden pews faced an altar with a large overhanging crucifix. A statue of Jesus was nailed into place, dressed in magnificent robes. On the left, there was a pulpit with a large floral arrangement underneath it. A choir stood on either side of an organ with rows of exposed pipes.

Hugh and Caroline found space in a pew about half way down the aisle to the left and settled in. Hugh forced out some polite greetings for the benefit of his neighbors before hunkering down for an hour of misery.

Hugh paid little attention to the first part of the service. When the old, doddery rector, Reverend Jeremiah Potts, climbed the pulpit and began to deliver a dismally boring sermon, Hugh's depression deepened and his imminent trial took over his thoughts. What was the worst thing that he could expect over the next few weeks? Probably a judgment that exceeded his policy limits. Most trial attorneys, however, felt it was counter-productive to put doctors permanently out of business. They preferred to keep them alive and twitching so they could keep filing fresh lawsuits year after year, like leeches slowly sucking the blood from their victims. Hugh imagined himself covered with dozens of the slimy things and drew some solace from what he had been taught in medical school: no good parasite kills its host.

To settle or not to settle? That was the question. Was it better for his insurance company to hand over enough money to enable him to return to his normal life or should he fight for his reputation and risk losing everything?

An obstetrical friend of Hugh's had once lived through a trial. For three weeks she had been forced to listen to a bunch of fancy lawyers in fancy clothes spout forth all kinds of fancy diatribe and lies. In the end, the jury returned a unanimous defense verdict. Did the doctor feel vindicated? Not at all. In fact, quite the opposite. She came away wishing she had settled long ago, thus sparing herself the worst experience of her life.

A signature. That's what it would take to put an end to this misery forever. An illegible scrawl of ink at the bottom of a settlement agreement. It was never too late to call it quits and sign such a document. In fact, he carried the papers wherever he went in the vague hope that he would some day have the courage to whip them out, scribble his name, and unload them onto Denmark before he changed his mind. The offer he was contemplating was a million dollars—the limit on his insurance policy.

Would Maxine accept it?

Probably not, but it was impossible to know for sure.

Suddenly a shaft of brilliant light shone from heaven above and transfigured the moth-eaten Reverend Jeremiah Potts into a much younger one with fiery eyes, fleshy face, and slickly combed black hair. He was wearing a sky blue suit and a purple tie. His fingers were festooned with gold rings.

One half of the congregation broke into rapturous applause while the other stretched their arms into the air, closed their eyes, and shouted with joy.

"Hallelujah!"

"Amen!"

"Thank you, Jesus!"

The band played a stirring tune. The choir cranked up to maximum decibels and blasted the congregation with their vocal cords.

"Brothers and sisters!" Potts called out, bringing his hands together. "Let's clap for *Jeeeee*-sus! Oh, I feel the Holy Ghost inside me. Yes I do!"

The music ended, the choir sat down, and the organ quietly throbbed on. Potts began preaching with fervor in his voice. "The word of God is oxygen for our souls and it will save us from our sins!" he said. "Let it flow through your bodies and take control of your lives! Look at your neighbors and tell them you feel anointed!"

A complete stranger in front of Hugh turned around, radiating holiness. "I feel anointed, Brother!" she squawked.

Hugh cringed.

"Thank you, *Jeeeee*-sus," continued Potts. "Thank you for doing something in this house tonight that will fertilize our faith and bring us to a defining moment. I feel an explosion about to take place. Miracles, signs, and wonders do happen. I want you to offer the Lord praise and glory in anticipation. The Lord provides! Are you ready for the flow?"

Hugh wondered what kind of flow the rector had in mind. Flows most familiar to him at the hospital included blood, urine, pus, cerebral spinal fluid, diarrhea, and vomit. Surely not one of those!

Potts had a message to deliver and seemed determined to do so in style. He set a chair in front of him and climbed on top of his pulpit. Once he had his balance he stamped his feet and waved around a Bible.

"Proclaim from the mountaintop: live for *Jeeeee*-sus!" he shouted. "Take His gospel to your neighbors and the fruit of your labors will be bountiful! Let those of us who are gathered here today witness of His infinite love! I ask you: are you ready to feel the spirit of the Lord?"

Men with silver name tags pinned to their suits passed around offering plates. The organ's throbs became more strident and the choir started humming.

"*Jeeeee*-sus died on the cross for your sins!" cried Potts. "He has shed his blood for you! Now it's time to keep to your end of the covenant! Harness the power of money and witness the miracles of the Lord! Give generously! Give now!"

Hugh stuck his hand into a pocket and found a lonely penny. He dropped it into one of the plates as it passed by. As soon as he did so, he was overcome by an epileptic discharge of insanity originating from the part of his brain most ravaged by juris psychosis.

"No!" he shouted, jumping to his feet. "Give that back to me! It's my last one! The lawyers will want it!"

He chased after the plate as it was whisked away, pushing past Caroline and stepping on black kneelers that resembled small elephant bags. When he reached the end of the row he tripped over somebody's legs and fell into the aisle, landing heavily on the carpeted floor. For a few moments he was dazed and saw stars. When his vision cleared, he found himself staring at a pair of shiny black shoes only inches from his face.

"And behold," announced a voice above him, "God has sent forth a soul lost in sin!"

Hugh ran his eyes up a sharply creased trouser leg and saw Jeremiah Potts glaring down at him with zeal. He attempted to stand up but didn't get far.

"Arise not!" commanded Potts, grabbing him by the shoulders and holding onto him. "Let me help you find peace in your heart!"

"That's impossible!" said Hugh, struggling to free himself. "I'm being sued!"

Reverend Potts was only interested in spiritual matters, not legal ones. "Brothers with the strength of Sampson!" he called, addressing the entire congregation. "Come hither! Hold down this poor wretch so I may save his soul from the depths of iniquity and deliver it to the Lord!"

The response was immediate. Several men hurried over and held Hugh down by his arms and legs.

"Let me go!" shouted Hugh.

"His name is Legion for he is many!" Potts told his followers. "Our brother knows not what he says or where he does!"

"Help me!"

"Hold fast, brethren!" The rector stretched out his hand. The brilliant light shining from heaven cast a five-fingered shadow across Hugh's face. "Beelzebub! Hear me, O Evil One! In the name of *Jeeeee*-sus, I command you to leave him!"

"No!"

"*Leeeeeave* him!"

"*No!*"

Caroline's voice suddenly rose above all others. "Hugh!" she cried. "Wake up! You're having another nightmare!"

Hugh's eyes flew open. He wildly looked around, clawing his way back to reality. The youthful, energetic Jeremiah Potts was nowhere to be seen. The old, withered one was back in the pulpit, staring at him with consternation—along with everybody else in the congregation.

Nightmares at home. Nightmares in his office. Now he was even having them in church.

"Oh God," moaned Hugh, rubbing his forehead. "That was a really bad one."

"Come on, Hugh," said Caroline, taking him by the arm. "We're leaving."

She led him outside, drove him home, and helped him back

into bed.

After dinner that evening Hugh sat in his favorite armchair by the fire and for the first time spoke openly with his daughters about the lawsuit. He explained to them that it was all a horrible mistake and that the lawyer suing him, Maxine Doggette, was only doing so because she held a personal grudge against him. Regardless of the circumstances, doctors were frequently sued these days due to the nature of their work and it was best to allow the legal system, however broken it seemed sometimes, to resolve these kinds of disputes. He confessed he wasn't himself these days—trying to make a tough decision whether to settle or not—and apologized for not giving them the attention they needed. It was important to remember that he loved them through thick and thin and that things would eventually return to normal.

"Don't pay any attention to the bullies at school," he said. "They don't have any idea what's going on and have no right to say the things they do."

"Thanks for clearing this up for us," said Anna, her upturned face glowing in the light of the fire. "When so many of my friends say the same thing about you, it can get very confusing. Now I know what to tell them."

"They're not *my* friends any longer," declared Marie huffily. "I'm going to find new ones."

Later on, after Hugh had hugged his daughters and watched them go upstairs to bed, he reached into his inside jacket pocket and pulled out the unsigned settlement papers he always carried around. He crumpled them in his hands and threw them onto the embers in the fireplace. They smoked for a while, then burst into flames with a soft puff. Within seconds they were consumed until nothing remained but ashes fluttering to and fro amongst the currents of hot air.

26

The next day, more than a year and a half since Jake the process server had rumbled up Hugh's driveway and humiliated him so spectacularly in front of his family, the *Winter vs. Montrose* trial began.

The weather was appropriately grey and depressing. Hugh met Denmark outside the Fourth Avenue entrance to the King County Courthouse and soon found himself irritated by his lawyer's optimism.

"This day marks the beginning of the end for The Dog," said Denmark as they waited in line to enter the building. "This time I'll beat her so badly, I swear she'll never sue another doctor again. Mark my words!"

They passed through security, rode an elevator to the eighth floor, and headed over to one of the courtrooms. Two sets of double doors led the way inside, one inner and the other outer. The architect's intention may have been to minimize noise filtering in from outside. When Hugh passed through them, however, he felt as if he was in a compression chamber, leaving behind a secure, familiar world and entering a self-contained war zone.

Aside from a handful of people in the public benches at the back, the courtroom was largely empty. A large wooden judicial bench dominated the far end. The judge's black leather chair stood on high, flanked by the flags of the United States and Washington, the sources of his power. Below the bench were two work stations belonging to a court reporter and a clerk. On the right a door led into a bailiff's office, and beyond that, the judge's chambers. A jury box ran along the wall to the left. Fourteen seats altogether. Twelve jurors and two alternates.

In the middle of this arena the plaintiff and defense teams had set up their positions. Two large tables were set together at right angles to form an L, the front lines where combat would take place. The plaintiff faced the judge, the defense the jurors—an equitable arrangement, agreed to by their lawyers after protracted and bitter negotiations.

Denmark helped himself to a comfortable seat behind the defense table and directed Hugh towards a wooden bench that ran along the wall behind him. "That's where you go," he told him, leaving no room for negotiation.

Hugh obediently sat down. The bench was as hard as rock and had a sharp edge along the top that dug into his back. How was he going to survive more than a month of this? As he searched in vain for a comfortable position he watched Denmark unpack his elephant bag. Out came folders, files, notepads, pens, a bottle of hand sanitizer, cough drops, breath fresheners, paper clips, a hole puncher, laptop computer, multi-colored Post-its, and a couple of colorful fishing lures. The last item he produced was a purple stadium cushion with a University of Washington Huskies logo.

"Here," he said, handing it to Hugh. "You'll need this."

Hugh slipped the cushion underneath him. It didn't provide much relief but was better than nothing.

A beefy female bailiff entered the courtroom from her office. "Please rise!" she cried. "The Superior Court for the state of Washington, in and for the county of King, is now in session, The Honorable Dudley S. Jenkins presiding."

Denmark, Hugh, and the spectators at the back stood up smartly.

Jenkins climbed the bench and faced the courtroom, his flowing black robes a symbol of his authority. He was short, in his early sixties, and scrutinized Hugh from across the room with hostile, unforgiving eyes.

Definitely no friend.

"Be seated," he commanded as he settled into his chair.

Denmark whispered that the man had been a medical malpractice lawyer for twenty years before his current position. "He's the most pro-plaintiff judge I've ever known," he groused. "Just our rotten luck to get *him*."

Hugh was about to add a cynical comment of his own when Jenkins started speaking.

"Does anybody know where Ms. Doggette is?" he asked, glancing at the clock above the jury box.

Barbara was about to say something when the compression chamber's inner pair of doors suddenly blew open and Billy appeared, so tall that his head barely cleared the wooden frame. Maxine swept in after him wearing a flamingo pink outfit and a black eye patch.

"Sorry I'm late, Your Honor," she said, not sounding sorry at all. "The traffic was horrendous this morning."

Jenkins gave her a welcoming smile. "I agree with you," he said. "The traffic *was* bad. In future, though . . ."

Maxine sat down at the plaintiff table and immediately delved into her notes, obviously uninterested in whatever the judge had to say about the future.

"See what I mean about a biased judge?" Denmark whispered into Hugh's ear. "If *I* had been late, he would have had me for breakfast."

"Why is Maxine wearing that patch over her eye?" asked Hugh.

"Something nasty is going on," he answered. "I caught a glimpse of it the other week. The skin is swollen and purple with big veins going everywhere. She can't open her eyelid without lifting it with a finger. The eye itself points off to the side like it's been knocked off kilter. When I asked about it, she made a cryptic comment about somebody trying to poison her. Could she be right?"

"Poison?" said Hugh, chuckling with skepticism. "That's ridiculous. Sounds more like a third nerve palsy to me."

"A what?"

"A third . . . Oh, never mind. Next time you get a chance, tell her to make an appointment with a doctor."

"I already did. She thinks none will agree to see her."

"I know one in Botswana who might."

After countless motions and countermotions—enough of them to give Hugh motion sickness—a hundred men and women of all shapes and sizes were herded into the courtroom like cattle. Red jury badges were pinned to their chests and they held numbered cards in their hands like bidders at an auction. When the last one was seated and the doors were closed, the judge leaned over his desk and glared at them as if he was a raptor and they were lunch.

"The United States of America only expects four things from its citizens," he declared, holding up a finger. "One . . . obey the law! Two . . ." He raised another finger into the air. ". . . pay your taxes!" And then another. "Three . . . vote in elections! And four . . ." A final fourth popped up. "Can anybody guess what the fourth one is?"

Not a moo from anybody.

"Jury duty!" he bellowed triumphantly. "Serving on a jury is the highest privilege an American has! Don't ever forget it!"

The process of choosing fourteen jurors from a pool of a hundred was lengthy and consumed the rest of the week. Denmark looked for educated people who had enough sense to see through Maxine's deceptions and lies and render a verdict based on the facts. Maxine, on the other hand, wanted them as dumb as rocks with no concept of science and medicine; ass-scratching simpletons who would more likely be swayed by the wrenching sight of a crippled victim. Her perfect juror: an old man who looked like he'd been press-ganged from the local park bench. Despite having been told nothing about the case, he already held a strong opinion regarding Hugh's guilt.

"Is this something the doc done?" he asked loudly, shaking his fist in the air. "'Cos my wife was lost the same way!"

The judge dismissed the man before Maxine could get her sticky fingers on him.

Questionnaires were filled out and analyzed. People were interrogated, either individually or en masse. Had they ever sued anybody? Half said they had. Had they ever *been* sued? Again, half. Were they satisfied with their medical care? All said they weren't. Was there anybody who would suffer undue hardship if they had to sit through a trial that was likely to last as long as five weeks? A forest of arms shot up all over the room: people with back-aches, jobs that wouldn't wait for them, and vacations that had already been paid for. One by one, they were each excused. When the fourteen were finally selected and seated in the jury box, Denmark seemed pleased with the result.

Hugh was aghast.

"I have a right under the Constitution to be tried by a jury of my peers!" Hugh whispered angrily into his lawyer's ear. "Just *look* at those people! Two are high school drop-outs. Only half graduated from college. None of them have any experience with medical issues. How will they possibly understand the subtle intricacies of a cervical intramedullary ependymoma case?"

"What did you expect?" Denmark asked, popping a breath freshener into his mouth. "Fourteen board certified neurosurgeons? All things considered, I think we've been pretty lucky."

"Lucky to have an unemployed construction worker, an eighteen year old who plays video games all day, and a tree-hugging hippie? Give me a break!"

"Things could be a lot worse."

Judge Jenkins asked the fourteen to stand up and raise their right hands into the air. While he was swearing them in, Hugh noticed that Maxine was gloating. Even with the eye patch covering her eye he knew what she was thinking.

Look at all the brain dead people I've managed to get onto the jury! They'll give me whatever I want!

*   *   *

Opening statements began on Monday morning of the following week.

As the jurors filed into the room, the judge clasped his hands together in front of him and his usual sour expression magically melted into one of magnanimous benevolence. The lawyers followed his lead and, had they been permitted to speak, would have wished them a very good morning, thanked them for serving, and told them to ignore what the other side had to say because they were a bunch of filthy scumbags.

The jurors looked resolutely ahead and avoided eye contact with the lawyers. When they sat down, they reached for the notepads and pencils that Barbara had given them and opened to the first page.

The judge took his seat and politely invited Maxine to begin her opening statement.

"Ladies and gentlemen of the jury," she said, standing up and addressing the jurors directly, "my name is Maxine Doggette and *that*—" She jerked her head towards Billy. "—is my assistant, Billy Barlow."

Billy looked up from his note-taking and treated the jurors to a goofy grin.

"I represent my clients, Mrs. Julie Winter and her husband, Gary," continued Maxine. "Julie hasn't arrived yet because she's paralyzed from the neck down and it takes her three hours to get ready every morning. Why is she paralyzed? Because she once had the misfortune to be the patient of the accused sitting before you in this courtroom: Defendant Hugh Montrose!"

A ramrod-straight finger pointed directly at Hugh. The jurors glared at him with undisguised hostility.

Maxine gave her words time to sink in before she went on. "Julie Winter and her husband, Gary, were once two of the happiest, nicest people you might ever meet. Gary teaches physics at a high school. Julie was a third-grade teacher. Both were as American as apple pie with two beautiful children. There was one problem though. Julie suffered from low back pain, severe enough to warrant an operation. The night after surgery, a tumor in her spinal cord—a tumor *nobody* could possibly have known about—caused paralysis in her arms and legs. Her orthopedic surgeon, Dr. Frank Clegg, an brilliant clinician and one of *Western Washington* magazine's distinguished Best MD's, ordered some tests. When he discovered the problem, he called Defendant Montrose."

Maxine began to strut up and down in front of the jury box like a model at a fashion show. "Now, the defendant is not just *any* doctor," she continued. "He's a neurosurgeon. He might very well be intelligent and highly trained, but, like all humans, he can still be negligent. In this case, he misinterpreted the MRI scan, obtained a history from a confused and medicated patient, performed an inadequate exam, and most negligent of all, chose not to offer Julie the only option that might have saved her from becoming permanently paralyzed: an immediate operation to remove the tumor from her neck. He didn't discuss the problem with any of his colleagues. Nor did he go to the library and research the medical literature. Julie and Gary trusted their doctor and waited. And waited. For *two whole days* they waited for Defendant Montrose to act. Finally, he did something. By then, of course, it was too late. *Far* too late. Any chance he had of reversing her paralysis was long gone."

Over the next thirty minutes Maxine outlined her case against Hugh, summarizing the witnesses she planned to call and the exhibits she would show. Dr. Frank Clegg would discuss the original lumbar fusion, a pathologist would explain what ependymomas were, a radiologist would show what they looked like on scans, and an oncologist would tell them how they were treated. Among non-physician testifiers, they would hear from Julie and Gary Winter themselves, some of their friends and relatives (onion-peelers, Denmark called them), a life care planner to outline what type of care she would need in the future, and an economist to estimate how much it would cost. The most important weapon in her armory was her neurosurgical expert, a man whose name she pointedly omitted to mention. Under the special trial-by-ambush rules imposed by the Washington State Supreme Court, she was not required to identify him before he took the stand.

"Ladies and gentlemen of the jury!" Maxine cried, sweeping her arms into the air in one climactic oratorical flourish. "I urge you to listen carefully to the evidence. Weigh the facts carefully in your minds. I am convinced that you can reach one and only one conclusion: Julie Winter was the victim of monstrous incompetence, shocking negligence, and pure, unadulterated callousness. You don't have the power to restore her limbs to their former function, but you do have the power to award the financial compensation she so richly deserves. Don't turn a blind eye to her pleas for justice! Give her family every dollar to which they are entitled! I implore you to find the defendant negligent. I humbly thank you for your attention."

After lunch, Judge Jenkins told Denmark it was his turn to speak. He stood up, took some notes out of his inside pocket, and cleared his throat.

"Ladies and gentlemen," he began, "my name is John Denmark and I have the privilege of representing Dr. Hugh Montrose and his wife, Caroline, the defendants in this case. I've met Mr. and Mrs. Winter and I want you to know that I agree with Ms. Doggette on one thing: they are indeed nice people. When you meet them yourselves I'm sure you'll see why. I'll also be the first to admit that a terrible thing happened to Mrs. Winter. She's now paralyzed and won't get any better. These are facts that are not in dispute. However, it's also true that when Dr. Montrose was called to help Mrs. Winter, she was *already* paralyzed and there was nothing he could have done to change that. In fact, *had* Dr. Montrose performed surgery at that time, as Ms. Doggette contends he should have, not only would she not have improved, it was very likely she would have gotten worse. And by worse, I mean she could have completely lost the ability to breathe on her own or use her—"

The inner doors of the compression chamber flew open with a loud crash and an emaciated Julie Winter suddenly appeared in her mechanized wheelchair. She nudged the joystick on her wheelchair with a gnarled knuckle and lurched into the courtroom. Gary followed close behind. Stopping every few moments so elephant bags could be hauled out of the way, she slowly made her way past the jury box and parked next to Maxine and Billy, neither of whom took the slightest notice of her arrival.

"Maxine is exhibiting her client like a freak at the circus," Denmark whispered angrily into Hugh's ear. "It's a well-known technique, especially in cerebral palsy cases. Been known to add lots of zeros to the end of an award."

When Julie and her husband had settled down, Denmark picked up from where he was interrupted. He presented a rough outline of the anatomy of the nervous system, using large poster boards that cost Grand National, Hugh later learned, more than fifty thousand dollars. Then he displayed Julie's MRI. Just in case they were unable to appreciate the tumor's gigantic size, he set up a normal study next to it. The contrast between the two was striking.

Unfortunately the jurors' concentration had been effectively shattered by the jarring sight of a paralyzed woman. Instead of paying attention to Denmark, they were looking at Julie, their eyes filled with sympathy.

After only twenty minutes Gary suddenly stood up, gripped the handles of Julie's wheelchair, and unlocked her brake as if he intended to take her out again.

"Your Honor!" cried Denmark in mid-sentence. "I must object to these interruptions in the strongest possible terms!"

"I object to your objection!" screamed Maxine, shooting to her feet and bringing her fist down hard. If she was aiming for the plaintiff table in front of her, she missed by a mile. Instead she hammered Julie's joystick. The wheelchair leapt forward and careened into Billy's elephant bag which was full of medical records and about as immovable as a block of granite. Julie was launched out of her seat, flew like a dummy through the air, and landed in front of the jury box with a sickening thud.

For a few moments of horrified silence, everybody sprang into action at once. Hugh started towards Julie. Maxine reached her first and barred his way. Expensive perfumes assailed his nostrils.

"Stay away from my client before you do her any more damage!" she hissed. "I'm a fully qualified registered nurse. I know how to handle emergencies!"

Billy dragged the heavy elephant bag aside while Gary guided the wheelchair over to Julie. They hoisted her off the floor and dropped her back into her seat. Maxine hovered around like a ferocious dragonfly, issuing orders and keeping Denmark and Hugh from getting too close.

Judge Jenkins gaped at the scene before him. When he remembered he was supposed to be in charge he ordered Barbara to escort the jury back to their room and announced a fifteen minute recess. Denmark and Hugh retreated to a remote corner outside.

"The Dog did that on purpose!" spluttered Denmark. "I was watching her!"

"Why would she do such a thing?" asked Hugh.

"What better way to demonstrate her client's helplessness? It'll elicit more sympathy than weeks of testimony. The whole thing was choreographed, right down to the smallest detail."

"You think the Winters were in on it?"

"I bet they rehearsed for days until it was perfect. Tell me something: how am I supposed to defend a client against somebody like Maxine Doggette?"

When the recess was over, Denmark and Hugh returned to the courtroom. Julie and Gary Winter were nowhere to be seen. Jenkins asked Barbara to fetch the jury. When they were settled in, Denmark resumed his opening statement. The fourteen men and women, however, were clearly kaput for the day. After a while Denmark puttered to an uninspiring close and collapsed dejectedly into his seat. He scribbled a note on a Post-it and passed it to Hugh.

This will be worse than I thought.

27

Maxine sat at her desk in her office, anxiously smoking a cigarette. Minimus was lounging on his velvet cushion in front of her, surrounded by medical supplies, a large make-up case, and numerous perfume bottles.

After an hour of careful preparation, Maxine was finally ready for the arrival of Professor Charles Mortimer. She had removed her black patch to give her eye some fresh air. A grotesque white ball bobbed around in a cauldron of engorged blood vessels, distorted eyelid, and crusty eyelashes. As if that weren't bad enough, something new was going on: a *whoosh-whoosh-whoosh* that sounded like a washing machine churning inside her head.

Maxine heard voices outside her office. Minimus jumped to his feet and whined.

Her neurosurgical expert had arrived!

The front door opened and Billy stepped inside, carrying an old battered suitcase. "This way, if you please," he said. "Ms. Doggette is waiting for you."

Professor Charles Mortimer shuffled in. When Minimus saw him he trembled with fear. Maxine picked him up and popped him into her pocket for safekeeping. Then she stubbed out her cigarette, slipped on her eye patch, and walked across her office to greet her expert.

Up close, Mortimer looked even worse than she remembered. He had dirty white hair and an ashen face covered with necrotic sores. A glob of glandular glue oozed from a corner of his mouth and stretched towards the ground. He was wearing a shirt with a collar that was much too big for his scrawny neck. His jacket looked as worn as he did, full of holes and saturated with stains. She took one look at the withered claw he held out for her and decided to shake it some other time. A powerful smell of rodents assaulted her nose.

"My dear Professor!" she gushed. "How simply *maah-velous* to see you again! I trust you had a good flight."

Mortimer regarded Maxine with mummified eyes. The drool separated from his chin and slimed the carpet below. "How's the symposium going?" he asked.

"The World Federation of Mouse Brain Research is having a most stimulating meeting!" said Maxine, grabbing a bony elbow and guiding Mortimer briskly towards her desk. "The scientists can't wait to hear your lecture this morning. Please make yourself comfortable. There's a lot we have to do first." She took hold of his shoulders and pressed him into a chair.

"How many scientists have come?" he asked.

Maxine thought of the jurors. "Fourteen."

"Only fourteen?" croaked Mortimer. "You said you'd make me famous!"

"And so I shall!" she said quickly. "Fourteen principle scientists serve on the Quality Assurance Committee. They sit together in a special box and evaluate each speaker before their official lecture. Of course, there'll be many other scientists sitting on the benches at the back of the room, enough to spread the word about your research all over the world and make you famous."

"How many others?"

"At least one hundred."

Mortimer broke into a thin smile.

Billy choked. "Ms. Doggette!" he urgently whispered.

"What is it?"

"Where on earth will we find a hundred scientists?"

"Later, Billy," said Maxine, silencing him with a finger to her lips. She returned her attention to the professor. "And now we have to do something about your appearance," she told him.

"What's wrong with my appearance?"

Maxine wanted to know what wasn't. "Presenting research papers these days is not unlike being an actor on a stage," she said instead. "You have to perform in front of an audience, which in this case happens to be the Quality Assurance Committee. You must remember your lines, pretend to be sad even if you feel happy and happy when you're sad. If you have to lie, be unabashed about it and sound convincing. Nobody will know the difference."

As he listened, Mortimer occasionally nodded. A fresh string of secretions dribbled from the corner of his mouth and drew circles in the air.

"And if you're going to be an actor, you'll need make-up." Maxine selected some brushes, compacts, and tubes of cream from the items on her desk. "You're very pale, you know. Obviously spending far too much time in the sub-sub-basement. With your permission, I'll fix that right now."

"I want to look my best when I give my lecture," said Mortimer airily.

"You're going to put make-up on him?" said Billy, blinking with disbelief.

Maxine dabbed a cotton ball into a bottle and smeared foundation across Mortimer's ghostly skin, obscuring his blemishes. Then she dipped a brush into a compact and vigorously applied powder to his scrunched-up face. White clouds billowed into the air. Her final touch: a layer of rouge for his cheeks, just enough to give the impression that some blood ran under his skin.

"There!" she said when she was finished. "You look at least twenty-five years younger. And now for your hair." She rummaged around and produced a can of Kiwi shoe polish.

"*Shoe polish?*" choked Billy.

"Works like a charm." Maxine opened it and scooped out a generous amount of the waxy substance with a rag. She smeared it into Mortimer's hair and spread it around. Within minutes, its whiteness was replaced by a rich brown luster.

"That's better!" she said, stepping back to admire her handiwork. "A real neurosurgical expert! Let me make you smell like one too."

She picked up a bottle of perfume from her desk, aimed the spray nozzle at Mortimer, and blasted him. The old man was engulfed in an orange blossom fragrance potent enough to eliminate the stench of rodents.

"And now it's time for your shots."

"His *shots*?" said Billy.

"Precisely!" Maxine selected a drug vial from her desk and flipped off its cap with her fingernail. She removed the wrapping off a small syringe and twisted a long, nasty needle onto its end. "You need something to dry you up so you don't keep drooling while you're in court," she explained to Mortimer. She jabbed the needle through the bottle's rubber stopper and pulled up clear, colorless liquid. "A small detail perhaps, but I can assure you that the Quality Assurance Committee can be distracted by such trivialities. Could easily make the difference between a win and a loss—excuse me, I mean acceptance and rejection." When she was ready, she ordered him to take off his jacket and roll up his sleeve.

"I don't want a shot!" he said, eyeing the advancing needle with alarm.

"Will you cooperate or not?"

"No!"

The needle flashed through the air anyhow and penetrated Mortimer's jacket. Maxine pressed the plunger hard with her thumb and emptied the contents of the syringe into his arm.

"*Owww!*" cried Mortimer, puckering his face in pain. "That hurt!"

Maxine yanked the needle out. "Next, I'll give you a powerful stimulant to perk you up," she said, reaching for another vial. She drew its contents into the same syringe and jabbed him again. Within seconds he was sitting up straight, looking alert and attentive for a change.

"Professor," she said, throwing the needle and syringe into the wastepaper basket by her desk, "you've had a chance to read my client's medical records and recently we've discussed them over the phone. Do you still remember anything about the case?"

"Of course I do," he answered, his voice already sounding stronger. "Can we talk about my lecture now?"

"First, I'll have to ask you some questions about Julie Winter," said Maxine. "You *must* say that if Montrose had operated on her spinal cord tumor right away she would have regained full neurological function and would now be leading a normal life."

"I feel strange," said Mortimer, his eyes charged with electricity.

"After I've finished, another lawyer named Denmark will ask you more questions and try hard to trick you into saying things you don't really mean. You mustn't let him get his way. Once the Quality Assurance Committee is certain you can present your point of view in a professional manner, they'll let you give your lecture. That's when you start down the road of fame and fortune. Do you understand?"

"My head is spinning."

"Remember to speak loudly and clearly so even the deafest members of the committee can hear you. When you're answering questions, look directly at *them*, not at me or Denmark."

Mortimer expanded his chest, drew in a deep breath, and flared his nostrils.

"Whenever you mention Montrose's name," continued Maxine, "don't call him Doctor. Always refer to him as *Defendant* Montrose."

Mortimer snorted like a race horse.

"You must sound convincing! Everything depends on it."

"I will, Ms. Doggette!"

"Good," said Maxine, satisfied with her preparations. "Now go and see my secretary in the waiting room. She'll give you something decent to put on. I have to speak to Mr. Barlow alone." She helped Mortimer to his feet and nudged him in the direction of the door. He tottered away, rubbing his sore arm.

"Ms. Doggette," said Billy as soon as they were alone, "what will happen when that old fool realizes we've tricked him and that he'll never be famous?"

"Him figure out what's going on?" said Maxine, snapping shut the make-up case. "Not in a million years. His mind's far too gaga for that."

"And what about the hundred scientists you promised him? Where the hell will we find them?"

"Don't be such a worrywart, Billy." Maxine stepped into a back room and returned with a thick wad of twenty-dollar bills. "Here's some money," she said, handing it over. "This is what I want you to do . . ."

After Billy had left to carry out his wackiest assignment yet, Maxine's office was quiet again, all except the annoying *whoosh-whoosh-whoosh* in her head. She retrieved Minimus from his safe haven in her pocket and set him on her desk. "Now I'm ready!" she said, looking into his black eyes. "Ready to show the world what kind of expert I can conjure from thin air!"

Minimus cocked his head to one side and whined.

"No, Minimus," she said, wagging a finger at him. "You know perfectly well little dogs aren't allowed in court."

His eyes grew large and beseeching.

"Don't look at me like that! I don't make the rules. The judge does." Maxine straightened up and reached for her elephant bag. "Stay here and guard my office against intruders. When I get back, I'll tell you what happened. Every little detail!"

She blew him a kiss and headed for court.

28

When Hugh met Denmark in the lobby of the Safeco Plaza building, Beelzebub was still raging inside his head. Not since his residency had Hugh experienced such exhaustion and stress. At least in those days he always knew that he would ultimately end up a better doctor for his patients. This time around, it seemed to serve no purpose at all. He had to force himself to believe things would turn out well in the end, if only to survive.

The sleep deprivation and churning anxiety were bad enough. Being thrown under a bus by another neurosurgeon was even worse. Hugh could understand why plaintiff lawyers habitually lied. They had an obligation to serve their clients and were supposedly doing their jobs. But a neurosurgical colleague? Somebody who had experienced the same hardships during training and should theoretically share common values? Why would such a person ditch his integrity, not to mention his reputation, so he could repeat the lawyers' lies under oath? Was it purely the corrosive power of money? An ego trip? A power grab? Or was it something else? There were so many unanswered questions. Hugh had a keen sense, however, that the key to fixing the broken medical liability system meant eliminating bogus medical experts first.

As usual, Denmark was primed for action, his blue eyes sparkling with energy. In one hand he was holding a cup of coffee, his high octane fuel for the day ahead. He towed along his elephant bag with the other.

"You look like a wreck," he said to Hugh with a look of disapproval. "Get any sleep last night?"

"About two hours. I'll never make it through the day."

"Drink coffee."

"Don't like it."

"Pity."

The weather outside was clear and cold. As Hugh and Denmark approached the courthouse they noticed a long line of people waiting outside the back entrance. At this hour of the morning there was often a crowd of lawyer ants waiting to get in, but never this big.

"What the heck?" said Denmark, abruptly stopping.

"Maybe there's a blue light special on filing lawsuits today," suggested Hugh.

Denmark dropped his empty coffee cup into a trash bin. "Come on, let's try the other entrance on Third," he said.

He led Hugh onto James Street and down a steep hill. When they turned the corner at the bottom they found themselves at the end of an even longer line. The people were wearing dirty, ragged clothes and worn-out shoes. A few were pushing grocery carts filled with junk.

"Well, knock me down with a stick," said Denmark quietly. "They're not even lawyers! They're homeless people!"

Hugh looked around and realized Denmark was right. He tapped on the shoulder of a man with disheveled grey hair, a beard, and no teeth and asked him where he was going.

"They're giving away money!" he answered, pressing forward. "All you have to do is watch a trial."

"Whose trial?" asked Denmark.

"How should I know?" said the man. "I'm just following everybody else."

Denmark and Hugh stayed in line and inched towards the security checkpoint inside the entrance. Once they passed through the metal detector they walked into a foyer packed with more homeless. Elevator after elevator opened its doors and was filled to capacity before either of them could get on.

"Looks like we'll have to walk up," said Denmark with a sigh.

Taking turns to haul the heavy elephant bag behind them, Denmark and Hugh climbed one flight of steps after another. As they slowly gained altitude, they wondered aloud where all those people were going. When they emerged onto the eighth floor, they had their answer.

"I don't understand," said Hugh, plowing his way into yet another crowd. "Why are they coming to *our* floor?"

"Not just to our floor, Hugh," said Denmark as he stretched himself taller. He was looking over a sea of heads at a faraway doorway. "To our courtroom!"

Sure enough, the nearer to Judge Jenkins' courtroom they pushed, the thicker the crush became. Outside the compression chamber they found Barbara in a high state of agitation.

"Go and watch some other trial!" she shouted at the people around her, struggling to make herself heard above the commotion. "This one's full up!"

Those at the front backed off while the ones at the rear pressed forward. The result was a chaotic crush with nobody going anywhere.

Hugh and Denmark battled their way through and caught Barbara's attention.

"Oh, there you are!" she said with relief. She let them slip through the compression chamber, then followed them in and locked the doors behind her. "I've been waiting for you to show up."

Inside, the public benches were crammed with even more people chatting animatedly amongst themselves. Flies circled over their heads and the stench of unwashed bodies permeated the atmosphere.

Maxine and Billy had already arrived and were sitting at the plaintiff table. She was throwing furious looks at him while he tried to appear busy fiddling with papers.

"Please rise!" said Barbara loudly, trying to make herself heard above the noise.

Everybody in court climbed to their feet.

"The Superior Court for the state of Washington," she continued, "in and for the county of King, is now in session, The Honorable Dudley S.—"

"I want to see counsel *now*!" shouted the judge from deep inside his chambers.

Maxine, Denmark and Billy hurried from their posts to see what he wanted. Hugh walked over to the bench behind the defense table, sat on his UW cushion, and made himself as comfortable as he could. After a while the lawyers returned.

"Maxine categorically denies knowing anything about these people," Denmark whispered into Hugh's ear. "Of course the judge believes her. He'll believe anything a plaintiff lawyer tells him! It's obvious to me she's lying, though. The man outside told us somebody was handing out money and I've already seen plenty of twenty-dollar bills being passed around in here. I just can't figure out why she's paying all these people to show up."

Judge Jenkins climbed the bench and glared at the throng assembled before him. "This is a free country and members of the public are allowed to watch trials," he said sternly. "However, be warned! If anybody causes a disturbance, I'll show them no mercy. Bailiff! Bring in the jury!"

The jurors entered from the jury room in single file and looked over the crammed courtroom with puzzled expressions. When they eventually settled into their seats they took out their notebooks and flipped to the appropriate page.

"Ms. Doggette," said Jenkins when it was quiet, "please call your witness."

"Yes, Your Honor," said Maxine, standing up. "Plaintiffs call Professor Charles Mortimer to the stand!"

Denmark gave Hugh a sharp look.

Hugh picked up his head and wearily shook it from side to side. No, he didn't recognize the man's name.

Billy left his seat, went to the compression chamber at the back of the courtroom, and held open both inner and outer doors.

Nothing could have prepared Hugh for what he saw next.

Mortimer was ancient! Maxine must have gone to great lengths to disguise his age for his wrinkly face was covered in make-up, his long hair was dyed a lustrous brown, and his cheeks were dabbed with rouge. He was wearing an expensive dark suit and a blue tie. When he reached the plaintiff desk he followed Billy's pointing finger and shuffled over to the witness stand.

Hugh was now wide awake. "What the hell is going on?" he whispered into Denmark's ear. A strong smell of orange blossoms wafted through the air.

Denmark shrugged. "Beats me," he said, staring at Mortimer. "I was expecting Odeus Horman. Who's this guy?"

The judge had dropped his pen and was also looking at Mortimer in disbelief. He quickly remembered his judicial poise, however, and told him to raise his right hand.

"Do you swear or affirm to tell the truth, the whole truth, and nothing but the truth?"

Mortimer's voice was surprisingly strong. "I do."

"Please be seated."

Mortimer sat down and peered at the jurors. "Excuse me," he said. "I'm Professor Charles Mortimer. Are you the members of the Quality Assurance Committee?"

Judge Jenkins quickly intervened. "The witness is not allowed to address the jury!" he said loudly. "You can only answer questions posed to you by counsel."

Mortimer regarded the judge long and hard as if he was trying to figure out who he was.

Maxine quickly stood up and started her questioning before he had a chance to ask. "Good morning, Professor Mortimer," she said. "Are you comfortable?"

Mortimer gave the judge a parting look of disapproval and turned to face Maxine. "Can I have some water?" he asked her.

"Yes, of course you can." Maxine snapped her fingers in front of Billy's face. He sprung to his feet and took Mortimer a jug of water and some paper cups.

The old man drained one cup, poured another, drained it again, and poured a third.

Maxine approached him. "What is your profession, sir?" she asked.

Mortimer fixed his eyes on the jury. "I'm a neurosurgeon," he answered, tilting slightly to the right.

"Where do you currently work?"

He tilted a few degrees more. "At the VA hospital in Miami, Florida."

"What do you do there?"

Suddenly he was leaning so far over Maxine worried he might fall out of his chair. "Research. Important research."

She looked anxiously at Judge Jenkins. "May I approach the witness, Your Honor?"

"You may."

She stepped up to the stand, gripped Mortimer's shoulders, and carefully set him upright again as if straightening a picture on a wall.

"Have you reviewed Mrs. Winter's medical records?" she asked him, retreating.

Now Mortimer started to tilt in the opposite direction. "I have."

"Do you know the standard of care for a reasonably prudent neurosurgeon in Washington State?"

He tilted some more. "I do."

"Have you formed any opinion as to the care that Mrs. Winter received from Defendant Montrose?"

Once again he looked as if he might topple over. "I have."

"Your Honor?"

Jenkins sighed. "Be my guest, Ms. Doggette."

Maxine set Mortimer straight once again, this time pressing him firmly into the witness chair before letting go.

"And what is your opinion, Professor?"

Mortimer drank three more cups of water before answering. "Defendant Montrose practiced below the standard of care," he gurgled, scratching his head. "He did an incomplete neurological exam, misinterpreted the MRI scan, and made an inappropriate decision not to operate right away."

"Doctor!" said Maxine, raising her voice for dramatic effect. "Do you have an opinion, to a reasonable degree of medical certainty, whether the breaches in the standard of care that you've outlined for us caused injuries to Mrs. Winter?"

Mortimer burped.

"Is that a yes, Professor?" asked Maxine.

Mortimer burped again.

"Let the record show that the witness answered in the affirmative," said Maxine, addressing the court reporter for a moment. "And what *is* your opinion?"

Mortimer bypassed the paper cup, picked up the water jug with his hands, and drank directly from it. When he was finished, he put it down, wiped his dripping mouth with his sleeve, and scratched his head some more.

"The breaches in the standard of care most certainly caused the injuries to Mrs. Winter," he said.

Maxine was now beaming. Perhaps her witness was as ancient as the pyramids but he was answering each of her questions just the way she wanted him to.

Denmark drew close to Hugh's ear. "Why's he drinking so much water?" he asked.

Hugh shrugged. "Maybe his brain's really a sponge."

"And look what's happening to his fingers. They're turning brown!"

Maxine cast aside her notepad and paraded up and down in front of the jury box like a pretentious chicken. She clucked a series of questions enabling Mortimer to express an opinion that Defendant Montrose had done an incomplete exam when he first saw Julie Winter at Columbia Hospital Medical Center. A small patch of numbness in one leg and an isolated toe reflex, as documented by a nurse in the chart, were supposedly proof she had never been quadriplegic.

"Since Mrs. Winter clearly wasn't completely paralyzed," said Maxine, raising her voice and engaging the upturned faces of the jurors one by one as she passed by, "she could have been helped by early intervention. Is that what you're saying?"

"That's what I'm saying," said Mortimer. "I think that if she'd had surgery right after Defendant Montrose first saw her, she would have been neurologically normal again. That means being able to walk, run, brush her hair, clean her teeth, have bowel movements, use her bladder. Everything like before." He lifted his jug of water into the air, tipped up the base, and drained what was left inside. Then he held it out at arm's length again. "More!"

Barbara obliged and he was soon guzzling again.

Maxine left the vicinity of the jurors and advanced upon her expert. "Do you hold your opinions to a reasonable degree of medical certainty, on a more probable than not basis?" she asked.

Mortimer put down his jug and frowned at her as if she was speaking gibberish. "Huh?"

"Do you hold your . . . What I mean is, are you sure?"

"Of course I'm sure!" he said indignantly. "Look, I've had enough of this nonsense!" He pointed at the rows of homeless at the back of the courtroom. "Those scientists have been kept waiting long enough! It's time I gave my lecture! That's why I'm—"

"Professor!" interrupted Judge Jenkins. "Not another word!" He turned to the jurors and asked them to wait in the jury room. After they had filed out, he returned his attention to Mortimer. "Scientists? Lecture? What the devil are you talking about?"

"Ms. Doggette will tell you!" he babbled excitedly, jabbing his finger in her direction. "*She's* the one who invited me to this symposium!"

Under the circumstances, Jenkins displayed remarkable patience. "This is not a symposium, Professor," he carefully explained. "This is a court of law. I'm the judge, the fourteen I just sent out are the jury, and, I can promise you, those people watching from the back definitely *aren't* scientists. We're trying a medical malpractice case and you just testified on behalf of the plaintiffs. So, if you don't mind, I would like to move on. Ms. Doggette, do you have any more questions for your witness?"

Maxine quickly approached the bench. "I have no more questions, Your Honor," she said, glancing nervously at Mortimer.

"Then we'll take a short recess before Mr. Denmark starts his cross-examination. Professor, you may step down."

Mortimer went nowhere. He was too busy staring at the judge in disbelief. "This *isn't* a symposium?" he spluttered.

"Definitely not," said Jenkins, shuffling papers.

Mortimer turned towards Maxine, his face now darkening.

"I can explain everything," she hastily told him. "Let's go outside where we can talk things over."

Mortimer would have none of it. "I came here to give a lecture!" he shouted back, rising to his feet.

"Yes, yes, yes, I know," said Maxine. "That comes later. But first, after the recess, it'll be Mr. Denmark's turn to ask you questions. Just as we discussed in my office this morning. Remember? After that, you may—"

"And I want to give it now!"

"I hate to break this to you, Professor," said Jenkins scornfully, "but there'll be no lectures in *this* courtroom. Not now. Not ever. Nobody here is the least bit interested in your research."

Mortimer staggered backwards. "They *aren't*?"

"Of course they are!" countered Maxine, desperately trying to regain control. "There's been a terrible misunderstanding! Come with me! I'll explain things . . . *outside*!"

Mortimer looked wildly back and forth between Judge Jenkins and Maxine, split on whom to believe. He became short of breath and clutched his heaving chest as if it hurt to breathe. "You have no right to treat me in this manner!" he gasped. "I'm an important neurosurgeon!"

The homeless crowd whistled catcalls and jeered. "You look more like Bozo the Clown to me!" shouted a man from the back.

"Order in the court!" shouted Jenkins, banging his gavel.

"I've saved thousands of lives!" continued Mortimer, sucking air in and out of his chest. "I've trained hundreds of residents! I've written *the* textbook. I've . . . I've . . ."

Mortimer's face suddenly turned blue and his eyes bugged out in a fleeting moment of terror. He sagged to the floor and rolled onto his back. The people in the public benches craned their necks forward to get a better look.

ANEURYSM

"I don't believe it!" moaned the judge. "Is anybody a doctor here?" He spotted Hugh. "Oh, yes. Defendant . . . Excuse me, *Doctor* Montrose. Please take a look at him, will you?"

Hugh left his bench and went over to Mortimer. He examined his pupils and palpated his neck with his fingers.

"He's dead, Your Honor," he calmly reported.

"*Dead*?" shrieked Maxine, jumping out of her seat. "He can't die! He hasn't been cross-examined yet! Everything he said on direct will count for nothing. We've got to *do* something!"

"What did you have in mind?" asked Hugh.

"CPR!" cried Maxine. "Chest compressions! Mouth-to-mouth resuscitation! Those sorts of things!"

Hugh looked at Mortimer dispassionately as he lay stretched out on the floor, his sunken, toothless mouth now drooling something black. The smell of orange blossoms had been replaced by the foul odor of death. A fly buzzed over from the homeless crowd, landed on his upper lip, and crawled up a nostril.

"You think he needs CPR?" he said to Maxine, jerking his thumb towards the corpse. "Be my guest. He's all yours."

Maxine shut up and sat down.

"Your Honor!" cried Denmark, rising to his feet. "In light of this turn of events, the defense makes a motion that the professor's testimony on direct be stricken from the record. I was never given the opportunity to cross-examine him!"

Jenkins frowned at Denmark and invited Maxine to make a counter-argument.

"I'm . . . I'm sorry, Your Honor," she replied, desperately wringing her hands together. "I'm too upset to think clearly right now."

"I understand, Ms. Doggette," said Jenkins kindly. "If you need more time—"

"Your Honor!" said Denmark. "Ms. Doggette doesn't need any more time. She knows as well as I do that her situation is hopeless. I repeat my motion to—"

"Mr. Denmark!" shouted Jenkins. "Sit down and shut—" He stopped himself just in time. "Uh, be quiet!"

"Yes, Your Honor," said Denmark, hastily retreating to his seat.

"Now, Ms. Doggette," said Jenkins, suddenly speaking softly and sweetly again. "I'm sure your expert's death has been very upsetting for you. When you *can* think, be sure to let me know. In the meantime, I'll have no choice but to consider Mr. Denmark's motion. I'll announce my ruling in the morning. Court is adjourned until then. And, if it's not too much to ask, will somebody *please* call an ambulance."

29

Professor Charles Mortimer's death blew a gaping hole through the middle of Maxine's case against Hugh Montrose.

She drove back to Castle Doggette in a state of high agitation, blaring her horn at cars that ventured too close and showing their drivers her middle finger. Minimus was waiting for her at the front door when she arrived. She stormed right past him, headed directly for the wine cooler in the basement kitchen, and plundered a bottle of Chardonnay. She poured out a glassful and gulped it down. The alcohol did nothing to settle her nerves.

"Damn!" she shouted, flinging the glass across the kitchen and shattering it against a far wall. "Damn! Damn! *Damn*!" She stormed to her bathroom upstairs, stood in front of her sink, and ripped off her eye patch. What she saw in the mirror startled her.

"Oh my God!"

Her right eye was a mass of misshapen and discolored flesh erupting from her socket. Now only a jumble of overlapping images was reaching her from the outside world. If Billy was poisoning her, she hadn't been able to figure out how. She was always very careful what she ate, quietly slipping Minimus samples from her plate before putting anything into her own mouth, then feeling vaguely guilty about it afterwards. As bad as things looked, however, she couldn't waste time worrying about them. She had a dire emergency on her hands: a case with no medical expert. If she couldn't find a solution to the problem within the next few hours, *Winter vs. Montrose* would be lost.

Maxine slipped the eye patch back on and left the bathroom, turning the light off behind her and putting the monster away for the night. She threw on a nightgown, helped herself to a couple of sedatives, and crawled into bed. Minimus watched cautiously from the other side of the room, afraid to go any closer. Sleep evaded her. Instead, she brooded and smoked for hours.

What was she to do? Forget about Defendant Montrose and move on to another medical malpractice case, or persevere against all odds and pray she can produce a rabbit from a hat? There was a third, even more extreme option: ditch her crusade against doctors and try something completely new—breeding Minimus, for example. She always thought it would be entertaining to introduce him to a bitch in heat and watch how he . . . well, *did* it with that miniature thing of his.

By three in the morning she decided to finish up *Winter vs. Montrose* before making any rash career decisions. Minimus' descendants would have to wait. She grabbed the telephone and called Clegg. He answered with an unintelligible grunt.

"Wake up, Clegg!" she barked into the receiver, the cigarette between her lips bobbing up and down as she spoke. "You're no longer testifying as a treating physician. I've promoted you."

"Huh?"

"You're now my medical expert!"

"How can that be?" he asked groggily. "I'm not a neurosurgeon."

Maxine had already considered that. "But you *are* a spine surgeon," she said. "That's good enough for me."

"Spine surgeons work with bones, discs, and joints. I don't know shit about spinal cord tumors."

"You're free to give an opinion on anything you want," said Maxine. "It's up to the jury to decide how much weight to give it. Besides, as my expert, you'll be compensated. I'll give you the usual amount for one day: ten thousand dollars."

"Excuse me," said Clegg, sounding irritated now. "You sued me *three* times. Remember?"

"Did I?" said Maxine, suffering from a sudden attack of amnesia. "If that's true, I can assure you it was nothing personal."

"It felt personal to me."

Maxine swore quietly to herself. Why were doctors always so thin-skinned about lawsuits? Sometimes it could be most inconvenient! Busily puffing on her cigarette, she plotted a way forward. "Twenty thousand then," she offered. "Not bad for a few hours of sitting around and doing mostly nothing."

"Forty or nothing," responded Clegg. "In cash."

Maxine almost choked. "You've got to be joking!"

"*And* immunity too, from the Winters and all other future medical malpractice lawsuits."

"Hey, I could put you on my Do Not Sue list!"

"Not good enough. I want a real contract. Something legally watertight. Meet me at eight in the morning outside the courthouse. Have the money and the documents with you. And don't try anything funny."

Maxine glared at the receiver she was holding in her hand and mouthed a string of silent curses at it. When she ran out of vocabulary she returned it to her ear. "For all that," she said, "I demand a guarantee you'll tear Defendant Montrose apart!"

Clegg chuckled. "Don't worry, Ms. Doggette," he said. "I promise a performance you'll never forget."

*   *   *

Later that morning Judge Jenkins met with counsel in chambers. He gave Maxine an apologetic look and announced his decision to strike Professor Mortimer's testimony from the record. Maxine fussed and complained but was unable to make him reconsider. Afterwards she took Billy to a café on the first floor, ordered a large cappuccino, and informed him about the change in plans.

"You know what that means, don't you?" she said with a sly, sideways look.

"Uh, no . . ."

"Since he's the expert now, *I'll* have to conduct the examination."

"You?"

"You're not qualified."

Billy suddenly became red-faced and watery-eyed. "Not qualified?"

"You're not allowed to examine an expert until you've proved you can handle an ordinary treating physician. And since you haven't yet—"

"What difference does *that* make? He's still the same witness!"

"Rules are rules."

"But I spent *weeks* preparing for Clegg!" shouted Billy, attracting unwanted attention from the other people in the café. "You *can't* take him away from me!"

If Maxine was feeling her normal self she would have told Billy to put a cork in it. Some center of critical importance inside her brain, however, seemed to have recently softened (How else could she have considered a career change?) and she hesitated just long enough to give him encouragement.

"I promise I'll do a good job," he quickly pleaded. "The jury will love every minute of it. They'll give us a verdict in our favor for sure!"

Maxine looked up at Billy long and hard, carefully assessing the risk of letting him have his way. Should a young lawyer with such limited experience be allowed to examine the medical expert? Eventually she was persuaded by his big, pleading eyes.

"All right, Billy," she said, shocked how easily she had caved in. "You can still examine him—"

"*Yes!*"

"You'd better not mess up a single question. Do you hear me?"

"I won't, Ms. Doggette! Not a single one!"

The people in the café returned their attention to their laptops. Maxine sullenly watched her cappuccino being prepared. After a few minutes she heard a small, timid voice behind her.

"Ms. Doggette?"

"Yes, Billy?"

"What kind of questions do you think I should ask? I mean, considering he's our expert now and not just a treating physician."

Maxine rolled her eyes. "Ask Clegg the same kind of things I asked Mortimer," she told him. "You *were* listening, weren't you?"

"Yes, but—"

"First, explore his background. Where he trained. Where he practices. That sort of stuff."

Billy whipped a notebook and pencil out of his pocket and furiously scribbled notes. "Where he trained . . ." he said, repeating her words aloud. "Where he practices . . ."

"When he's loosened up, ask him if he's familiar with the standard of care of a reasonably prudent spine surgeon in Washington."

"Standard of care. Reasonably what?"

"Prudent!" said Maxine, taking her cappuccino from the barista and gulping it down. "Make him say Defendant Montrose practiced below the standard of care and caused Julie Winter's injuries."

"What if he doesn't want to?" asked Billy, writing PRUDENT in capital letters and heavily underlining it.

"Oh, he'll want to all right," said Maxine, thinking of the large brown envelope she handed him only an hour before. "I've taken care of everything."

Maxine threw her empty cup into the trash and returned to the eighth floor. Billy followed close behind, frantically formulating questions appropriate for a medical expert and scribbling them into his notepad as each one came to mind. Today the courthouse was relatively empty. The homeless had returned to the streets and the building was once again the domain of lawyer ants and their clients. In the courtroom Denmark was smiling from ear to ear, obviously delighted that the judge had ruled in favor of his motion to strike Mortimer's testimony. Hugh squirmed behind him, searching for the least uncomfortable way to sit on his wooden bench. Julie showed up for the first time since she was catapulted out of her wheelchair.

Gary was at her side, hanging onto her hand tightly as if he was afraid the same thing might happen again.

"Please rise!" cried Barbara just as Maxine walked in. "The Superior Court for the state of Washington, in and for the county of King, is now in session, The Honorable Dudley S. Jenkins presiding."

Jenkins swept into court, more sour-faced than usual. He climbed the bench and invited Barbara to bring in the jurors. Once they were settled, he begrudgingly instructed them to disregard everything Mortimer had said before his death and told Billy to call his witness.

Billy stood up and buttoned the middle button of the jacket—something he had learned from countless lectures on *Perry Mason* at his law school. "Plaintiffs call Dr. Frank Clegg to the stand!" he announced dramatically.

The inner doors of the compression chamber opened. Clegg entered and was sworn in by the judge. When lowered his bulk into the witness chair, its wood creaked ominously underneath him. His black eyes surveyed the courtroom, resting on Hugh for a moment before they hastily flicked away. The two hadn't spoken since the day he transferred Julie to Columbia Medical Center and whatever collegial relationship they might have had in the past, however slight, was clearly over.

Carrying his notebook with him, Billy approached Clegg. When he was ready, he cleared his throat and read his first question from the list he had prepared.

"Dr. Clegg," he said, "would you tell the jury your full name and business address?"

Clegg provided the information.

Billy took out a pen and put a check mark against the question he had just asked. "You're a spine surgeon. True or false?"

"True."

Billy made another check mark. "Would you tell the jury about your education and experience?"

Clegg described his extensive training.

"You first met Mrs. Winter in your clinic at the Emerald Spine Institute. Fair statement?"

"I suppose I did," said Clegg.

"Just answer yes or no."

"Yes."

Check. "What history did she give you?"

"She told me she had low back pain."

Check. "Did you then perform a neurological examination on her?"

"No."

Billy paused and frowned. "You *didn't* examine her?" he asked, flipping through the pages of his notebook as if searching for the answer his witness was supposed to have given.

"No, I didn't," said Clegg firmly.

"Why . . . why not?"

"These chronic pain people never have anything significant on their exams," explained Clegg, "so I didn't bother."

Billy's confusion deepened. "But you documented in the clinic record that you did!" he said, scratching his head with his pencil. "Is this your new truth?"

"It is."

"Let's move on," said Billy, hoping the jury wasn't paying attention. He proceeded to the next question. "So, what recommendations did you make?"

"I ordered an MRI scan and a lumbar myelogram to see what was wrong with her back."

Check. "And the MRI was obviously abnormal. You agree with me, don't you?"

"No, I don't. It was normal."

"Normal?" cried Billy. Clegg had departed from the script again! "But you told my client that one of her discs was severely diseased!"

"Mr. Barlow!" interrupted Jenkins.

"*His* words," blurted Billy. "Not mine!"

"Just ask the witness questions."

Billy quickly returned his attention to Clegg. "If the MRI was normal, why did you recommend an operation?"

Clegg broke into a vicious grin. "To make money, of course. Why else?"

A gasp arose from the jury. They *were* paying attention.

Ever since Billy began his questioning, Maxine had been slowly turning a deeper shade of red. Now she was shaking like a pressure cooker. The alcohol, nicotine, sedatives, insomnia, and caffeine were having a synergistic effect and were threatening to blow the lid off her head.

"To make money?" said Billy, throwing his notebook onto the plaintiff table. "But that's not what we agreed you would say!"

"Mr. Barlow!" roared Jenkins. "Remember you're in a court of law. Conduct yourself accordingly!"

Billy cringed. "I'm . . . I'm sorry, Your Honor," he said. "What about the myelogram?" he asked Clegg, grasping at straws. "Weren't *those* films abnormal?"

"No, they were normal too," answered Clegg, his voice growing louder as if he was building up to something. "But the spinal fluid obtained from the myelogram wasn't. The protein was too high."

"And that was because of the pain and inflammation in Mrs. Winter's back. Correct?"

"High protein has nothing to do with pain and inflammation."

"But that's what you told me when we had lunch together at *Joe's Diner*!"

Denmark jumped to his feet. "Objection!" he cried. "Hearsay!"

"Sustained," ruled Jenkins.

Billy took a step closer to the stand, his face rapidly draining its color. "But you said—"

"I lied to you!" shouted Clegg, exploding out of the witness chair. "The protein was high because there was a tumor somewhere in her nervous system!"

Maxine rocketed to her feet. Her good eye on the left was popping out of her head. God only knew what the other was doing under her patch. "What's this about spinal fluid protein?" she demanded.

"Don't you understand?" cried Clegg. "I didn't bother to check the lab results! If I had, I would have discovered Julie Winter's tumor. A neurosurgeon could have taken it out and she wouldn't be paralyzed now!"

Jenkins grabbed his gavel and banged it on his desk. "Order in the court!" he shouted.

Clegg wasn't finished yet. Now he turned to the jurors, smiling maliciously from ear to ear. "Dr. Montrose wasn't negligent!" he told them with a loud, booming voice. "*I* was! Ladies and gentlemen, *Ms. Doggette sued the wrong doctor!*"

Julie cried out in anguish. Ashen-faced, Gary grabbed the handles to her wheelchair and propelled her towards the exit. They knocked over several elephant bags along the way, spewing stacks of loose papers across the floor. When they reached the compression chamber, they flew through it with a loud crash.

Maxine marched over to Billy. "You've known about this spinal fluid thing all along, haven't you?" she seethed. "Why *the hell* didn't you tell me?"

Billy was suddenly seized by a spasm of throat-clearing and was temporarily unable to answer.

"Stop making that horrible racket and answer my question!"

"I forgot about the lab report!" Billy coughed and spluttered. "I didn't find it again until much later! I kept it to myself because I was afraid you'd get mad at me!"

"I give you a tiny bit of responsibility and you manage to screw up the whole case! You're nothing but a *lipless coward*!"

Judge Jenkins banged his desk even harder. "*Ms. Doggette!* That's *enough*!"

"It wasn't my fault!" shouted Billy. "Clegg told me a bunch of lies about degenerated discs and break-down products!"

Maxine delivered her final blow with precision. "Billy, you're fired!"

Billy looked stunned as if Maxine had just slugged him in the face with a fully loaded elephant bag. "Fired?"

"*Fired!*"

"You can't—"

"*Get out of my sight!*"

Murderous hatred suddenly filled Billy's eyes. His chubby cheeks turned bright red and his receding chin disappeared from view altogether. "I'll . . . I'll . . ." he stammered. "I'll get you for this!" He shoved her aside, grabbed his elephant bag, and headed for the compression chamber. For the second time in as many minutes the court was treated to the sound of slamming doors.

"Good riddance!" Maxine yelled after him.

Jenkins pointed a shaking finger at Maxine. "Ms. Doggette! I'm warning you!"

Maxine ignored the judge and confronted Clegg instead as he sat in the witness chair. "And what the hell do you think *you're* playing at?"

"I've sworn to tell the truth," he sneered, glaring back defiantly.

"You're in a court of law, testifying under oath on behalf of the plaintiffs!" shouted Maxine, shaking a fist at her medical expert. "You're not supposed to tell the truth!"

"*Ms. Doggette!*" roared Jenkins, banging his gavel over and over again. "That's an *outrageous* thing to say!"

Maxine whipped around. "Shut up, you pompous little prick!" she screamed at him. "Stop making so much goddamned noise with that stupid hammer of yours! Are you blind? Can't you see I've got a rogue witness on the stand?"

Doubtlessly The Honorable Judge Dudley S. Jenkins had never been called a pompous little prick before, at least not by anybody in his own courtroom. His eyes bulged and the gavel in his hand was all of a sudden hanging motionless in midair.

Clegg stood up, towered over Maxine, and gave her a victorious smile. "Remember all those lawsuits you filed against me?" he asked. "Three in one year. Put me through hell, you did. My life was changed forever. Well, from this day on, you and I are even. And don't even *think* about suing me ever again. Remember . . ." He pulled some papers from his inside jacket pocket and held them up high for everybody to see. "You granted me immunity. Hah!"

Denmark had been watching the mayhem unfold before him with alternating delight and disbelief. Now he launched himself into the air with a look of grim determination as if he was running the final few yards of a grueling marathon.

"Your Honor, I make a motion that the case against my client is dismissed!" he said, pointing his finger directly at Hugh just in case there was any doubt as to whom he was referring. "The plaintiffs haven't produced a shred of admissible evidence that proves he was negligent!"

"*No!*" screeched Maxine, rushing towards the bench with arms outstretched.

Judge Jenkins finally found his voice. "I am delighted to grant your motion, Mr. Denmark," he declared, glowering at Maxine with fury in his eyes. "The case against the defendants, Hugh and Caroline Montrose, is hereby dismissed!" This time he brought down his gavel so hard it broke. With the loud, splintering crack of a stubborn bone flap being pried open, *Winter vs. Montrose* was history.

"*Yes!*" cried Denmark, flinging his arms triumphantly into the air like a champion prizefighter.

"As for you, Ms. Doggette . . ." said Jenkins, trembling with rage. "I find you in contempt of court! I've got something special waiting for you—a cell in the King County Jail. Bailiff! Call the sheriff's office downstairs! Tell them to send up a couple of deputies immediately! Ms. Doggette will be spending the next *two weeks* in custody!"

Maxine suddenly let loose a bloodcurdling scream, gripped her temples with her hands, and lurched against the clerk's work station, knocking a long row of white exhibit folders onto the floor. She staggered backwards and collapsed into a heap.

A long, shocked silence ensued.

Eventually Judge Jenkins sighed long and hard. "Not *again!*" he said, looking thoroughly exhausted, "Dr. Montrose, would you mind . . ."

Hugh had been watching the chaotic events over the last few minutes in open-mouthed shock. Now he went over to Maxine, checked her breathing and pulse, and found both to be normal. As a precaution, he told Barbara to send for medics before she contacted the sheriff's office. Then he retreated into a far corner, pulled out his cell phone, and called Caroline to give her the news of his victory.

Clegg climbed down from the stand, gave Maxine a look of sheer contempt as he walked past, and left court a free man.

Denmark hurried over to the jurors and quizzed them about their impressions of the trial. At first they paid scant attention to him, focusing instead on Maxine with looks of deep concern.

"There's nothing wrong with her," he assured them, waving dismissively in her direction. "She's faking. I guarantee it."

Gradually he garnered the jury's attention with his questions and was just getting warmed up when the medics arrived. They fastened a plastic collar around Maxine's neck, slipped a spine board underneath her, and lifted her gurgling onto a gurney. Then they wheeled their patient through the compression chamber and out of the courtroom.

30

Fighting back tears, Julie drove her wheelchair wildly down the steep sidewalk outside the courthouse. The grey clouds that had been hanging heavily over Seattle all day had finally opened up and rain was falling. She was soon drenched, her dark hair plastered across her face. Flashing pedestrian crosswalk signs meant nothing to her. She careened across several intersections, looking neither left nor right. Horns blared. Cars swerved to miss her. Somehow she made it through each one without getting killed.

Gary ran after her, calling her name and begging her to stop. The more he yelled, the harder she pushed her joystick, oblivious to the danger. She shot between an elderly couple with walking sticks and knocked them tottering in opposite directions. At the bottom of the hill she ploughed into a big puddle at full speed. Her wheelchair suddenly decelerated underneath her and she was thrown out of her seat, landing in dirty water with a huge splash.

"*Julie!*" shouted Gary. He reached her within seconds and scrambled to raise her head above the water so she could breathe. "Are you alright?"

"Clegg's a bastard!" she gasped. "A dirty, rotten bastard!"

Gary lifted her out of the puddle and laid her on the sidewalk. Pedestrians pretended not to notice. If Julie had been any normal person with a functioning thermoregulatory system he could have taken her somewhere and changed her into dry clothes. But she was quadriplegic and had as much control over her body temperature as a lizard. The water in the puddle had been cold and she was in danger of severe hypothermia. Gary dialed 911 on his cell phone, asked dispatch to send an ambulance, and prayed it came quickly.

"Look what he did to me!" said Julie, her abdomen rising and falling as she worked hard to get air into her lungs.

"Here, take this!" cried Gary, struggling out of his raincoat and throwing it around her shoulders. He put his arms around her and rubbed her to provide a small measure of warmth.

"Can he imagine what it's like being this way?"

"Julie, don't distress yourself. It'll only make things worse."

"Doesn't he care about other people? Not even a tiny bit?"

"Forget about Clegg!" said Gary, wiping hair from her eyes.

"And what about Maxine? She should have known about the spinal fluid protein but she didn't! What kind of lawyer misses important information like that? I don't care if Billy misled her! She's still responsible!"

"If you have to blame somebody," said Gary, "blame me!"

"No, Gary," said Julie, shaking her head. "I'll never—"

"You must!" he said, tightening his hold on her. "*I'm* the one who insisted you should see a doctor in the first place. And when Dr. Jones sent us to Clegg, I missed the warning signs—all those tests done in a single day, no second opinion, surgery scheduled so quickly. They should have been obvious to me, but they weren't."

"You did what you thought was right," said Julie, catching her breath. "Clegg conned us."

"Maxine was another big mistake of mine," he continued as he heard the wailing of an ambulance in the distance. "When she first called me, she claimed to be the best medical malpractice lawyer in the country. And I actually believed her! If it was really true, then why did she sue Dr. Montrose when Clegg should have been the defendant? She must have had some private agenda of her own and was simply using us."

"Gary! There's no point—"

"What will we do now?" he continued, choking back tears. "Our savings are gone. My unemployment benefits will soon run out. We'll be evicted from our home. The poor children . . . I've failed them, haven't I? I've let you down too. It's all my fault!"

"*No*, Gary," said Julie firmly. "You're not responsible for everything that went wrong. That's just the way things go sometimes. We can't look back. Let's pick up the pieces and move on. Ours is a strong family. If we hang together, we'll get through anything."

"Get through anything? Even *this*?"

"Even this."

An ambulance turned a corner, drew up to the sidewalk, and stopped. The doors opened and a couple of medics came over with their gear.

"Now let's go to the hospital before I catch pneumonia," Julie said to Gary. "I promise I won't dive into any more puddles."

31

After he spent an hour squeezing every last impression from the jurors, Denmark invited Hugh to dine with him at a nearby Italian restaurant. The lights were low and the music soft. Denmark basked in the warm afterglow of his stunning victory, reminding Hugh over and over again that he had not only beaten The Dog for the first time but had done so under the auspices of a judge who had been so blatantly biased against him.

"I can't believe Maxine collapsed at the end like that," he said, shoveling a forkful of spaghetti into his mouth. "What a finale! She was obviously faking. That much I'm sure of. Mark my words: she'll be busy filing an appeal tomorrow. Not that one will do her any good, of course." When Hugh didn't respond, Denmark frowned at him. "What's the matter? Where's your appetite?"

Hugh had long ago abandoned his own plate of spaghetti. "I'm sorry, John," he said, clasping his hands around a candle jar for warmth. "I know I should be celebrating with you, but I feel completely empty inside."

"That's because you're still suffering from juris psychosis," said Denmark, washing his food down with a swig of Chianti.

"How can that be?" asked Hugh. "The trial's over."

"You had type I before," said Denmark, jabbing his fork at him. "Maybe you've got type II now."

"What's type II?"

"Sometimes when doctors spend too much time around lawyers," explained Denmark, "they suffer paradoxical psychological problems, mistaking the occasional lack of abuse as an act of kindness and developing positive feelings towards them. When the trial is over, they go back to their medical practices suffering from a bizarre and inexplicable desire to return to the courtroom. It's similar to the more commonly known Stockholm syndrome that can occur between hostages and their captors."

"That's not it," said Hugh. "I never want to set foot inside the King County Courthouse again."

"How about type III then?" asked Denmark, spearing the pile of spaghetti on his plate with his fork.

"What's that?"

"Some physicians get so depressed over lawsuits they want to quit practice forever," he explained, rotating the fork and winching noodles on board. "It's the fastest growing kind of JP these days. If the current trends continue, soon there won't be anybody left, especially from high risk specialties like neurosurgery and obstetrics."

"No, that's not it either," said Hugh, tilting the jar in his hands and watching the molten wax shift around inside. "Is there a type IV?"

"Not as far as anybody knows," said Denmark, lifting more food into his mouth. "Tell me what's bothering you. Maybe we can author a ground-breaking paper for the psychiatric journals."

"For one thing, I can't help feeling sorry for Maxine."

"You're so gullible!" cried Denmark, confidently chewing away. "I promise you there's nothing wrong with her."

"No, I'm not talking about her health," said Hugh. "I'm talking about *her*."

"Sympathy for vanquished plaintiff attorney?" said Denmark, looking up at the ceiling with a professorial air and rubbing his chin. "I suppose that *might* be classified as type IV."

"If she's got an ounce of insight," continued Hugh, "can you imagine how disturbing her life must be to her? Maybe even frightening. And don't forget: she doesn't have any friends or family to help her with her problems. Just a rather ugly dog."

Denmark slurped up the last of his noodles and pushed away his plate. "She's got problems alright," he said, finishing his wine and blotting his mouth with his napkin. "Lots of them, in fact. She's unstable, moody, unpredictable, self-destructive, impulsive, manipulative, and has a crappy self-image. Let's see . . . Have I left anything out?"

"She hates herself."

"No doubt that too," agreed Denmark. "Maxine Doggette has been the same for years. You can't change her, unless you know how to do a brain transplant."

"I've no intention of changing her," said Hugh. "If I did, she wouldn't be Maxine Doggette any longer. No, I just wish there was a way she could learn to feel more comfortable inside her own skin. Perhaps she would stop hating doctors and find something more useful to do with her life."

"Maxine will never stop hating doctors," declared Denmark. "That's what gives an ounce of meaning to her miserable existence. And as long as there are people around like Julie Winter who feel they have to file medical malpractice lawsuits, she'll always have work to do."

"Talking about Julie Winter," said Hugh, releasing the candle jar and pushing it back to the center of the table, "she's somebody else who's bothering me."

"What? Sympathy for the vanquished plaintiff too? This is sounding more and more like a possible type IV!"

"I'm being serious, John," said Hugh. "There's no more deserving victim on the planet and yet she wound up with doodly-squat. Do you think our so-called justice system served her well? I hardly think so. Did you see her face when she left the courtroom? God, it was terrible! I'll be haunted by the memory for the rest of my life. I wish I could help her somehow. As a matter of fact, I've been having a few ideas lately along those lines."

"Like what?" asked Denmark, flashing Hugh a look of apprehension as if ideas weren't good things to have right now.

"Why not establish a society that offers certification for neurosurgeons who want to give fair and balanced opinions in medical liability cases?" he suggested. "Not prostitutes like Odeus Horman and or senile retirees like Charles Mortimer. I'm talking about normal, actively practicing neurosurgeons who would testify in accordance with the proper standards of medical practice and the literature. If such a society was able to develop a name for itself, it could be a valuable resource for plaintiff and defense lawyers alike. What do you think?"

"How would that help Julie Winter?"

"If somebody decent and reputable stood up for her instead of the screwballs we've seen over the last couple of days, wouldn't she have been more likely to win her case? Don't you think an expert who has been certified by his peers would carry more weight in a court of law?"

"If you're being serious, then I'll be too," said Denmark, sounding just a little bit peeved at the thought of Julie Winter robbing him of his victory. "Our justice system isn't perfect but it's all we have. Maybe Julie got the short end of the stick but sometimes that's the way the cookie crumbles. Sure, she's a nice person, but don't forget she chose to sue you and came perilously close to ruining your reputation and your career. You don't have an obligation to do anything for her. Expunge her from your mind. Think about more important matters, like what we're going to have for desert." He reached for a menu and opened it.

"I suppose if I've gotten nothing else from this damned lawsuit I've learned how big and far-reaching the medical liability crisis really is," said Hugh with a sigh. "Maybe it's too much to hope for, but wouldn't it be nice if my idea had a small part to play in solving the problem? High quality expert medical testimony might mean fewer lawsuits and trials. Over time, physicians may feel secure enough to waste less money on worthless tests and procedures. Perhaps this runaway healthcare train that all Americans are riding could be slowed down and brought under control. Taxpayer money could be spent on more important things. We could save Medicare!"

"Fancy some tiramisù?" asked Denmark, his face hidden behind his menu.

"You haven't been listening to a word I've been saying," grumbled Hugh.

"Of course I have. Something about trains."

Hugh's cell phone rang. Dave Holz was on the other end of the line.

"Hugh!" he said. "Thank God I found you!"

"I'm not on call for the ER tonight," said Hugh, his thumb hovering over the red hang-up button.

"But I have a patient for you."

"Not interested."

"You will be after I tell you who she is."

"No I won't."

"It's Dog-breath . . . Dog-face . . . Whatever the hell she calls herself."

Hugh pressed the phone closer to his ear. "*Who?*"

"You know—that redheaded nurse attorney bitch who gets off from suing doctors."

"Dog-*gette*?"

"That's it! She's here! In my ER!"

"Really?" said Hugh, noticing Denmark lower his menu and start watching him with acute interest. "I was there when she collapsed in court. My attorney says she's faking."

"Sorry, Hugh," said Holz, "but she's definitely not faking. We did a CT angio and it shows she has an aneurysm."

"*Oh my God!*" whispered Hugh, closing his eyes and seeing the images loom bright in his imagination. Little white lines branching throughout the brain like twigs on a bush. A berry was growing from one of them. The thing had already leaked some blood and now it was threatening to burst. The diagnosis made sense. Aneurysms sometimes compressed cranial nerves and caused eye problems. Denmark had said hers was pointing off to one side and was associated with a drooping eyelid. So she *did* have a third nerve palsy.

Those damned medics! Why the hell did they take her to *his* hospital?

Denmark scooted closer. "What's going on?" he asked, his voice filled with urgency.

"Maxine has a cerebral aneurysm and it hemorrhaged," Hugh answered.

Denmark's mouth fell open.

Years of training and experience automatically kicked in and Hugh found himself focusing on the problem at the other end of the phone line. "What's her neurological status?" he asked Holz.

"Very much intact. The woman thinks she's surrounded by her enemies and that they're out to kill her. My nurses can't get close; she keeps throwing things at them. Thank God she's under arrest and chained to the bed, otherwise she would be tearing the place apart!"

"I suppose that's a good sign."

"She's a raving lunatic, Hugh! Come quickly before somebody gets hurt!"

From the information he had been given, Hugh knew that Maxine was neurologically stable and could still be transferred out. It would mean losing an aneurysm case, an especially painful sacrifice after spending more than a week in the barren wastelands of the King County Courthouse. The urge to purge that woman from his life, however, overrode all other considerations.

Hugh put his cell back to his ear. "Send her packing to Harborview," he said. "They'll take good care of her there."

"She refuses to go anywhere," said Holz. "She's demanding to see you."

"Why me?"

"She says you're the best."

Hugh felt like burying the phone in his unfinished spaghetti. "I'm the best?" he shouted. "Has she already forgotten that she devoted the last couple of years of her life to proving I'm the worst?"

"She insists it was nothing personal."

"*Nothing personal?*" spluttered Hugh, fighting for control. He searched for an appropriate way to respond. "Not everybody gets to pick the doctor they want," he finally said after reviewing and rejecting several less diplomatic options.

Holz's voice grew more serious. "Be reasonable, Hugh," he said. "She's not just anybody. She's The Dog! Consider what'll happen if we kick her bony butt out of here? As soon as she recovers, I promise you, she'll bombard us with lawsuits."

"Now *that's* a real possibility," conceded Hugh. A ruthless, scorched earth, leave-no-prisoners-behind policy towards his colleagues on the medical staff was well within her capabilities. He wasn't anxious to expose them to such dangers unnecessarily.

"Can you hold for a minute, Dave?"

"Sure."

Hugh quickly explained the situation to Denmark.

"I've always predicted that woman would self-destruct one day," he responded solemnly. "And now it's finally happened. A brain aneurysm, no less. How appropriate!"

"The ER doc wants me to come to the emergency room and see her."

Denmark's face suddenly turned the same reddish color as the tomato sauce remnants on his napkin. "Don't think for a minute you've got any obligation to see that woman!" he spluttered. "You're not on call. Insist she goes to Harborview!"

Hugh pursed his lips and said nothing.

"You're not actually considering it, are you?" continued Denmark, transitioning seamlessly to plum purple. "Because if you are . . ." He slammed his fist on the table. The plates around it jumped. ". . . I strongly counsel against it! As your lawyer . . . As your *friend*, I absolutely forbid it! It's simply too dangerous!"

Hugh had a far off look in his eyes. "I wonder if I can . . ."

"If you can what?" asked Denmark suspiciously.

"If I can find a way to fix that woman."

"What the devil do you mean?"

"Fix her *permanently*." A shiver ran down Hugh's spine. "Yes, maybe there *is* a way!"

Denmark looked alarmed. "I hope you're not planning to murder her in the middle of an operation! If you are, you'll never get away with it!"

Hugh smiled at his lawyer. "Poke the thinnest part of the aneurysm with a micro-dissector when nobody's looking?" he asked. "Suddenly the country is deprived of its most notorious medical malpractice lawyer. I can see the reaction now: physicians everywhere pouring into the streets and rejoicing. Champagne parties and fireworks. Is that what you mean?"

"Something along those lines, yes."

Hugh rolled his eyes and lifted the phone back to his ear. "Dave? Are you still there?"

"I am. Will you come?"

"I'll be there as soon as I can."

The sense of relief at the other end of the line was palpable. "I knew I could count on you!"

Hugh hung up and noticed Denmark staring at him with astonishment. "I know what I'm doing," he reassured him.

"No, you *don't* know what you're doing!" cried Denmark. "You could end up in prison for the rest of your life! Is it really worth it? Think of your family!"

"I *am* thinking of my family," said Hugh, scraping back his chair and standing up. "And the family of every human being within suing range of that woman."

Denmark was far from mollified. He also rose to leave, grumpily declaring that if Hugh wasn't going to take his advice any longer he might as well celebrate his victory with somebody else.

Hugh laid a hand on his lawyer's arm. "Let's not end the evening like this," he said. "I want to thank you for everything you've done for me, especially for showing me that not *every* lawyer is a blood-sucking parasite."

The compliment, such as it was, placated Denmark.

"And another thing," continued Hugh. "When are you next going fishing?"

"Not soon enough. Why?"

"Because when you go out again, I want to come with you."

"You know how to fish?"

"Actually, no. But I would love to learn from a world class expert."

This time the compliment struck home. Beaming from ear to ear, Denmark grabbed Hugh's hand and shook it warmly.

"If it's the last thing I do, Hugh," he declared, "I'll teach you to be the second best fisherman in the state of Washington!"

32

Shit-canned!

Maxine must pay, swore Billy under his breath as he left the courtroom.

Pay with her life.

She had dogged him relentlessly and was a back-stabbing liar. And now she'd had the nerve to fire him. She knew perfectly well that that would put an end to his career. And what a stellar career it would have been! Fame, riches, Super Lawyer status, the cover of *Time* . . .

He blundered into a revolving door, pushed way too hard, and was sucked into the moving parts so fast he lost his footing and was sent sprawling. Something caught his elephant bag and ripped it open. Legal papers exploded into the air and scattered everywhere.

"Damn!"

He showed the bemused security guards his middle finger and hobbled to a parking garage outside. Where was his rusty, piece-of-crap car? When he found it, his hands were shaking so badly he had trouble getting the key into the ignition. The engine started with a cough and a shudder. He threw the gear shift into what he thought was reverse, stomped on the gas, and plowed into the car parked in front.

"Crap!"

He became red and sweaty as he wrestled with the gears. When he trod on the accelerator again, he leapt backwards and smashed into the car behind. On the third attempt he sprung loose from the parking place and raced for the exit. Tires squealed as he flew around corners. Sweat ran into his eyes and impaired his vision. He never saw the mechanical arm at the exit and blasted through it, spraying the garage with splinters of wood.

At his apartment he grabbed a double-barreled shotgun from a closet. From a maintenance shed outside he took a plastic container full of gasoline and a box of matches.

Now he was ready.

Billy drove to the Doggette law firm first. He dashed wildly around, searching every room. To his bitter disappointment, the place was deserted. No Maxine anywhere. He opened the top drawer of her desk and took out the black leather notebook she had once shown him. He also found her video camera and some microcassette tapes, stuffed everything into his pockets, then smashed the certificates and diplomas hanging on the walls with the butt of his shotgun. "You won't get away from me!" he screamed, his eyes filled with hatred.

Minimus suddenly ran into the room.

"Hello, you ugly freak," said Billy, thrusting the business end of the shotgun into his face. "How would you like to be blown into a billion atoms?"

The little dog bared a cosmetically perfect set of teeth and growled.

"But why waste ammunition on something as puny as you?" said Billy, lowering his weapon. "I have a much better idea. Let's have a barbecue, shall we?"

He opened the gas container and splattered its contents over the furniture. A match flared and arced through the air. Flames leapt up with a whoosh. Scorching heat blasted against his face like a desert wind.

"There's the fire . . ." said Billy, backing away. When he'd seen enough, he rushed out of the office, slammed the door in Minimus' face before he could escape, and howled with laughter. "*. . . and you're the meat!*"

Next stop, Castle Doggette. He drove there as fast as his old rattletrap could go, flying past wailing fire engines headed in the opposite direction. When he arrived, he searched the entire building with his shotgun cradled in his arms.

Again, Maxine was nowhere to be found.

He went to the Great Hall and heaved the two yellow armchairs to a spot underneath the heavy window drapes. He wrenched open the doors to the antique bookcase, grabbed books by the handful, and threw them on top of the chairs. He added the shelves, and then the bookcase itself.

Was there anything else that would burn?

His eyes fell on Maxine's nude portrait above the fireplace.

Perfect!

Billy yanked the painting off its hook and dumped it on top of the pile. Her sultry eyes glowered at the ceiling above. He poured out the remaining gasoline from the container and tossed another match.

Once again flames leapt into the air. They hungrily spread up the drapes and licked the wooden rafters near the ceiling. Maxine was quickly consumed. Billy imagined her writhing in hell and felt his body tingle with delight.

He ran to his car and drove away. He *had* to locate her. But who could tell him where she was?

Barbara the bailiff!

He dialed her cell phone number.

"Where did Ms. Doggette go?" he asked as soon as she was on the line.

"Ms. Doggette?" asked Barbara. "Don't you know?"

"Know what?"

"She collapsed a few minutes after you left the courtroom."

"Collapsed?"

"Passed out. Fainted. I don't know what exactly. Mr. Denmark claims it was all an act. We called the medics anyway. They came and took her away."

"Where did they go?" he asked.

"Columbia Medical Center."

Billy hung up and sped towards a freeway that would take him downtown.

So far, he had destroyed Maxine's office, her home, and her horrible dog. Now it was time to find Maxine at the hospital and destroy *her*.

33

Hugh passed through the entrance to Columbia Hospital Medical Center's ER, his face etched with determination. He found Holz anxiously pacing up and down inside.

"Thank God you're here!" said Holz, gripping him by the shoulders. "I can't tolerate that awful woman any longer. Either transfer her to Harborview or admit her to your service. Doesn't matter which. Just get her out of my ER!"

"Where is she?"

"Shut up in there," said Holz, jerking his head towards the trauma room. "Your resident managed to take a peek at her—"

"Before she threw me out," said Richard Elliott, walking over from the nurse's station.

"Show me her CT angio," said Hugh.

The three doctors huddled around a monitor. Hugh clicked through the images and identified telltale blood at the base of Maxine's brain. A thick vessel traveled up her neck—the internal carotid artery. Once inside the skull it ballooned into a round aneurysm that resembled the head of an octopus—larger than he had dared to imagine. A tangle of smaller blood vessels was looped around its neck like tentacles.

Hugh noticed evidence of blood escaping from the base of the aneurysm and feeding directly into the surrounding venous drainage system—a rare phenomenon known as a carotid-cavernous fistula. Her veins downstream were engorged and swollen from the abnormally high pressures within. No wonder her eye was trying to climb out of her head!

"A real challenge," he said, studying the information on the screen. "The aneurysm will have to be dealt with first since it's the main threat to her life. We'll do a craniotomy and clip it."

"You don't want to use coils?" asked Richard.

"No. It's really big and the neck looks too wide. Later on, when the dust settles, we'll plug the fistula from the inside with a balloon. Has anybody broken the news to her yet?"

"I was saving that for you," said Holz with an apologetic look.

"Gee, thanks," said Hugh. "Maybe it won't be as bad as all that. She's probably terrified. How would *you* feel if you've dedicated your entire career to tormenting medical professionals only to find yourself in an ER depending on them to save your life?"

Before Holz could answer, Hugh went over to the trauma room. A sheriff's deputy stood guard outside the door. When he saw Hugh coming, he nodded curtly and opened it for him. They both ducked as a plastic bedpan flew out and clattered down the hallway.

"Get out of here!" screeched a familiar voice from inside the room. "You won't make me piss in one of those things and you *sure as hell* won't stick any needles into me! I know what you're up to! You can't hide anything from me!"

A nurse ran out, fighting back tears. She ripped off her ID badge, flung it away, and fled down the hallway.

Hugh took a deep breath, gave the deputy a here-goes look, and stepped through the doorway.

Maxine was sitting bolt upright on a gurney with one of her ankles handcuffed to the footboard. Her black patch was gone and for the first time Hugh could plainly see her right eye. It was juicy, colorful, and bloated just like the giant hemorrhoids he used to lop off when he was a surgical intern. The lid was partially closed. Underneath, the globe was protruding and cocked to the side.

When Maxine saw Hugh she jumped as if startled, then ogled him with her other eye. "You're here?" she said, astonished.

"You sent for me."

"I wasn't expecting you to show up."

"If you're having second thoughts about this, I'll go home. It's been a long day."

"No, stay!" said Maxine. "It's just that . . ." She faltered, then began again. "I was sure you wouldn't come, considering everything I've put you through over the last couple of years."

Hugh was intrigued. Had the aneurysm performed the physiological equivalent of a bifrontal lobotomy when it hemorrhaged? Entirely possible, especially if it had bled upwards into the brain like anterior communicators sometimes do. Or was Maxine was up to her old tricks again, playing the repentant sinner in order to get what she wanted?

"Why don't you just tell me what happened?" he suggested, taking a step closer. "Was it a sudden, severe headache?"

Maxine lay back down and rested her head on a pillow. "The worst one in my life. And I've got terrible nausea. *And* a stiff neck. Bright lights bother me too."

Hugh gently nodded. The symptoms definitely fit the diagnosis of a subarachnoid hemorrhage. "Your scans show you have a brain aneurysm," he said.

"Really?"

"You need an operation to fix it."

"An *operation*?"

Hugh explained things in simple terms. "If you don't have one, you'll likely have another hemorrhage. I need to put a clip across the neck of the aneurysm and isolate it from the normal circulation. That way it'll no longer be a threat to you."

"Are you saying I could *die* from this thing?"

"If it bleeds again, yes."

She examined Hugh suspiciously as if she thought he was playing some kind of cruel joke on her. Eventually her eye broke away and gazed at the ceiling instead. "It'll take more than a silly brain aneurysm to stop me," she concluded.

Hugh came nearer until he was standing right next to her. From this close he could see that her pupil on the right was fully dilated, a prominent feature of third nerve palsies. "You're afraid, aren't you?" he said.

"Afraid?" said Maxine. "Why should I be afraid?"

"All patients are afraid when I tell them they need a life-saving brain operation," answered Hugh. "There's no reason why you should be any different. Listen, I know you've never been very good at setting aside personal grudges, but I am. I'll do the best I can for you, regardless of who you are and what you've done in the past."

Maxine gave him a look filled with contrition and humility. No Oscar-winning actress could have performed so well and Hugh instinctively knew that her feelings were genuine.

There was a knock on the door and Richard walked in.

When Maxine saw him the window into her soul suddenly slammed shut and she became agitated once again. "Don't come any closer!" she cried, the handcuffs around her ankle rattling with alarm. "Dr. Montrose will be the surgeon operating on me. Not you!"

Richard was careful to maintain a safe distance. "*Are* you going to operate on her, Dr. Montrose?"

"I suppose so," sighed Hugh. "Let the OR know we'll be up in a few minutes. Tell them we'll need plenty of blood on standby."

"You heard him!" said Maxine, waving Richard away with her hand. "And make sure it's been properly screened for nasty diseases! Now get out of here!"

When Richard withdrew, Hugh looked down at Maxine. "Surgery has risks, you know," he told her. "I'm obliged to inform you what they are."

"I know all about the risks," said Maxine, looking away as if she was trying to seem uninterested.

He listed them as he walked towards the door. "Infection, hemorrhage, stroke . . . Only one really matters though."

Her eyes sought him out. "Oh? Which one is that?"

Hugh stopped and turned around.

"There's a reasonably good chance I might kill you," he said casually, then left the room.

34

Hugh took the hair clippers from Val the circulating nurse, switched them on with his thumb, and plunged them into the mass of red curls before him. The chattering blades were quick and efficient. They cut one swath after another from the front of Maxine's scalp to the back, exposing an ever-widening tract of stubble. Within seconds she was completely bald. Hugh dumped her unique plumage into a pile on the floor.

"Save it," said Hugh.

"I know, I know," said Val as she gathered it up and stuffed it into a plastic bag. "If she dies, the mortician might need it."

Next, the Mayfield. Hugh picked up the heavy clamp and fastened three sterile spikes onto the ends of its arms. He carefully positioned them around her head and squeezed as hard as he could. The spikes penetrated her scalp and bit into her skull. The beeps coming from the anesthesia machine accelerated as her body reacted to subconscious pain.

The anesthesiologist dialed up the gases and her vital signs soon returned to normal.

Hugh covered Maxine with blue paper drapes. The scrub tech, Lori, positioned a tray stand over her and neatly arranged the most commonly used instruments on its flat, rectangular surface. Val hooked up the monopolar, bipolar, and suction, then tested the air drill. She connected Hugh's headlight to a light source and helped with a quick sponge count. Then came the time-out: a mandatory procedure when everybody in the room stopped what they were doing and checked if they were about to cut open the correct patient or whether some other poor, unsuspecting bastard had been inadvertently wheeled into the wrong operating room.

"I hope you have plenty of blood on standby," said Hugh to the anesthesiologist after everybody in the room agreed they had the right woman on the table. "This could get messy."

"Yes, sir. Four units of packed cells hanging and ready to transfuse."

"Good. Let's get started." Hugh pressed the blade of his scalpel into Maxine's scalp and felt the edge of its blade run over hard bone.

The first fifteen minutes of the operation were routine. Hugh drilled burr holes in the skull with a high-powered craniotome and connected them with a saw. Next he placed an elevator under the bone flap, pushed down on its handle, and heard the usual loud, splintering crack as bone separated from bone. A fine jet of blood from the middle meningeal artery sprayed Hugh's magnifying loupes with dozens of tiny red dots—Maxine's special way of lashing out at him even while she was under anesthesia. Val wiped him clean with an alcohol prep pad.

Richard entered the room with wet arms held out in front of him. "I'm making a big mistake getting involved in this case," he said as he accepted a towel from Lori. "On the other hand, if I pass up this opportunity to rearrange the brains of a trial lawyer, I'll kick myself for the rest of my life." When he was gowned and gloved, he drew closer and peered at the operative field with feigned shock. "My God! She *does* have a brain! Does that mean she has *feelings*?"

Hugh pulled in the microscope and adjusted the zoom and focus. A sight for sore eyes greeted him: glistening brain covered with an intricate network of tiny arteries and veins. Using ever smaller and finer instruments, he spelunked down the crack between the frontal and temporal lobes, edged along the lesser wing of the sphenoid bone, and approached the aneurysm's location. A big one like Maxine's wasn't hard to find. He spotted the thin, transparent dome bulging towards him before any of the usual landmarks.

"Jeez!" muttered Richard, looking at a tornado of blood spinning angrily inside. "That's an F-5."

Hugh only knew of one way to approach aneurysms, both big and small, and that was *carefully*. First he dealt with the relatively easy obstacles, clearing away surrounding debris and sucking out small blood clots. As work progressed, the pieces of the puzzle gradually joined together into a more complete picture. Although the dome of the aneurysm was big and multi-lobular, its neck was narrower than expected and looked as if it might accommodate a regular straight clip.

Hugh took a probe from Lori, explored the crevices on either side of the neck, and identified the artery from which the aneurysm arose. Holding his breath and hoping the thing wouldn't pick this moment to rupture again, he compressed the dome and found the third cranial nerve, the source of Maxine's drooping eyelid and paralyzed eye muscles.

"I've got the anatomy pretty much worked out," Hugh said to Richard. "Now it's time for the kill." He exchanged the probe for a clip applier loaded with a silver-colored permanent straight clip. He opened its jaws and slowly advanced them towards the neck of the aneurysm as if he was defusing a bomb. If he wanted to murder The Dog, as Denmark had feared, this was his perfect opportunity. Nobody would ever know he'd done it intentionally.

Hugh chuckled to himself. What an absurd idea Denmark had had! A neurosurgeon could no more sabotage an aneurysm in the operating room than a defense lawyer could intentionally betray a guilty client in open court. Erasing the unwelcome image of rupturing aneurysms and life-threatening hemorrhages from his mind, he slipped the blades of the clip into the crevices on either side of the aneurysm's neck and released the applier. The tornado of blood inside the dome fizzled into nothing.

Maxine would live to sue another day.

Hugh heard the door behind him open. Lori was suddenly looking over his shoulder, her eyes wide and staring. He twisted around to see Billy standing tall in the doorway, dressed in ordinary street clothes and a raincoat—a bizarre sight in the sterile surgical environment. He was gripping a double-barreled shotgun in his hands.

"What the—" exclaimed Hugh, unable to believe his eyes.

"I've come for Ms. Doggette," Billy snarled.

"Y-you can't come in here!"

"That's her under the blue paper stuff, isn't it?"

"Yes . . . No! It's somebody else!"

"You're lying," said Billy. He took a few steps closer, raised his weapon, and pointed it directly at Maxine's head.

Everybody scattered. Only Hugh stood his ground.

"I was a happy lawyer before I ever worked for her," said Billy. "I had harmless dreams and ambitions like anybody else. All I wanted was to learn how to be good at medical malpractice. Instead of teaching me what she knew, she made my life hell; humiliated me, insulted me, treated me like crap! And when she finally gave me something important to do, she sandbagged me and stole everything that was rightfully mine!"

"Put the gun down, Billy," urged Hugh. "We can talk about it outside."

"The time for talking is over," said Billy, edging even closer. "Now's the time for killing."

"Don't do it!"

"Bye-bye, Ms. Doggette."

Hugh launched himself at Billy and struck him the instant he pulled the trigger. Orange flame flashed from one of the barrels with a deafening roar.

Billy missed Maxine by a mile and hit the anesthesia machine instead. The inhalant canisters blew up, spraying glass and metal fragments far and wide. Clear and colorless liquids poured from the wreckage and splattered onto the floor.

"Get away from me, Dr. Montrose!" shouted Billy as he grappled with Hugh. His considerable height gave him an overwhelming advantage and he sent Hugh sprawling into the microscope. "I've got nothing against you! I'm here for Ms. Doggette!"

"Billy!" yelled Hugh, disentangling himself from cables and counterweights. "Listen to me! It's not too late! Put the gun down!"

Billy raised his shotgun again and held it within inches of Maxine's open head. The liquids on the floor, however, were rapidly vaporizing and filled the atmosphere with highly potent anesthetic gases. He blinked hard and his hands shook. Even so, the muzzles never wavered far from their target. He was so close, he couldn't possibly miss.

Hugh hurled himself at Billy a second time and, like the first, crashed into him just as he pulled the trigger. A blast roared from the other barrel. All four bags of packed cells hanging on the IV pole exploded, showering the operating room with blood.

The gases were now overpowering. Billy tottered around. His eyes rolled up into his head and his lids fluttered closed. He collapsed onto the back table, sending dozens of instruments clanging to the floor.

Hugh saw Richard, Val, and Lori crumple to their knees, coughing and fighting for air. Moments later he felt an intense burning his own throat and a terrifying sense of breathlessness. His legs gave out from underneath him and he yielded to swirling clouds of blackness.

35

"For God's sake, somebody get me out of this thing!"

Hugh's eyes flickered open. When the fuzziness cleared he realized he was lying on the cold, hard floor of the operating room, gazing at Maxine's shaved head above him. It was still firmly clamped in the Mayfield, one pin embedded in the forehead and two in the back.

When he looked around he was shocked by what he saw. The room looked as if a torrential rainstorm had just passed overhead, drenching it not with water but with sweet-smelling blood. Everything was dripping red: ceiling, overhead kettle-drum lights, OR table, microscope. Bodies were littered around, unmoving in the shambles. He recognized Richard slumped over the back instrument table. His arms dangled towards the floor. Blood was even dripping from his fingertips. Val was crumpled against the pedestal of the microscope with Lori twisted into a knot underneath her. The anesthesiologist was stretched out near the shattered remains of his machine.

Hugh realized what a crowded marketplace must look like in the aftermath of a suicide bombing. First he ran his hands over his body, checking to see if any of the blood was his own. When he was satisfied he was unharmed he willed himself to his feet. A hammer was pounding an anvil behind his eyes. He steadied himself against the suction machine and waited until the pain eased.

Maxine had pulled out her breathing tube and ripped off her drapes. Now she lay spread-eagled on the table, naked and exposed, her head firmly locked in place. The trapdoor in her skull was still open. Her brain was in plain view, pulsating rapidly.

When Hugh saw Billy propped against a wall, a shotgun across his knees, everything suddenly returned to his memory: the weird sight of him wearing street clothes in an operating room, the first shotgun blast shattering the anesthesia machine, the second ripping apart the bags of blood.

"My head's stuck!" moaned Maxine. "I can't move it! Somebody help me!"

Hugh took a deep breath. The air was fouled by anesthetic gases that irritated his windpipe and made him cough.

"Who's there?" cried Maxine.

"It's me," croaked Hugh, fighting a wave of nausea. "Dr. Montrose."

"Thank God!" she said, her healthy eyeball swiveling towards him. "What happened? Is that Billy over there?"

Billy was snoring loudly. His face was covered with red spots as if he had developed a fulminant case of measles.

"That's him alright," said Hugh.

"What's he doing with a shotgun? Oh my God! He went postal, didn't he?"

"You could say that."

"And he killed all these people!" wailed Maxine.

Hugh was quite certain nobody was dead. When Billy destroyed the anesthesia machine, its inhalants escaped and merely sent everyone in the room to sleep. The spikes penetrating Maxine's scalp acted as a painful stimulus and she had been the first to wake up. He was about to inform her that the four people scattered across the floor would soon be rousing when she abruptly cut him off.

"Why can't I move my head?" she asked. Her right hand wandered up to her craniotomy opening. Before Hugh could stop her she poked a finger into her brain. Her opposite arm shot into the air as if it belonged to a puppet on a string.

"What's the matter with my arm?" said Maxine, staring at the curious way it was jerking around.

"*No!*" shouted Hugh, horrified. "Your operation! It's not finished yet!"

"What do you mean?"

"Your head's still open!"

Puzzled, Maxine poked around some more. When it dawned on her what the squishiness was she shrieked with terror and withdrew her finger. Her arm dropped to the table with a thud.

Hugh lurched towards the wall phone and slipped in a puddle of sticky blood. He regained his balance, grabbed the receiver, and called the operator. Within seconds he was speaking to the nursing supervisor.

"Page the on-call back-up team to come to the hospital STAT!" he shouted over and above the ruckus Maxine was making. "I need an anesthesiologist, circulator, and a scrub tech! *Now!*"

The supervisor hesitated before she responded, no doubt peering through her reading glasses and checking the clipboard she always carried around with her. "But it says here you already have a team, Dr. Montrose," she said flatly. "You're not allowed to have two."

"Mine's asleep! I need one that'll stay awake!"

"Sleeping during an operation? I'll have to file a report about that."

"Call hospital security too! And the police! Hurry!"

Hugh slammed down the phone and stumbled towards Maxine. Another wave of nausea suddenly hit him. He doubled over, put his hands on his knees, and threw up what little food he'd eaten at the restaurant. When he was finished, he wiped his mouth and slowly straightened up again. "Help's on the way," he told Maxine once he had the strength to speak again.

"Get me out of this horrid thing!" she screamed, grabbing the Mayfield with both hands and shaking it. "I can't stand it anymore!"

Hugh furiously reviewed his options. If he released her from the clamp she might stampede out of the operating room in a panic. He imagined the ludicrous image of a stark naked medical malpractice nurse attorney rampaging through the hospital, her brains spilling from her skull like beans from a tin can. No, not the wisest option. Neither could he dispatch her back to sleep. The anesthesia machine had been totally destroyed. He supposed he could haul one over from another room and hook her up to it. No—

far too risky, he decided. If Maxine ever had the notion to sue him for practicing anesthesia without the proper credentials he wouldn't have a leg to stand on.

The best course of action, he figured, was to stay put until help arrived.

With nothing better to do, Hugh grabbed a bloody drape off the floor and covered Maxine with it. "The aneurysm's clipped now," he said, thinking the news might calm her down a bit. "The worst is over. In a few minutes another anesthesiologist will get here and put you back to sleep."

"You're doing this on purpose!" shouted Maxine, anything but calm. "You're keeping me clamped because you hate me! Admit it!"

Hugh knew there was only one response to such an accusation; a comeback so apropos he was sure that even Maxine would get the point. "You're wrong about that," he said. "I can assure you, it's . . ."

Maxine met his glassy gaze. "It's what?" she sobbed. "*What?*"

"It's *nothing personal.*"

Maxine's screaming reached a new level of intensity. "It feels personal to me!" she bawled. "Get it off! What are you waiting for? An apology? Okay! I'm sorry for suing you! Is that what you want to hear? I only did it because you said I was dreadful! I *despise* that word. I couldn't help reacting the way I did!"

When she realized she wouldn't get what she wanted by shouting, she took some deep breaths, wrestled for control, and tried something new.

"Listen to me, Dr. Montrose," she said, a little quieter and more measured now. "Let me be perfectly honest with you. Lately I've been thinking about making a change in my life. I have to do *something*. How can I keep going on like this? But I don't know even know where to begin." She reached out with her arms and spread her fingers as far as they would go. "Now get me out of this damned clamp!" she implored him. "*Please!*"

Hugh stared at Maxine, hardly believing what he'd just heard. Did The Dog just admit she wanted to make a change in her life? Was her tough outer crust crumbling under pressure, revealing a frightened little girl inside? It certainly looked that way, if only for a moment, and he felt compelled to react in a positive way.

"Okay," said Hugh. "I'll unclamp you as long as you promise not to run away. Agreed?"

"Agreed!"

"Do you promise to keep your promise?"

"Yes!"

"Maybe I should have you sign something first."

"*Get on with it!*"

"Okay. Here goes . . ." Gripping the Mayfield with his left hand, Hugh first released the complicated system of joints and screws that kept it connected to the operating table. The mechanical arm fell away and suddenly he was carrying the combined weight of Maxine's head and the clamp. "Take some more deep breaths. In . . . out. In . . . out. Ready?"

"Ready!"

Hugh supported Maxine's head with his right hand, then twisted the main screw counter-clockwise with his left, released the clamp, and lifted the three spikes out of her scalp. "There!" he said, laying the ugly contraption aside. "Better now?"

Maxine shuddered with relief.

"Good," said Hugh, encouraged that she wasn't making a wild dash for the hills. He had her scoot down on the operating table and slipped a pillow under her head to make her more comfortable. "Everything's going to be okay. You'll soon be well again." He instinctively took Maxine's cold, bony hand into his own and gave it a reassuring squeeze.

Maxine started to shiver. She screwed her good eye tightly shut and began to whisper. Hugh drew close until his ear was inches from her lips. The sound of shouts in the hallway outside was growing louder and he had to strain to hear her words.

"I'm so afraid . . ." she was repeating over and over again. "I'm so afraid . . ."

36

When the new anesthesiologist and the rest of the surgical team arrived, Maxine was quickly dispatched back to sleep and Hugh closed up her head. While he was busy sewing her various tissue layers back together the bloody bodies around him arose from the dead one by one and staggered outside. Billy was arrested in the hallway, read his Miranda rights, and hauled off to jail in handcuffs.

Maxine's postoperative course was plagued by complications. Pressure built up in her head and Hugh was forced to insert a ventriculostomy to drain away the excess CSF. The arteries at the base of her brain went into spasm and she suffered a devastating stroke, losing use of the left side of her body. On the sixth post-operative day she oozed infected pus from her wound, proving that people should never poke a finger into their own brains unless they're wearing a sterile glove.

As Maxine suffered each complication, Hugh gave it all the attention it deserved. When she became infected, he removed her bone flap. The source of the problem thus eliminated, her fevers abated and she quickly improved. Unfortunately she was left with an ugly defect on the side of her head; a cave big enough inside for bats to breed. She couldn't have it repaired until a few months had passed and every lingering bug had been wiped out with antibiotics. In the meantime the eyesore remained and drew awkward stares wherever she went. The overlying skin pulsated with her heartbeat and people were able to judge the state of her emotions by monitoring the rate at which it did so.

When the infection was gone, Hugh took her to surgery for a third time to remove the ventriculostomy and replace it with a shunt—a permanent tube that allowed CSF to run down to her abdominal cavity where it was absorbed back into her system. He treated the spasm in her arteries by closely managing her blood pressure and fixed her carotid-cavernous fistula with his catheters. Physical and occupational therapists were consulted. They helped her out of bed and got her going again.

As emotionally traumatizing these complications were for Maxine, they paled in comparison to how she felt when she learned that Billy had destroyed her home and her office. Even worse, Minimus was missing. She had last seen him in her office early in the morning on the day Clegg testified. She told him—like she always did whenever she left for the courthouse—that animals weren't allowed to go to court. To make up for it (Didn't the wronged always deserve compensation?) she left him with a bowl of Honey Nut Cheerios piled extra high and plenty of Perrier water to enjoy while she was gone. Nobody had seen him since. The fire chief came to the hospital to tell her that her dog could never have survived the inferno and, since he was so small, his remains were not likely to be recovered either. Maxine wailed with anguish and fell into a deep depression.

Maxine had neither family nor friends to console her. When the doctors and nurses saw her lying alone in her room they felt sorry for her and went out of their way to treat her well. Paradoxically, the nicer they were, the deeper her depression became. She had spent her entire life dogging medical people like them to death and yet here they were, putting all that aside for the sake of their common humanity. Their kindness made her own legal profession seem so petty and vindictive.

A week later, the fire chief showed up in Hugh's office carrying something in his hand that looked like a diseased and bedraggled Mexican sewer rat. After cleaning off layers of dirt and ash Hugh recognized Minimus. Miraculously, he was alive and unharmed. Somehow, so said the chief, he had crawled into a storage closet where a powerful sprinkler right above him had kept the flames at bay. He had lived off the food and water Maxine had left him and yapped when he heard firemen clearing away the mountains of debris around him. Flagrantly breaking all hospital rules regarding animal visitation, Hugh took him to the intensive care unit and returned him to Maxine. She hugged her beloved Chihuahua and sobbed with relief for hours.

A month after her aneurysm surgery Maxine was transferred to the Bellegrove Rehabilitation Center. When she arrived she was dog-tired and hardly capable of managing for herself. For some unknown reason her hair was growing back extremely slowly and did nothing to hide her scars and the sunken crater. The nurses didn't recognize her even though they had seen and spoken to her many times in the past. A team of physical and occupational therapists helped her make good progress with respect to her physical impairments. First she learned how to use a walker and then graduated to a cane. Her appetite returned and she regained some of the weight she had lost. Mentally, though, she was a shadow of her former impetuous self. She spent most of the time huddled in a chair by the window, clinging to Minimus and sullenly watching the grey clouds slowly drift past overhead.

After she was discharged from rehab she returned to Castle Doggette and saw for herself the results of Billy's rampage. She was heartbroken by the scene that greeted her. All that remained of the stately building were blackened walls, a portion of the basement, and the adjoining garage. Even now, two months after the fire, the stinging smell of smoke still lingered in the air. Her collection of videocassette depositions—the possession she treasured the most— was gone forever, a twisted tangle of molten plastic buried somewhere beneath the ashes. So were most of her clothes, perfumes, and precious jewelry. She bought a few supplies from a local store, suppressed her phobias from her childhood, and moved into what was left of the basement.

Billy was charged with attempted murder and arson. He was held in the downtown King County Jail pending trial. The evidence against him was overwhelming and few people doubted he would be sentenced to a lengthy prison term in the state penitentiary. At first he spent his days in his cell shouting that his victims—an ugly woman with red hair and an even uglier dog with virtually no hair at all—had both deserved to die. Later on, when the seriousness of his predicament eventually sunk into his feeble brain, he finally did what Maxine had always feared most: betray her to the authorities. He showed his prosecutors the video tapes and black leather notebook he had taken from her desk drawer that proved her involvement in extortion and corruption.

As Maxine's medical problems gradually improved with time, her legal problems worsened. A wide-ranging investigation into her business practices was launched and dozens of healthcare professionals were interviewed, including Henry Harrison, the anesthesiologist, and Giles Thompson, the neurosurgeon. Endless stories of blackmail and bribery poured into the public domain like a river of raw sewage and the outlook for Maxine's future looked very doubtful indeed. Things grew even worse when the Washington State Bar Association began proceedings to disbar her.

As she contemplated her dramatic downfall, Maxine would often sit on a chair in front of her ruined castle, cradle Minimus in her arms, and smoke endless cigarettes. On one of those days—a Sunday afternoon it was—an old Chevy Chevelle from the sixties rolled up her driveway, a cloud of blue smoke slipstreaming along behind, and pulled up in front of her. The engine coughed and spluttered, then idled with a loud gurgling noise. The driver, a dirty young man with greasy hair, satanic tattoos, and body piercing rolled down the window and looked at her with uncertainty in his eyes.

"Ms. Doggette?"

"Yes?"

"Is that really you?"

"Of course it is," she said, sighing with frustration. Her baldness was throwing everybody off these days. "Who are you?"

"Don't you recognize me?"

Maxine shaded her eyes against the sun. "Aren't you Jake, one of my process servers?"

"No. I'm Jake, your *favorite* process server!"

Which was probably true, Maxine privately conceded. She used to love the way this weirdo dope fiend invaded the front yards of freshly-minted defendants on their weekends off and humiliated the shit out of them in front of their families. Nothing wrong with a smidgen of drama at the beginning of a case, she always believed. Just enough to give her victims a tantalizing taste of things to come.

"Why are *you* bothering me?" she asked.

"I have something special just for you! Let me see if I can find it." Jake rummaged through a pile papers in the back seat and selected a batch that had been stapled together. "Here it is! Congratulations, Ms. Doggette! Now *you're* being served!"

Maxine flung away her cigarette, dumped Minimus, and stood up. She snatched up a nearby cane and hobbled over to the car. "Is this some kind of sick joke?" she demanded.

"No, Ms. Doggette," said Jake. "There's a couple called Gary and Julie Winter who've filed a lawsuit against you. Says so right here in the complaint: *professional negligence, legal malpractice, failure to name the correct defendant.* Failure to name the correct defendant? How did you let *that* happen? Aren't lawyers supposed to name everybody in sight, then gradually let them off the hook one by one when the facts become clearer? Called the shotgun approach, if I remember correctly. Thought about going to law school myself once—"

"Give me those!" snapped Maxine, reaching out. When Jake handed over the papers, she quickly scanned through the first few lines.

SUMMONS

IN THE SUPERIOR COURT OF WASHINGTON FOR THE COUNTY OF KING

JULIE WINTER AND GARY WINTER, wife and husband, plaintiffs v. MAXINE DOGGETTE, individually.

TO THE DEFENDANT:

A lawsuit has been started against you in the above-entitled Court by JULIE WINTER AND GARY WINTER, plaintiffs.

"Outrageous!" shouted Maxine, crumpling the papers in her hand and throwing them away. "They can't sue *me*!"

"Looks like they just did," said Jake, striking a match and lighting a cigarette. Throwing Maxine a disparaging look, he added, "And if you want my humble opinion, it's not hard to see what gave them the idea."

"How dare you speak to me like that!"

"Don't get pissed off with me, lady," said Jake, blowing a cloud of smoke towards the roof. "I'm only doing my job. Speaking of which . . ." He jerked his head towards the papers in the back seat. "Lots of other lawsuits to deliver before quitting time. Got to go. Have a great afternoon!"

Jake drove off, leaving behind a puddle of black oil on the driveway.

Maxine stared after him, shocked that after suing thousands of people in her lifetime somebody was now, for the first time ever, actually going after her. Unbelievable! After all the beastly things that had happened to her recently, this was the last straw!

Remembering where Gary and Julie Winter lived, she stormed to her Rolls in a rage.

The Winter home was more run-down than ever before. There were weeds and peeling paint everywhere. A large FOR SALE BANK OWNED sign was posted outside. When Maxine screeched to a halt in the driveway she spotted the family near the old camper at the bottom of the garden. Julie was in her wheelchair, enjoying the sunshine and sharing a joke with her children. The lower half of a man's body, dressed in mechanic's overalls and boots, was sticking out from underneath the engine. An open toolbox lay by his feet. The family's chocolate Labrador, Rolo, was lying on the grass nearby, chewing a bone.

When Julie spotted Maxine limping towards her she stopped laughing and frowned as if she wasn't sure who she was without her trademark red hair. Rolo sniffed the air and growled. Gary slid out from underneath the camper and struggled to his feet.

"Maxine?" he said, wiping his hands on a dirty rage and throwing it away. "How you've changed!"

"Restrain that animal before he bites me!" said Maxine, pointing her cane at Rolo.

"Changed for sure," responded Gary. "But only on the outside. What are *you* doing here?"

"I demand you drop your lawsuit against me!"

"So you've just been served, have you, Maxine? Or should I call you Defendant Doggette now?"

"Don't get cheeky with me!"

"I can't talk to you," said Gary, unafraid. "At least, not directly. Don't you remember? It's one of your stupid rules. Plaintiffs and defendants aren't allowed to—"

"I don't have time for childish games!"

Now Julie spoke up. "We're suing you because we need the money," she said. "Since we were unable to get a single penny out of Dr. Montrose's insurance company, we decided to try yours instead. After all, you *did* sue the wrong doctor."

"How was I supposed to know about the spinal fluid protein?" protested Maxine. "That maggot Billy Barlow kept the results to himself and never told me! I can't be responsible for the harebrained stunt of an imbecile!"

"Nevertheless, you're ultimately responsible," said Gary. "We put our trust in you and you let us down. Now we're entitled to compensation. Our new lawyer suggested fourteen million dollars."

Maxine staggered backwards. "*Fourteen million?*" she cried, leaning heavily on her cane to steady herself. "No jury would ever dream of awarding you that much money!"

"Why not? It's the same amount you demanded from Dr. Montrose."

"That's different!" shouted Maxine. "He's a doctor. I'm a lawyer."

"Why should *that* matter?"

"Lawyers aren't obliged to play by the same rules as everybody else!"

Julie nudged the joystick on her wheelchair and turned to confront Maxine. "You may think you're something special," she said, her eyes smoldering with hostility, "but as far as I'm concerned, you're nothing but a fraud; one who couldn't even win a slam-dunk case for a paralyzed client. What does *that* say about your professional abilities? Hopefully you're not too deranged to know."

To be sure they were biting words, especially coming from somebody who was usually as mild-mannered as Julie. Maxine lost all semblance of control. With a terrifying howl, she raised her cane into the air and attacked her. Gary, Patrick, and Jennifer jumped into the fray, locked their arms around her, and dragged her away. Rolo chased after her, barking furiously and nipping at her heels.

"Get out of here!" shouted Gary, shoving Maxine in the direction of her car and hurling her cane after her. "You invited yourself into our lives. Now we're inviting you out again. Never come back! Do you hear me? *Never!*"

Maxine snatched her cane off the ground and shook it at the Winters. "You're making a big mistake!" she said. "You won't get a dime out of me! Your lawyer had better realize who he's up against! I know how to deal with my enemies! Just ask any doctor!"

"*Go!*"

"All right, I'm going!"

Maxine limped away as fast as her weakened legs could carry her. When she reached her Rolls Royce she leant against the hood for a few moments to catch her breath and let her pounding brain slow down. While she was recuperating she saw Gary get into the camper, jam a key into the ignition, and crank the engine. An almighty KA-THONK startled her. The camper shuddered violently and plume of smoke billowed from the engine. Thick black oil poured from somewhere underneath and formed a small lake on the lawn.

Maxine stood up straight and cupped her hands around her mouth. "Serves you right, you *jerks*!" she yelled. Then she climbed into her car, slammed the door shut, and returned to the ruins she called home.

37

That night, Castle Doggette erupted with the noise of mass destruction—smashing plates, splintering wood, and shattering glass interspersed amongst agonized howls and the crudest of cursing. The few things that had somehow survived the fire were now being finished off in a relentless orgy of violence. An elephant bag with a wire mesh window and padded walls flew out of an upper window and disintegrated on the patio below, kicking up clouds of billowing ash. It was followed by piles of ruined clothes, a bent ceiling fan, and a badly damaged mattress. Later on, a Rolls Royce Phantom crashed through the back wall of the garage, sending chunks of wooden framing and sheet rock flying through the air. A bald woman was clutching the steering wheel, wailing the lamentations of a patient who had just seen their hospital bill for the first time. The car roared across a patio, careened into a swimming pool with a gigantic splash, and sent a tidal wave to the far end. As it slowly sank, a window opened and the woman wriggled out, climbed from the pool, and staggered back to the house.

After that, things settled down. Somewhere inside the basement of the castle a door slammed shut and a naked light bulb switched on, casting shadows from a small window. Heart-wrenching sobs pierced the cool air and were carried far across the glassy smooth reservoir below. As the hours passed by they gradually faded away and silence finally reigned amongst the old growth sentinels that towered towards the stars.

When dawn eventually broke in the east, Mount Rainier coalesced from the darkness and its pristine glaciers bloomed pink in the rays of the rising sun.

The basement door fell off its hinges with a loud crash and Maxine stepped outside, a cigarette hanging from her lips. Her eyes were inflamed and swollen, her clothes dirty and torn. In her hands she was carrying the charred remains of a big, boxy computer. One end of a rope tied around it while the other was fastened to her ankle. She slowly limped across the lawn towards the reservoir. Minimus followed, his big black eyes filled with sadness.

Maxine suddenly whipped around. "Go back inside!" she told him harshly, speaking around her cigarette and sending puffs of smoke sputtering into the crisp morning air. "You can't come where I'm going."

Minimus whined.

"That won't work either!" she shouted at him. "You're better off without me!"

Minimus edged tentatively forward.

Maxine stepped onto the wooden dock and advanced along its length. When she reached the end, she stopped and surveyed the reservoir. It had been slowly drained over the last few weeks and now the water was only a couple of feet deep. Not a chance of drowning today, she figured—something that should be obvious to any human being, although hopefully not to a dog with a brain the size of a plump raisin.

"This is where we part company," Maxine told Minimus who had stubbornly followed her. "You needn't worry about your future. I've left you everything in my will. You'll be well taken care of."

Minimus cocked his head and frowned.

Maxine took one final drag from her cigarette. "Farewell, Minimus!" she cried. "Farewell, cruel world!" She screwed her eyes tightly shut and stepped off the dock. Instead of being pulled into the abyss by the computer, however, she landed on her feet in shallow water, the cigarette still hanging from her mouth.

With a desperate howl, Minimus flung himself off the end of the dock. He plopped into the water below, shifted his little legs into high gear, and paddled towards his mistress. By the time he reached her he was panting hard.

"Minimus!" she cried, spitting out her cigarette. "Let me die alone!"

He propelled himself around in circles, yapping furiously. His agitation quickly exhausted him and he started to sink.

Maxine let the computer tumble from her hands and plucked him out of the water. "You would risk your own life to save mine?" she asked, her voice trembling with emotion. "You must really care for me!"

For a few moments Minimus lay in the palm of her hand like a clump of soggy seaweed, catching his breath. When he had sufficiently recovered, he looked up at his mistress with great depth and resonance behind his eyes. Whatever he was thinking, he gave her a strange, unfamiliar feeling of warmth inside. Was it love? She had a sudden urge to open up and share everything with him. What difference did it make if he was only a tiny Chihuahua? She was so deprived of companionship, he could have been a dung beetle and she would have felt the same way.

"Oh Minimus!" she said, choking back tears. "Everything has gone to the dogs. Absolutely *everything*! My home and office are in ruins and my business is finished. My bigass hole—" She pointed to her healing craniotomy wound to make sure he knew which hole she meant. "—freaks anybody who comes too close. The entire world is after my blood. I'm being prosecuted for all kinds of crimes and the Washington State Bar Association wants to disbar me. And my clients! Or rather, my *ex*-clients! Boy, are they pissed!"

Minimus licked her hand with his little pink tongue.

"Why, oh why did my parents have to die in that plane crash long ago?" she continued. "Ever since then, I've been forced to endure nothing but rejection and loneliness. You, of all dogs, should know what that's like. Remember the Humane Society?"

Fear filled Minimus' eyes and he shuddered.

"I'm sorry," she said with a sigh, bending down and kissing the tuft of hair on his forehead. "I didn't mean to scare you like that. Let's go inside and see if I can find some Cheerios. There's nothing more pitiful than a hungry Chihuahua."

Dragging the computer along the bottom of the reservoir with her ankle and holding Minimus securely in her hand, Maxine slowly waded back to shore.

38

Hugh lounged in his office with his feet propped on his desk. He was holding a rag doll in his hands. It bore an uncanny resemblance to Maxine, right down to the curly red hair and the brightly colored clothes.

Denmark had found it on a fishing trip to the Caribbean, added a black patch over the right eye, and sent it to him. He enclosed a knitting needle and a witty note telling him that the doll was just the thing to help him overcome the lingering effects of juris psychosis.

To inflict pain, stick needle all the way through, he wrote. *For best results, simultaneously mutter curses under your breath.*

After Hugh's trial was over, his obsession with practicing defensive medicine melted away like pack ice in summer. He started liking his patients again and treating the Joyce Parkers of the world with the same honesty and respect he'd always shown them in the past. MRI and CT scanners that had been threatening to blow their gaskets from excessive use resumed a regular schedule. The length of hospital stays shortened, the ICU was returned to patients who actually needed it, and health insurance companies worried a little less about imminent bankruptcy.

There was a knock at the door.

"Come in!"

Sandra, the office manager, appeared. "You asked me to bring Ms. Doggette to you as soon as she arrived for her clinic appointment," she said.

"So I did," said Hugh. "Thank you."

Maxine pushed past Sandra and limped in. She was wearing a drab grey pullover with a matching skirt; no sign of her usual designer clothes, make-up, or jewels. Not even a hint of perfume. Her hair was still short, her black patch was gone, and her right eye was back to normal. The sunken area on the side of her skull pulsated smoothly. A half-smoked cigarette hung from her pale lips. Minimus was peering out of a pocket, his tiny black nose twitching as he explored the air in the unfamiliar office.

"There's just one thing left for you to do," she said. "Fix this damned hole in my head. After that, we'll be done with each other forever."

Hugh stood up, approached Maxine, and gave her a friendly smile. "Thank you for coming," he said, clasping both hands behind his back and studying her head wound with the eye of a seasoned expert. "Your infection is completely gone," he observed. "How's your double vision?"

"Gone too."

"And the whooshing sound?"

"Look," said Maxine impatiently, "I'm not here to . . . Good grief!" Her mouth dropped open and the cigarette fell from her lips. "What's *that*?"

Hugh picked up the doll from his desk. "It's you."

"Me?"

"That's right. Another Maxine Doggette. A true replica in every detail. I've even given her your name. She's a gift from John Denmark. He told me to stick a knitting needle through her if I ever lose my grip on reality again. Supposed to cause you excruciating pain and make me feel better. Hey, let's see if it works!" Keeping one eye trained on the real Maxine, Hugh pierced the stuffed one's abdomen. "Feel anything?"

"That's not funny!"

He withdrew the needle and tried again, this time simultaneously muttering curses under his breath. "How about now?"

Maxine snatched the doll away from Hugh. She was about to throw it away when a tortured look suddenly filled her eyes and she held onto it instead. "Please don't stick her again."

"It's only a doll."

"I don't care! It upsets me!"

Her reaction surprised Hugh and he wondered what it meant. "Ok, I won't then," he said, returning to his chair behind the desk. Obviously time to change the subject. "I have a question for you. Do you have any recollection of what happened in the middle of your aneurysm surgery?"

"No," replied Maxine. A string of drool oozed from the weak side of her mouth and reminded Hugh of the late Professor Mortimer. Her look of embarrassment suggested she knew what he was thinking.

"So you don't remember waking up with your head immobilized in a Mayfield clamp?"

"Definitely not," said Maxine, quickly wiping the drool away with the back of her hand. "I've been told Billy walked in and tried to kill me with a shotgun. Hardly surprising he failed. That nitwit couldn't do anything right. But I don't have any personal recollections. Why do you ask?"

Hugh paused as he organized his thoughts. "During the brief time you were awake," he eventually continued, "you said some things . . ."

Maxine's eyes widened with alarm. "What kind of things?"

"For one, you apologized for suing me."

"Did I? That's strange. I've never apologized for anything before."

"You also confessed that you wanted to change your life but didn't know how."

Judging by Maxine's sudden pinched, withdrawn expression, Hugh knew he had struck a sensitive nerve. Hoping to capitalize on the moment, he quickly made his point. "I have a proposal for you."

"What kind of proposal?"

"A partnership."

Maxine choked. "A *partnership*? You and me? How absurd! We're complete opposites! What on earth are you talking about?"

Hugh returned behind his desk and took his seat. "I agree it sounds improbable," he said, "but give me a chance to explain. I've been spending a lot of time thinking about a pet project of mine lately. My idea is to establish a non-profit organization that sets a national standard for the quality of neurosurgical experts."

Maxine gingerly lowered herself into a chair opposite and sat the doll in her lap. "So you weren't impressed by the late Professor Charles Mortimer," she said, looking chagrin.

"No, I wasn't," said Hugh, finding himself under the unsettling impression that he was speaking to two Maxines, one large and the other small. "How *did* you dig up that old relic anyhow?"

"My usual testifier, Odeus Horman, referred me to him."

"You must have been really desperate."

"I was."

Hugh was encouraged by the conversation's civil tone. "Anyhow," he continued, hoping it would continue, "the main idea behind my organization is to provide lawyers on either side of a lawsuit a reliable source of neurosurgeons certified bullshit-free by their peers."

Maxine gave a skeptical grunt. "You'll never stop medical experts lying in exchange for money . . . or other things."

"Perhaps not," said Hugh. "But maybe we can compete with them."

"How?"

"By practicing and promoting a strict code of conduct," answered Hugh. He held up a finger the way he had seen Judge Jenkins do it in court. "One . . . *our* expert opinions will be based on generally accepted standards of care and the scientific literature." Another finger flew into the air. "Two . . . *our* experts will be in active practice. Three . . ." He raised his third finger. ". . . *our* experts must be board certified. Four . . . *our* experts may not earn more than a certain small proportion of their gross practice income performing medical-legal work."

"That would definitely make it harder for the Odeus Hormans of this world to stay in business," said Maxine.

Hugh leaned forward and rested his elbows on his desk. "I can think of all kinds of ways we could put such a society to work," he said. "For instance, we could give plaintiff lawyers the information they need in order to make a decision whether or not to proceed with a case. Don't you think they would prefer to know the odds of winning ahead of time, instead of risking a bunch of money on something that could likely be a bust? Or if a case *does* go forward, members could provide expert testimony for either side. Since their membership in the organization and certification as a neurosurgical expert are admissible in a court of law, having a legitimate expert on one's team could give a lawyer a distinct advantage over an opponent who doesn't. Wouldn't you agree?"

"I see what you're getting at," said Maxine thoughtfully. "But how do you keep doctors you don't like from becoming members? Suppose somebody like Odeus Horman wants to join."

"I considered that too," said Hugh. "Applicants must be vetted and sponsored by existing members. The board of directors accepts all those who qualify and certifies them as neurosurgical experts. Membership automatically expires after every five years and a renewal application has to be submitted. That way, the rank and file's ideology should stay relatively pure."

"So basically you're proposing a national organization that offers accreditation to neurosurgical experts," said Maxine. "But what does it have to do with me? You mentioned a partnership."

"So I did," said Hugh. He stood up, stepped to his window, and looked outside. The brick wall across the alley looked the same as it always did so he turned away and gazed at Maxine instead. He spotted her brain pulsating against her soft scalp a little faster now. "Putting this organization together and making it run smoothly will be a monumental task," he told her. "There will be strong opposition from trial lawyers. They'll do everything they can to quash it no matter how much sense it makes. I have neither the time nor the expertise to fight back. You, on the other hand, are eminently qualified."

"You want *me* to help you?"

"Yes. You have the experience and inside knowledge to beat trial lawyers at their own game and get the job done. That would make you an invaluable asset for our organization. You can use whatever tactics you wish as long as they're legal and your loyalties remain with us. If you're looking for an opportunity to change your life, then I'm offering it to you. I could also help you through any difficulties along the way. What do you think?"

Maxine glanced down at Minimus as if looking for advice from her little friend, then fixed Hugh firmly with her gaze. "Nobody has ever gone out of their way to be kind to me," said Maxine, her quickening brain pulsations betraying her rising emotions. "At least not since I was eight years old. So why you? And why now?"

Hugh sighed. Never one who liked to be sentimental about anything, he had hoped he wouldn't have to explain himself. "Alright, Maxine," he said reluctantly. "Honestly, I don't think you're as bad as you seem. By forgiving you in my heart and helping you to turn your life around, I'm betting I can find an ounce of goodness somewhere inside you and coax it out into the open."

Maxine probably recognized the truth when she heard it and after decades of self-loathing it must have shaken the foundations of her soul. Her eyes suddenly became watery and she buried her face into her hands.

"The old Maxine Doggette everybody loved to hate might morph into one they might actually like," continued Hugh after a poignant silence. "Maybe you'll even make some friends. Doesn't that sound more appealing than staying the way you are?"

Maxine peaked out from between trembling fingers and nodded. Her brain hammered against the inside of her scalp as if trying to climb out.

"So you would like to join us?"

She nodded again, this time more vigorously.

"Splendid!" cried Hugh. "In that case, let's put the past behind us and start building a new, improved Maxine Doggette today." He helped her to her feet. "We can begin by repairing that God-awful hole in your head. Would you like that?"

"Yes . . . *Please!*"

"Not a problem." He guided her towards the door. "Let's go outside and ask Sandra to set a date for surgery. And when she's done that, we can talk some more about our new organization. I've had a bunch of new ideas recently and was wondering if I could get your opinion about one or two of them. Perhaps we could go down to the local café and—"

"Dr. Montrose?" Maxine meekly interrupted.

"Call me Hugh."

"I was wondering . . . Hugh . . ." She broke off and wiped a tear away from her eye.

"Yes?"

Maxine picked the doll out of her lap and held it up. "I was wondering if you would let me have this."

Her request puzzled Hugh. The doll obviously signified something important to her but he had no idea what. Resisting the temptation to pry, he gave her a pleasant smile instead.

"Of course you can have it," he said. "What use is it to me? The darn thing doesn't even work. Denmark should demand a refund."

"Thank you!" She slipped off the eye patch and gave it back to Hugh. "You can keep this," she said. "She looks better without it."

"Agreed," said Hugh. "And you'd better call her something else. This planet isn't big enough for two Maxine Doggettes."

"I've already chosen another name."

"You have?"

"Yes," said Maxine, breaking into a pleasant smile of her own—the first one Hugh had ever seen. "I'll call her Rosie."

39

Ten years after honoring Hugh with the Radcliffe Trophy for his work with cerebral aneurysms, BRAIN awarded it to Doctors Against Medical Litigation Abuse (DAMLA), a non-profit organization he founded shortly after the conclusion of *Winter vs. Montrose*.

DAMLA was a dazzling success. In the beginning, it simply offered certification to neurosurgeons who gave expert opinions for either side in disputes related to neurosurgery. In return, they pledged to abide by a well-defined code of conduct and give only high quality testimony that was consistent with national standards of care. As soon as DAMLA's members were being called to the stand and their credentials presented to juries, the harlot testifiers could no longer compete and crawled back under the rocks from whence they came. Odeus Horman was among those who found themselves without work and was forced to evaluate workers' compensation claims for the rest of his career.

DAMLA soon expanded its membership to include physicians from all specialties, not only neurosurgeons. Thousands of them saw a chance for real change in the medical liability crisis and joined in a gratifying display of support. A national movement was born and became powerful enough to challenge the rampant litigation abuse that had been running amok for decades. The end result was a significant drop in the number of frivolous lawsuits, expensive trials, biased judges, clueless juries, prostitute testifiers, and jackpot verdicts. Direct beneficiaries included plaintiffs who had valid claims and defendants who were innocent of negligence. The public viewed DAMLA as a positive non-partisan force that served the cause of justice.

One big surprise was DAMLA's effect on the practice of defensive medicine. With their future more secure, physicians were wasting far fewer dollars trying to protect themselves from lawsuits. Health insurance companies were given a reprieve and reduced their premiums. Family budgets breathed a sigh of relief. Medicare's life expectancy was extended a few years, giving politicians extra time to hash out a solution. A modicum of sanity was introduced into America's healthcare system and the country pulled back from the brink of disaster.

Like the decade before, the BRAIN special award ceremony was being held in the Grand Ballroom of the Seattle Excelsior. A thousand neurosurgeons and their spouses from all over the world sat around scores of tables in front of a brightly lit stage. The Radcliffe Trophy was set on the same refectory table as before with BRAIN's officers arranged around it in their traditional semicircle.

The table closest to the stage was reserved for Hugh. He was flanked by Caroline and his grown daughters, Anna and Marie. Sometimes it was easy to forget that the families of neurosurgeons go through their own private little hell when lawsuit shit hit the fan. The members of his own family were no exception. They had watched Hugh change from somebody they knew to somebody they did not and suffered deeply as a result. Succumbing to the ravages of juris psychosis hadn't been an option for them. Instead, they stayed strong inside and had given Hugh the support he needed. For that and many other things, he would always love and honor them.

Julie and Gary Winter, together with their own grown children, Jennifer and Patrick, occupied four more places at the table. They had been dumbfounded when, one sunny day a few months after the end of *Winter vs. Montrose*, Maxine pulled up in front of their squalid homeless shelter in a huge wheelchair-accessible RV and honked its horn. A door on its side had automatically opened, a lift unfolded, and Minimus hitched a ride to the ground, hopping around and yapping with excitement. Maxine had appeared at the open doorway and had enthusiastically motioned Gary, Julie, and their children to come inside. A few minutes later, surrounded by luxury accommodations and every modern amenity, she had offered a heartfelt apology for making a hash of their case and handed them the keys to the RV. Then she sat down at the dining table, whipped out a pen and a check book, and with a contrite smile across her face wrote a check for fourteen million dollars—more than enough to take care of their financial needs for the rest of their lives.

"W-why are you doing this?" Gary had asked, barely able to speak as he watched the string of zeroes in the amount box grow longer and longer.

"I want to help," explained Maxine as she signed her name. "I'm only sorry I didn't do something for you sooner."

Gary and Julie ditched their legal malpractice lawsuit against Maxine, bought their home from the bank, and moved back in. They hired a full-time rehabilitation nurse who was experienced taking care of quadriplegics and knew how to make the daily bowel protocol tolerable. Harvey the RV was towed away and replaced by the much larger Harvey the RV Jr. When they finally went on their long-postponed camping trip to Yellowstone National Park, they sent Hugh a couple of postcards, letting him know how happy they were.

As soon as the Winters returned and Julie settled into her new life, she bought a specially equipped van and hired a driver so she could make trips into town and visit her old school again. The students were ecstatic to see her, showering her with flowers, presents, and hugs. They wasted no time asking when she would come back to work. Soon afterwards she took a step in that direction when she became a volunteer teacher three days a week. When she proved how useful she could be, the principal gave her a part-time position.

Gary never returned to teaching high school physics. Instead, he was inspired to start a non-profit organization of his own that advocated the disclosure of hospitals' patient-outcome statistics so consumers and payers could have an objective way of assessing the care that was provided. What were the chances of making it through heart surgery without dying? What was the average length of hospital stay after having a back operation? What was the readmission rate for all the major diagnoses? And that wasn't all. He wanted such disclosures to be tied to the performance of individual physicians. Which ones, on average, had the best results? Which ones had the worst? Forget about subjective Best MD cronyism. Well meaning perhaps, but totally worthless. He and his organization demanded simple numbers that were only capable of telling the truth.

His goal was simple: no future patient should ever have to go the same hell Julie had experienced. Fusion factories like the Emerald Spine Institute and knife-wielding cowboys like Frank Clegg either had to radically reform themselves or be driven out of business.

John Denmark, looking dashing in black tie, occupied the last seat at the table. After winning *Winter vs. Montrose*, he felt that he had reached the peak of his career and promptly retired. He spent his days traveling the world, reeling in fish of every description. His most recent adventure had been off the coast of Australia where he had caught a male blue marlin that weighed two hundred pounds. Like the salmon in his office, he stuffed it and mounted it on a wall in his house.

When it was time to present the Radcliffe Trophy the house lights dimmed and a hushed silence descended over the vast ballroom.

The president, an egg-head with a horseshoe rim of white hair, stood behind the podium and took notes from his pocket. He located Hugh sitting at his table and smiled at him. "Ladies and gentlemen of BRAIN," he said, "please welcome Dr. Hugh Montrose who will accept the Radcliffe Trophy on behalf of DAMLA."

The members rose from their seats and applauded.

Hugh gave Caroline a kiss, shook Denmark's hand, and bounded up the steps into the spotlights. He accepted the silver cup from the president and stood behind the podium.

"Fellow BRAIN members," he began when the ballroom was quiet again. "Thank you very much for awarding the Radcliffe trophy to DAMLA this year. A great honor indeed! The members are very grateful." He paused a moment to collect his thoughts, then continued when he was ready. "The lawyers love to tell us it isn't personal, don't they?" he said with a playful smile.

A smattering of agreement arose from the crowd.

"Ten years ago," he continued, "I went through my first medical malpractice lawsuit and it opened my eyes to a tort system that benefits few people aside from trial lawyers and professional testifiers. Everybody kept telling me not to take things personally, but unfortunately I did. After all, my integrity as a physician was being seriously questioned. I should have remembered that it's only about money. Nothing else."

Everybody applauded.

"Something else I took personally: what happened to the plaintiffs, Julie and Gary Winter. When I won my trial, I resumed my work where I left off. Life went on pretty much as before. Julie and Gary, however, didn't have the option of returning to their normal lives. Not only was Julie irreversibly damaged by a medical mistake but she was also denied a single penny of compensation. I often complain about the way I was treated, but in the end she was by far the bigger victim.

"When I saw how unfairly the system treated defendants like me and plaintiffs like the Winters, it was my ambition to do something about it. But what? Lots of other efforts towards reform had failed—stifled by self-serving trial lawyers and their lackeys in politics. We needed a smart, new approach; something revolutionary that would circumvent the opposition. When I examined the problem, I realized that its Achilles heel was the medical experts who think they have the right to say anything under oath. Compete with them and the situation might improve. That's when I had the idea of establishing DAMLA.

"At this point," continued Hugh, breaking into a broad smile. "I am joined by somebody who made DAMLA what it is today. Ladies and gentlemen, I have the distinct honor and pleasure of presenting to you Ms. Maxine Doggette, accompanied by her wonderful Chihuahua, Minimus!"

Curtains parted and Maxine walked onto the stage. Aging had been kind to her face. It was softer and more sophisticated now, complying with the rules of nature rather than violating them. Her facial droop was indiscernible and the sunken crater on the side of her head had been skillfully repaired. Her red hair was as dazzling as ever and contrasted beautifully with the bright green evening gown she was wearing. In her hand she was holding Minimus who grinned at the sea of upturned faces before him. The tuft of hair on his forehead had matured into grey, making him look exceptionally wise.

The people gave them both a thunderous standing ovation that seemed to last forever. Maxine smiled and waved back, then joined Hugh at the podium. She hugged him and waited for the applause to die down.

Hugh spoke again once he could make himself heard. "This is the second time Maxine Doggette has honored us with her presence," he said. "No doubt many of you will remember the first. She followed through with her threat to sue me and soon I found myself fighting for my survival in the King County Courthouse instead of taking care of patients. I often wondered why I had to endure such hardship. During my darkest moments I made myself believe that there was a purpose to it all. With the benefit of hindsight, it turns out there was—one that I could never have predicted."

The Grand Ballroom was so quiet Hugh could hear air blowing from ducts in the ceiling high above.

"After my trial was over," he continued, "I invited Maxine to work for DAMLA. Why did I do it? My rational side told me she had the experience and inside knowledge to get things done. As it turns out, I was right about that. There was another reason though: I wanted to get to know her better, to understand who she is. I was glad—and nervous, of course—when she accepted the job.

"As you might have predicted, Maxine's personality didn't suddenly change when she joined DAMLA's staff. She was still the same old cantankerous, bombastic trial lawyer, seeing everything in black and white and always getting people's attention. She bossed us around as if nobody else's opinion mattered, argued incessantly, and almost quit a couple of times. With our help, however, she gradually learned how to work with others around her and changed from a one-woman extravaganza to a fully integrated member of our team. All the best ideas were hers. Nothing was too outrageous. Our opponents didn't stand a chance. Over the years, nobody has worked harder or more effectively than Maxine to make DAMLA the winning organization that it is today. It's been a pleasure and an honor getting to know her."

Once again everybody clapped loudly, then fell silent as Hugh invited his guest to the microphone.

"Good evening, everybody!" said Maxine. "It's been a long time, hasn't it?"

Friendly laughter rippled through the audience.

"You can all relax now," she continued. "Every physician in the country has a permanent place on my Do Not Sue list. I'm through with filing lawsuits. When I went after Hugh Montrose ten years ago I got much more than I bargained for. I lost the trial and let down my clients, Julie and Gary Winter, two people who had put their trust in me. I also ruptured a brain aneurysm and suffered all kinds of complications. My home and my office were both destroyed. Minimus barely escaped with his life."

Tears welled in Maxine's eyes. She gave her dog a loving squeeze.

"Over time," continued Maxine, "I was able to put a lot of things right again. When I was charged with extortion and corruption, I pled guilty, paid huge fines, performed community service, attended endless psychotherapy, and served a suspended sentence. The Washington State Bar Association was also merciful and punished me in every way short of permanent disbarment. I even gave up smoking cigarettes. Eventually, with your help, I was able to claw my way to respectability. That was the roughest time in my life. An atonement as difficult as there has ever been."

Maxine pulled a handkerchief from her sleeve, dabbed a tear that was trickling down her cheek, and spent a moment collecting herself. "Just like Hugh," she continued when she was ready, "my own hardship has also had a hidden purpose. That's the way things often turn out, isn't it? As I settled into DAMLA I made real friends. For the first time since my parents died when I was eight years old I actually found happiness again. I realized that it has nothing to do with being the Queen of Med-Mal or living in a castle. Neither is it about being a Super Lawyer or seeing your face on the cover of *Suing for Dollars*. Having lots of money isn't the answer either. Happiness is about giving and not taking, forgiving and not hating. It's about loving your family and friends, and living every day to the fullest."

The people concurred and gave Maxine another standing ovation.

"And one more thing!" cried Maxine above the tumult. "Never let lawyers get between you and your patients! God bless you!"

Hugh gave Maxine a hug, petted Minimus, and adjusted his microphone. "Thank you very much," he said to her audience. "Thank you for giving Maxine a much warmer welcome than the last time she was here!"

Everybody laughed and cheered.

Suddenly Hugh's pager went off. He unclipped it from his belt and read the message. *Twelve year old female with ruptured aneurysm in ER. Come immediately. Holz.*

A child with a ruptured aneurysm!

Hugh stepped back from the podium, called Holz, and clamped his cell phone to his ear. "What's the situation?" he asked, plugging his opposite ear with a finger so he could hear.

Holz was a seasoned ER physician and yet he sounded shaken as if he had finally met his match. "She's a beautiful child," he reported. "Awake and crying from the terrible pain in her head. The CT scan shows a huge aneurysm extending into her right temporal lobe. The worst one I've ever seen. Lots of subarachnoid blood. The parents are scared to death of losing her. I don't know what to tell them. Are you available? Please say yes!"

Hugh looked at the smiling, clapping crowd. He was the star of the banquet—a once-in-a . . . no, *twice*-in-a-lifetime event. If he wanted to stay and share his big moment with his family and friends, he certainly could. After all, he wasn't even on call that night. His partners could take care of the problem.

Powerful gravitational forces, however, were pulling him inextricably into a vortex that led back to the hospital. Being in the spotlight meant nothing to him. At heart he was an aneurysm hunter, most at home in the quiet sanctuary of the operating room carefully dissecting his way through the jungle of nerves and arteries at the base of a human brain. Nothing compared to the thrill he felt when he found the aneurysm he was after and moved in for the kill.

Did the girl in Columbia's ER need him? wondered Hugh. Or did *he* need *her*.

Hugh told Holz he was on his way and handed the Radcliffe Trophy to Maxine. "Take care of this for me," he said. "I have to go to the hospital."

"You trust me with this thing, Hugh?" she asked, winking at Minimus.

"Sure I do," he said. "As far as I'm concerned, it's half yours."

Without another word, he waved goodbye and rushed from the stage.

Made in the USA
Lexington, KY
07 December 2012